DELORES FOSSEN

CHASING TROUBLE IN *Texas*

HQN

Recycling programs for this product may not exist in your area.

ISBN-13: 978-1-335-13698-5

Chasing Trouble in Texas
Copyright © 2020 by Delores Fossen

That Night in Texas
Copyright © 2020 by Delores Fossen

This edition published by arrangement with Harlequin Books S.A.

For questions and comments about the quality of this book, please contact us at CustomerService@Harlequin.com.

HQN
22 Adelaide St. West, 40th Floor
Toronto, Ontario M5H 4E3, Canada
www.Harlequin.com

Printed in U.S.A.

CONTENTS

CHASING TROUBLE
IN TEXAS

CHAPTER ONE

IN HINDSIGHT, Austin Jameson realized he should have taken off the pink tutu and matching tiara and ditched the disturbing-looking stuffed bunny before he answered the door. After all, he was a cowboy with a hardworking reputation that didn't involve such things.

Live and learn.

He'd just been in such a hurry to make sure the knocking wouldn't wake up his twin girls that he'd forgotten about the "costume" that the twins had talked him into wearing for their bedtime story. But Austin remembered it when he faced the visitor at his door.

The sun had already set, but the porch light made it easy for Austin to see the tall lanky guy in a white Stetson and jeans, complete with a giant's-eye-size rodeo buckle. The light also made it easy to see the big truck and horse trailer parked all the way at the end of his driveway. It wasn't surprising that Austin hadn't heard the truck what with the voices—and yes, hopping around—he'd come up with to make the otherwise dull story, *The Fairy Princess's Magic Rabbit*, a hit with his girls.

The man who'd no doubt driven that truck had his right hand lifted in midknock. He looked dumbfounded, too, and that's when Austin got that hindsight and remembered what he was wearing.

Austin supposed he could take off the tutu and tiara and

offer some kind of explanation to dispel any rumors about him going off the deep end, but his dignity had already been shot to hell and back. Besides, this guy—this stranger—wasn't anyone he felt the need to impress.

However, Austin couldn't say that about his visitor.

Obviously, this guy had come to impress, *or something*, since he was holding on to the reins of a Shetland pony that was standing by the porch steps. The pony was draped with a flower garland and was wearing a straw hat and yellow cardboard sunglasses. Austin wasn't sure what to make of that get-up. Judging from the expression on the Shetland's face, it didn't know what to make of it, either.

Apparently, the pony had had its dignity shot to hell, too.

"Uh, I must have the wrong house," the guy said, shaking his head and backing away.

"Yeah," Austin agreed.

And he wondered why the guy hadn't checked that little detail before getting the pony out of the trailer. It wasn't as if Austin's ranch was on the beaten path. Heck, neither was his nearby hometown of Lone Star Ridge. People who usually made it out this far knew where they were going.

"I was looking for Austin Jameson," his visitor added a moment later.

Austin gave the guy another once-over. He still didn't recognize the pony whisperer, but since Austin raised horses, he had done business with a lot of people in the six years that he'd owned his ranch. Sometimes, folks brought him horses that needed adoption, but he didn't think that was the case here.

"I'm Austin Jameson," he said. "And you are?"

The confusion vanished from the guy's face, replaced by what Austin was certain was a flare of anger in his eyes. "You're the guy McCall left me for?"

Now, Austin was the one who was confused. He only knew one person named McCall, and she hadn't left any guy for him. In fact, he hadn't seen McCall in years. This idiot had to be talking about someone else. "McCall Dalton?"

"That's the one," he snapped, jabbing a finger at Austin's chest.

Again, Austin regretted the tutu and tiara because it obviously gave this lunatic the impression that he couldn't kick ass. He. Could.

"Who the hell are you?" Austin snarled. He tossed the bunny in the foyer and stepped out on the porch so he could close the door behind him. He didn't want his girls, Avery and Gracie, hearing any of this.

"I'm Cody Joe Lozano." The guy spat it out as if that was something Austin should have already known. He hadn't known, but it did sound kind of familiar. "And you're gonna tell me where McCall is."

"Lower your voice," Austin warned him, and he tried to get a whiff of the guy's breath. No scent of alcohol, but that didn't mean he wasn't drunk. Or high. "My kids are asleep."

"Kids?" he snarled. "You're married?"

"I'm a widower, not that it's any of your business. Why would you think I'd know where McCall is?"

"Because you were her boyfriend," he said without hesitation.

As explanations went, it was more than a little thin.

"I saw you two on TV, on the reruns of *Little Cowgirls*," Cody Joe added with the curl of his lips.

Again, it was thin on the explanation. "So did thousands of people," Austin pointed out.

Hell, Austin hoped he wasn't dealing with one of those "fans" of the reality show *Little Cowgirls*, which had indeed starred McCall and her sisters, the three of them triplets and therefore even more intriguing. It had been a while, years, but every now and then such a fan would come around. And yeah, Austin had been her boyfriend.

Sort of.

McCall's very brief, occasional TV boyfriend, anyway.

But *Little Cowgirls* had been canceled eighteen years ago when McCall was fifteen. She'd left Lone Star Ridge after high school graduation, and Austin could count on one hand how many times he'd seen her since then.

The last Austin had heard, McCall was a counselor of some kind and was living in Dallas, but he wasn't about to tell this idiot that. Austin didn't want Cody Joe going to look for her.

"Where's McCall?" Cody Joe demanded, jabbing his finger at Austin again.

"Get that finger away from my chest and get off my porch. Take your pony with you. And for Pete's sake, get the stupid-assed hat and glasses off him. You're humiliating him."

Cody Joe looked back at the Shetland, and it was as if that one glimpse drained the fight from his body. "McCall likes horses." His breath was now a weary sigh.

Well, she had when she'd lived in Lone Star Ridge, and it was possible that she'd wanted a pony when she was a kid. But Austin didn't think she would appreciate this particular gift from this particular guy.

Cody Joe swatted at a mosquito buzzing around his head and used his forearm to swipe sweat off his forehead. It might have been nearly eight-thirty, but the June temps were still in the high eighties.

"I've got to find her," Cody Joe went on, his voice more of a whine now. "I've got to tell her how sorry I am. I still want her to marry me." He fished around in his jeans pocket and came up with an engagement ring, one with a diamond so big and sparkly that it could have triggered a seizure.

Austin was torn between just kicking this moron off his porch and trying to get to the bottom of this. If Cody Joe was some kind of crazed stalker, then he needed to call the sheriff, who just happened to be his brother.

"Are you saying you were engaged to McCall?" Austin asked.

Cody Joe shook his head, leaned against the porch railing and groaned, the sound of a man in misery. "I was this close to getting her to say yes." He held up a small measured space between his thumb and index finger. "But I messed things up, *bad*. Miss Watermelon just looked so good in that red bikini bottom and watermelon-seed pasties, and I lost my head."

Austin didn't bother to get more details on that story. He got the picture.

While Cody Joe kept up his "pit of despair" mutterings and sank down onto the porch, Austin texted his brother, Sheriff Leyton Jameson, to come out to his place and bring a breathalyzer. And some handcuffs in case Cody Joe objected to a sobriety test. He added for Leyton to keep this quiet. No way did Austin want this getting around when he had so much at stake.

Hell. His whole life was at stake.

Anything that hinted at trouble could come back to bite him in the ass, and Cody Joe had trouble written all over him. So did the pony.

"Help me find McCall," Cody Joe grumbled on. "I know she came back here to her hometown 'cause I heard Boo talking to her on the phone."

Again, Austin didn't ask for clarification, not even to figure out who the heck Boo was. He'd never heard anyone including a toddler whine this much, and since he was the father of two three-year-old girls, he was more than qualified to ID an excessive whiner.

The Shetland started eating the petunias—after it pissed on the walkway. Austin ignored that and used his phone to do a search on Cody Joe Lozano in case the guy was an escaped mental patient.

But no. It was worse.

Cody Joe was a stinkin'-rich champion bull rider who'd been dubbed Hot Steel Buns. That meant he was likely sane and was just an ass. In Austin's experience, whining, heartbroken, cheating asses could be more unpredictable and dangerous than an actual mental patient. Especially when the ass had an obsession with the woman he'd cheated on.

While he continued to search, Austin spotted a tweet about Cody Joe and Miss Watermelon, but before he could get much past the picture of the blonde with Dolly Parton breasts and, yes indeed, watermelon-seed pasties, he heard the rustling at the side of his house. His first thought—a really bad one—was that either Avery or Gracie had woken up and come out through the back door. He definitely didn't want his girls to see or hear any of this.

But it wasn't Avery or Gracie.

It was a brunette who was using the flashlight on her phone to navigate the yard. She was dressed more like the fairy princess who'd been in that lame story he'd just read to his kids. Her long white shimmering dress hugged her breasts and billowed out over her hips like the top of a soft-serve ice cream cone. She also had a tiara, one a heck of a lot better than his, and a satin sash angled over her chest that proclaimed her Miss Watermelon Runner-Up.

"Austin," she murmured.

If the bunny from *The Fairy Princess's Magic Rabbit*

had come hopping around the corner, Austin wouldn't have been more surprised.

"McCall," Austin murmured back.

"McCall," Cody Joe said. Not a murmur, more like a whine of relief, and he sprang up, heading to the side of the porch toward her.

"No," McCall snapped, narrowing her eyes at Cody Joe. It probably would have looked more menacing if she hadn't had on a kilo of sparkly eyeshadow lighting up her eyelids. "If you try to touch me again, so help me I'll kick you in the nuts, and I'm wearing very pointy, very hard shoes."

Wisely, Cody Joe stopped in this tracks, proving that he perhaps wasn't a complete idiot, after all.

Austin didn't make a move to go to her, either. In part that was because he was stunned. Not only because McCall was indeed at his place as Cody Joe had thought she would be. Stunned, not only because of her strange outfit, either. But what was the most surprising of all was that he'd never heard McCall sound as if she might do some actual nut-kicking. When she'd been on *Little Cowgirls*, she'd been dubbed the nice one of her triplet sisters. Later on, Prissy Pants had been what folks called her.

Too prissy for Austin, that was for sure, which was why their "relationship" had never gotten past the peck on the lips stage.

Well, she'd definitely shed some of that prissiness.

"But, McCall—" Cody Joe tried.

"No," she repeated. "You don't speak to me unless I say so, and I'm not saying so. And you won't grab me again, either."

She pointed to the bruises on her left arm. Fingerprint bruises. Since the marks had no doubt come from Cody Joe, that made Austin want to kick his ass, and he wouldn't need pointy shoes to do a damn good job of it.

Still huffing, McCall turned toward Austin. "I can explain," she said, motioning toward her clothes. She eyed his tiara and tutu. "I'm guessing you can, too."

"I was reading to my girls."

He yanked off the tiara, tossing it into the rocking chair on the porch, but there wasn't a dignity-saving way for him to get out of the tutu without tearing it—something that would cause Gracie to cry. It'd taken some time and effort to shimmy it over his jeans.

"It's a costume for a charity fundraising beauty pageant," McCall said, pointing to her sash. "It's pinned on from the back, and I can't get it off. I didn't want to rip the dress because I can eventually put it in a charity auction."

Unlike some of the things Cody Joe had said, Austin wouldn't have minded hearing the story behind that, but he was pretty sure the tale would end with Cody Joe nailing the winner of the contest and getting caught.

And then bruising McCall.

"I bought you that pony you always wanted," Cody Joe blurted out. "I called a friend after you left, and he brought it right over for me. It's a peace offering."

The look McCall gave him was the Super Bowl and World Series of earth-searing glares. "Shut up. And get the ridiculous hat and sunglasses off that poor animal. It's humiliating."

"That's what I said," Austin agreed in a grumble.

While Cody Joe took care of the de-humiliation of the pony, McCall again turned back to Austin, and he could see her fighting to rein in her temper and turn off the laser rays she'd just shot at Cody Joe.

"I'm sorry," she said to Austin. "The contest was in

San Antonio, and when…things got ugly—" the laser rays drilled into Cody Joe again "—I decided to come home."

That made sense. Sort of. San Antonio wasn't that far from Lone Star Ridge, but his house sure wasn't her home. Home for her was Granny Em's place on the other side of town. It was a ranch where *Little Cowgirls* had been filmed and where McCall and her siblings had lived until they'd each moved away to go to college.

"While I was driving to Granny Em's," McCall went on, "I realized I didn't want her to see me like this. It would have upset her."

True, and since Em was in her late seventies, McCall probably hadn't wanted to risk an upsetting. "So, you came here?" Austin asked that tentatively, letting her know that he would indeed like some filling in on this part.

McCall nodded. Apparently, her tiara was pinned on, too, because it didn't shift even a little on her long cocoa-brown hair. "I left my rental car on Prego Trail and walked here."

She fluttered her fingers in the direction of said trail. It was on the outer edge of his property, and it hadn't gotten the name from that particular brand of spaghetti sauce. But rather because it was where the local teenagers went to make out, which resulted in some of them getting knocked up.

"Uh, why exactly did you come here?" Austin came out and asked her.

"Temporary insanity," she muttered, but then he saw her do some steeling up to look him straight in the eyes. "I thought about going to my sister, but Sunny isn't home."

No, she wasn't. Because Sunny was away on a romantic weekend with his oldest brother, Shaw. And since Sunny and Shaw were now engaged and planning to marry and have kids, it was almost certain that there were some knocking-up rehearsals going on.

"I didn't have any other clothes with me and didn't want to go walking into the inn like this." McCall motioned to her dress again. "I knew if I did, word would just get back to Granny Em. So, I decided to come here. I know you've got kids, but I thought maybe I could stay on the sofa or something until morning."

"You didn't have to hide out from me, McCall," Cody Joe declared. "You should have come to me so we could talk things—"

Hiking up her dress in a way that no one could call lady- or fairy-princess-like, McCall climbed onto the porch and aimed her foot at Cody Joe's balls. And yep, those heels were definitely pointy.

"Say one more word to me," she warned him, "and it'll be months before you can ride another bull or screw around with another beauty queen. You made an embarrassing laughingstock out of a charity event that would have pulled in thousands of dollars for troubled kids." She didn't yell, but the intensity grew with each word. "And it was all caught on camera."

She rummaged through a side pocket of the dress, came up with her phone and thrust the photo on the screen at Cody Joe. Whoever had taken the picture had captured Hot Steel Buns in action, complete with a watermelon-seed pasty stuck on Cody Joe's cheek. The beauty queen's tits were visible, too. Of course, it would have been hard for them to not be seen even it hadn't been a wide angle shot.

The caption on the picture was: "Little Cowgirl's cheating cowboy sampling some melons at the annual Saddle Up for Tots Fundraiser. Hope the tots didn't get a peek at this!"

"One more word," she emphasized to Cody Joe.

Oh, Cody Joe wanted to say something. Austin could see the man practically biting his tongue, but he kept his jaw locked and mouth closed. Good thing, too, because he must have known there was no excuse he could give her that would allow him to leave with his nuts intact. But even if McCall didn't hurt him, Austin might still kick his ass for putting those bruises on her.

"Anyway," McCall said as she shifted back to Austin. Clearly still fighting for her composure, she lowered her dress. "I really am sorry. I didn't know Cody Joe would come after me here."

"He said something about hearing you talking to *Boo* on the phone," Austin provided.

McCall nodded and looked as if she wanted to give herself a kick for allowing that to happen. "Again, I'm sorry." She paused, met him eye-to-eye. "I'm sorry about your wife, too. Zoey was a wonderful person."

Yeah, she was, and despite the "distraction" going on around him right now, Austin had to put up a fight to keep himself from slipping back into the dark place with just the mention of Zoey's name. Grief was a greedy bitch, and even though Zoey had been dead for a little over a year now, grief wasn't done getting a pound of flesh from him.

McCall broke the eye contact, murmured another apology, making Austin think that she could see right through him. Well, she was a counselor, after all, so maybe that gave her some kind of insight. If so, he'd shut it down. He'd had fourteen months of pity, and it didn't help. It only dragged him back to places he didn't want to be.

"Cody Joe will leave now and take the pony with him," McCall went on. "He won't come back, and he won't try to contact you or me again. I'll go back to San Antonio and get a hotel room."

She aimed another glare at Cody Joe. "I want to end all of this—*quietly*."

At that exact moment, there was the sound of approaching vehicles. It didn't take long for those vehicles to come into view. Leyton's cruiser was in the lead, no sirens or flashing lights. Right behind it, though, was a San Antonio PD cruiser with its blue lights slashing through the darkness.

And right behind that were two news vans from TV stations in San Antonio. Broadcast vehicles, complete with satellite dishes that would no doubt make it easy to turn all of this into a breaking news story.

Any chance of *quietly* had just bit the dust.

CHAPTER TWO

"DON'T WORRY, MCCALL," the woman in the stripper outfit called out when she stepped from one of the news vans. "Everything will be okeydokey."

McCall was reasonably sure that nothing about situation this would be okey or dokey.

Austin must have realized that, too, because he started muttering curse words under his breath. While he propped his hands on his hips, he stared at the circus that was now playing out in his driveway and front yard. It didn't matter that this wasn't his circus, nor his monkeys. Before this was over, McCall was going to owe him a thousand apologies along with cleaning up some metaphorical monkey poop. First, though, she had to diffuse a very ugly mess.

Wadding up the sides of her dress so she could walk without tripping, McCall started toward the people who were pouring from the vehicles. Three cops, two cameramen and two people she guessed were reporters because they had microphones.

Leyton was a welcome sight—especially since he hadn't arrived with sirens blaring, and unless he'd changed a lot over the years, he'd be levelheaded and reasonable. That wouldn't make this hunky-dory, okeydokey or less poopy, but at least it wouldn't add any more monkeys to the circus.

Her assistant, Rue Gleason, aka Boo, might be of help, as well. Definitely not a circus monkey on most days. Too bad, though, that Boo was giving this tawdry mess even more tawdriness in her stilettos, sequined halter top and red micromini leather skirt that stopped only an inch below her crotch. Since Boo still had on the Miss Watermelon Participant sash, maybe it had been pinned to her outfit, too. Of course, knowing Boo, maybe she just liked wearing it.

"Why are the San Antonio cops and news crews here?" McCall asked her. She tried to keep her voice to a whisper and hoped that Boo did the same.

Boo didn't. "I wasn't going to let that weasel-balled turd get away with grabbing you like that. I told a cop friend I met at the fundraiser, and he said he'd come and arrest Cody Joe. A reporter heard me talking to the cop and offered me a ride out here. The reporter said he was coming even if I didn't give him directions or anything."

Boo sent a steely look at Cody Joe, who was heading in their direction. So were Austin and the Shetland pony. That only upped the urgency to get rid of the problem—the cop—that Boo had obviously seen as a solution.

McCall didn't want a San Antonio cop to arrest Cody Joe because it would just end up making more news than it already had. Plus, he hadn't "grabbed" her for the purpose of bruising her but had rather tried to hold on when she'd turned to walk away from him. Yes, that was pretty much the same thing, but if McCall had thought for a second that he'd been trying to hurt her, she would have kicked his nuts all the way into his throat.

"I'll issue a statement in the morning. For now, I want you to respect my privacy and leave," McCall said, aiming that at the reporters.

She kept her voice level and noncombative because she'd already had enough bad press for one night. While flying off the handle would feel good, temporarily, it could end up costing the foundation even more money in donations.

"I want you to go, too," Austin added, "and since I own this property, and you're trespassing, that leaving will happen right now."

"Say, that's the guy from *Little Cowgirls*," one of the cameramen said.

McCall groaned. In all the years *Little Cowgirls* had been on the air, Austin had appeared on-screen only about a half dozen times, but he'd gotten a ton of fan mail. His good looks had played into that. Still would with his tousled nearly black hair and sizzling blue eyes. The man looked like a rock star—even in that tutu.

"I'm sure you want to tell your side of the story as to what happened between Cody Joe, you and Miss Watermelon," one of the reporters shouted to McCall.

"Leave now!" Leyton snarled, tapping his badge and holding up a pair of handcuffs that he took from a clip at the back of his jeans. Unlike McCall, Leyton didn't bother with a level or nonconfrontational tone. He was all pissed-off cop.

The cameramen didn't stop filming, but they did walk backward to their vans, and once they were inside, they slowpoked their way down Austin's driveway. Heaven knew how bad the spin would be that they'd put on this story, and first thing in the morning, McCall really did need to do some damage control.

"I'm Officer Gary Hatcher," the cop said. "I'm here to take Cody Joe Lozano into custody for an incident that happened at the Miss Watermelon beauty contest in San Antonio's jurisdiction. I was in pursuit," he added to Leyton, "so that's why I crossed into Lone Star Ridge."

Officer Hatcher grinned at Boo, and McCall instantly knew why he'd taken such an interest in going *in pursuit* and bringing Cody Joe to justice. He was lusting all over Boo. Of course, plenty of men did.

"Sorry, but I gotta take you in," Hatcher told Cody Joe. He shook his head, scratched it, smiled. "But I gotta tell you, I'm a hell of a big fan of yours. That ride you did on Gray Smoke up in Austin was one of the best I've ever seen."

"Well, thank you. I appreciate that. Always good to hear from a fan." Cody Joe turned on his thousand-watt smile that McCall suspected he'd been practicing since he had first cut teeth.

Of course, he'd had to practice that smile around that silver spoon in his mouth, and it had paid off. A trust fund rodeo champion with movie star looks and charm that often got breaks mere mortals didn't. However, it appeared getting out of this arrest was one break Cody Joe wasn't going to get.

"But I still gotta take you in," the cop added to Cody Joe with plenty of regret. Regret which eased up a little when Boo winked at Officer Hatcher. "Just come on with me, and we'll try to get this all straightened out as fast as we can." He shifted his attention to McCall. "You'll need to come, too, and press charges 'cause Boo here said that Cody Joe assaulted you."

"I didn't. It was just a misunderstanding, that's all." Cody Joe didn't lose an ounce of his charm with that denial. "I didn't want her to leave before I explained things."

"No explanation needed," McCall countered. "I got the picture when I saw your jeans hiked down over your hips and your hand in Miss Watermelon's bikini bottom."

There'd be actual pictures of that, too, since McCall hadn't been alone when she'd gone into the ladies' room at the rodeo arena and found Cody Joe on the verge of banging the contest winner against the feminine hygiene products dispenser. A few attendees who'd just needed to pee had been right behind her. So was one of the biggest donors of the fundraiser, Elmira Waterford, who'd simply wanted to powder her nose before the next round of publicity photos.

Elmira, who was the mother of the contest winner that Cody Joe had been about to nail, hadn't taken things well and had ended up needing medical attention because of hyperventilation and a panic attack.

It'd been while Elmira was breathing into a discarded Chick-fil-A bag McCall had pulled from the trash that Cody Joe had insisted this was all a misunderstanding and that he needed to speak to McCall alone. McCall had resisted telling him to do anatomically impossible sex acts with himself and had held her ground about not leaving with him. That's when he'd grabbed her. That's also when she'd stomped on his boot to get him to back off.

While the drama of the night was still playing out in her mind and would continue playing out in the press, McCall started that damage control now. "I won't be pressing charges if Cody Joe leaves and agrees not to come here again."

And once Cody Joe was gone and she did some serious groveling to Austin, McCall would do the same.

"But, McCall, I really need to talk to you," Cody Joe protested. He started to move toward her, but Leyton blocked his path. "I need to make things right," he hollered over Leyton's shoulder.

Apparently, Cody Joe was going to continue to act like a fool tonight, but McCall didn't get a chance to show him her shoe as a reminder of what would happen if he touched her again. That's because the sound behind them caught everyone's attention.

Girl squeals.

McCall turned to see the twin girls in pj's run out the front door, onto the porch and then down the steps. The girls were identical except for their hair. One had a halo of dark blond curls bouncing around her head. The other had a choppy bob that appeared to be in the growing-out stage.

That gave McCall a déjà vu moment of when her own sister Hadley had cut McCall's hair. It'd been used in an episode that the producer had joked was "Why Badly Hadley Can't Be Trusted with Scissors."

"A pony!" the girls squealed in unison. That was accompanied by giggles, jumping up and down and immediate attempts to pet the pony.

Obviously, these were Austin's kids, and it was also obvious that this wasn't something he wanted them to see because he hurried to them. McCall did the same. Well, she hurried as much as the dress allowed, but she wasn't sure if the Shetland was skittish and might knock the girls down.

Austin made it to the girls well ahead of her, and he scooped them up like footballs in each of his arms. "You should be in bed," he said, but there was no anger in his voice.

"But we woke up 'cause we heard loud talking," the girl with the longer hair proclaimed. "Santa got us a pony!"

The twin with the shorter hair got a puzzled look as if she might have realized Santa didn't bring gifts in June, but then her gaze landed on McCall. Her eyes widened. "It's the fairy princess," she said in awe.

McCall smiled at her but didn't get a chance to explain that she was merely a fake fairy princess before the other girl asked, "Where's your magic bunny?"

"She brought her magic pony instead," Austin answered without missing a beat. "Princess McCall, this is Avery." He kissed the nose of the one with longer hair. "This is Gracie." He gave the other a kiss on her cheek. "But now that you've met the princess and her pony, you have to go back to bed. That's the fairy tale rules, and we can't break them."

The girls groaned, of course, and the one with the longer hair declared, "Rules suck."

"Yeah, they do on many occasions," Austin agreed. "You still have to obey them."

He turned and headed toward the porch, holding the girls in such a way that he was clearly trying to keep their little eyes and attention away from what was going on beyond the pony and the princess. But "rules suck" Avery pointed at the driveway. "Nuckle Leyton," she squealed. "I wanta see Nuckle Leyton."

"Tonight, Uncle Leyton's part of the fairy tale police. So is the other guy in the uniform. They're here to make sure we don't break fairy tale rules." Austin didn't offer explanations for Cody Joe and Boo.

Avery gave her father a flat look as if she clearly wasn't buying that. Gracie gave a little wave and shy smile to Leyton, who was now walking toward them.

"Let me put them back to bed," Leyton volunteered. "Then you can finish up here with…Princess McCall. I'll read you a story," he said to the girls when they started to protest about having to go to bed.

All protests stopped, even though the twins both cast longing glances at the pony. Since Austin raised horses, McCall wouldn't have thought a pony would have been a big deal, but it obviously was. Maybe because it'd been a surprise and was still wearing the flower garland. The "magic" part might have played into it, too.

"I'll talk to your dad and the pony and see if it can visit you sometime soon," McCall said to try to console them. It worked. The girls cheered.

"Read us two stories," Avery insisted. She cuddled against her uncle when Austin passed off the girls to Leyton. "And we get ice cream."

"Nice try." Leyton took hold of Gracie, too. From the looks of her droopy eyes, the excitement for her had run its course, and she'd likely be asleep as soon as her head hit the pillow. "Yes to the two stories, but nope to the ice cream.

"FYI." Leyton lowered his voice and leaned in closer to Austin. "Howie and Edith will get wind of this."

Austin nodded, groaned and looked as if he wanted to start digging the hole to bury himself in. It took McCall a moment to realize that she recognized the names. They were Howie and Edith Marygrove, Zoey's parents.

"Shit," Austin muttered once Leyton had the girls out of earshot and back in the house.

She didn't know the specifics as to what was going on, but McCall remembered Granny Em mentioning something about Zoey's parents wanting to raise the twins. Crap. If there was some kind of custody struggle going on, this free-for-all certainly wouldn't help.

"I'm so sorry," McCall said. "I honestly didn't mean to involve your girls in this."

He didn't give her a "that's okay" or any other sign that he wasn't riled to the bone about this.

"If you think it'd help, I could talk to Mr. and Mrs. Marygrove and explain none of this was your fault," McCall pressed.

Austin slid glances at her, Cody Joe, the cop and Boo. "Just wrap this up. I want as little getting back to them as possible."

That was her cue to get moving again, so with Austin on her heels, McCall went back to Cody Joe and Officer Hatcher.

"As I was saying, if Cody Joe leaves now, then I won't press charges." McCall motioned toward the Shetland. "And if Austin agrees, you'll leave the pony for his daughters. Send me a bill and I'll reimburse you for the cost."

Even with the blue lights from the cruiser swirling across his face, McCall saw the glimmer go through Cody Joe's eyes. A glimmer that let her know he thought this was a time to bargain with her.

"The kids can have the pony as a gift," he said, "if you'll give me another chance and forget all about what happened in San Antonio."

It was such a ridiculous attempt at bribery that McCall couldn't even muster up another round of temper. Boo could, though. She made a sound of outrage and lunged toward Cody Joe, but Officer Hatcher hooked an arm around her waist and held her back.

"You were going to marry this guy?" Austin said, tipping his head to Cody Joe, who was attempting his "gotta love me" grin.

"No." McCall couldn't say that fast enough. "But we were a couple," she was forced to add.

"A couple of what?" Austin asked.

A burst of air left her mouth, not quite a laugh, but it was as close as she would come to one tonight.

Austin turned and looked at her. The blue lights were swirling on his face, too, but she didn't see a glimmer there. However, she did see the hot cowboy who'd once been her biggest crush.

"Cody Joe and McCall are cofounders of the Saddle Up for Tots Foundation," Boo pointed out. "Cody Joe's the poster-boy celebrity, and his name brings in a lot of money."

Austin made a sound to indicate that explained a lot. It did. But it didn't explain why the foundation was so important to McCall. Or that she'd known from the get-go that Cody Joe was irresponsible. However, this was the first time he'd put the foundation in the center of what would almost certainly be a scandal.

"Me and you together can still pull in a lot of money for those kids," Cody Joe went on, obviously trying to sell an unsalable plan. "I love you, McCall. Just give me another chance."

Deciding that he just wasn't going to get it, that he'd done something that couldn't be undone, McCall shook her head and turned to walk back to Prego Trail. Cody Joe made another move toward her, and this time it was Austin who stepped in. He caught on to Cody Joe's arm, but all of Cody Joe's charm vanished, and he tried to push Austin away.

Enough was enough.

McCall turned to give him another "kick to the nuts" threat, but Cody Joe took a swing at Austin. He missed. Then he pulled back his fist to try again. Boo, McCall and Officer Hatcher all went rushing in.

And Cody Joe's punch caught the cop right in the face.

A wise man would have stopped right there and started apologizing, but Cody Joe decided to lunge at her again. Since now both Austin and Officer Hatcher had hold of him, his momentum sent them forward.

Toward Boo and McCall.

They all went to the ground, landing in a tangled heap of bodies. McCall's shoe did indeed land in the area of a man's nuts but not Cody Joe's. Instead, she connected with the cop's. He howled in pain, and McCall wanted to do the same when Boo's seriously hard elbow slammed against her cheekbone.

There was some cursing from all of them, coupled with the sound of the pony, who was neighing over the melee.

But there was another sound, too. A car engine. A moment later, a sleek silver Mercedes came to a stop, the tires kicking up the gravel in the driveway, and the headlight spotlighting the human heap.

McCall managed to crawl out on all fours. So did Austin. His mouth was bleeding, the tutu practically ripped to shreds, but he'd clearly fared better than Officer Hatcher. His nose was gushing blood, there was a cut on his forehead, and he was using both hands to clutch his balls while he writhed in pain and rolled from side to side.

"Shit," Austin grumbled, and he groaned as the two people stepped from the pricy car.

Howie and Edith Marygrove.

His former in-laws.

And McCall could tell from their horrified expressions that this circus had gotten a whole lot more monkey crap.

CHAPTER THREE

AUSTIN HEARD MCCALL muttering something about monkey crap right before she asked him if she should try to smooth things over with Zoey's parents. He didn't even have to think about his answer to that.

No.

Because any smoothing-over attempt would be a waste of time.

Normally, Edith nitpicked his parenting—everything from lax bedtime hours to the twins' food choices. But Edith would take this many, many steps past the nitpicking stage. There'd been a brawl in his front yard, and while the girls hadn't actually witnessed it, thank God, they'd seen and heard enough to have their night disrupted.

"I'll deal with them," Austin told McCall.

Her shoulders dropped, so did her expression, and she nodded in a gesture that he had no trouble interpreting. Resignation and regret. Yeah, he was right there on the same page with her. But he also had a side order of pissed off added to everything else he was feeling.

"I'm sorry," McCall called out to no one in particular, and using the flashlight on her phone again, she motioned for her assistant, Boo, to follow her.

His former mother-in-law had no doubt noticed Boo's choice of clothing and would nitpick about that, as well. It didn't matter that Austin hadn't a) chosen Boo's clothes, b) invited anyone other than Leyton here tonight, or c) wanted any of this to happen. There'd be hell to pay and he was the payer.

Maybe he was just stalling, but Austin watched as McCall traipsed through the yard and into the line of trees that concealed the trail. He couldn't hear what Boo was saying to McCall, but Austin doubted there was anything that could be said that would console her.

Officer Hatcher did some consoling, though, in his own cop way. He handcuffed Cody Joe and put him in the back seat of the cruiser.

"You have to help me, Austin," Cody Joe said, saying Austin's name as if they were old friends. That, of course, caused Howie and Edith—especially Edith—to harden their expressions even more.

Austin resisted shooting Cody Joe the bird or barking out that the only help he'd give him was a kick to the ass to get him out of there faster. Instead, Austin just waited and watched as the cruiser pulled away before he turned to Edith and Howie. They were wearing "church clothes." A suit coat, jeans and bolo tie for Howie. A yellow dress and matching shoes for Edith.

Since it was a weekday, they likely hadn't come from church but a meeting or some kind of social function. Along with owning a cattle ranch, Howie was the mayor, and Edith was on any and all committees in Lone Star Ridge. If there was a baby shower, book club or guild meeting, Edith would be there and almost certainly chairing or hosting it.

Considering they were grandparents, they weren't old, only fifty-four. They'd had Zoey when they were twenty-three and apparently hadn't been able to have other children. Austin figured that played into the woman's obsession with the twins. That, and losing Zoey.

Of course, losing Zoey played into a lot of things.

"McCall had some personal issues," Austin volunteered, knowing his in-laws would want an explanation. "A cop from San Antonio followed one of those *issues* here and arrested him."

"McCall Dalton," Edith grumbled. There was no "old friends" tone for her. "The girl who was on that TV show?"

"Little Cowgirls," Howie supplied. "Did McCall and the girl with her lose a bet and have to wear those costumes?"

Austin frowned at Howie's guess. "No. They were in a contest for a fundraiser."

"She was dressed like a hooker." Edith again, and yeah, she grumbled that, too.

"That was McCall's assistant," Austin explained. Well, unless Edith thought a fairy could be a hooker. "I need to go inside. Leyton's with the girls."

Edith's disgust turned to horror. "Oh, I hope he doesn't have on his gun and badge. It'll scare the girls."

"No gun." Not a visible one, anyway, since Leyton used a slide holster in the back of his jeans to carry his service weapon. "And the badge won't scare them." In fact, the twins liked to use it to play various games about sheriffs and bad guys, but he wouldn't mention that to Edith.

Edith hurried ahead of them, not actually running but close. She wasn't an athletic woman and wasn't in tip-top shape, but she always seemed to be able to move fast when it came to her grandchildren.

"Is there anything you can tell me about this situation that'll help calm Edith down?" Howie asked once Edith was far enough ahead that she couldn't hear them.

"Nope. McCall got into a tight spot and ended up here."

When Austin reached the pony, he took the reins and hooked them around a porch post. Once he got Edith and

Howie to leave—whenever the heck that would be—he'd put the Shetland in the barn, give it some feed and deal with it tomorrow.

"A tight spot that involved Cody Joe Lozano?" Howie asked, keeping his voice low.

So, apparently Howie had recognized the rodeo star, and here was one area that Austin could clarify. "Cody Joe put bruises on McCall. She got away from him and came here because she didn't want to worry Em."

"Shit," Howie mumbled.

That was Austin's sentiments exactly, and it still riled him that he hadn't given the idiot a solid punch.

Howie stopped on the porch, turned and faced Austin. "Are you starting up with McCall again?"

Despite the way he'd phrased that, Howie didn't seem to be passing any judgment on the "starting up" if that was indeed what was happening. The man was likely just wanting to know what he was up against when they faced Edith. Some of the time, it felt as if Howie and he were on the same side, but Austin knew Howie wouldn't try to rein in his wife and risk disharmony in his marriage.

"No," Austin assured him. "I'm not seeing McCall."

The moment he issued that quick denial, he felt the slide of heat go through his body. But it wasn't necessarily heat for McCall, he assured himself. It was just because it'd been so long since he'd been with a woman. McCall was attractive.

Damn attractive.

However, he didn't have time for a relationship with a woman who appeared to have more on her plate than he did.

Howie and he went inside, and they made a beeline for the girls' bedroom where they knew they'd find Edith. Leyton appeared to be holding her at bay by staying close to the beds where Avery and Gracie were sacked out. That was something at least. The events of the night hadn't wired them up enough to keep them awake.

Leyton put his finger to his mouth in a stay-quiet gesture, one that just Edith needed because she was the only one of them doing something that might disturb the girls' sleep.

Edith adjusted the covers that in no way needed adjusting, brushed back their hair from their faces. Again, no adjustment had been needed. And finished it off by brushing kisses on their heads and murmuring, "Everything will be okay now. Grandma Edith is here."

"Gracie's hair is taking its time growing back," Howie remarked.

It was indeed, and Austin figured that would earn him another nitpick since Avery had been the one to cut her sister's hair. Not a good cut, either. It had been done with plastic scissors but looked as if Avery had used a weed whacker. Gracie hadn't minded, had actually seemed to enjoy the shorter style, but Edith hated it.

Secretly hated it, anyway.

Since his mother-in-law had never been able to tell the girls apart, this gave Edith the advantage of being able to do that. However, Edith would never admit it.

Walking backward so that she could keep her eyes on the twins, Edith crept out of the room, and once she was back in the hall with Leyton, Austin and Howie, Austin eased the door shut.

"Gracie's poor hair," Edith remarked. There was an unspoken tsk-tsk after that. "You really should have been more careful, Austin." She paused only long enough to draw breath. "In case McCall and that man come back, the girls should spend the night with us."

Austin had already anticipated that demand, and he shook his head. "The girls have preschool tomorrow."

Not the best excuse since they'd be up by six and wouldn't have to be at school until ten, but Austin limited the sleepovers to Friday or Saturday nights. And he never allowed two nights in a row. The girls didn't press for that, either, preferring to be home with him, but Edith certainly did some pressing.

Austin suspected if the woman kept the girls for more than one night, she'd only push for more and more until she could squeeze Austin out of the picture and into the background where she thought fathers belonged. It was an old-fashioned notion that Austin had no intention of passing on to his girls.

"I need to head out now," Leyton said, checking the time and then looking at Austin. Austin gave him a nod to let him know that he'd be okay, that he didn't need moral support to face down whatever Edith was about to dole out. "I'll run by Em's and make sure McCall got there okay," Leyton added.

Austin thanked him. A genuine thanks, too. And no, it didn't have anything to do with the slide of heat he'd felt. Austin was genuinely worried about McCall.

He walked with Leyton to the door, closing it behind him, and when Austin turned back into the living room, he saw Edith at the fireplace. As usual, she was looking at photos on the mantel, a row of shots taken of Zoey, him and the twins.

The last twelve years of his life were on that mantel. Zoey and he had started dating when they'd been twenty, and there was a photo of them on the first vacation they'd taken together. Another photo of Austin at her college graduation. Then a wedding shot of them the following year. The pictures after that were all of them with the twins that they'd finally managed to get after a couple of years of fertility treatments. The girls had been born the week of Zoey's thirtieth birthday.

Then two years later she was dead.

Of course, there were no pictures of her after the breast cancer had started to ravage her body, but Austin could see it just as clearly as if it'd been in a silver frame on that mantel. He saw it, too, most nights when he closed his eyes to sleep. No reprieve in sleep, either, because she was in his dreams. Just once, he wished his dreams would be of any of the moments actually captured on that mantel.

Edith ran her fingers over Zoey's face in one of the pictures, and then she backed away, turning toward him. There were tears in her eyes, and Austin was neither surprised by them nor immune to them. Edith's heart was broken, too, and seeing her tears always brought the grief down harder on him.

"I'm glad Zoey wasn't here to witness what went on tonight," Edith said, and there was a bite in her voice now. "It would have upset her."

No, it wouldn't have. Zoey would have had a good laugh about it. Well, not a laugh about her pissed-off parents, but Zoey would have spun it into a story to tell the girls. That's what she'd done with other turns and disasters that life had thrown at them.

But the girls wouldn't remember that.

Because Zoey had died when they were barely two years old, they wouldn't remember their amazing mother. And sometimes that realization felt like a fist that had just squeezed all the air out of him.

For better or worse, he'd married Zoey. They'd gotten plenty of the "better," and now he was dealing with the "worse." Of course, she'd left him plenty of the "better" with their daughters.

"Leyton said McCall would be at Em's," Edith threw out there. "Does that mean she'll be staying for long?"

Austin shook his head. "I couldn't say." Though he was certain he'd soon know because the gossips would spread anything there was to be learned.

"Well, I hope not," Edith went on. "Lone Star Ridge doesn't need the kind of publicity that McCall or the rest of the Daltons brought to this town."

Edith was no doubt referring to the fact that McCall's sister Sunny had recently had her teenage diaries stolen by a reporter, and the reporter had then published a sexually charged entry from one of them.

"McCall didn't have anything to do with that," Austin explained. "She's a counselor. A respectable one who does charity fundraisers."

Edith's raised, overly plucked eyebrows let Austin know either that didn't matter or she didn't believe him. "She comes from a family with questionable ethics and an equally questionable reputation," Edith argued.

It was an okay argument, considering that McCall's parents were basically money grubbing assholes who'd exploited their triplet daughters through not only the reality TV show but also later when they'd taken most of the money that the show had earned. But McCall's grandmother, Em, was a decent person who'd always tried to do right by her grandchildren.

"I don't think Avery and Gracie should be exposed to someone like McCall or her family," Edith went on.

That crossed a huge line, and it caused Howie to huff. The man would have no doubt interceded at least in some small way, but Austin beat him to it.

"My brother Shaw is engaged to McCall's sister," Austin quickly reminded her. "Sunny will definitely be part of the girls' lives and mine. From time to time, McCall might be, too."

"But her brother and other sister are on the cover of those trashy tabloids," Edith snapped.

He couldn't argue that. Her brother, Hayes, and other triplet sister, Hadley, had definitely gotten into their share of trouble. But Austin was pissed now that Edith had taken up McCall bashing.

"I didn't know you read the tabloids," Austin remarked.

Oh, Edith didn't like that, and Austin instantly regretted not putting a gag on himself. After all, many would see what'd happened tonight at his place as a scandal. One that had gotten some news coverage. One that would fuel the gossips for a decade or two. While none of it would actually hurt Gracie and Avery, it wouldn't help.

There was fire in her eyes when Edith walked closer to him. "All of this should prove that you can't raise the girls on your own. Our granddaughters," she emphasized. "For once do what's best for them because if you don't…"

She trailed off when Howie took hold of her arm. "Edith." It was a mild warning for her not to say something she might regret.

But Edith said it, anyway. And there wasn't regret in her voice.

"It's time for Howie and me to visit our lawyer," Edith insisted. "I want to make it legal and petition for custody of Gracie and Avery."

MCCALL WOULD HAVE kicked herself if she'd thought she could do it without tripping over her own feet and damaging the fairy dress even more than it already was. If she could get out the grass stains from the scuffle in Austin's yard, she could still donate the dress and maybe get some money to add to the Saddle Up for Tots Foundation.

Maybe.

And it was just as likely that anything connected to that would be as toxic as typhoid and that potential donors would want zilch to do with it.

Damn Cody Joe. Damn Miss Watermelon.

And McCall had to damn herself, too.

Because she was ultimately the one guilty of round two of this ugly fiasco. She'd been the one to get the harebrained idea of running to Austin's. She'd been the one who told Boo where she was heading and that made it possible for Cody Joe to overhear the conversation and go after her. That, in turn, had set the events of the night into a terrible motion, including the news vans and Cody Joe's arrest.

McCall could only hope that Austin would forgive her and that this wouldn't cause any trouble for him. Howie and Edith certainly hadn't looked pleased, but maybe once he explained that none of it had been his fault, they wouldn't give him grief about having a tawdry ruckus right in front of his and his daughters' home.

"Hey, I recognize that mailbox shaped like a little red barn," Boo said, getting her attention as McCall made the turn onto the road that led to Granny Em's ranch. "It was in some of the episodes of *Little Cowgirls.*"

"Pretty much everything you see will have been in the episodes," McCall remarked.

After all, the show had been on for twelve years, following the sisters from age three to fifteen when the show had thankfully gotten canceled. Of course, at the time there hadn't been much thanks because it'd ended in yet another scandal when Hadley had gotten caught joyriding in a stolen car.

"Yep," Boo agreed. She pointed to the two-story yellow Victorian just ahead. "The house looks just like it did on TV."

It did from what McCall could see with the headlights of her car, and it was a reminder that it'd been over a year since she'd come back. Unlike Hadley and her brother, Hayes, McCall hadn't left Lone Star Ridge with a chip on her shoulder the size of Texas and vowing to stay gone. McCall loved Em and, yes, loved the ranch, too, but life—and the mess that it had become—had gotten in the way.

McCall groaned when she stopped in front of the house and saw Granny Em in the doorway, clearly waiting for her. The gossips had already gotten out the word, and McCall was reasonably sure "word" would continue. Ready to face the music, and Granny Em's questions, she got out and went up on the porch.

"I hope you aren't scared of bats," Em greeted. She pulled McCall into a hug and kept her there in her arms.

If McCall had been given a thousand or more tries, she wouldn't have guessed Granny Em would say that. Not with all the other juicy bits of news there was to discuss.

"Uh, bats are kind of creepy," McCall said when she realized Granny Em was waiting for an answer.

"They are." Em let go of her at the exact moment McCall saw a bat flutter past the house. "But they're good for eating mosquitos so I bought two dozen and had them delivered."

McCall knew all about Granny Em's mosquito hatred, but the topic of conversation had her worrying. Was Em in denial? Or, heaven forbid, was she getting senile? A third possibility was that she simply hadn't heard about what had gone on at Austin's, but that theory was dispelled when Leyton pulled into the driveway. He didn't stop. He merely gave them a wave and headed on out.

"He's just checking to make sure you got here from Austin's," Em remarked in a discussing-the-weather tone. So, if Granny Em knew that, then she likely knew the rest.

"Cool. I love bats," Boo said, coming up on the porch. "They're like little black dragons."

That was McCall's cue to make introductions. "Boo, this is my grandmother, Em. Boo is my assistant."

Em pulled Boo into a hug, too, and some of the tension in McCall's stomach started to settle. It would come back when she started to deal with the aftermath of Cody Joe and Miss Watermelon, but for now she could be in a place where she wouldn't be judged.

Well, *maybe* she wouldn't be.

"Boo and I need to stay the night," McCall said.

"Of course you do. I just tidied up your rooms." Em stepped back into the foyer, tugging them in with her. "You know you can stay as long as you like. You being here might help Austin, too. He's still down and blue about losing Zoey. I'm betting once he's had a good night's sleep, he'll be glad you're here."

McCall figured there was zero chance of that, and stopping by Austin's was on her to-do list for tomorrow. Not so she could try to help him with his grief but because she wanted to apologize again and see if there was anything she needed to do for the Shetland that Cody Joe had left behind.

"You two go on up to your rooms and get settled while I make us a snack," Em instructed. She looked at Boo. "I've put you in my grandson's old room, but you'll have to be on the lookout for magazines with naked people in them. Even though he hasn't lived here in seventeen years, every now and then we still find some of his old stash of *Playboy.*"

"Oh," Boo said, and wisely left it at that.

"If you do find some," Em went on, "bring it to me because sometimes there are good articles in them."

Boo settled for a nod.

After getting kisses on their cheeks, Boo and McCall

started up the stairs. It wasn't late, but McCall was suddenly exhausted and wished she could just shower, find something comfortable to put on and fall into bed. But she owed Granny Em some time. And besides, Em might be able to help level her out so that she could actually fall asleep without rehashing the events of this memorable night.

"Your room's down there," McCall said once they were in the upstairs hall. "But we need to talk before we see Granny Em again." She motioned for Boo to follow her, and they stepped into McCall's childhood bedroom.

Aka Purgatory. At least, that's how McCall thought of it.

The large loft-style area was divided into three sections, one for her and each of her two sisters. It was more than a mere bedroom, though. It was a display of the labels the producers had put on them. Sunny was Funny Sunny with her posters of boy bands and comedians. Her area was bright and fun, just as they'd wanted Sunny to be.

And the polar opposite of Badly Hadley.

Her area was painted black, though Hadley herself had done that, and her boy band/comedian alternative was a stack of science fiction graphic novels. What many people didn't know was that Hadley never slept here after the show had been canceled. She'd made a "nest" in the attic and even the storage closet, leaving her bedroom space as a warped time capsule.

"Wow, just like on TV," Boo remarked, her gaze skirting around the room and settling on McCall's area.

Unlike her sisters, McCall hadn't gotten any fun or edgy props. Her posters were of Princess Diana and Mother Teresa, and the stack of books had authors like Jane Austen and Emily Brontë.

"Wow," Boo repeated. "You left it just like it was when *Little Cowgirls* was still on."

Yes, McCall had. That's because at the time she hadn't realized that it was just that—props. She'd been so brainwashed by her mother, the greedy over-the-top Sunshine, that McCall had thought this was her true self instead of some image that the show's producers wanted the viewers to see.

"Prissy Pants," Boo muttered.

That had indeed been McCall's nickname. And for a while, Pissy Pants, when she hadn't made it to the bathroom in time during preschool. McCall had sworn off apple juice ever since.

"Uh, before you go look for porn, which I know you'll do…" McCall started. She sat on her bed. "There are some things I don't want my grandmother or anyone else in Lone Star Ridge to know."

Boo nodded and dropped down next to her. "You mean you don't want anyone to hear about your relationship with Cody Joe being staged because you thought it'd get more donations for Saddle Up?" *Relationship* went in air quotes. "Because that would be bad for Saddle Up's reputation."

Reputation could have gone in air quotes, too, because McCall was afraid there wasn't much of that to salvage. Still, she'd try.

"Yes, I don't want anyone to hear that," McCall agreed. And Cody Joe likely wouldn't spill it, either, because he had apparently developed feelings for McCall. A weird twisted set of feelings that involved cheating on her while still intending to ask her to marry him.

"And you don't want your grandmother or anyone else to know that your therapy practice is basically talking to old people who can still get it up," Boo went on.

McCall frowned. Then sighed. She hadn't talked over any details with Boo about her counseling sessions, but one of the clients, Mr. Bolton, had shared plenty with Boo while he'd been waiting for his appointment.

"Yes, we should probably keep that between us, as well," McCall agreed.

However, it was true that the bulk of her clients came from the Peaceful Acres Retirement Village that was next door to her clinic. And yes, the majority of those clients seemed to want relationship and sex advice. Some were just lonely and wanted her to listen.

"Oh, and I thought of something else." Boo clapped her hands as if she'd won a prize. "You don't want Em to know about my past because she might not approve of me having worked at a strip club."

McCall realized she should have written down a list instead of just believing there was one thing she didn't want to get out. But yes, Boo's past career should probably stay hush-hush because if it came out, then McCall would get questions about how she'd met someone in that profession.

And that led her to the main point of this conversation.

"Whatever you do, don't mention Peekaboo," McCall told her.

"Got it." Boo made a locked lips motion over her mouth. "I'm guessing folks around here wouldn't understand, huh?"

No, they wouldn't, and she didn't especially want to explain that Peekaboo was a strip club.

And the former Prissy Pants McCall owned it.

CHAPTER FOUR

"WE COULD NAME him Rose," Gracie said as she studied the pony through the slats of the stall.

Austin studied the Shetland, too, but not with the same gleam in his eyes. Heck, his sister, Cait, was sort of gleaming, too.

Crap.

He definitely hadn't planned on becoming the owner of Cody Joe's failed bribe to McCall. But here it was the morning after the fiasco, and the pony was not only still there, his girls were also trying to come up with names while it chowed down on the remainder of the flower garland that was on the floor of the stall.

Even more, Austin was holding ownership papers that Cody Joe had couriered over. Ownership papers with a handwritten "I'm sorry about what happened, man" sticky note attached.

That was one apology Austin had no intention of accepting. It might not be the adult thing to do or serve as a good example to his twins, but Cody Joe had done the unforgivable and caused a crapload of trouble. Not only for McCall but also with Edith and Howie.

Thanks to the idiot's antics, Edith might carry through on her threat to try to get custody of the girls.

Austin had to believe that she wouldn't win, that he hadn't done anything that would warrant losing his kids. But a battle like that would put a wedge between Zoey's parents and him, and the girls would end up being the biggest losers. Austin would never ban Edith and Howie from seeing Gracie and Avery, but talk about a major strain to have to be civil to the people who were trying to rip his heart to pieces.

"How about Charley Horse?" Cait suggested, drawing Austin's attention back to the pony naming. "Or Unicorn?"

Neither Gracie nor Avery showed any enthusiasm for those choices, but Avery's eye gleam got gleamier. "We could name him Poopy Head."

Austin gave her a warning glance that shifted to more than a glance to Cait when Avery added, "Aunt Cait called somebody that."

Cait looked remorseful for about half a second. Then she shrugged. "Hey, it could have been worse." She patted Avery's arm. "But it's best not to use words like that until you're at least six."

Austin didn't want her saying things like that at six, either, but for Avery three years from now was a lifetime away. Besides, if that was the worst thing that came out of her mouth, he could live with it. Edith, however, would use it as fodder to prove what a bad father he was.

"It's nearly time to go to preschool," Cait announced, glancing at her watch. "You can work on pony names when you get back home. You need Leyton or me to pick them up after school?" she asked Austin.

And this was one of the many reasons why he loved his sister—despite her poopy head language. Cait stepped up to the plate to try to make things easier for him. Leyton, Shaw and his mother, Lenore, did, too. But Cait had gone above and beyond, and it wasn't as if she didn't have her own life. In addition to being a deputy sheriff, she also raised and boarded horses and gave riding lessons. Still, she worked it into her schedule to drive the girls to preschool at least once a week.

"No, I'll be able to get them," Austin told her. He didn't have any meetings today. He did have some paperwork and training to do with a couple of the horses, but he could work that in while the girls were gone for these four hours.

Cait took hold of Avery's and Gracie's hands to get them moving away from the pony and out of the barn. "Go inside and get your backpacks," she instructed. "Make as much noise as you can doing that so I'll know how excited you are."

Normally, the girls loved preschool, but it was obvious they didn't want to leave the unnamed pony. Yep, they'd be keeping the Shetland.

Groaning and grumbling a little and not looking anywhere on the excited scale, the girls started out of the barn. "Can we play cops and bobbers on the way to school?" Avery asked Cait.

Bobbers, not robbers. A little change that Gracie had made when she'd mispronounced it, and it'd stuck. The game didn't entail fake guns, nor equally fake violence or even any running around. It was more of a bossy dialogue that involved lots of giggling and role playing phrases like "You'll never get away with this" and "I was born ready." Occasionally, there was even a "Book 'em, Danno," something they'd gotten from Cait, who loved watching reruns of the old *Hawaii 5-0*.

Of course, any and all phrases used would be peppered with more mispronounced words or made-up ones that could only come from a three-year-old's vocabulary.

"Sure, we can play," Cait agreed. "I'll be the bobber."

Avery frowned. "But you're the cop. And I wanta be the bobber. It's more funner."

"Yeah, it is." Cait patted her head. "But in every life, a little rain must fall."

Even though it was highly likely that Avery didn't have a clue what that meant, she got the gist of it and rolled her eyes. Eyes that were a genetic copy of Cait's and Austin's.

Gracie had already started to walk to the house for her backpack, and Avery ran to catch up with her. "We could all be bobbers," Avery concluded.

"Don't worry," Cait assured him. "Next week, she'll want to be something else. Like be a lion tamer or a flame-thrower." She paused until the girls were out of earshot. "You want to talk about the poopy head bull rider who might have screwed you and McCall six ways to Sunday?"

Austin hadn't believed for a second that Cait wouldn't have heard about that. Heck, it was probably all over social media. For certain, it was all over town, and he hoped the girls wouldn't get wind of any of it at preschool. Of course, the big topic for three-year-olds would be the pony and not the poopy head bull rider who'd almost nailed Miss Water-melon and then made an ass of himself.

"No, I don't want to talk about him," Austin assured her. "I'm hoping I don't ever have to talk about or see him again."

Cait made a sound of agreement, and like him, she kept her attention on the twins as they went inside after their backpacks. Austin and she started strolling in that direction.

"Leyton said that first thing this morning Cody Joe checked himself into a sex addiction clinic in San Anto-nio," Cait provided. "And according to the statement he made, he's doing that with the hopes of getting his life back on track, and that includes being with McCall."

Austin still didn't want to talk about Cody Joe, but that last bit of info latched right on to his attention. Not in a good way, either. He thought of McCall. Of her bruises. Of the dejected expression she'd had the night before when she'd walked away.

Then he thought of her breasts.

Shit.

That was definitely a man-thought that he wouldn't be sharing with his sister. Or anyone else for that matter.

"You think McCall wants to be won back?" Cait asked.

"No." He got another hit of hindsight and realized he should have at least hesitated as if giving it some thought that it in no way needed. McCall would be a fool to get back with that, well, fool.

"Is that because you're interested in…rekindling un-requited stuff with her?" Cait pressed.

This time he made sure he didn't hesitate. "No." He didn't want Cait to get started with any matchmaking.

He wasn't ready for that.

Hell, he wasn't ready for life yet. Not when he was still grieving for Zoey. Not when he hadn't forgiven himself. If he'd just insisted that she have a more aggressive treatment sooner, that might have beaten off the cancer. But he hadn't insisted because she'd wanted to be able to spend as much quality time as possible with him and the girls. Now, that decision was a daily punch to his gut and bite to his ass.

"Leyton also told me about Edith being pissed off," Cait went on. "You want me to try to talk to her and maybe smooth things over?"

For the third time in this short conversation, Austin repeated his "No." He muttered a thanks, though. "You'll just lose your temper and end up snarling, 'Bite me.'"

"True. You want me to see if Leyton or Shaw will talk to her? They're good at that sort of thing." Cait snorted. "Probably because they've had to deal with so much crap from the poopy head in our own gene pool."

Yep, no doubts about that.

Their father, Marty Jameson, was a country music legend, and it'd netted him lots of groupies. Instead of just signing autographs, though, Marty had made it a habit of nailing said groupies and knocking them up. Even though Marty and Austin's mom had divorced years earlier and Marty no longer lived at the ranch, every other year or so, a "love child" would show up.

In fact, Leyton was one of them.

Leyton had not only stuck, but Austin's mom, Lenore, had actually adopted him shortly after Marty and she had divorced.

"Don't ask Shaw or Leyton to talk to Edith," Austin insisted. "I'll give her a day or two to settle and then talk to her myself." He reached the side door to his house just as it opened and the twins came running out.

"Bobbers," Avery squealed. "We all get to be bobbers!"

"Apparently, I have a bank heist to pull off." Cait gave him a bop on the arm and turned to take hold of the girls' hands. She stopped, though, at the sound of an approaching vehicle.

Austin stopped, too, and while he didn't recognize the dark blue car, he sure as heck recognized the woman who stepped out.

McCall.

She wasn't wearing a fairy dress today but rather snug jeans and a white top that would have been plain and ordinary on anyone else. But McCall wasn't the plain and ordinary type. Nope. She filled out those jeans and top in a way that reminded him that she was a woman.

One with breasts.

And a great ass.

She gave them a tentative smile and started their way. Austin just watched the sway of her body as she moved. The way the morning breeze fluttered her hair. And he choked on his own breath.

Cait slapped him on the back and grinned as if she knew exactly what he was thinking.

Maybe rekindling unrequited stuff wasn't such a bad idea, after all.

OH, MY.

That was McCall's first thought, and that was an *oh, my* on a couple of levels. For one, she hadn't expected an audience for the face-to-face apology she needed to give Austin. For another, she hadn't expected to feel the punch of, well, lust.

She wasn't normally a luster. Or rather it didn't usually hit her like a sack of bricks, especially when she'd seen the object of her lust—Austin—just the night before. But that'd been in the dark, during the middle of the crap-storm that Cody Joe had created. Now, here he was looking like something that the cowboy gods had created to make sure women lusted.

It was working.

"The fairy lady," one of the girls squealed. Avery, she remembered. She broke away from Cait's hand and ran toward McCall. Her sister, Gracie, was right behind her. "You don't got on your fairy dress," Avery quickly pointed out.

"It's at the dry cleaner. This is my fairy cowgirl outfit. And this is my magic lasso." McCall pointed to her empty belt loop. "You can't see it because it's invisible."

The words had just rolled out of her mouth, and McCall's gaze flew to Austin to make sure that he let his children believe in such things as fairy tales. Also known as story lies. Of course, the night before he had been wearing a tiara and tutu so she'd figured it'd be okay for her to dabble in pretend things.

"Can I borrow the rope to play bobbers?" Avery asked.

"Nope," Cait quickly answered. "No magical stuff in my SUV. Besides, Fairy Cowgirl might need her lasso—" she

winked at McCall, then slid her brother a glance "—for rop-
ing things."

McCall smiled but blushed, too, and she was thankful for
the hug when Cait pulled her in for a hard one. "Welcome
home, McCall." Cait pulled back and looked down at her
nieces. "McCall is a triplet. That means there are three of
them who all look alike. Twins plus one."

That didn't seem to impress the girls nearly as much as the
magic rope. "Can we play bobbers now?" Avery asked Cait.

"Yep. We gotta go, or they'll be late for preschool."

McCall stepped to the side as Austin kissed both girls,
and while Avery babbled, "Book 'em, Danno," she and her
sister went to the SUV with Cait.

"Remind the teacher not to let Avery bring home any
scissors," Austin called out.

Cait gave him a thumbs-up, strapped the girls into their
car seats and then drove away.

"So, that's what happened to Gracie's hair," McCall remarked. "Hadley used to give me haircuts, too."

She gathered her breath and turned to him, but because
it was hard to hold on to her breath while looking at the
cowboy gods' finest creation, McCall just ended up glancing away.

"I'll bet you're here to tell me how sorry you are," he said.

McCall nodded. "Not just about last night. I should have
called before I came over because I interrupted your time
with your children. But I was afraid if I called, you wouldn't
answer."

"I would have answered," he assured her. "What happened last night wasn't your fault."

McCall had to look at him again to make sure that wasn't
lip service. It didn't appear to be. In fact, he smiled at her.

And her toes tingled.

That smile had more power than any magical fairy rope. Heck, it was possibly more powerful than a million turbo engines.

"Come inside," Austin said. Except he didn't just say it. He drawled it as if his words were slow and sweet. "We can have a cup of coffee and trade summaries of the gossip we've heard. Then we can sort out what's bull and what's really going on."

It seemed so…civil. Except for the sizzle of heat that she felt, and this time McCall thought Austin might be in on that sizzle, too.

She followed him inside and lingered a bit to look around while Austin headed for the kitchen. It was an open floor plan so she didn't lose sight of him. Didn't lose sight of the photos on the mantel, either.

Zoey.

His children.

The life the four of them had once had.

That cooled the sizzle down a little. Once, Zoey and she had been friends. Well, they had been after they'd worked out their somewhat competitive "situation" with Austin. Mc-Call wondered if Zoey had ever mentioned that to him and decided probably not. McCall wouldn't mention it, either.

Tearing her attention away from the mantel, she made her way through the living room. There were definitely signs of the girls here. A toy chest on each side of the fireplace, a stack of kids' books on the coffee table and a pair of pink sandals next to the sofa. The room was cluttered but not messy. This was a well-lived-in home.

"Cream? Sugar?" Austin asked, holding up the coffeepot.

She shook her head. "Just black." And while Austin poured, she took a seat at the granite snack bar.

"Cody Joe had a courier bring over ownership papers of

the Shetland," Austin said. He took a seat, too, across from her with the snack bar in between them.

Cody Joe was probably trying to suck up to Austin. Maybe because he thought Austin had some kind of influence over her. Cody Joe wouldn't be pleased to know that some influence was there if you happened to count sexual attraction.

No, Cody Joe wouldn't be pleased about that.

"Are you okay with keeping the pony?" she asked. "If not, I can deal with it."

He sipped his coffee, looking at her from over the top of his cup. "The girls are picking out names for it."

"Oh." She smiled. "So, you'll be keeping it."

"It looks that way. How about you? Are the gossips right that Cody Joe's antics will cost your foundation lots of money?"

That erased her smile. "It will. Cody Joe called this morning to assure me that he'd make up for that." She paused to have some of her coffee. "Did you know he's supposedly in a sex addiction clinic?"

Austin nodded. "I heard. Is it for real? Does he have a sex addiction or just stupid judgment?"

"The latter," she answered without hesitation. And here's where she thought she owed him an explanation if only so Austin wouldn't think she was an idiot. It was one of those "secrets" that McCall had insisted for Boo to keep to themselves.

"Cody Joe and I used to date," she said, "but for the last six months or so, our relationship's been more of a prop." McCall was certain she was going to have to add a lot more explanation than that.

"You mean like we were in eighth and ninth grade when the *Little Cowgirls* honchos wanted you to have a boyfriend?" he threw out there. "A boyfriend who'd keep up your goody-goody image?"

She nodded. So, Austin hadn't had any trouble grasping that. "Cody Joe loves his mother, Alisha, and she's a huge supporter of the foundation. She insisted that he stay *attached* to me. So do other large donors of the foundation and some of his fans."

"Seems like Cody Joe wants to be attached to you, too," Austin pointed out. "He came here last night to get back together with you."

"Maybe. But I think what he really wants is to make sure Alisha's not thoroughly pissed off at him. As opposed to partly pissed off at him for that stupid stunt he pulled with Miss Watermelon."

Austin paused, studied her. "So, what will you do?" he asked.

Good question, and she had absolutely no good answer, just the hope that this would all blow over. She didn't have to tell Austin that, though, because his phone rang, and he frowned when he checked the screen.

"Sorry, but I have to take this," he said. He set down his coffee and started toward the back of the house. Maybe where he had an office.

McCall was about to offer to go outside so he could have some privacy, but her own phone dinged with a call. She'd turned off the ringer because way too many people had been trying to get in touch with her about Cody Joe. But the caller was Willard Bolton, and she was reasonably sure this didn't have anything to do with the Miss Watermelon debacle. He was a client from Peaceful Acres Retirement Village. And while this call likely wouldn't be an emergency, McCall took it, anyway, with the intention of setting up a phone or Skype session with him for later in the day.

"Is forty-five seconds really too short for sex?" the man immediately asked.

McCall wasn't at all surprised by the question. Along with several other clients in the retirement village, Mr. Bolton often wanted advice on the active sex lives they wished to continue. Admirable, she supposed, since Mr. Bolton was in his mid-eighties and didn't seem to have trouble finding sexual partners.

"Well, is it too short?" he pressed. "I've been timing myself, and forty-five seconds is the average."

Thankfully, he didn't get into the specifics of how and why he was timing himself. "I'm with someone right now, but I'd be happy to discuss this with you later today. Does one o'clock work for you?"

"No. I don't care if anybody you're with hears this. My lady friend's with me right now, and she said if I couldn't last longer than forty-five seconds like the last time, then she's leaving. I think forty-five seconds is fine as long as we both get our bells rang. Isn't that right?"

McCall sighed. "Did your lady friend get her *bell rang* last time?"

Silence. For several long moments. "Uh, maybe."

Which meant no. "I'd think if you had rung her bell, then she wouldn't have said you need to last longer. Mr. Bolton, we've discussed this before, remember? I explained that some women need more time than men during sex." And she was betting nearly all women needed more than forty-five seconds, but McCall kept that to herself.

More silence. "What if I can't give her more than forty-five?" he said, and he'd lowered his voice to a whisper. Probably because the lady friend was hearing this.

They'd discussed this, too, and McCall didn't know if Mr. Bolton was having memory issues or if he just hoped that she'd give him a different opinion if he asked again. For the sake of his lady friend, though, McCall wasn't going to give him a thumbs-up on anything under a minute.

"Foreplay," McCall emphasized, setting her coffee on the countertop. "If you make that good enough for your partner, then she might not complain about the duration."

"Foreplay?" he repeated. "That's the kissing and touching stuff you told me about?"

"Yes, the kissing and touching stuff is foreplay. Women generally need that sort of thing," she verified. "Aim for at least five minutes."

"Five minutes?" he protested. "That's too long. A man my age can't waste that kind of time."

"A man your age won't get his bell in place to be rung if you don't at least try. Kisses and touches," she emphasized. "When you're done, text me if you still want a phone appointment. Goodbye, Mr. Bolton."

She hit the end call button before he could say more, turned around, and her heart landed in her kneecaps when she saw Austin standing there. He wasn't talking on his phone, either. Instead, he was looking at her as if he'd just heard everything she'd said.

McCall quickly went back through her part of the conversation and realized—yes, she'd just talked about sex in front of Austin, a man who sexually charged the air just by breathing.

"One of my clients," she said, slipping her phone back into her jeans pocket.

"Same here." He held up his own phone before he put it away. "Clearly, your conversation was a lot more interesting than mine."

McCall felt herself blush. At least, she hoped it was a

blush and not a flush. She didn't need any part of her body getting in on this renewed crush she had for Austin.

"I should just be going." She fluttered her fingers in the direction of the front door.

"You're sure?" he asked.

Oh, it was not a simple question. It sent another zing through the air. A zing that hit her midbody as if he'd just done the full five minutes of kissing and touching.

This was stupid. She shouldn't be tempted. Even if she was the sort to have casual sex—and she wasn't—this kind of casual sex could quickly turn complicated not just for her but for Austin.

"Yes, I'm sure," she said, hoping that she sounded a lot more certain than she felt.

McCall turned, forced her feet to get moving, and was well aware that Austin was right behind her. If he touched her, she might ditch all the "quickly turn complicated" rationale.

She'd just reached the door when someone knocked on it. McCall froze. Austin did, too. And even though the lust for him had only been in her head, she suddenly felt guilty, as if they'd been caught doing something wrong.

Something that would have definitely lasted more than five minutes.

Austin stepped around her to open the door, and her guilt went up a notch. Austin's father-in-law, Howie, was on the porch. The man blinked, obviously surprised to see her.

"I just dropped by to apologize to Austin," she quickly said, hoping that he hadn't thought she'd spent the night. "I'm really sorry," she added from over her shoulder as she went outside.

Even though she didn't look back, McCall had no trouble hearing what Howie said. "Austin, we have to talk. *Now.*"

CHAPTER FIVE

AUSTIN STOOD IN the doorway and watched McCall hurry away as if she'd just been scalded. Maybe in a way that's exactly how she felt. He'd been out of the romance loop for a while, but he still recognized an interested woman when he saw her.

McCall was definitely interested.

Hell, he was interested in her, too, but there were too many obstacles in their paths. Obstacles that five-minute foreplay and good sex weren't going to fix.

Still…

"If you look at her much longer, you might start drooling," Howie remarked, getting Austin's attention.

He certainly hadn't forgotten that Howie was standing right there or his *we have to talk now* demand, but Austin had let McCall temporarily distract him. Drooling wasn't likely but a possible hard-on was. That's why Austin tore his attention from McCall and closed the door so he could regain his focus and face down Howie.

"I'm not letting Edith and you take my kids," Austin said right off. Best to get that out of the way. "And you know that's not what Zoey would have wanted, either. Zoey knew I was a good father. Hell, I'm still a good father."

Howie sighed, went to the kitchen and helped himself to a cup of coffee. "I know Zoey wouldn't have wanted it, but Edith doesn't see things that way. She wants what's best for Avery and Gracie."

"I'm what's best for them," Austin snapped. "They're my kids, not yours and Edith's."

Howie nodded as if that's exactly what he expected Austin to say. Probably because Austin had already voiced several variations of that with the hopes that it might finally sink in. This wasn't his first rodeo with an overbearing grandmother who thought she was acting in the best interest of her grandchildren. Edith had been singing the same tune for nearly a year.

"Edith is still grieving," Howie said, going to the mantel to look at the pictures. "We all are," he added before Austin could remind him of that. "You lost your wife. Edith and I lost our only child. Avery and Gracie lost their mother."

Austin sighed, too. "I want to cut Edith and you some slack because I know how much both of you loved Zoey. How much you miss her. But I'm not going to hand over my kids to help make that better for Edith and you."

Howie turned around to face him. His forehead was bunched up, and there was worry all over his expression. "I think I've calmed Edith down for now. She did call our lawyer first thing this morning, but she hasn't pulled the trigger yet on filing a petition for custody."

"A petition she'll lose." Austin couldn't tone down the snarl in his voice.

"Maybe." Howie looked him straight in the eyes. "Courts and judges don't always play fair. Edith's family has a lot of contacts, a lot of pull."

Yeah, and that's what caused Austin to lose sleep at night and twisted his gut into a knot. Edith was old money. Old power. In contrast, Austin was the son of a washed-up country music singer with the morals of an alley cat.

"You would actually help Edith try to take my kids from me?" Austin demanded.

Howie sighed again. "No. But Edith's my wife, and I love her. I won't take her side on this, but I won't take yours, either."

"Sounds like a wishy-washy load of bullshit to me." The temper came like a flashfire.

And it cooled just as quickly.

Austin had to force himself to remember that Howie had been a darn good father. A good grandfather, too. A good enough one that he might be able to keep Edith in check.

"You said Edith had calmed down," Austin reminded him. "Any chance of keeping it that way?"

"Maybe." Howie wearily scrubbed his hand over his face and repeated it. "My advice would be to keep everything, uh, low profile."

Austin didn't have to guess what Howie meant by that. "You mean I shouldn't open my door in case an idiot bull rider is standing on the other side." Yep, there was plenty of sarcasm in his voice.

"I know that wasn't your fault," Howie quickly assured him. "From what I'm hearing, it wasn't McCall's fault, either." He paused. "By the way, why'd she come here to you?"

Austin shrugged as if the answer were obvious. "We're old friends." But it was possible it was more than that. Or it could be the unexpected heat between them was causing him to think that. "Zoey and McCall were friends, too."

Howie stared at him for several long moments. "And there's nothing more than *friendship* going on between McCall and you?"

"No," Austin quickly answered. Because dirty thoughts about five-minute foreplay and sex didn't count.

"Too bad," Howie mumbled.

It was a good thing Austin hadn't just had a gulp of coffee because he would have gotten choked on it. "Excuse me?"

Again, Howie's gaze came to his. "It's true that McCall

had an unconventional upbringing as Edith pointed out, but I did some internet searches on her. She's a do-gooder. She's made something out of her life."

She had indeed. "I pointed that out to Edith, too. She didn't seem convinced or impressed."

"Well, I showed her the articles on McCall's foundation. Showed her the pictures that McCall had taken with some of her donors. Edith knew some of them."

Because Edith and those donors had run in the same "silver spoons in their mouths" circles. And Austin suddenly saw where this was going. It was going in a direction that caused him to mentally curse.

"Now that Edith knows McCall hobnobs with rich people, she might be the kind of woman Edith would approve of," Austin grumbled.

"She might," Howie agreed, "and before you get your back up about that, consider this. One of Edith's biggest gripes is that she doesn't believe a man should be raising two little girls by himself. You don't buy that. Hell, I don't buy that. But Edith does, and if you had someone like McCall in your life, then maybe that would make Edith hush about trying for custody of the girls."

It was too late—Austin already had his back up. "You want me to get together with McCall to appease Edith?"

"No." Howie said it not only quickly but also with a firm voice. "That'd just be a side benefit. I want you to get together with McCall—or some other woman—because you deserve to be happy, Austin. You deserve to find love again."

And just like that, all the wind went out of his pissed-off sails.

Austin mentally fumbled around with what he should say to that. Heck, maybe he wasn't ready to be happy or to find love again. Maybe his girls weren't ready for that, either. But that wasn't what came out of his mouth.

"I haven't asked out a woman in years," Austin grumbled. "Not since Zoey."

Howie set his coffee cup down and patted Austin on the back. "Well, maybe it's something you oughta consider."

ALL THINGS CONSIDERED, the third text that McCall got on her way from the grocery store to Em's was very unexpected. She hadn't checked her phone during her quick shopping trip to get some things for Em, but now that she'd pulled up in front of the house, she could see that the first had been from Mr. Bolton.

Apparently, he hadn't been able to pull off a five-minute foreplay.

The second text had been from Dottie Purcell—who'd been on the receiving end of Mr. Bolton's quick-trigger love-making. Since Dottie was also her client, McCall would soon respond to both the woman and Mr. Bolton. But for now, it was the third text that got her attention.

If you're still in town on Friday night around six, do you want to have dinner at my place? Fairy dress and tutu optional. Austin.

McCall wasn't even sure how Austin had gotten her number, but she didn't have to guess why he'd asked her out. It was that blasted heat again. Good grief. She'd thought that with Austin having his hands so full with his kids he wouldn't have even tried to make time for her.

She smiled.

Then she frowned.

Groaning, McCall went through a flurry of emotions

that were more appropriate for a teenage girl than a grown woman. A grown woman with a multitude of her own problems.

McCall grabbed the grocery bags and got out of her SUV to go inside, but the moment she reached the door it opened. Not Granny Em or Boo but rather her grandmother's part-time housekeeper, who always seemed to have a full-time stick up her rear.

Bernice Biggs.

"Your sister and that weirdo assistant of yours are here," Bernice immediately informed her.

Since everything the woman did or said seemed to be coated with a thick layer of disapproval, McCall merely smiled and did something she was certain would confuse Bernice. McCall dropped a quick kiss on her cheek.

"Thanks for letting me know," McCall said, and her voice was coated with as much glee as she could muster. It was a decent accomplishment, considering there wasn't much glee in her life right now.

Well, except for Austin asking her out on a date.

Obviously, she'd have to figure out how to handle it, and by handle it—she'd have to tell him no without hurting his feelings. It wouldn't be easy, but Austin didn't need the kind of trouble she could bring to his life.

McCall made her way to the kitchen to put up the groceries, and she found the three women seated at the breakfast table. Boo, Granny Em and Sunny. Her sister immediately got up and pulled McCall into a hug that she very much needed. The rest of their family might qualify for the supreme dysfunctional label, but Sunny and she were still close. And normal-ish.

McCall was about to ask Sunny how her romantic weekend with Shaw had gone, but Granny Em spoke first. "Austin called me and asked for your number. Did he get in touch with you?"

Granny Em's question brought silence and stares, all aimed at McCall. She nodded and hoped she didn't have to get into why Austin had wanted her number.

"Good," Em declared, grinning. "Because he's gonna ask you out on a date. He didn't come out and say that, but I could hear it in his voice. He sounds pretty smitten with you."

That brought on more silence and stares, again aimed at McCall. Obviously, they were waiting for her to explain how Austin could have become so smitten with her when she'd been back in Lone Star Ridge less than twenty-four hours.

"Not smitten," McCall corrected, and because she was in the company of people she trusted, she could be honest. "It's lust."

"Ah," Granny Em said, giving an approving nod, and Sunny and Boo added nods of their own.

"Lust is a good way to start," Boo commented.

"A good way to keep things going, too," Sunny said, giving McCall a playful jab with her elbow.

"Yes, but that might not be good for Austin. Because of Edith," McCall added, and she left it at that.

Judging from the next round of nods, the women had already gotten wind of Edith wanting custody of Avery and Gracie. McCall hoped the woman failed. She didn't believe Edith was a bad person, but Austin had a right to raise his own children.

Pushing all of that aside, McCall turned to Sunny and took a long look at her. "I don't have to ask if you're happy. I can see it all over your face."

"I am indeed over the moon," Sunny confirmed, but she didn't smile. "And I don't have to ask if you're feeling crappy. I can see it all over your face." She slipped her arm around McCall's waist. "Why don't we go for a walk and you can tell me all about it?"

"It's hotter than a hen laying hard-boiled eggs out there," Em interrupted. "Y'all just stay in here and have your *feeling crappy* chat. I've downloaded some new music I want to listen to."

"Oh, can I listen, too?" Boo asked.

"It's okay," McCall assured her assistant. "You can stay."

"No, I really want to listen to the music," Boo insisted. Her mouth stretched into an exaggerated grin. "Did you know Em has sort of trashy taste in tunes?"

McCall and Sunny both made sounds of agreement without a trace of surprise. Granny Em did seem to enjoy listening to the more explicit songs, and McCall wasn't at all sure that Em didn't know exactly what those lyrics meant.

"So, tell me about your hot affair with Shaw," McCall prompted Sunny after Granny Em and Boo were out of the room.

Sunny's smile was delicious and decadent. "You know I've been in love with him since I was old enough to know why I got tingles in my nether regions whenever I laid eyes on him."

McCall had indeed known that. The "smitten" label had definitely been true in Sunny's case. "What about the differences you two had?" McCall asked as she started putting up the groceries. "You've always wanted kids and Shaw didn't."

Sunny's smile only intensified. "He's changed his mind on that. We're going to wait a few months until we're married, and then the knocking-up sex will begin."

Well, that a huge change for Shaw. McCall remembered him not being fond of kids since he'd had to deal with so many of his siblings and half siblings. As the oldest of the

Jameson clan, a lot of responsibility had been placed on Shaw's shoulders, and his father certainly hadn't stepped up to the plate to help. Still, it sounded as if Shaw had figured out that he would have parenting help if he had a child with Sunny.

"I'm very happy for you," McCall said. She paused putting up the groceries to give her sister another hug.

"But?" Sunny asked after she pulled back.

"No buts," McCall assured her.

However, there was one. McCall was indeed happy for Sunny and Shaw, but a little piece of her was sorry that she hadn't found that kind of happiness. It wasn't jealousy. Okay, maybe it was, just a little. But it was frustrating that a therapist couldn't heal herself.

"I know that look." Sunny studied her eyes. "Using one of Granny Em's sayings—you look lower than the basement of a gopher hole."

McCall tried to change her expression. Tried to brighten up. Because there was no way she wanted to bring Sunny down anywhere near a gopher's basement.

"Any chance Austin could be the cure for what ails you?" Sunny asked.

McCall shouldn't have been surprised that her sister had seen right through her. Sunny and she had always had a telepathy type thing going on. Some people would have said that's because they'd shared the same womb for the first eight months or so of their lives, but since McCall had no such connection with Hadley, that wasn't it. It was probably because Sunny and she were more birds of a feather. Family and doing the right thing were important to them.

Unlike Hadley and Hayes.

Their Hollywood lives put them in a different sphere than Sunny and her. That and their crappy attitudes toward life. McCall and all her siblings had been subjected to the same insane upbringing, but it had sucker punched Hayes and Hadley more than it had Sunny and her.

"Well?" Sunny nudged when McCall stayed quiet.

McCall took out her phone and showed her the "dinner date" text from Austin, and it caused Sunny to squeal with delight. And give her another hug.

"No, I'm not all gushy because we could be hooked up with brothers," Sunny assured her. "I'm gushy because I think Austin could scratch an itch for you that hasn't been scratched in a while."

"I don't doubt that," McCall admitted. Austin definitely looked like an itch scratcher. "But there's a problem."

Sunny continued to study her. "You mean Zoey?"

"She could be part of it," McCall admitted, and then paused. "I remember Zoey and Austin together, and it was nothing like what I had with him. Everything that Austin and I had together was part of a script." Well, that was true on his part, anyway. "But it was the real deal with Zoey and him."

Sunny slid her hand over McCall's. "It was. They were very much in love. But surely you don't think Austin should keep on being in love with her even after she's gone?"

"No, but part of him will always love her." McCall shook her head to cut off any assurances from Sunny that Austin could and would have a life after Zoey. "If Austin gets involved with me, that could end up hurting him."

"You mean because of what happened last night with the bull rider?" Sunny asked.

"No." McCall dragged in a long breath. "It's because of something I did when I was in college. Also, because of something I own."

Apparently, triplet telepathy wasn't working so well on

this because Sunny just looked confused. "Uh, what exactly did you do and what do you own?"

Best just to say this fast, and over the years McCall had sort of rehearsed it. She'd known that someday she would have to tell Sunny or Granny Em. "I ran short of money when I was in grad school so I worked in a gentleman's club called Peekaboo in Dallas."

Sunny's mouth fell open, the stunned surprise all over her face. Then she gasped. Then laughed. "You were a stripper?"

McCall understood the shock. After all, she'd been the "good" Little Cowgirl. "No, but I was a waitress there, and I wore a very skimpy outfit that barely covered my nipples and my butt. It was so skimpy that customers often mistook me for one of the strippers." Thankfully, the place had good bouncers so things never got out of hand.

"Wow," Sunny said, not disapproval but with awe. "But you were able to watch the strippers and see what they do?"

That was a big yes. McCall hadn't had a choice about the watching and seeing since the women had been "performing" on the stage that jutted out onto the floor. The very floor where McCall had served drinks.

"Yes, I got to see a lot of the shows and routines," McCall settled for saying. Ditto for getting plenty of behind-the-scene glimpses of the women shoving and prying themselves into costumes.

Sunny's eyes seemed to light up. "Do you think you could teach me some moves the strippers used? Shaw would *appreciate* something like that."

And this was why she loved Sunny. No judgment. Granny Em probably wouldn't, either, but McCall couldn't say that for the rest of the town.

Or even for Austin.

"I'd like to keep this on the q.t.," McCall went on, "but

yes, I'll teach you a few moves." She winked at Sunny, but then McCall's expression got a lot more serious. "There's more." Again, best to say this fast. "I became close friends with the owner of Peekaboo, Lizzie Marlow, and when she passed away last year, she left the strip club to me. According to the terms of the will, I can't sell it or give it away."

No gasp this time, but Sunny stared at her for some long moments, no doubt trying to absorb everything. McCall knew her sister would have questions, and then Sunny would soon come to the conclusion about the owner of a strip club getting involved with Austin.

It'd be a bad idea.

Wouldn't it?

Of course it would. Well, unless McCall kept things to a fling, but heck, that would be bad, too. He was recovering from a horrible ordeal, and while sex might give him a temporary lift, it wouldn't solve anything.

"Very few people know about me owning Peekaboo," McCall went on when Sunny didn't say anything. "Boo knows. So do the strippers who work there." She frowned. "And Cody Joe."

She could *thank* one of the strippers, Marla Devereaux, for spilling that to him. Apparently, the woman hadn't taken McCall's warning of "keep this hush-hush" to heart and had spilled when Cody Joe and she had crossed paths. That path crossing had likely involved sex, but at least Marla and Cody Joe hadn't let the ownership info leak to anyone else.

"Wow," Sunny repeated, the word coming out with a gush of breath.

McCall nodded. "I know. It's a lot to absorb, a lot to take in."

Sunny mimicked her nod and kept her gaze locked with

McCall's. She could see Sunny trying to process all of this. "I have a question," her sister finally said.

Of course she had a question, maybe more than one. Sunny probably wanted to know how she thought she could go on keeping a secret like this. Because after all, secrets-keeping took its toll. And it would especially take a toll if McCall had to watch everything she said, everything she did.

"Funny Sunny time," her sister announced. "Why do strippers wear panties?" Sunny followed with the punch line before McCall could even think to venture a guess. "To keep their ankles warm."

The laughter burst from McCall's mouth, and she thought that it might have been the first time she'd found a Funny Sunny actually funny. She would have asked her sister when she'd added adult humor to her comic routine, but all laughter faded when her phone beeped with a call, and McCall saw the name on the screen.

Alisha Lozano.

"Cody Joe's mom," McCall muttered. She would have preferred to let this go to voice mail, but it could have something to do with the foundation.

"You need some privacy?" Sunny asked.

McCall shook her head. She might want her sister's shoulder if this turned out to be bad news. Plus, she'd basically just bared her soul to Sunny so there would be no need to keep hush-hush anything said in this phone conversation.

"McCall," Alisha said the moment that she answered, "I need you to forgive Cody Joe." The woman's tone wasn't what anyone would consider friendly, but this seemed even more brusque than usual.

"Forgive him!" McCall tried to clamp down the dart of temper that hit her like a boulder. *Remember the foundation*, she told herself. Remember that this woman could make things better or worse. For the sake of the foundation, Mc-Call needed *better* to happen.

"Forgive him?" McCall repeated once she got her teeth unclenched. "Exactly what does forgiving him entail?" That had also come out as a snarl, and she had to rein that in. "Are you thinking maybe a statement to the media?"

Because if so, McCall could muster up that lie if she kept reminding herself it was for the good of the foundation.

"For starters, but you'll also have to do something more personal than that," Alisha readily supplied. "A media statement will go a long way in soothing over things with our donors."

"I had already planned to do a phone interview with the press," McCall agreed. She had a reporter friend who could help with that. "But what do you mean about *something more personal*?"

"Forgiving Cody Joe, of course." Again, no hesitation. "*Really* forgiving him," the woman emphasized. "That means you should be visiting him in the clinic so that everyone knows you two are still a couple."

Another temper dart jabbed at McCall. "Cody Joe and I haven't been together in months. You know that."

"Yes, I know that my son apparently had some wild oats to sow. Well, the oats are all sown," she said like gospel. "I've spoken to him, and now he understands that it's time for him to settle down."

It took McCall a moment to get her jaw unclenched. "With me?"

"Of course. Who else? Cody Joe and you are perfect for each other. I couldn't ask for a better wife for him."

McCall knew she should be used to the woman's steam-roller attitude, but it was pissing her off more today than usual. "Cody Joe got caught about to have sex with Miss Watermelon," McCall pointed out. "I'm not going to forget the damage that caused to the foundation and possibly to my therapy practice."

"That'll all blow over." Again, it was Alisha's gospel tone. "I expect you to mend this rift with my son."

This time, McCall's jaw locked, and she could have sworn she actually saw red. "And if I don't?"

"You will," Alisha declared. With that order, she ended the call.

McCall stood there, staring at her phone, and when her fingers began to cramp, she eased up her grip. Eased the reins on her temper, too, and that temper flew right to her fingers.

She pulled up Austin's text, her gaze skimming over the words again.

If you're still in town on Friday night around six, do you want to have dinner at my place? Fairy dress and tutu optional. Austin.

McCall didn't tamp down anything she was feeling when she typed, I'd love to have dinner with you. Pink tutu, okay?

And before McCall could change her mind, she hit Send.

CHAPTER SIX

"On a scale of one to ten, how sure are you about this dinner date with McCall?" Shaw asked.

"Ten," Austin immediately answered.

It was a lie, of course, and while he didn't like lying to his brother, he also didn't want to admit that his confidence rating was more like a three or four. But if Austin said that to Shaw, he'd have to justify why he'd asked McCall out. Shaw would get the attraction/possible-sex angle. Heck, he would even get the part about Austin wanting to catch up with an old friend.

What Shaw wouldn't get was this had an "appease Edith" element to it.

Austin felt like crap for having that play into this, even if the playing into it was in a very small way. He'd indeed thought about seeing McCall, but there was little chance he would have acted on it this fast had it not been for Howie's *maybe it's something you oughta consider.*

While Austin waited for his brother to respond, he continued cooking and keeping his well-tuned parental ear turned in the direction of the girls' bedroom. The twins were supposed to be stuffing their backpacks for their overnight with Uncle Shaw and Aunt Sunny, but if it got too quiet, Austin would need to check on them. For now, there was enough giggling and excited chatter that all was well. When you had three-year-old twins, silence and quiet usually weren't good things.

"Ten?" Shaw repeated with all the skepticism of a big brother or a jaded parole officer.

Austin looked up from the pot of red sauce he was stirring and lifted his eyebrow. "You've got reservations about me seeing McCall?" He didn't wait for an answer from Shaw. "Because if so, you're kind of late. She'll be here in about fifteen minutes."

Unless she'd changed her mind. If she had or if she had doubts about doing this, he normally would have heard about it through the town grapevine. But Austin hadn't told anyone other than members of his immediate family about the dinner date so there was no gossipy fruit on the vine. Apparently, McCall had kept things quiet, too.

Shaw shrugged. "It just seems like McCall's got a lot going on right now. I'm surprised she'd want to fit in a dinner date."

Austin stared at him and considered something. Shaw was bedmates with McCall's sister so it was possible McCall had expressed her doubts about this date through a sisterly gabbing session. Doubts that Sunny would have then passed on to Shaw.

"Since I need to get some water boiling and then put on my tutu," Austin said, "maybe it's best if you cut to the chase. Are you worried about McCall or me?"

Shaw opened his mouth, stopped and did some gaping. "Your tutu?"

"It's tonight's dress code," Austin said with a straight face. McCall had no doubt meant that "Pink tutu, okay?" part of her text as a joke, but Austin thought it might be a good icebreaker.

"I'm not worried," Shaw insisted after a long pause. It seemed as if he changed his mind a couple of times on what to add to that. "I just don't want you or McCall hurt."

Austin wanted the same thing, but he didn't see a chance of that happening. "It's dinner," he reminded Shaw. "I'm sure McCall's no more interested in falling for me than I am in falling for her."

That seemed to be what Shaw was waiting to hear because he nodded. So did Austin. But then his brother shrugged and added, "I'm surprised McCall's stayed in town this long. Figured she'd be here just overnight like usual when she visits Granny Em."

"Well, there was nothing usual about this visit. McCall's sort of hiding out from the press."

At least, that was Austin's take on it. Shaw was right, though. Over the past decade and a half since McCall had graduated from high school and left, her trips to see Granny Em had usually been only for a night or two. McCall had been here for nearly a week now and probably wouldn't be staying much longer.

A reminder that didn't settle well in Austin's gut.

Of course, her life wasn't here. It was in Dallas with her perhaps odd counseling practice. In fact, she could be planning on going back to that life and her home this weekend. If so, this date could be her way of saying goodbye.

Shaw snapped his fingers, getting Austin's attention. His brother stared at him, cursed softly. "You've got a glazed look in your eyes."

"It's from the red pepper flakes I put in the red sauce," Austin said without missing a beat.

"It's from lust," Shaw argued. "Just a reminder that you might have forgotten—dicks don't always make good decisions. Don't let yours get in on any decision you make with McCall."

Austin thought, all in all, that it was sage advice. Not necessarily advice that any functioning male had ever taken, but he made a sound to let Shaw know he'd heard those words of wisdom and would act accordingly. In other words, if McCall wanted sex, Austin would have sex with her.

To shift the subject, Austin was about to add another thanks for Shaw agreeing to take the girls for the night, but the giggling and running feet stopped him. Apparently, Avery and Gracie had changed the subject for him and were ready to go.

Sort of.

"Where the heck did they get the makeup?" Shaw asked, eyeing their red lips, green eyeshadow and attempted pink rouged cheeks.

"It's not makeup," Austin said. "It's Magic Markers."

Austin gave the girls his best glare while secretly admiring, well, whatever it was they were doing. It appeared to be some sort of attempt at costumes, complete with glitter winter knit caps that covered their heads. They were both wearing tutus, as well, which meant he wouldn't be able to use one to impress McCall with his wit and complete confidence in his masculinity.

Outside, he heard a car turning into his driveway. McCall probably. Well, unless Cody Joe had returned for a repeat performance.

"Uh, will Magic Marker come off with soap and water?" Shaw asked.

"No," Austin answered. "But hand sanitizer works."

This was a déjà vu situation except the last time the girls had resorted to Magic Marker makeup, he'd been on the receiving end of the "makeover." That's when he'd been dumb enough to try to take a nap while the girls were supposed to be watching a movie.

"I'll get the hand sanitizer," Austin muttered, but the girls immediately objected.

"We want the fairy lady to see us all pretty," Avery insisted with Gracie joining in on that.

To Austin, it seemed as if there was some other agenda behind that simple demand. But he shrugged and went to the door to answer it when he heard the knock. It was indeed McCall. So, not only hadn't she canceled, but she was even a little early.

And she was also wearing a pink tutu over her jeans.

"The fairy lady!" the girls squealed before Austin could even get out a greeting. They swarmed toward McCall and hugged her legs as if greeting an old friend. And McCall hugged them right back.

"Did you put that makeup on for me?" McCall asked.

Gracie and Avery eagerly bobbed their heads.

"Well, it's lovely," McCall declared. "Hello, Shaw." She hugged his brother, too.

No hug for Austin, but the smile she gave him was plenty enough. Of course, her mere breathing seemed to be enough to remind him that he was glad she hadn't canceled.

"Something smells great," McCall remarked, sniffing the air.

"Pasta sauce," Austin supplied, "and I baked some breadsticks."

"We getta have pizza," Gracie piped in.

"With Nuckle Shaw," Avery finished.

"Yep, Sunny's picking up the pizza for us now. Come on, girls," Shaw said to them, but the twins didn't budge.

"I'm Gracie," Avery volunteered, looking up at McCall.

And Austin got it then. It was the reason they'd dressed alike and were wearing the hats to cover their hair. They were attempting a switcheroo, and they usually got away with it with almost everyone but Cait and him. Now, though,

McCall eyed Avery with what Austin was pretty sure was skepticism.

"Okay, Gracie," McCall said, and she gave the girl a wink. She winked again when she greeted the real Gracie and called her Avery.

Again, the twins stared at her with some awe. Austin did, too. The girls were indeed identical in looks—except for their expressions. Austin had gotten very good at reading those, but most people didn't see the differences.

"Time to go," Shaw repeated. "There's pizza, movies and a clean house waiting for you two to mess up."

That caused some jumping up and down and giggling as if it were a fine joke, but there would indeed be some messes made. It came with the territory.

Austin kissed the girls goodbye, but there was no need to give them reassurances that he'd be at Shaw's first thing in the morning to get them. This would be a fun outing for them, and they'd likely beg him to stay even longer with their uncle. Shaw, in turn, would be more than ready to hand them back over to Austin.

"I feel overdressed," McCall remarked, motioning toward her tutu, after Shaw and the girls had left.

That gave Austin an excuse to skim his gaze over her body while he shut the door. He could hear the water boiling on the stove, but he didn't hurry. Unfortunately, McCall noticed the slow as molasses gaze-skimming because her eyes met his when he finally lifted them.

"So, why exactly did you ask me to dinner?" Her voice had some smoke in it, and the sound created a stir in his body. Of course, his once-over of her had done some preliminary stirring, too.

Austin considered how to answer that, and he figured this wasn't the time for the truth—that Howie had put the notion of it in his head. Nope. That wouldn't play well, and besides, Austin had taken the notion and run with it. Not because of Howie or Edith. But because it was something he'd wanted to do.

He wanted to do this, too.

And he leaned in and brushed his mouth over hers.

It barely qualified as a kiss, but that didn't mean it had no punch to it. It did. Man, it did. A punch that was hard enough to make him remember that he shouldn't have done it. A punch that was coated in guilt. Not just because he'd maybe gotten McCall here under false pretenses but because of those pictures on the mantel.

Because of Zoey.

Part of him still felt married to her, and that part of him pulled back. He would have stepped away from her, but McCall caught on to the front of his shirt and dragged him to her. Specifically, dragging his mouth to hers. Of course, she really didn't have to exert much energy to get him heading in that direction. Apparently, lust and attraction could override even a double dose of guilt.

This second kiss wasn't much more than a touch, either. At first, anyway. But she pressed harder, leaning in until the stiff netting of the tutu pressed against the front of his jeans. As if that weren't enough contact, she touched his bottom lip with her tongue before she broke the contact and let go of his shirt.

"All right," she said as if surprised by some experiment she'd just tried. Then she muttered some profanity. "I'd hoped I wouldn't feel that as much as I did." McCall looked up at him. "We didn't kiss like that in middle school when it was scripted."

"No," he agreed. Then Austin added some truth by giving her back her own words. "I'd hoped I wouldn't feel that as much as I did."

She nodded and licked her lips as if tasting him there. That didn't stop his body from begging for more. Nope. Didn't help at all.

"Is there something I can do to help with the meal?" she asked, clearly switching them to a more comfortable subject. One that wouldn't cause an uncomfortable fit in the crotch of his jeans.

"No, thanks." He motioned for her to follow him into the kitchen. "I got it under control."

McCall followed him. "So, are Howie and Edith giving you grief about seeing me, or are they in favor of it?"

Austin hadn't expected to have such a frank conversation with McCall. Especially not coming on the heels of two kisses.

"Howie's in favor. I'm not sure about Edith. What about Em and Boo? Are they in favor or against you being here right now?"

"In favor," she answered without pausing a beat. "However, Cody Joe's mother wants me to remain pure and in-wait for her son. I didn't accept your dinner invitation because I was pissed off at her for saying that," McCall added. Then she shrugged. "All right, maybe that played into it just a little."

Austin smiled. "Maybe Howie's pushing played into me asking you out. He thinks I should get on with my life."

She made a sound of understanding. "So, does Howie only want you to date in general, or did he decide I was a good enough candidate for something more?"

"I think it's more of the second than the first."

"Ah. Got it." She nodded. "In his mind, it wouldn't be good for Avery and Gracie for you to date a string of women. Howie would prefer you to focus on only one, and he's willing to overlook my unconventional upbringing."

The woman had a way of boiling everything down to the gist. "That sounds about right. And while we're getting everything out in the open, you should know that I invited you here to keep the gossipers at bay. If we'd gone to the diner or any other place in public, everyone around would have watched our every move."

McCall nodded. "I understand. If you hadn't suggested we come here, then I would have invited you to Em's."

Mercy, it felt good to be honest with her, and it made him realize just how much he'd missed conversations like this. How much he missed just sharing a meal with another adult who wasn't in his gene pool.

Austin reached on top of the fridge to get a bottle of red wine from the rack he kept there, but when he pulled out the bottle, something fell to the floor. He instantly knew what it was, but since it fell right at McCall's feet, he couldn't get to it before she did. She picked it up, handing it to him. However, there was no doubt that she saw the caption on the front of the greeting card.

Life is all about asses.

Below the caption was the image of two guys with their backs to the camera. They were jumping to emphasize both their seriously out-of-shape asses and the bareness of them. McCall didn't open the card, but if she had, she would have seen the punch lines of *You're always covering it, saving it*, etc.

McCall smiled, but it quickly faded when she saw what had to be a way too serious expression on his face.

"It's from Zoey," he explained, taking the card.

"Oh." Her expression went in a serious direction, too, and she backed away as if to put some distance between the card and her. Or maybe the distance was from Austin. "I remember she had a sense of humor."

"Yeah. She did," Austin managed to say.

It took him a couple of seconds to tamp down the sudden lump in his throat. The sizzle of the boiling-over pot helped with that, and Austin laid the card back on top of the fridge, set the wine aside and took care of the bubbling water that was spreading over the cooktop.

"Uh, when Zoey found out the treatments weren't going to work, she left some cards with Edith and Shaw so they could give them to me and the girls," he said. It was easier to tell McCall this when he wasn't looking at her. "At first, we got them once a month, but they've tapered off. Zoey dated the envelopes so that Edith and Shaw would know when to deliver them. I'll be getting another one soon."

McCall's silence felt a little like a shrink's kind of silence. As if she was analyzing everything he'd just told her.

"Shaw doesn't think the cards are a good idea," he went on. "He thinks it draws out my grief."

"Does it?" she asked, but she waved off the question when he turned back toward her. "My guess is the grief is there no matter what."

Bingo. It was there when he woke up, when he drew breath, when he was falling asleep at night in a bed he'd once shared with his wife.

"It's getting better," he insisted. Austin kept his gaze on her while he turned back to open the wine.

"You're waiting for me to ask a counselor question, aren't you?" McCall concluded.

"Well, you are a counselor," Austin reminded her. He poured her a glass of wine and handed it to her. "But maybe I was waiting for you to ask something, well, more personal. For instance, wine or beer? Cats or dogs? Boxers or briefs?"

McCall grinned. "Boxers. Well, unless you've switched preferences in the past eighteen years. I accidentally got a glimpse of you changing clothes for a scene when they were filming *Little Cowgirls*."

It took him a moment to pick through his memories and figure it out, but he did recall a time when he'd come over to deliver something his mom had asked him to bring to Em. The cameraman had asked Austin if he'd change into a pair of jeans that hadn't been torn at the knees. "Date jeans," the guy had called them, and he'd even had Austin's right size. What Austin hadn't known was that McCall had gotten a glimpse of that.

"Accidentally?" he questioned when he saw her dodge his gaze.

She huffed, made a show of rolling her eyes. "Okay, I peeked. Good Girl McCall wasn't always good."

For some stupid reason, that made him hope that she wasn't always good in other areas, too.

Like sex.

But even if it didn't mean that, even if things never went past this dinner date, Austin liked flirting with her. Liked getting to know the woman his pretend girlfriend had become.

"Tell me about this foundation you help run." Austin put the pot with the water for the pasta back on the burner.

"Saddle Up for Tots." McCall sipped her wine. "Cody Joe and I started it about two years ago. His mother actually pressed for him to be part of it," she quickly added. "And Alisha Lozano put a lot of money into getting it off the ground."

"Enough money to offset Cody Joe acting like an ass?" Austin took the salad he'd already put together from the fridge and set it on the table.

"Sometimes it's enough," she admitted, then paused. "The foundation's important, and what he did could cause us to lose donations that could save kids."

He heard the edge of anger in her voice but didn't ask her about it. Austin just kept working on finishing the meal while she continued.

"I had a client." McCall stared into her wine as she spoke. "She was the mother of two young children and in an abusive relationship. I tried to help her, but the truth is, I was way out of my depth. Six years of college doesn't necessarily prep you for something like that."

His chest tightened, and he hoped like hell this didn't have the bad ending that it felt like it would have. "They're alive?" he had to ask.

She nodded, swallowed hard. "But all three of them got hurt when her husband and the children's father decided to show them how much he loved them by beating them. Both the mother and the kids had to be hospitalized, and that's when I decided to do more than just try to use my counseling degrees to get her head on straight. Saddle Up for Tots funds shelters and services for families with young children trying to get back on their feet after being in abusive or bad situations."

Oh, there was that damn lump in his throat again. "Good Girl McCall," he managed to say.

She shrugged. "That's me." McCall lifted her chin, maybe trying to lift the dark mood that'd settled over the kitchen. "I fought it for a long time, you know," she went on. "Because Good Girl McCall was the label the producers of *Little Cowgirls* gave me."

"Badly Hadley and Funny Sunny," he said. "Guess they couldn't think up one for you that rhymed."

"No, and Hadley and Sunny didn't fight theirs. They

more or less slid right into the roles. I, on the other hand, secretly pigged out on junk food and looked at porn."

Well, that got his attention. "Porn?"

She nodded. "Hayes had a stash of magazines in his room. Let me tell you, it was a real surprise to my first lover when I tried to put some of those moves on him."

Austin laughed and was extremely happy when McCall grinned. Mercy, she was a picture sitting there in her pink tutu and with her mouth stretched in a wide smile. And Austin knew then exactly what he had to do. He went to McCall, sliding his hand around the back of her neck.

Complicating the hell out of things, he kissed her.

CHAPTER SEVEN

UH-OH.

That was McCall's first thought. For just the flash of a second, she knew this wasn't a smart thing for Austin and her to be doing. But the flash became a wonderful scorching heat that zinged through her.

His mouth was incredible. So much more than when they'd been kids. Of course, her woman's body could feel a whole lot more, too, and Austin was making sure she got a full dose of those feelings.

McCall felt herself moving and realized she was getting off the seat and going straight into Austin's arms. That gave them some chest-to-chest contact, but the tutu became sort of a chastity belt. Probably a good thing. Because McCall figured she was going to need all the chastity help she could get to stop this from going further than a making-out session.

Austin made the most of the kiss, deepening it so that she got the jolt of his taste. There was the hint of the wine, but the rest was all man. A reminder that she didn't need because McCall could feel the muscles stirring in his well-toned chest. Of course, her breasts were doing some stirring, too, and she knew it wouldn't be long before both her breasts and she wanted a whole lot more.

She eased back to give herself a moment to catch her breath, but she kept her mouth hovering next to his.

"Too fast?" he asked. "Too slow?"

"Too right," she answered honestly. And that was Mc-Call's cue to step back even more.

She immediately saw those sizzler blue eyes. A color so wild and rich that it seemed as if she could dive right into them.

"Too right sounds…promising," he drawled.

"Yes," she admitted, and she was about to tell him that, for both their sakes, they had to go slower, but she was saved by the bell. Or rather by the ding to indicate she had a text. She'd intended to turn off her phone, but maybe it was a good thing she hadn't.

McCall had to reach under the tutu to pull out her phone from her pocket, and she bit back a groan when she saw the name on the screen. Willard Bolton.

"Sorry, it's a client," she muttered to Austin. "I can answer it later."

"No. Go ahead if you need to. I'll finish the pasta."

McCall hesitated but read the message when Austin went back to the stove. Then she wasn't able to bite back the groan.

The lady I'm with has bazookas that drop darn near to her waist, Mr. Bolton had texted. What the heck am I supposed to do with them?

It was times like this that McCall wished she'd become a data cruncher. Or limited her clients to those with real emotional problems. Of course, in Mr. Bolton's mind, this was a problem, and it was real. He probably didn't realize that many men over eighty would love to get a chance to ogle bare breasts, no matter their current location on the body.

Most women lose firmness in their breasts as they get older, McCall texted back. Don't bring it up because it might embarrass her. Just touch or kiss them as you normally would.

She stopped, then remembered this was the man who had trouble with foreplay. His "normally" probably wasn't anything to write home to Mom about. So, McCall added, For at least five minutes.

Five??!! was the response she got back from Mr. Bolton a few seconds later.

Five, she verified. And I'm sorry, but I won't be able to answer any other texts or calls from you tonight. Contact me tomorrow for a phone consult if you need it.

McCall was certain Mr. Bolton would feel as if he *needed* it; though, at times, like now, she thought that maybe the man just enjoyed having someone else know that he was still sexually active. It was something she'd need to address with him if these foreplay questions continued.

She started to put her phone away, but it dinged again with another text. Thankfully, not from Mr. Bolton this time but rather from Boo.

Sorry to bug you while you're with the hot cowboy, but there was a grabby-feely at Peekaboo tonight, Boo's message said. Delia grabbed and felt right back in her usual way. Someone called the cops, and Arnette is dealing.

McCall sighed. Delia's *usual way* was to kick a guy's balls if he got too *grabby-feely* with her. The woman was good at the job, but she stood her ground. McCall admired that. Well, she did when cops didn't get involved. But Arnette Middleton was the club manager, and she would handle this.

Hopefully, anyway.

Keep me posted, McCall texted back, and she hoped she wasn't going to have to go to Dallas tonight. The press was still on her heels, and she didn't want one of them seeing her go into the club.

When she finally managed to put her phone away, McCall saw that Austin was smiling. "I'm thinking you lead a very interesting life," he said.

She scrounged up a smile. "You have no idea."

He didn't. Austin had gotten an inkling of her clients from her other conversation with Mr. Bolton, but he didn't have a clue about Peekaboo. And that's why those kisses had been a horrible idea. She might not be able to stop her physical reaction to Austin, but she could protect him by backing off.

"I'm so sorry, but I'll have to eat and run," she said. "Something really important came up."

He managed to keep his smile in place, but she saw the disappointment in his eyes. Disappointment was a lot better than suspicion, though. A lot better, too, than his realizing that just being with her might give Edith some extra firepower.

Austin nodded and drained the pasta he'd just finished cooking. "If you like, I can fix you a plate to go."

McCall jumped right on that. "Yes, thank you. That'd be great. Everything looks so good, and I know you went to a lot of trouble. Not just with the meal but with arranging for Shaw to take the girls."

He dismissed that with a shrug. "I like to cook. And as for Avery and Gracie, they've been wanting to stay overnight there for months. Plus, this'll give Shaw and Sunny some parent creds." Austin was saying all the right things, but the disappointment made it to his voice, too.

She watched as he put some pasta and sauce in a plastic container. Austin did the same to some salad and the breadsticks. When he had that all bagged up, he held it out to her.

Then he kissed her.

Good grief. McCall melted again. No way could she just tamp down her response, and she even heard herself make a soft moan of pleasure.

"Just checking," Austin said when he pulled back from her.

She didn't ask what that meant, but maybe he'd thought her "eat and run" was bogus. Which it wasn't. Something had indeed come up—her remembering why this wasn't a good idea.

He walked her to the door, kissing her again. This time, though, it was only a peck on the cheek. A friendly goodbye, but McCall's body was already zinging with the overwhelming desire to get his mouth back on hers again. Still, she forced herself to walk away, got in her car and started the drive back to Granny Em's.

Obviously, it was time to leave Lone Star Ridge.

The thought of that washed over her like a kind of filmy grief and disappointment. She'd been anxious to leave after high school, but it felt, well, right to be here now. In part that was because of Austin. Because of Granny Em, too. But feeling right could blow up in her face.

Since she no longer felt festive enough to wear the tutu, McCall yanked it off before she got out of her car at Granny Em's. She'd have to explain the canceled dinner, but she wouldn't sulk. Well, maybe not. She could dive right into solving the possible problem at Peekaboo to help take her mind off Austin's kisses and the look on his face when she'd walked out.

McCall went around the house and in through the kitchen door, but she immediately came to a stop. There, at the breakfast table, sat Boo and Granny Em. Boo was only in her underwear—a hot-pink bra and matching panties—and

Em was wearing a full outfit. Jeans, shirt, boots and even a sweater. Judging from the cards they were holding and the stash of pennies on the table, they were playing some sort of game.

"Reverse strip poker," Boo quickly supplied.

Em made a sound of agreement but kept her attention on the cards in her hand. "It's something I used to play with a fella I was seeing way back when. Everybody starts in their undies, and you get to add an item of clothing when you win a hand."

"Em was telling me about it," Boo said, picking up the explanation. "And I thought it'd be fun to learn how. I'm clearly not very good at it." She motioned toward her skimpy attire. Then Boo frowned, got to her feet and started putting on her clothes. "What went wrong with the dinner?"

Granny Em looked up at McCall, too, and after she eyed the bag of food, she also stood.

Obviously, Boo wouldn't have mentioned anything to Granny Em about Peekaboo so McCall went with Mr. Bolton as an excuse. "A client needs my help. I didn't want to discuss things with him in front of Austin so he made me a to-go bag."

A bag that McCall put in the fridge. Her appetite was nil right now, and she hated that Austin had gone to all the trouble to make her a delicious-looking meal.

Granny Em studied her in only the way that a wise grandmother could do, and she sighed. Then she coughed. She also tightened the sweater around her, pinching it at the neckline as if she were cold.

"Maybe it's a good thing you came home early," Em muttered. "I'd wanted to talk about you and Boo staying here for a while longer. Maybe for the rest of the summer."

McCall studied her in only a way that a skeptical granddaughter could do. "Are you sick?" Just in case she was, McCall used the back of her hand to check Em's forehead. It felt like a normal temp to her.

"No, not sick," Em assured her. "Just down. I've been down a lot lately."

McCall never remembered Granny Em being depressed, but maybe she was. "When's the last time you had a checkup?"

Em dismissed that with a wave of her hand. "Nothing's wrong with my body." But she coughed again. "It's just it's not so lonely with Boo and you here."

McCall released the breath she'd been holding. Granny Em wasn't sick, and this was likely a ploy to get her to stay. "Sunny's living just a few miles away," McCall pointed out

"Yes, but Shaw will have her knocked up soon if he hasn't already, and I'd like someone here with me for a while." Her eyes met McCall's. "Would it be too much to ask if you could stay on just a little longer? If not for the summer, then how about a couple more weeks?"

McCall wanted that. But she thought of Austin. "Gran, I have clients—"

"Boo said you can do those on your phone or your computer," Em interrupted. "She said it's how you take a lot of appointments even when you're in Dallas, that it's easier for the clients who don't get around so well on their own."

"Boo's just a font of information tonight," McCall muttered, and she shot her assistant a quick narrow-eyed glance.

"She is," Em agreed, "and she's such a big help to me. Not many young people want to spend time with an old woman."

McCall could practically hear the violins whining out a sad tune. And she knew when she was being played.

"Sleep on it," Em went on before McCall could say anything. "I'm going to turn in early. I get so tired these days."

With that, her grandmother dropped a kiss on McCall's cheek and headed out of the kitchen toward her bedroom.

McCall watched her go, and the moment she was out of earshot, she whirled back toward Boo. "Did you and Em work this out so I'd stay here and hook up with Austin?" she came out and asked.

"Yes," Boo admitted without hesitation. "I could see how happy you were about going to his place for dinner. Sorry, though, that my text interrupted things. Still, that doesn't mean you can't hook up with him again soon."

McCall sighed. She had one word for her assistant. "Peekaboo."

Boo smiled, and there was a slyness to it. "I'm guessing we're not playing a game with me or your hands would be over your eyes."

McCall leveled a very flat look at Boo. "Peekaboo," she repeated.

"Yeah, yeah. You don't want Austin or anybody else to know about it, but honestly, it's not a sleazy place. Not with the changes you've made, anyway."

McCall had indeed made some changes. Unpopular ones with the old customers. She'd done away with lap dances and had invested in some new costumes that she believed had a more tasteful slant. The Victorian maiden garb, for instance, had replaced the naughty schoolgirl. She had also paid for dancing lessons that had taught the performers to go for more subtle moves rather than relying on hip grinds.

The end result was still the same—the strippers would, well, strip down to G-strings and pasties—but there was a little more class to it now. That said, Peekaboo was what it was. A strip club.

"I would have just closed the doors to the place if Lizzie

hadn't made me promise that I wouldn't," McCall said, thinking out loud.

"And you were secretly hoping that the changes you made would run the business into the ground," Boo piped in.

Yep. McCall had indeed hoped for that, and it's why she'd insisted on the historical costumes. In the end, though, it'd just brought in more customers who had heard there was "something different" going on at Peekaboo.

"I think I've come up with something that'll take care of you owning Peekaboo," Boo added a moment later.

McCall automatically dismissed it before she even heard it. "You know I can't sell or give away the club," she reminded Boo.

Boo got a look in her eyes. Possibly an insane look. "Of course, but there's nothing that says I can't be the club owner."

McCall actually leaned in to sniff Boo's breath. "Have you been drinking?" Because that's exactly what Lizzie's will had said, that no one other than McCall could own it.

"No." Grinning as if she'd discovered the secret to world peace and calorie-free Snickers bars, Boo caught on to her shoulders. "I went online and got the paperwork started for a name change. In about six weeks, I can become Mc-Call Dalton."

McCall did no such grinning, and she stared at Boo. "And who will I become?"

"You'll stay McCall, too, and you'll keep calling me Boo. But this way, if the subject comes up, I can say I'm the owner of Peekaboo. Don't pooh-pooh it," Boo said when McCall started shaking her head. "You've always wanted a way out, and I'm handing it to you."

McCall was ready to start some pooh-poohing, but she stopped. "This can't be legal."

"It's not illegal," Boo argued. "Think of it like tit rouge."

McCall blinked. "Excuse me?"

"Tit rouge. It's something I used to do when I lost one of my pasties or the darn thing just wouldn't stay on. I'd just cover my nipple with bright red cream rouge, layering it on thick enough to make it no longer look like a nipple."

McCall didn't consider herself dense, but she wasn't sure she was following this. "What does tit rouge have to do with Peekaboo?"

"Everything." Boo gave her that grin again. "I'll be like the cover-up to your exposed nipple. If anything leaks about you being the owner of Peekaboo, I can say nun-uh, I'm the McCall Dalton who owns the club."

Now, McCall huffed. "And how will you explain why your name is the same as mine?"

"Easy peasy. I could say I was a fan of *Little Cowgirls* and this was sort of my homage to you. Don't pooh-pooh it," Boo warned her again. "In fact, don't say anything else about it. Just sleep on it, and while you're sleeping, consider this. This tit rouge could be your ticket to getting into Austin Jameson's jeans."

CHAPTER EIGHT

"GOD, THIS IS GOOD," Cait mumbled around the mouthful of cold pasta she'd just gobbled up.

Austin frowned at his sister and kept packing the twins' snacks for preschool. Cait was standing in front of his fridge, eating right from the plastic storage container where Austin had put the pasta after his semifailed date with McCall.

"I fixed that three days ago," Austin reminded her. "It's probably ready to be tossed out."

"Nope. It's still prime stuff." She wolfed down a few more bites, made some sounds to indicate it was delicious and then helped herself to a leftover breadstick.

"Who needs a garbage disposal with you around," Austin grumbled.

Cait wasn't the least bit offended by his comment and washed down her scrounged breakfast with some apple juice. "So," she said, turning back toward him, "want to tell me how things are going between McCall and you?"

This was an easy question to answer. "No." Besides, there was nothing to tell. McCall had cut their date short, and other than a text the following day to apologize, again, he hadn't heard from her.

He added the bagged snacks to the girls' backpacks and listened to make sure they weren't getting into any trouble. Avery and Gracie were arguing over whether to wear pink or white panties so all was well. It was a usual argument since neither girl wanted to dress alike—unless they were trying to pull a switcheroo, that is—and that included likeness in their underwear choices.

"You're sure you don't need some kind of dating advice?" Cait asked. She put both her fork and apple juice glass into the dishwasher.

"From you?" He added the appropriate amount of brotherly snark to a kid sister who didn't exactly have a stellar track record when it came to dating.

Again, she took no offense. "I'm a woman. I might be able to help you get into McCall's head."

He wouldn't mind getting in McCall's head. Or her bed. But obviously McCall had a different notion about that.

Austin silently cursed himself. He shouldn't have kissed her. Especially shouldn't have kissed her three times. That had likely sent her running, and now he might not get another chance to be with her. Not just for sex, either. *Any chance.* That was too bad because while it sounded like a cliché, he enjoyed her company. McCall was like a breath of fresh air in his life that needed something fresh.

"Yoo-hoo!" someone called out.

Edith. Definitely not the bringer of fresh air, and she was obviously already on the porch.

"Crap," Cait said under her breath. "Do you need me to run interference for you?" she asked him. "I could pretend I've got to puke or something."

"No. It's okay." Well, it actually wasn't. He didn't like Edith dropping in unannounced—literally. The woman didn't even knock on the door. She just came right on in.

"I wanted to see the girls before they left for school," Edith said. "Good morning, Cait," she rattled off in the same breath. She looked at Austin. "Then you and I need to talk."

Cait groaned, rubbed her stomach, but Austin cut off any fake puking attempt by giving his sister a hard look.

"I got pink panties," Avery announced, coming out of the bedroom with Gracie right on her heels. Avery lifted her dress to show them the outcome of what had obviously been an intense debate.

"Very nice," Austin told her, and he motioned for them to do a turn around so he could make sure they weren't wearing anything inappropriate. It was a lesson he'd learned when Avery had once tucked a pair of his boxers in the armpit of her dress to pad a seam that was bothering her. Today, however, all the clothing they were wearing belonged to them.

"Can we play cops and bobbers?" Avery asked when her attention landed on Cait.

"Absolutely. I got the cuffs ready. First, though, you need to say hi and goodbye to your grandmother."

"Hi!" the girls squealed. Austin didn't think their enthusiasm was as much for Edith, though, as it was to speed up them getting out of there to do the fun ride and game with Aunt Cait.

Edith gathered them up in her arms, kissing them. Then she complained once again about Gracie's haircut along with reminding Avery not to lift her dress and show people her "undies." When Edith moved on to complaining that the girls shouldn't be playing *cops and bobbers*, that's when Austin gave Cait the signal that it was time for them to go. That way, only he'd have to be on the receiving end of Edith's grievances.

"Head 'em up, move 'em out," Cait announced to the twins.

The girls grabbed their backpacks, gave Austin and Edith some cheek kisses and left running out the front door with Cait.

"Honestly, I could drive the girls to school," Edith murmured while Cait raced the girls to her SUV. His sister pretended to stumble at the last second so that Avery and Gracie could get ahead of her and win.

He left the front door open so he could watch them get in the SUV and drive away. "They enjoy being with Cait. You want some coffee?" he immediately added to cut off anything else Edith had to say about that.

"No. I suspect you're busy so I won't keep you."

It was a light day for him, some tax paperwork, checking the back fence and looking in on the new part-time ranch hand he'd hired to do some training with the horses. Still, he had no intention of letting Edith know he had time to draw out this chat any longer than necessary.

"I know that Howie came by to talk to you," Edith continued. "He told you that he'd convinced me to wait and see if he and I still needed to fix this situation with the twins."

"Fix this situation," Austin repeated. That was a pretty sterile term for what was essentially a hotter than hell button for him. "My daughters are fine."

Austin knew it was a mistake to let the anger creep into his voice, and into him, but it was hard when Edith called his daughters a situation that needed to be fixed.

Edith made a sound that could have meant anything. Or nothing. "Howie seemed to think you'd be interested in seeing McCall. By seeing, I mean—"

"I know what you mean," Austin said, cutting her off. He didn't want to discuss McCall with Edith.

But apparently Edith had a different notion about that. She gave a weary nod and sighed. "McCall's attractive, and there's no need for you to remind me of all the good things she's done."

Now, it was Austin's turn to sigh, but it wasn't as weary

as it was slicked with frustration. "Edith, could you just cut to the chase and tell me exactly what you're trying to say?"

Her gaze nailed his, and her chin came up. "Now that McCall's staying in town for a while, I'm guessing that means you'll be seeing her."

Curiosity replaced his frustration. "Who told you that McCall was staying for a while?"

"Em," she readily answered. "I saw her at the diner this morning, and she said McCall was staying at least until the end of the month, maybe through the entire summer."

Well, this was a nice turn of events. At least, it could possibly be nice if McCall didn't continue to brush him off.

"Now that she's staying," Edith went on, "Howie seems to think the two of you will get involved again. Well, you should know I have concerns about that. There are all kinds of stories about how messed up child actors become when they grow up. Plus, McCall doesn't have a good mother role model."

That was some BS slathered in with the truth. Yeah, some child actors became screwups. And McCall didn't have a good mother. But she had Em, and Em was as good as gold.

Austin took a moment to consider how to respond to that, and he finally just went with his gut. "You say you want the girls to have a mom, that they should be raised in a home with two parents, but I'm starting to believe you feel you're the only mom they should have. You can't be their mom, Edith."

That, of course, tightened her jaw, but damn it all to hell, he was tired of this.

"I want what's best for them," Edith said, the hurt in her voice.

"So do I, and FYI, I believe I'm doing what's best for them."

Edith pulled out the big guns then. Tears sprang to her

eyes. The woman was a walking, talking definition of frustration because her crying always got to him.

Thankfully, the sound of an approaching vehicle got Edith blinking hard, trying to stave off the tears. It also got Austin out of saying anything else that would just make this worse. Besides, his visitor was someone he actually wanted to see.

Shaw.

"I'll be going," Edith quickly said, and while giving her eyes a wipe, she headed out to her car, muttering a hello to Shaw as she walked by him.

Shaw arched an eyebrow. "I'm guessing you haven't had a good start to your morning."

"Well, it was going pretty good until Edith showed up." He waved off any questions Shaw might have about that. "Did you know McCall was planning to stay in town for a while longer?"

His brother nodded. "She told Sunny a couple of days ago. Em wants McCall there because she's been feeling blue. Or so she says. Sunny thinks it's because Em's trying to matchmake McCall and you."

Austin couldn't help it. He smiled.

"And I can see that's got you all worried and torn up inside," Shaw remarked. His eyes got heavy with concern as he took an envelope from the back pocket of his jeans and handed it to Austin.

Austin immediately knew the reason for his brother's concern. It was because this was another card from Zoey.

Shaw swore under his breath. "Are you okay?"

This time Austin didn't have a quick answer. There was always a mix of emotions when it came to getting the cards. Seeing anything that Zoey had touched made him feel closer to her. It soothed him just as if she'd actually touched *him*. But the soothing wouldn't last.

"How many more of these did she give you?" Austin asked, taking the envelope.

"One more, and no, I'm not going to tell you when I'm supposed to give it to you. That was Zoey's rule, and I promised her I wouldn't break it. It's a damn bad rule," Shaw added in a grumble. "You want me to stay while you read it?"

Austin shook his head, and he kept his attention on the envelope while Shaw did more cursing and went back to his truck. Part of him knew his brother was right. This was prolonging the grief, but mercy, it felt good to have something like this from the woman he'd loved all the way to the marrow.

As he always did, Austin took his time opening the envelope, savoring the way it felt in his hand, and he brought it to his nose. No smell. There never was. And it made him ache more than a little that he could no longer remember Zoey's scent.

He smiled when he pulled out the card and saw a buff bumblebee wearing tighty-whities and working out with weights. On the outside, Zoey had written, "Be brave, Honey Bee."

Honey Bee. It wasn't a term of endearment she'd ever used with him, and maybe that was the point. The cards were likely meant to make him laugh. To cheer him up. That would hardly happen if they took him back to specific memories of them.

But there was something specific inside the card.

Usually, Zoey just signed her name or drew little hearts. This time, though, she'd actually written something.

"Austin, if you haven't already done it, you need to get on with your life. Find someone nice, someone who'll make you happy and will be good to our girls. Not Mandy Tupper-man, though. I still haven't forgiven her for flicking a booger in my hair when we were in kindergarten. Oh, and not Ve-ronica Stiller, either. Those fake boobs of hers look good but will bruise your chest. Of course, if you are with Mandy or Veronica right now, then just forget what I've said and carry on. Bye, Honey Bee."

Austin stared at the card for a long time. Until the words started to swarm in front of his eyes.

Bye.

That was a first. Of course, she'd told him goodbye with her dying breath, but it was different seeing it written down. Different, too, because Zoey had written this goodbye be-fore she'd left him.

He swallowed hard. Blinked hard, too. Shaw wasn't the only one who'd made a promise to Zoey. Austin had told her that he'd keep the crying and outward grieving to a mini-mum. For the sake of the girls. For his sake, as well. But at the moment, the grief was all he could feel.

Austin grabbed his keys, headed for his truck and drove away. He wasn't even sure where he was going until he took the turn to Em's. This was a bad idea, but that didn't stop him. He kept going until he parked at the end of the driveway.

Putting the card in the glove compartment, Austin got out intending to go onto the porch and knock on the door. Then he heard McCall's voice. Not coming from inside the house but rather from the side yard.

He kept walking and soon saw her sitting in a rope swing beneath one of the massive live oaks that dotted the prop-erty. She had her phone sandwiched between her shoulder and ear, her arms hooked around the ropes, and she was twirling around while she talked.

"I know," she said to whoever was on the other end of the phone line. "I know," she repeated on a heavy sigh.

Her back wasn't actually to him, more of her side, which meant if she glanced in his direction, she'd see him. She should see him, Austin reminded himself. McCall should see him and know that this—whatever this was—was no longer private. But he stood there, watching.

And listening.

"I kissed him, Sunny," McCall said, not with disgust but rather apology in her voice. "Zoey's probably going to figure out a way to punch me for that." She looked up at the sky. "Not too hard, though. Zoey, you always knew I had a thing for Austin."

Now, Austin *really* listened. Talk about a flood of feelings. The woman he was lusting after was talking to his late wife. About him. About how hot he was.

"I keep going back to those dice," McCall went on. "The ones Zoey and I rolled when we were in ninth grade. Remember? Of course you do," she said, answering her own question.

But it didn't answer anything for Austin. What dice? He didn't remember either McCall or Zoey ever mentioning that.

"I swear, I think Zoey cheated," McCall said. "The dice were loaded or something, but I never called her on it. I knew she had a thing for Austin, too. So when she rolled box cars and I rolled a five and a three, I just accepted that she'd won. Some prize, huh?" McCall gave a little snort. "The winner takes Austin."

What the heck? They'd rolled dice for him? That nearly brought Austin out from the side of the house, but his feet suddenly seemed magnetized to the ground and his ear was magnetized to McCall, who just kept talking.

"Now, I'm back here and kissing him. *Three times*," Mc-Call emphasized. "If I'd stayed, I would have kissed him three thousand times." She sighed. "I've already mentioned that he's really hot."

Yeah, that had come up, and while Austin thought this might make him a perv, he doubted he'd tire of hearing McCall say that.

"And Zoey's and his girls," McCall went on. She lifted her head enough for Austin to see her smile. "They're amazing. So smart and funny." She paused, obviously listening to whatever Sunny was saying. "Yes, that's a problem."

Problem, he mentally repeated. Maybe McCall was talking about the mess with Cody Joe. Or maybe the fact that he was a widower. Then again, it could simply be a problem because her life wasn't here in Lone Star Ridge. It wasn't as if he could pick up and move to Dallas to be with her, and it was likely the same for McCall.

So, why did he still want her?

Why was he mulling over how to make this work?

"I don't think tit rouge is going to fix this," McCall said.

Austin's head whipped up so fast that he heard his neck pop. WTF was tit rouge? Better yet, how was he going to explain why he was just standing there gawking at McCall and listening in on her conversation? And he was going to have to explain that soon because the neck pop had obviously alerted McCall.

On a startled gasp, McCall's gaze speared in his direction. "Austin. Oh, God. How much did you hear?"

CHAPTER NINE

WELL, CRAP.

That was McCall's first thought, quickly followed by a string of mental profanity that she was glad didn't actually fall out of her mouth. Clearly, she'd already said too much.

Maybe.

And maybe Austin hadn't heard anything she hadn't wanted him to hear.

"I'll have to call you back," McCall quickly said to Sunny. Then she stood and faced Austin. "Hi," she croaked out.

"Hi, back." No croak for him, and he was smiling. Sort of. Mainly, though, he was just looking confused.

This was tricky territory, and McCall wasn't sure if she should just come out and ask him what he'd heard or if she should wait for Austin to speak. She didn't get a chance for either, though, because her phone rang. At first, she thought it was Sunny wondering why she'd hung up so fast, but it was Mr. Bolton's name on her screen. McCall checked the time and realized this was the phone appointment she'd set up with him.

"Uh, I need to take this call. Sorry," she added. "It's a client."

"No problem." He tipped his head toward the house. "I'll just go inside and see how Em's doing."

So, Austin was staying, and that meant he almost certainly would question her about what she'd told Sunny. Mc-

Call gave him a nod, tried not to look panicked, but she went back through her side of the conversation with her sister. Yes, she'd said plenty, maybe even enough for Austin to figure out that she was the owner of a strip club.

For now, though, McCall had to push that aside and take the call from her client.

"Mr. Bolton," she greeted.

"I can't talk long," he immediately told her. "I got a hot date lined up."

McCall checked her watch. It was barely ten in the morning, hardly the hour for a hot date. Then again, at Mr. Bolton's age he might not want to waste any time.

"We can reschedule," McCall offered. "How about tomorrow morning at the same time?"

"That works. Well, unless this date turns to be a sleepover. If that happens, I'll text you. And don't worry, I plan on doing the five-minute stuff with her just like you told me."

"Good—" That was all she managed to get out before Mr. Bolton continued.

"This one doesn't appear to have saggy knockers so I might take even longer. Of course, the saggy ones took a while for me to work my way down. I swear, they drooped a good ten inches."

That was an image that McCall was certain would stay in her head for quite a while. "I'm glad things worked out for you and your partner. I'll call you tomorrow morning at ten," McCall said, and she hit End.

Gathering her breath, she went straight into the house, ready to face whatever questions Austin had. Or rather hoping she was ready. But Austin was nowhere in sight. Instead, a tight-faced Bernice greeted her in the foyer.

"You've got to stop Em and your weirdo flake of an assistant from playing that stupid reverse strip poker game," Bernice complained. "They were playing it again in the kitchen when one of those Jameson boys came in."

McCall groaned. The Jameson boy was obviously Austin, and she hoped he hadn't gotten an eyeful to go along with the earful he'd already gotten from her. She made her way to the kitchen and did indeed find Em and Boo at the table.

Good grief.

Like before, Em was more than fully clothed since in addition to her jeans, top and sweater, she was also wearing her Stetson and a red bandanna tied around her neck. In contrast, Boo had on a loose camisole and a pair of equally loose men's white boxers that were likely something Hayes had left behind. The outfit was skimpy, but she had more covered than she had the night McCall had walked in on them. Apparently, Boo had figured out that because she wasn't very good at reverse strip poker, she should start the game with more than a demibra and panties.

Austin snagged McCall's gaze, and he smiled. "It bears saying again. You lead such an interesting life."

She welcomed the smile rather than any immediate questions he could have tossed at her, and since Em and Boo showed no signs of ending their game, McCall motioned for Austin to follow her.

"FYI," McCall said to get it out of the way, "Granny Em claims she's been blue, but I think it's a crock. Don't let her talk you into doing anything you don't want to do."

By the time they made it into the living room, Austin's smile had definitely faded. "But she used the blues to talk you into staying in town?"

"Pretty much. Shaw told you I was staying?" she asked.

Austin nodded. "And Edith."

He strolled to the large bay window and looked out. He

certainly made a picture standing there in his incredibly well-fitting jeans and with the sunlight streaming over him. A cowboy Greek god.

"You'll be able to run your business from here?" Austin asked.

McCall could have sworn her heart skipped a beat or two. Then she realized he was talking about her counseling practice.

"For the most part," she answered. "There are some non-client things that need to be done like checking on the office, but Boo can make trips back to do that."

Boo would also need to include Peekaboo in those checks. And Boo also wanted to do the name change in Dallas, which was why she'd be flying back tomorrow. A quick in and out, Boo had assured her. Even though there was no real reason for Boo to stay here in Lone Star Ridge, McCall was thankful that she was because Em seemed to enjoy her company. It was also nice for McCall to have an ally who knew the whole truth about her.

"Coming here is always like stepping into a time machine," Austin remarked several moments later.

McCall walked to him, looking out at the ranch as he was doing. "Yes," she agreed.

There must have been something in her voice or body language that alerted him because Austin looked at her, his eyebrow already raised. "Bad memories?"

"Some," McCall admitted.

No need to spell them out. Austin likely knew some of the exploitation games her mother, Sunshine, had played. The woman had been willing to do whatever it took to keep the ratings high. Then, once *Little Cowgirls* had been canceled, their father had walked out, taking a lot of the money the show had earned with him.

"What's a good memory you have of this place?" he pressed.

That caused her to smile. Leave it to Austin to turn her mood around so fast. There were plenty of happy times here, as well, but one came quickly to mind. Maybe because she had a view of where it'd taken place.

She pointed to the corral next to the barn. "You taught me to ride there. It was a gray mare named Smoke that you'd brought over from your family's ranch."

"It was scripted," he admitted, "but you're right—it is a good memory."

Funny, for a second she'd actually forgotten the scripted part, but yes, the producers would have arranged that since they'd still been trying to set Austin up as her boyfriend.

"Shaw taught Sunny to ride," she went on. Probably also scripted. "Leyton tried to teach Hadley."

And that was another good memory for her. Probably not for Hadley, though, since she hadn't taken to riding the way Sunny and McCall had. However, Hadley had taken to Leyton for a while until Leyton had decided that he didn't want the bad-boy reputation that he would have almost certainly gotten had he stayed connected with Badly Hadley.

McCall pointed to the barn. "I used to sneak up in the hayloft and read Jane Austen novels. That's a good memory."

His eyebrow came up again. "Why'd you have to sneak to do that? If I remember right, you had those kinds of books in your room."

She nodded. "They were props, meant to go along with my Good Girl McCall image. It was sort of rebellion that I wouldn't read them whenever a camera was nearby, but I loved the books. So, I read them in secret."

Austin chuckled. "That explains something Shaw told

me. He said you used to disappear for a while every afternoon after you got home from school. He thought you were sneaking off to meet someone."

McCall hadn't known that anyone, especially Shaw, had noticed her doing that. "I guess you could say I was sneaking off to be with me. The real me. Ah, the identity crisis of a TV kid," she added with some drama. Still, that particular guilty pleasure had been one she'd savored.

Austin shifted a little, pointing to the garden shed. "I kissed you there."

Her forehead bunched up. "Was that really a good memory for you, since it was scripted, I mean?"

"Hey, I was a teenage boy. Even scripted kisses were a good thing." He shrugged in a "what are you going to do" gesture. Then he paused. "You and Zoey actually rolled dice for me?"

She sputtered out a breath and then cursed herself for not being better prepared for the question. Austin had thrown her off with the easy conversation. Well, this wouldn't be so easy.

"We did," she admitted. "Obviously, Zoey won."

"With boxcars," he said, letting her know that he'd overheard that part of the conversation, too. "And you thought she cheated by using loaded dice."

"Yes, but I don't blame her. I would have done the same if I'd thought about it." The moment the words left her mouth, McCall realized they were a mistake. She'd just confessed that she had indeed had the hots for him. The *real* hots. "I'm sorry. I hope that doesn't make you feel weird or anything."

"Maybe a little."

She hoped that Austin wasn't playing a mental game of what might have been. Probably not, though. Without Zoey, he wouldn't have his daughters. Plus, she had no doubts, none, that he'd loved his wife. In fact, that's likely what he was thinking about right now.

Or not.

"What's tit rouge?" he asked.

McCall was certain she became the human definition of a deer caught in the headlights. Her brain froze for a moment, too, so she couldn't pick back through the memory of the conversation with Sunny to try and figure out specifically what he'd overheard.

"It's, um, breast makeup," McCall managed to say, actually motioning toward her own chest.

He grinned, and my oh my, if she hadn't had wobbly knees from his question, that particular expression would have unsteadied her in a major kind of way. It was a flirty expression that only emphasized his hot face.

"Makeup," he repeated, adding a tinge of skepticism to that hotness. "I'm guessing it didn't fix certain problems."

She sucked in her breath, remembering then exactly what she'd said to Sunny. *I don't think tit rouge is going to fix this.*

Well, it certainly wouldn't fix this heat between Austin and her. Wouldn't help the issue with her secrets, either. She could blurt out that she owned Peekaboo and had once been a waitress there, but he might tell his brothers. It might get around, and that was something she didn't want any donors of the foundation to hear.

"Uh, Austin, it's probably not a good idea if we see each other," she threw out there.

By degrees his grin faded. His breathing became slow and even. "Don't."

That one word was all he said while he kept his suddenly intense eyes on her. McCall thought of arguments she could give him to support them "not seeing each other." Their complicated lives. The fact that she'd be going back to Dallas soon. The problem with Edith wanting custody. But she said none of that because Austin robbed her of her breath by leaning in and brushing his mouth over hers.

"Give me a chance, McCall," Austin whispered against her lips. "Give *us* a chance."

She figured she could blame her response on temporary insanity. Insanity caused by her extreme reaction to Austin's kiss.

"Okay," she whispered back.

There'd be hell to pay for this, later, but for now, McCall slid right into the kiss.

AUSTIN FELT AS uncomfortable as a flasher in an igloo.

It'd been a while, nearly a decade, since he'd had to buy condoms, and that certainly wasn't something he'd wanted to do in his own hometown where the gossips would get wind of it and start speculating.

About McCall and him.

That's why Austin was at the Pump and Ride, a badly named convenience store/gas station just off the interstate exit. It was a good ten miles from Lone Star Ridge, which put some much needed distance between him and that potential gossip pool.

He didn't think it was being presumptuous of him, either, to be prepared like this. No. It might have been a while since he'd needed condoms—or been with a woman other than Zoey—but he was pretty sure he'd read the signals right.

Okay.

That one-word response from McCall had caused Austin to smile for days. McCall had not only muttered it when he'd asked her to give them a chance, but she had also agreed to go on a date with him. Of course, he'd played dirty by kissing her and continuing to kiss her until she'd said yes, but hey, all was fair when it came to something that he felt was right.

Well, right-ish, anyway.

There was still the guilt. Still the part of him that would always feel married to Zoey. But the other parts of him were totally on board with moving on and seeing where things could go with McCall. He'd asked her to give them a chance. Now, he was telling himself to do the same thing.

Austin grabbed a box of condoms from the shelf. Then grabbed two. Then three. Obviously, his dick was pushing these particular purchases, but he was going with the notion of being prepared in case one date led to another. Then another and another.

Of course, dates didn't equal sex, but Austin thought McCall and he were on the same page about that, too. And if not, then he'd just consider this a boost to the local economy. He was carrying the boxes to the register when Austin saw something that had his knees locking up and his stomach pitching.

Howie.

Sonofabitch. The man was at the magazine rack, his back to Austin, so Austin just stayed put, hoping that Howie wouldn't turn around.

He turned around.

Their gazes collided, and while Austin was damn sure there was a guilty gleam in his own eyes, there was guilt all over Howie's face, too. Austin looked down at the magazine Howie had in his grip, and he expected to see a copy of a nudie magazine. But it was a copy of *Needlepoint Monthly.*

Howie glanced at the boxes of condoms. Austin glanced at the magazine. The seconds crawled by, and Austin tried to figure out what was going on here. If the magazine was for Edith, there'd be no need for Howie to come to the Pump and Ride. It was something he could likely buy at the grocery store in Lone Star Ridge. That meant the magazine was for this hard-nosed rich rancher who probably didn't consider needlepoint an acceptable hobby.

Howie gave him a crisp nod and hurried to the cashier.

Just as the door opened, and Boo came in.

Both Howie and Austin groaned. Boo did, too, and then she huffed along with throwing her hands up in the air in a frustrated gesture. She stormed past Howie and Austin, and while Howie was checking out as if his pants had suddenly caught fire, Boo went to the back of the small store. A few seconds later, she came back with a box of tampons.

"I don't want to buy them in Lone Star Ridge because people will know my business," she grumbled, eyeing the condoms.

"I don't want to buy them in Lone Star Ridge because people will know my business," Austin repeated.

She nodded, made a sound of agreement. "I don't like people looking at me funny."

Boo's hair was like an orange volcano erupting on her head. It was nearly the same color as her lipstick and nail polish, both of which didn't outshine the neon pink gym shorts and top she was wearing. Austin didn't want to tell her that in a small ranching town, people were already looking at her funny.

"McCall told me that she was going out with you," Boo added a moment later, her gaze sliding down to the condoms. "I won't mention those."

"I appreciate that." The quantity would either scare McCall off or make him seem like a horny braggart. "How is McCall?" he asked.

"Fine." Boo said it so fast that it made Austin wonder if it was really true. "I was in Dallas earlier in the week. Taking care of some business," she added in a mumble. "But I think she enjoyed spending time with her grandmother."

Yeah, McCall probably had enjoyed that, but there was something… "What's tit rouge?" he came out and asked.

Boo looked at him as if he'd hit her on the head with a hammer. "Makeup," she said with a squeak, and after several moments of hesitation, "And I really gotta go." She hurried toward the counter but then turned around. "Be nice to McCall, okay? She's a good person, and I don't want her hurt."

Since that last part seemed genuine and hadn't been said to insult him or deflect him from her half-assed tit rouge answer, Austin nodded. He had no intention of hurting McCall, but then again, good intentions didn't always lead to the best.

He paid for the condoms, got a grin and thumbs-up from the acne-faced clerk and Austin started the drive back to his house. He'd have at least two hours to work with some new horses he'd bought. Then he could pick up the girls from preschool. Kinsley, his fifteen-year-old half sister, and his mom, Lenore, would be coming over to give the twins a cookie-baking lesson. Austin would have to work for part of the time they were there, but it'd give him a chance to catch up.

Especially with Kinsley.

His most recent half sibling had found out she was a Jameson less than two months ago, and she was still settling into the family. Ironically, his mother was at the top of the list of those who were helping with the settling.

Austin wasn't sure how Lenore managed to do it, but she genuinely cared about her cheating ex-husband's "love children" who continued to show up at the family ranch that Shaw now ran. The first had been Leyton, and while most women would have resented the proof of her husband's cheating, Lenore had ended up adopting Leyton after his birth mother had abandoned him. Austin thought she might end up doing the same to Kinsley. Unless Shaw and Sunny adopted her first, that is.

All thoughts of that, however, went to the back burner when Austin pulled into his driveway and saw the sleek black Range Rover parked in front of his house. He hadn't been expecting company, but it could be someone on business.

In this case, the person was on his porch. A man in one of the wicker chairs. He had his long, jeans-clad legs stretched out in front of him, his arms folded over his chest and a black Stetson covering his face. The guy looked as if he was taking a nap.

Since he didn't want to meet a *guest* while carrying a plastic bag filled with boxes of condoms, Austin left it in his truck and walked to the porch. "Can I help you?" Austin asked, and for one bad moment, he thought this might be Cody Joe.

Nope.

Yawning, the man sat up, automatically sliding his hat back on his head, and he stood, then stretched. It'd been a while since he'd seen him, but Austin had no trouble recognizing McCall's brother.

Hayes Dalton.

He wasn't the absolute last person on earth Austin had expected to see, but it was close.

"Austin," Hayes greeted.

His voice was a mix of gravel and smoke—a combination that apparently served him well in his badass role on a TV series called *Outlaw Rebels* about a motorcycle gang. His looks had no doubt done some serving well, too, since he had a "been there, done that" vibe with his messy black hair and sleepy blue eyes.

"Sorry I didn't call first, but I didn't have your number," Hayes said. "We need to talk."

Austin didn't bother keeping the profanity to himself or under his breath. "This is about McCall?"

Hell. He hadn't expected her brother to get in on warning him not to hurt McCall, the way that Boo just had. But Austin immediately rethought that. From what he'd heard, Hayes didn't have a lot to do with any of his sisters. That included Hadley even though both Hayes and she lived in Hollywood.

"It's about McCall," Hayes verified. "We have a problem."

Austin cursed again, but he also got a buzz. "Does this have anything to do with tit rouge?"

Obviously, it didn't—if Hayes's bunched-up forehead and frown were any indication. "Uh, no. At least, I don't think so. What the hell is tit rouge, anyway?"

Austin waved that off since he wasn't sure he had the answer, either. "What problem do we have?"

Dragging in a heavy breath, Hayes keyed in the password on his phone. "I want us to work this out, and I don't want you taking it out on my sister."

That was as puzzling as tit rouge. "Rumor has it that you don't give a damn about much other than yourself."

"True," Hayes admitted. "But I give a small damn about my sisters, and because I do, you and I are going to fix this."

Hayes turned his phone in Austin's direction. There was a photo on the screen, and even though Austin took a moment to look at it, he shook his head, not sure what he was seeing. Then it hit him.

Oh, shit.

CHAPTER TEN

McCall PACED ACROSS her bedroom while she listened to her client, Mrs. Clara Eidelman, talk about her cat, Ol' Blue Eyes. McCall liked cats, didn't usually mind hearing about them, but for the past six months, it had been the sole topic of conversation between Clara and her.

"Frank just loves it when I dangle yarn in front of him," the woman continued. "And he really likes it when I play music from his namesake, Frank Sinatra."

McCall knew that, too, because Clara brought it up every conversation. "Mrs. Eidelman, if you don't have any issues you want to work through, then maybe you should consider taking a break from therapy."

That was also something McCall brought up every conversation, and she'd long since stopped charging the woman for these sessions.

"But I do love talking to you," Clara assured her. "It's nice to be able to talk to someone who loves cats as much as I do."

"Yes, that is nice to find someone with shared interests." Again, it was a repeat of what she usually said, but today, McCall added to that. "For instance, maybe someone there at Peaceful Acres Retirement Village? Maybe Mr. Bolton?"

Clara made a hmmp sound. "He's only interested in s-e-x." And yes, the woman spelled it out. "I know the women who put out around here, and I don't want to be one of them."

McCall could understand that, but she didn't think Mr.

Bolton would press for sex unless it was offered. Plus, it might help him if he did find a friend who was interested in something other than falling into bed with him.

"If not Mr. Bolton, then maybe someone else?" McCall threw out there.

"There's nobody here who loves Ol' Blue Eyes as much as I do," Clara insisted.

That was very likely true, and it didn't just apply to the residents of Peaceful Acres but to everyone in the entire universe. "Yes, but you could maybe *find* someone who shares your interest in cats. Then that would make both Ol' Blue Eyes and you happy."

"Maybe," Clara said as if actually considering it. McCall wished that she would, but she figured that their call next week would go pretty much the same as this one.

"Just give Mr. Bolton or anyone else there five minutes of conversation," McCall went on. "If at the end of the five minutes you don't want to keep talking, then just politely explain that you should go and take care of your cat. Five minutes," she emphasized. "I really think it's a good idea."

"You do?" Again, the woman sounded as if she was considering it. "All right. I guess, then, I'll give that a try. But what happens if Mr. Bolton wants to have s-e-x? I'm not sure I'm ready for that." She paused. "But I might be ready for a kiss or a hug. I used to like kisses and hugs."

McCall had to wonder how long it'd been since the woman had had either of those things. Hugs that didn't involve the cat, she mentally amended. It'd probably been decades.

"You don't have to have sex. Just talk, and if talking leads to kissing and hugging, take your time to figure out if that's what you want," McCall explained. "Use the sixty-minute rule for that. For sixty minutes only kiss and hug, nothing more. Make sure you keep on all your clothes, too, so you're not tempted."

And if Mr. Bolton was on the receiving end of that one hour, it would seriously slow him down—which was a good thing, as well. After all, he seemed to be on the receiving end of too many kisses and hugs, ones that didn't have any emotional connection whatsoever. While that was fine for an occasional hookup, Mr. Bolton had made it his norm, and he'd likely done that to avoid intimacy.

"But what if he wants more?" Clara asked. "What if I want more?" she amended.

McCall couldn't help but smile. The woman just might take this and run with it. "Then wait for at least a day until you decide on more. That way you can be sure that's what you really want."

"Five minutes of conversation. Then sixty minutes of the other stuff if the talking is okay," Clara repeated. "I might be able to do that. I'll let you know how it goes."

McCall ended the call and hoped for the best. She put her phone away and went to her laptop to put in notes about the session, but her phone rang.

Austin.

She went through the little stomach flip-flop that she usually got at the thought of him. Then McCall tamped down her breathing before she answered.

"I need a big favor," Austin immediately said. "I'm tied up with something right now, and I need someone to pick up the girls from preschool."

McCall was both surprised and pleased that he'd asked, but he continued before she could say that.

"I can call somebody else if you're too busy, but I'd like for it to be you," he went on. "Then you and I can talk once

I get back to the house. I can tell you why I need you to do this."

Well, that sounded intriguing, and since she needed to talk to him, too, this could work out for both of them. This time, though, she'd have to make sure she told him about Peekaboo before he got into what he wanted to say.

"I can go get the girls," she assured him.

"Good. Thanks. But you'll have to use my truck because it's got the car seats in it. It's parked in front of my house, and I left the keys under the seat."

McCall blinked in surprise. Lone Star Ridge wasn't exactly a hotbed of crime so it didn't surprise her that Austin had left the keys like that, but it did surprise her that he hadn't taken his truck wherever it was he'd gone. Again, it was intriguing.

"No problem," she told him. "Just let the school know that I'll be picking them up, though. They probably have rules about that sort of thing."

"Will do. Thanks, McCall." He sounded flustered and harried, and she got confirmation of that when he quickly ended the call.

McCall grabbed her purse and hurried downstairs to tell Em and Boo that she was heading out. When she didn't find them, she left them a note and went out to her SUV.

The drive to Austin's didn't take long, but along the way she started to speculate about why Austin had sounded so urgent about talking to her. Maybe something had come up with Edith. Another custody threat. Or he could want to see her to tell her that their dating was a bad idea.

That put a twist in her stomach.

But she couldn't deny that it was indeed a bad idea. That's why she had to tell him about Peekaboo, and then Austin would know that she was someone he should avoid. Of course, that only twisted her up even more.

By the time she'd gotten his truck and driven to the school, McCall felt as if she'd bathed in a big tub of dread. That eased some when she spotted Avery and Gracie waiting in the pickup area with Adelle Carson, their teacher who was someone McCall had known from childhood. The girls jumped up and down when they spotted McCall get out of their dad's truck.

"The fairy lady," they squealed in unison. They rushed toward her, giving her a hug. That certainly helped with McCall's otherwise dreary mood.

"McCall," Adelle greeted. "I didn't know you knew the twins so well."

McCall caught the unspoken text in that. Adelle obviously thought Austin and she were *involved*. She didn't know if Adelle would spread that as gossip, but if so, there was nothing McCall could do about it. Plus, the gossip would soon die down when folks didn't see Austin and her together.

"I've been to Austin's place a couple of times," McCall settled for saying, and she got the girls moving toward the truck.

"Can we play fairy princess?" Gracie asked just as Avery said, "Can we play cops and bobbers?"

"Well, I'm not a cop like your aunt Cait, and I'm not really a fairy princess, but we can play fairy tale rules."

That got a groan from Avery and a look of disappointment from Gracie.

"We each get to be the fairy princess and come up with our own rules," McCall amended.

After a few moments for the girls to process that, McCall's suggestion brought on claps and excited wiggles, which made it a little hard to get them in the child restraints in the back seat of the double cab pickup.

"But there are rules for the rules," McCall added. "You can't make a rule that makes someone feel bad or makes them say things they really don't want to say. In fairy tale land, everybody should be happy."

The girls stayed quiet a moment, clearly considering that, but then the clapping returned.

"I'll start," McCall said once she was behind the wheel. "My fairy tale rule is that Gracie has to tell me her favorite color."

"Reen," Gracie immediately said, mispronouncing *green*.

"Great choice. And now it's Gracie's turn to make a fairy tale rule," McCall instructed while she drove back toward Austin's.

Gracie took a moment, and after glancing in the rearview mirror, McCall could see the girl's face screwed up in concentration. "Avery's gotta tell me her favorite color."

"Red," Avery quickly answered as if anticipating the question. "Now, it's my turn to do a law?"

"It is," McCall assured her.

"Fairy lady's gotta tell me her favorite color," Avery said.

Obviously, there was a theme here, and McCall answered, "Blue."

The game continued with favorite foods and drinks, and it ended with favorite books as McCall pulled to a stop in front of Austin's. She didn't see any sign of Austin, but McCall recognized the car parked in his driveway.

Edith.

"We don't gotta go with Grandma Edith, do we?" Avery immediately asked. "Can we make that a fairy tale rule?"

"We wanta stay with you," Gracie piped in.

Obviously, the girls weren't happy about seeing their

grandmother, but Edith apparently wasn't happy to see Mc-Call, either.

"Is something wrong?" Edith asked the moment McCall opened the door. "Why isn't Austin here?"

"Nothing's wrong," McCall assured her. "Austin just got tied up with something and asked me to pick up the girls."

Clearly, Edith didn't approve of that. "He should have called me. He shouldn't have bothered you with that." And she proceeded to help the twins out of their car seats.

"We want the fairy lady to babysit," Avery grumbled.

"Well, there's no need. I'm here now." Edith smiled despite the girls' mutual groans and grumbles. "Go on inside and put up your backpacks," Edith instructed. "I'll be there in a second or two to fix you a snack."

That was no doubt the woman's way of letting McCall know that she had some things to say to her in private. Things that McCall didn't especially want to hear. That's why McCall didn't stay put. With Edith right on her heels, she followed the girls inside.

Obviously, Avery and Gracie had a routine because they went straight to their rooms, discarding their backpacks on the floor and kicking off their shoes. The moment they were done with that, they ran into the adjoining bathroom.

"They'll be fine in there," Edith assured her. "And this will give us a chance to talk. If we talk fast, that is."

McCall sighed. "Look, I know you don't think much of me because of my upbringing, and I know you don't approve of me seeing Austin—"

"I was wrong," Edith said, cutting her off. "I didn't think you'd be right for Austin, but I've reconsidered it."

McCall was stunned to silence and she was betting it wasn't very often that Edith admitted anything like that. "Why?" McCall asked.

Edith shrugged, her gaze landing on anything but Mc-Call. "I know how your mother pushed you girls into that TV show, and you were too young to do anything about it."

Pushed was a very polite way of explaining things. Since the show had started when McCall and her sisters were only three, they'd had no say in it. No say in the antics that Sunshine had pulled, either, to boost the ratings and keep the show on the air for over a decade.

"I also know about your foundation," Edith went on. "From what I've heard, it does great work."

"It does," McCall assured her. Then she waited for the other shoe to drop. McCall was certain there was a "but" in all this praise and that Edith was about to tell her to get lost.

"Austin is still grieving," Edith continued. "I don't want that. I don't want him grieving for Zoey forever. But I want Zoey's daughters to have a good home. Zoey reminded me of that when I got a card from her yesterday."

McCall didn't ask for details about the card, but she suspected Zoey had left cards for her mom as she'd done for Austin.

"Anyway, you have my blessing to see Austin," the woman muttered in a barely audible whisper. A whisper that got drowned out when the girls came running out of the bathroom.

"Your blessing?" McCall repeated, stunned. However, she didn't have time to say more because Avery and Gracie stopped right in front of her.

"Fairy tale rules," Avery announced, her gaze nailed to McCall. "We want you to fix our snack."

"And watch a movie with us." That from Gracie.

McCall didn't respond because at that exact moment, she heard the footsteps behind them.

Austin was standing there.

And judging from his raised eyebrow, he'd obviously heard what his daughters had said.

"Well," Edith said, muttering that, too. "I'll just be going." She kissed the girls, gave Austin's arm a squeeze and walked out.

"Daddy!" the girls squealed, apparently already forgetting fairy tale rules. Or not. Avery took her hand and started leading McCall into the kitchen.

"We played fairy tale rules," Avery babbled to her dad.

"Did you now?" Austin asked, smiling.

"Yep," Avery verified. She took McCall to the fridge and even opened it for her. "You gotta do stuff in fairy tale rules. I want cheese and grapes, please," she added to McCall in the same breath.

"I can get that for you," Austin offered, only to be told, "No," by both girls.

"We want the fairy lady to do it," Gracie said in her quiet, shy voice. "It's my fairy tale rule."

Austin put his hands on his hips. "The fairy lady might have other things to do."

"I don't. No fairy tale chores on my to-do list right now," McCall assured him, but she hadn't forgotten that Austin had wanted to talk to her.

And she needed to talk to him.

She had to come clean about why she couldn't continue to see him. Ironic that she needed to do that on the heels of getting Edith's seal of approval.

McCall soon learned that snack prep wasn't a big deal. That's because Austin or someone had everything already sorted out, cut and washed in plastic storage containers and bags. McCall got out some green grapes that had been halved—probably to prevent choking—some cheese cubes and two small boxes of milk.

Avery, Gracie and, yes, Austin watched as she arranged the food on small plates that she took from the cabinet, and she hoped that Austin didn't think she was doing this to prove her domestic skills. No need for that even if she hadn't been on the brink of putting an end to this scalding-hot attraction with him.

Well, the attraction would almost certainly stay. But she had to bow out of his and the girls' lives.

"I didn't know Edith was coming over," Austin said as he helped her carry the plates to the coffee table. He picked up the remote, turned on an animated TV show that he'd recorded. This was obviously the routine because the girls sat on the floor, their attention on the TV while they ate.

"Little pitchers have big ears," he reminded her. Austin caught on to McCall's hand and pulled her onto the sofa next to him. "But if we whisper, we might be able to talk."

McCall considered that a moment. Considered, too, that Austin might not question her too much about this "breakup" if his daughters were right there. When she nodded, he turned up the volume on the TV, which pleased the girls because they clapped and continued to munch on their snacks.

Austin took out his phone and opened it up to a picture. For a moment McCall was about to ask why he'd shown her that, but then it was as if her entire brain screeched to a very noisy halt.

Oh, God.

It was a slightly out of focus picture of her wearing her skimpy waitress outfit when she'd worked at Peekaboo. Whoever had snapped the photo had caught her just as she'd leaned down to put some drinks on a table, and the leaning had caused her to practically spill out of the swatch of a tube top. In the background was a dancer—one in a G-string and pasties—working the pole.

Her gaze flew back to Austin's, and she expected to see some anger and even confusion on his face. There wasn't any. But there was something else that she couldn't quite put her finger on.

"How'd you get that?" she asked. There was no need for her to lower her voice because a whisper was the best she could do with what little air she had managed to get into her lungs.

Austin looked her straight in the eyes. "Hayes gave it to me."

"Hayes?" That didn't make sense, and it took a while for it to register in what was left of her brain. "How would he have gotten it, and why would he have given it to you?"

"Your brother came by earlier," Austin explained, "and he messaged me a copy of it then. We had some business to take care of, and he dropped me off here."

Again, that didn't make sense, and this time McCall didn't even attempt a whisper. Or speech of any kind. She just shook her head and sat there, taking several long moments to rein in all the thoughts flying through her head. She hadn't seen her brother in several years, and yet he'd come here to give Austin that photo.

Why?

That was something McCall very much wanted to know but first things first. She had to woman-up. "Yes, it's me. I worked as a waitress in a strip club when I was in college."

Austin studied her a moment, his expression still giving away nothing, and he nodded. "I remember Em telling my mom that Sunshine and your dad had taken most of the money from the accounts set up for you and your sisters."

McCall made a soft sound to indicate that was true, but she hated that, even after all this time, it still caused a flood of resentment. Her parents had indeed taken the money, and they'd done it legally because of the way they'd set up the contracts for *Little Cowgirls*. That meant McCall had had to work her way through college along with taking out some student loans.

"I don't understand why you have this picture," she admitted.

Austin gathered in his breath but then hesitated when Gracie looked back at him. He smiled at her and then waited for her to turn back around before he said anything. "A man named Jason Pierce sent Hayes the photo. Pierce lives in San Antonio now but was apparently in the strip club years ago when he sneaked a picture of the stripper."

Since cameras weren't allowed in Peekaboo, that explained the odd angle and blurry image. Still, this guy had managed to get her in the shot without McCall even realizing it.

"Pierce kept the picture," Austin went on, "and when he recently showed it to a girlfriend, she recognized you. She didn't know you," he quickly added.

"She recognized me from the TV show," McCall filled in, and she got a very bad feeling about this. "This Jason Pierce tried to blackmail Hayes?"

Austin nodded. "Hayes thinks Pierce got in touch with him because he figured Hayes would have money to pay him off."

McCall bit her lip to make sure she didn't curse because she couldn't be sure that would come out as a whisper. Damn it. "How much does Pierce want?"

"Ten grand."

Considering how much Hayes made, or rather how much he was rumored to make, that wasn't a huge amount to him, but it certainly was to her.

"Hayes also wanted me to go with him to San Antonio so I'd be a witness to what Pierce had to say. And be a witness to him making the payment. That took longer than I thought it would so that's why I asked you to pick up the girls."

Again, she had to bite her lip and rein in the anger. "Hayes shouldn't have paid him a penny. The guy will probably just tap him for more."

"I don't think so. Hayes recorded the conversation and said if he came back with another demand or if he published the photo anywhere that he'd turn the recording over to the cops. Then Pierce could be arrested for extortion."

McCall shook her head, not at all certain that would work, but maybe it would. Still… "How did Hayes know you'd even care about me being in that picture? Why did he come to you and not me?"

"The reporter did an article about Cody Joe and that night you were here," Austin quickly answered. "Hayes got wind of the story and assumed you and I were together. And as for why he didn't come to you, he didn't want you to know. He figured you had enough to handle what with the mess with Cody Joe."

That eased her anger even more. And upped her frustration. Her brother should have come to her. He shouldn't have tried to shelter her.

But it didn't surprise her that he had.

Hayes played up his bad-boy image, but just weeks earlier, he'd run interference for Sunny by helping her get back some items that Sunshine had managed to get her hands on.

"Obviously, I didn't listen to Hayes about keeping you out of the loop on this," Austin went on. "It didn't feel right not letting you know."

"Thank you for that." She paused. "I just wish Hayes would have at least come in so I could see him."

"He said he had to get back to shoot some scenes. Plus, I don't think he wanted to explain why he was here because he would have had to let you know about the picture and blackmail."

McCall nodded and glanced at the girls. They were still watching the TV show, but they only had a few more bites to go and they'd be finished with their snacks. Once that was done, they might pay more attention to Austin and her than they were doing right now.

It was time to tell Austin the rest of the truth.

"There's more," he said before she could even get started. "Boo saw me buy three boxes of condoms at the Pump and Ride."

McCall hadn't thought she could be surprised again so soon. However, she'd obviously been wrong. Her mouth didn't actually drop open, but it was close.

"Yeah," he said as if acknowledging her surprise. "FYI, Howie saw me, too. Clearly, the Pump and Ride was a busy place today. I just didn't want one of them to say anything about it to you and blindside you."

"Three boxes," she muttered. "Wow."

She had to fight a smile, which was crazy, considering there really wasn't anything to smile about. Still, she felt a little flattered that he thought they were going to be burning up the sheets. Of course, the smile and the flattery didn't last.

"We've both had a past, McCall," he said. "That picture doesn't bother me. The fact that you worked at that club doesn't bother me. What would bother me is if you decided that it or anything else was so bad that you wouldn't allow yourself to at least see where things were going with us."

Mercy. That was the right thing to say. Of course, it was also what she wanted to hear. She blamed that on the three boxes of condoms. And the heated look Austin was giving her. She wanted to dive right in, kiss him and put at least one of those condoms to good use.

"In my mind, I'm doing very dirty things to you right now," he drawled.

McCall smiled. "In my mind, I'm doing those dirty things right back to you."

The corner of his mouth lifted, and he seemed to be moving in closer. But then he stopped, his gaze turning toward the TV. Or rather toward his daughters.

Avery and Gracie had obviously finished their snacks. And the girls were staring at Austin and her.

"Fairy tale rules," Avery said with a sneaky smile on her face. "You gotta kiss our daddy."

McCall knew she should resist, but Austin was right there. Even knowing it was a mistake that both Austin and she would soon regret, she leaned in and obeyed the rules of the game.

Of course, the kiss was off the charts. It was easy to feel the simmer and flames with Austin. However, it was easy to feel other things, too.

Deeper things.

Like the emotions that tugged at her heart. Maybe it was because she'd had such a crush on him in school, but those old emotions seemed to be playing into this and adding another layer to the heat. Not good. Lust was one thing. But lust with feelings that could turn to something much, much more was bad.

McCall eased back, met his gaze and gave herself a few seconds to savor the sensations. Then she checked to see how the girls were reacting. They were still both staring at Austin and her, and they probably would have launched into another round of fairy tale rules if something on the

TV hadn't snagged their attention. Apparently, seeing their daddy kiss her couldn't hold a candle to the cartoon ducks who'd started to dance. That got Avery and Gracie up and dancing, too.

"I need to go," McCall said to Austin. "Would you walk me out?"

Judging from his grin, he thought that was going to lead to more kisses. Sadly, it wouldn't. But McCall did dance her way to the girls and gave them a goodbye hug before she took Austin by the hand and led him onto the porch.

"I'm going to say this fast," she started. "Then I'm leaving. If you never want to see me again, I'll understand."

That put some worry lines on his forehead. "If this is about that picture—"

"It's more than that," she interrupted, but McCall had to take a deep breath before she finished. "I'm the owner of the Peekaboo strip club where the picture was taken."

The moment the last word left her mouth, McCall turned and hurried off the porch and to her car.

CHAPTER ELEVEN

"FAIRY TALE RULE," Avery said, tugging on Austin's hand. "We getta have ice cream for dinner. And candy. And no vegge-tables. And pizza."

Austin looked down at her and gave his daughter his best "not a chance" face. He'd already made their dinner—it was sitting in the microwave. Baked chicken with potatoes and carrots. Still, since Cait was babysitting tonight, there was a chance some ice cream and candy would be involved.

"Be good for Aunt Cait, and I'll take Gracie and you to the Lickety Split tomorrow." It was the only ice cream parlor in town and the girls' favorite. He knew that from the way they squealed.

"Take us tonight," Avery insisted.

Austin shook his head. "I'm going to see McCall. The fairy lady," he added.

That got a mixed reaction including suggestions from Avery that the fairy lady could go with them for ice cream. Aunt Cait, too. But Austin would have to nix that idea. He needed to talk to McCall, and he didn't want his girls around for that.

Of course, it was entirely possible that McCall wouldn't want to talk to him. That was the risk he was taking by just showing up at Em's. After all, she'd left darn fast a few hours earlier when she'd delivered her bombshell.

I'm the owner of the Peekaboo strip club.

In hindsight, Austin should have called out to her. Or gone after her. But the news had left him stunned just long enough for her to make her speedy exit. It was an exit she obviously intended to stick to, which was likely why she hadn't responded to the texts he'd sent her.

Thankfully, she hadn't left town. He knew that because he'd called Em and she'd told him that McCall was in her room and that she'd seemed upset. His visit might only add to her being upset, but Austin was determined to talk this out with her.

Maybe that would help him figure out his own feelings, too.

He couldn't imagine what had prompted McCall to own a strip club. It certainly didn't mesh well with the high-society folks who donated to her foundation. But maybe the club was somehow funding the foundation, too. Still, he could see why she'd want to keep something like that a secret. Could equally see why she'd end things with him because the trouble something like that could cause him.

So, why was he going to McCall?

That was a question Austin had asked himself most of the afternoon, and he came up with only one answer: because he wanted to see her, that's why. As answers went, it wasn't a very good one. But maybe it was the only answer that mattered. McCall could be all twisted up in knots over what she'd told him, and he wanted to talk that out with her.

"Pizza delivery," Cait called out from the porch.

That sent the girls running to open the door, and yep, there was his sister, balancing a pizza box in one hand while she held a plastic grocery bag in the other. A bag that no doubt contained something sugary. Probably candy and ice cream.

Austin sighed. "At least make sure they brush their teeth

after eating whatever it is you've brought them. And they have to eat vegetables first."

That brought on a duo of groans from Avery and Gracie, though they must have known it was coming. Cait knew it, too, and while yes, she indulged the girls a lot, she'd make sure they ate the right stuff before getting the junk food.

Austin took the grocery bag, glanced inside and saw the ice cream, popcorn and two kids' books. All the items definitely got the girls' attention when he took them out and put the ice cream in the freezer.

"Thank you for doing this," Austin murmured to Cait. And she knew he didn't mean bringing the food and books.

"Hey, anything I can do to further your love life," she whispered back while the girls started flipping through the books. Cait set the pizza on the counter. "This is about your love life, right? It's about McCall?"

Austin nodded. No way would he spill to Cait about Peekaboo. That wasn't his secret to tell, but other photos could turn up of McCall working there. If so, it could blow up in her face and add another layer of embarrassment and hurt on top of what Cody Joe had already doled out to her.

"Stay out as late as you like. Even all night since I can bunk here," Cait added, still whispering. "Do I need to have the safe sex talk with you?"

Austin ignored her and didn't mention the brand new condom he now carried in his wallet. He wasn't expecting sex—okay, maybe he was hoping for it—but he was pretty sure that wouldn't happen. Heck, it was possible McCall wouldn't even see him. If so, he'd just drive around for a while so that the girls could have time with Cait.

Gracie and Avery were already engrossed in the books so they barely looked up at him when he kissed them goodbye. Austin went to his truck and started the drive to Em's.

Along the way, he tried to figure out what he was actually going to say to McCall if he got the chance to speak to her, but nothing he came up with sounded right. Best just to see her and take things from there.

He was relieved when he saw her car parked on the side of Em's. Relieved, too, when he spotted the light on in her room on the second floor. There were no lights on, though, in the front of the house so he went to the back, hoping to have a quick word with Em to find out how McCall was doing. The lights were definitely on in the kitchen, and he could hear laughter. Not McCall, though. It sounded like Boo.

Em answered his knock right away, and Austin saw that she was wearing a full assortment of clothes, including a sweater and two cowboy hats stacked on top of each other. Unlike Boo and McCall. They were seated at the kitchen table, and Boo was in her underwear again.

McCall wasn't faring much better.

She was in her underwear, as well, a plain white bra and panties, but she was scrambling to put on a robe that she'd had draped over the back of the chair. Boo barely spared him a glance. Instead, her attention was on the poker hand that she had spread out on the table. The hand—three kings—beat the other two hands on the table, and those no doubt belonged to Em and McCall.

"Finally!" Boo declared, giving a victory whoop. "I won."

She was grinning, but she was the only one in the room who was. Em was studying Austin as if she wasn't sure what to do with him. McCall looked mortified.

Austin was certain he just looked aroused.

Even though McCall and he had dated way back when, he'd never gotten past the point of a few kisses with her.

He'd definitely never seen her in her underwear. Of course, there was that picture of her in the waitress outfit, but it was different with her in the flesh. And he was certain the image of the real her would stay in his head and the rest of his body for a long, long time.

"I can dish you up a plate of lasagna," Em offered, "but I'm guessing you're here to talk to McCall?"

He nodded and kept his attention on McCall, to see if she was going to nip this visit and the talk in the bud. For a few snail-crawling moments, that's exactly what he thought she might do, but then she motioned for him to follow her. She also scooped up the stack of neatly folded clothes on the counter. Probably clothes she'd intended to put on if she won any hands.

"This way," McCall whispered. "But I don't want Granny Em to hear our conversation."

Em but not Boo, which meant her assistant already knew about Peekaboo.

"Your grandmother's certainly good at poker," Austin commented as he followed her into the front room that Em called the parlor.

He hadn't expected McCall to stop midway there, but she did and turned toward him. "Em said she was once involved with a guy in the mob and that he taught her how to play. Have you heard anything about that?"

Judging from the tightness of her mouth, that was bothering McCall. A lot. But he had to shake his head. "When it comes to Em, the only man I've ever heard about was your grandfather. From what I recall people saying, Em moved here after they got married."

"Yes, and until tonight I don't remember her ever mentioning anything about the mob." McCall stopped and waved that off when she glanced down at her robe. "Sorry. Let me put on some clothes, and then we'll talk."

He wanted to tell her to skip the clothes but figured that wasn't a smart idea. Knowing what she was wearing beneath the robe was distracting, and instead of talking—something they needed to do—he'd be thinking of other things. Like kissing her again.

When they got to the parlor, she shut the door. "Turn around," she instructed.

Austin did that, but he soon realized there was a problem. He could still see her in one of the wall mirrors. *Clearly* see her when she tossed aside the robe. Yeah, that was definitely a distraction. The best kind of one if they'd been about to have sex, that is. Since they weren't, Austin closed his eyes.

"I thought you'd have run for the hills by now," McCall said. "You *should* have run for the hills," she amended. "No way will I fit into the image of the woman Edith wants in your life."

And there it was. All laid out for him. Edith definitely wouldn't think McCall was right for him. And maybe she wasn't. But Austin wanted to make that decision for himself.

"Tell me about the club," he said. "How'd you end up owning it?"

Austin heard her drag in a long breath. "A woman named Lizzie Marlow owned the place when I was a waitress there. She had a good heart but was awful with paperwork, managing schedules and such so I helped her. When she died, she left Peekaboo to me. Unfortunately, she set up the terms of the will so I can't sell it or give it away."

He let that sink in and found himself smiling a little. It was so like McCall. She'd helped someone out and had ended up getting more than she'd bargained for. More than she wanted.

"Boo was a stripper there," McCall went on. "That's how I met her. When she wanted to go into a different line of work, I hired her as my assistant."

Well, that explained a lot. It might be stereotyping, but Boo did dress like a stripper.

Austin jerked a little when he felt McCall touch his arm to get his attention, and when he opened his eyes, he saw that she was wearing jeans and a red top.

"It doesn't matter that I inherited the place or that I don't want it," she went on. "I'm still the owner of a strip club, and if anyone around here finds out, that could end up hurting you."

Austin wanted to deny that. But it could hurt him even if it shouldn't. And that pissed him off more than a little. It wasn't fair. Then again, he'd learned the hard way that life sucked in the being-fair department.

"FYI, Boo is legally changing her name to mine," McCall said. "But she's doing that only so she can cover for me if anyone finds out I'm the owner. It's a bad cosmetic attempt to hide the truth."

He went back through the conversation he'd overheard between McCall and Sunny. "Tit rouge?"

She made a soft gasp of surprise, followed by a nod. "Yes. That's what Boo calls the name change. I call it an unnecessary deal that'll solve nothing." She stared at him. "Austin, I'm really sorry."

He wasn't sure exactly why she was apologizing especially since owning the club was out of her control.

"I've got baggage, too," Austin settled for saying. "Just being around me puts you under Edith's eagle-eye scrutiny. I'm sorry that she came over to my house this afternoon—"

"She basically told me that she was giving me her blessing so I could keep seeing you," McCall interrupted.

Oh.

Well, Austin hadn't expected that, and he immediately saw the irony of it.

"Yes," McCall said as if she knew exactly what he was thinking. "Edith gave me her blessing right before you came in after wrapping up the photo payoff with Hayes. By the way, I've talked to Hayes to let him know I'll give him back every penny that he paid that blackmailing creep."

Austin figured she would say exactly that. He knew, too, that Hayes wouldn't want or accept payment. He hadn't spent much time with Hayes, but Austin recognized brotherly love when he saw it. Hayes was trying to protect his sister, something that Austin would have done for Cait.

"I'm really sorry," she repeated. On a weary sigh, she dragged her hands through her hair, pushing it away from her face.

He could have told her that this wasn't her fault. That she'd simply been trying to earn a living when the photo had been taken by the blackmailing creep. He doubted that would help. Doubted, too, that a kiss would help, either.

But that's what he did.

Austin could blame this fresh punch of heat on seeing McCall in her bra and panties, but the truth was, he simply wanted to kiss her. Wanted to feel her mouth on his. Wanted to feel her against him. So, he slipped his arm around her waist, pulled her to him and kissed her.

He made it long, slow and deep because he was afraid this might be the last kiss he ever got from her. In fact, he expected her to push him away and remind him of all the reasons why they shouldn't be doing this.

She didn't.

McCall made that silky sound of pleasure in her throat. Sort of a *hum* and an *mmm* combined as if she'd just tasted something damn good. Austin figured he could make the same sound because the taste of her definitely worked for him. The woman fired him up in the hottest kind of way.

The firing up continued when he moved in closer, tightening his grip on her until her body slid against his. Everything lined up just right. Her breasts against his chest. The zipper of her jeans in the general vicinity of his. The contact and her mouth were more than enough to send the heat flaming high.

"Edith," she said with her mouth still against his.

Obviously, she was reminding him that Edith would revoke her blessing if she learned the truth about Peekaboo, but at the moment that just didn't seem important. Actually, not much of anything other than kissing and touching seemed important. Still, Austin eased back to give her a chance to tell him to back off.

Her breath came out in little gusts, hitting against his mouth. Her face was flushed. Her eyes glazed. All good signs for making out but not for conversation.

"If Edith finds out…" she murmured.

He stopped the rest of what she was about to saying by kissing her neck. Austin hadn't known it would be so effective, but he got proof that it was when McCall's *hum* and *mmm* got deeper and louder. Her head lolled to the side, exposing her neck like an offering to a vampire. Austin didn't bite. Well, not too hard, anyway. But he made sure both of them got the most out of that particular kiss.

Still making that sound of pleasure, McCall caught on to his arms, her fingers digging in, but he soon realized that was just to bring him even closer. She moved. He moved. And they moved together in such a way that made Austin very glad there was a sofa nearby.

But McCall might not be ready for that.

He had to force himself to remember that. It got through to his brain just fine, but his dick was having a lot of trouble with the notion.

"Granny Em and Boo are in the house," McCall said. That reminder was also a breathy murmur complete with more of her body pressing to him.

Austin managed to make a sound to let her know he was aware of that, but that was an easy fix. Keeping hold of McCall, still kissing her neck, he backed her across the room until he could reach the door and lock it.

The click of the lock must have pulled McCall out of her lusty haze because she lifted her head and met his gaze.

"If we have sex right now, how much will it mean to you?" she asked.

Well, hell. At the moment he was barely capable of human speech much less answering something like that. Was she asking if this would be just sex?

Maybe.

At least, that's what he'd want it to be until they figured out if there could be anything deeper between them. But sex was a start. He was sure of that. Or maybe again, that was his dick talking.

"I don't know," he answered honestly. He could practically feel his dick wanting to kick him for it, too.

She nodded as if that was the exact answer she expected. "I'm not analyzing you…us," she amended, "but I don't want to jump into anything that you could regret."

"I won't regret it," Austin blurted out.

McCall smiled, gave his erection a nudge with a part of her that could do some serious nudging. "Let's just be sure. I care about you too much to screw this up for you."

Austin repeated his mental, *Well, hell.* Now, there was caring too much? He wasn't sure that was possible at this stage, but he thought he knew what she meant because he cared about her, too.

"Sixty minutes of making out," she said.

No "Well, hell" this time, but Austin did manage a "Huh?"

"It's what I tell my clients who aren't sure if they should be doing more than kissing. I suggest sixty minutes of making out. No sex, no clothing removal," she emphasized. "Then wait at least a day to see how you feel."

Austin didn't have to think about this answer. "I know how I'll feel—frustrated and unable to walk."

She smiled again. "Yes, but then you'll know better how you feel."

Again, he had a quick answer. Or would have. He could have repeated the part about being frustrated. But McCall took hold of the front of his shirt, gathering it up in her hand and pulling him to her.

"Come with me," McCall said, her voice that damn silky siren's whisper. "And let's get our sixty minutes started."

CHAPTER TWELVE

THIS WAS THE very definition of playing with fire. McCall knew it. So did Austin. But that didn't stop her from taking Austin by the hand, and it definitely didn't stop him from going right along with her as she led him outside.

"Where are we going?" he asked, stealing a kiss on her neck as they went down the porch steps. "We can't go to my place because the girls are there with Cait."

"We're going parking," McCall explained. She might be thirty-three years old, but she didn't think she could fool around with her grandmother just a couple of rooms over. "We can go to Prego Trail."

Austin went a little stiff, probably in surprise, but McCall still got him to his truck. "I never went there when I was a teenager."

"Neither did I. Since I own it now, I go there a couple of times of year just to check on it, but it wasn't a spot I used for making out."

Now, she was the one who was surprised. "You didn't take any girls there?" Of course, what she really wanted to know was had he taken Zoey there. If so, they'd need a change of venue since she didn't want to tap into those kinds of memories for him. Some places were more of a punch than a tap.

He was smiling when he shook his head. "Going to a place called Prego Trail never appealed to me, not when it was much prettier scenery to park by the creek bank. But the trail is closer," he quickly added. "I'm thinking *closer* is better."

Yes, it was. Though it took less time to walk there than it did to drive. Still, they shouldn't be out in the open when things got hot and heavy between them. Plus, the good thing about using his vehicle was that he'd be driving and it'd give them some time to cool off. Maybe even give them some time to come to their senses.

Or not.

Austin kissed her when he started the engine, kissed her again before he put the truck into gear. Then, going at turtle speed as he drove down the road, he sneaked a few more kisses. Those might have been short, but they were still scalding enough to singe her eyelashes.

"Prego Trail is over a mile away," Austin grumbled.

Considering his suddenly urgent tone and the steamy lust in the truck, McCall probably shouldn't have unhooked her seat belt so she could give him some neck kisses. And she used her tongue. That seemed to be the tipping point for Austin because he cursed and pulled to the side of the road. The moment he had his truck in Park, he hauled her to him.

And that's when the real kissing began.

Mouth-to-mouth. Deep and extremely satisfying. Well, satisfying in that it sent her need level spearing through the roof. Mercy, she wanted him, but this was the kind of heat that could lead to a lot more than making out. That's why McCall finally leaned back when she had to break for air. Of course, she couldn't lean far because she was sandwiched between Austin and the steering wheel.

She automatically glanced around. They were alone on the road, and they were far enough from town that anyone driving there wouldn't be able to see them. That didn't mean, though, someone couldn't come driving up.

That only added to the thrill.

Which obviously wasn't good. She definitely didn't need

for Austin and her to get caught acting like horny teenagers. Or horny adults for that matter.

"We didn't get to do any of this when we were fake dating," she reminded him, saying the first thing that popped into her head. Clearly, she should have come up with something a whole lot better.

"We can make up for that, and this time it won't be fake." Oh, there was that drawl. The slow husky voice that pulled her right in. Then again, his breathing could pull her in, too.

"The clothes have to stay on," she reminded him.

Her breath was gusting. Her body on fire. And the only reason she'd said that to him was to force herself to remember that it was one of the rules. Rules that she'd laid out.

Stupid rules.

Really stupid, she decided when Austin went after her neck again. But he didn't just kiss. No, not Austin. He was obviously a multitasker when it came to this sort of thing. While his mouth was busy on her neck, his hand got plenty busy on the front of her shirt. He touched her breasts, cupping her, swiping his thumb over her very hard, very erect nipple.

"I didn't check the time to see how we're doing with our sixty minutes," she said. The comment was mixed with moans, and lots of rustling-around sounds as McCall wiggled closer to Austin.

Using the F-word, he told her what he thought of their time limit. Or maybe he was telling her what he wanted to do to her. Either way, McCall didn't protest. She just let him touch and didn't blink when he ran his hand under her shirt and pushed down the cups of her bra. It wasn't clothing removal, not really, but it was just as effective. And it whittled down even more of her quickly dwindling willpower.

"We should slow down," she managed to say despite everything inside her yelling that slow wasn't the way to go here.

Austin did stop kissing her, but he didn't move his fingers that were now pinching her nipple. "Sixty minutes," he said. McCall knew the tone of someone trying to convince themselves that he could get through this.

She nodded. "It's hard..." Then she had to laugh because there was indeed some hardness going on. His erection was pressed against her thigh. "I mean, in high school it was easier to say we can't do this."

"Really?" There was just enough moonlight for her to see the corner of his mouth lift into a smile. "And how easy is it now?"

"Not easy at all," she admitted. "I'm pretty sure you'll be really good at sex. You're certainly a good kisser." She paused. "I just need you to be sure."

McCall figured his silence meant he was coming up with a whopper of an argument. One that would toss the rules and get them at least partially naked. But he kissed her again. And slid his hand from her breasts down to her jeans. Not inside them. However, his fingers created some mind-blowing sensations even through the fabric of her jeans and panties.

"I want you to be sure, too," he drawled.

There might have been clothing barriers between his touching and the center of her body, but it was almost as effective as him being inside her.

Almost.

McCall was certain full-blown sex with Austin would be off the pleasure scale. For now, though, he was doing an amazing job taking her to the point of begging.

"You want about fifty more minutes of this?" he asked.

She wasn't sure she could take five more seconds without having what she was sure would be an amazing climax, but McCall didn't like that it would all be one-sided. That's why she ground herself against his erection. It was incredibly easy to find, and she pushed his hand out of the way to give them both the contact.

This was so high school.

So good, too.

It felt naughty, necessary and incredible all at once. Austin upped that, too, by hooking his arm around her butt and moving her in just the right way. The right pressure. The right place, and just like that, the orgasm was on her before McCall could do anything to stop it.

She heard herself make a gasp of pleasure, and the climax rippled through her. Except it was much more than ripples. It stole her breath. Turned her body limp. And she collapsed against him.

McCall took a moment to come back down so she could do the same to Austin, but when she pushed her hips forward again, he stopped her. The kiss he gave her was different from the other ones. There was no urgency in it. Just a long slow kiss that felt like icing on top of the cake of a climax he'd just given her.

"I want you to be sure, too," he repeated. Then his gaze connected with hers. "Come and see me tomorrow and let me know what you decide."

With that shocker barely out of his mouth, Austin moved her off his lap and turned around to take her back home.

AUSTIN WAS TRYING very hard to focus on work. And it wasn't as if he didn't have plenty of that.

As soon as Edith and Howie had picked up the girls for their usual day out with them, Austin had dived right in and done some training with three of the horses. That had taken all of the morning. Then going over the bills and contracts had taken nearly an hour, but he could have done that in half the time if he hadn't been checking his phone every few minutes to see if McCall had texted him.

She hadn't.

He tried, and failed, not to read too much into that. After all, it was only early afternoon, and maybe she was using the time she needed to think about what'd happened in his truck.

I want you to be sure, too.

Yep, that's what he'd told her, all right, and it'd been the right thing to say. At the moment, though, with his body in knots and his mind on McCall, he was wishing he hadn't offered her an out. He didn't want McCall taking an out. He wanted her in his bed. Or in his truck. Hell, he just wanted her.

Cursing himself and his honorable streak, Austin signed the contract that'd taken him way too long to read and process. Callen Laramie, a cattleman in nearby Wrangler's Creek, wanted to lease one of Austin's pastures that he wasn't currently using. Callen wanted to bring in some quarter horses for the rest of the summer and into the fall. It'd give Austin some solid revenue for his ranch along with establishing business ties with Callen. Signing the contract was a no-brainer, but it had apparently taken Austin's brain longer than usual to figure that out.

Austin scanned the signed contract, fired it off to Callen's office and then he practically jumped up from the desk when he heard some movement in the front of the house.

"I'm heading out now," Sharla Beech called out to him. Not McCall but rather the housekeeper he had come in once a week. "You've got company," she added. "Someone just pulled up."

Finally. That was Austin's first thought, but he tried to tamp down everything he was feeling so he could go to the front door. Then he had to tamp down some serious cursing when he saw his visitor. Again, it wasn't McCall.

It was Cody Joe.

Austin couldn't say that Cody Joe was the absolute last

person on earth he wanted to see, but he was in the top five. His father, serial killers, door-to-door salesmen and his in-laws topped that list.

"Hey, Austin," the man greeted. He smiled as if there was something to smile about. "How's that pony?"

Austin skipped the niceties and went with a snarled question. "What are you doing here? Aren't you supposed to be in rehab or something?"

"*Was* in rehab," Cody Joe corrected, walking toward the porch where Austin was standing. "I got switched to being an outpatient so I can finish up my counseling."

Austin didn't know how long inpatient treatment was supposed to last for a sex addiction, but it didn't seem as if Cody Joe had been there nearly long enough. Plus, Cody Joe still had that cocky-assed smile, the kind that made Austin think that he believed therapy was all a joke, anyway.

"So, how's the pony?" Cody Joe repeated. "What'd your kids name him?"

Austin had no intention of explaining that the girls hadn't actually agreed on that, and the Shetland was being called Rose-Poopy Head. So, he went with a repeat of his own question. "What are you doing here?"

"Well, I was wondering if McCall was around so I could talk to her about, um, some things," Cody Joe went on. "I was just at her gran's place, and she said she thought Mc-Call was coming over to see you."

"She's not here." But maybe that meant she was heading to his place. If so, seeing Cody Joe wouldn't make her visit pleasant. At least, Austin didn't think it would. Mc-Call had seemed awfully pissed off at Cody Joe for costing her foundation donors.

"Any idea where I can find her?" Cody Joe pressed. "It's real important that I talk to her."

Austin shook his head, and even though Cody Joe came up on the porch, Austin didn't invite him in.

Cody Joe sighed and pulled off his hat so he could rake his hand through his hair. "I really messed up with her, and I need to fix things." He looked Austin straight in the eyes. "Can you help me fix things?"

Austin wasn't sure whether to groan or huff so he did both. "How or why would you think I'd do that?"

Cody Joe didn't seem offended by the question or Austin's growled tone. "Because you're McCall's friend."

That was the lamest excuse in the history of lame excuses. "Yeah, she's my friend, and I don't want her hurt." Hell, that's what last night was all about—not hurting McCall—and he damn sure didn't want this idiot stepping in to do more damage.

Of course, Austin might not have a say in that.

He'd given McCall some thinking time, and she just might use that time to decide that she didn't want him any more than she wanted Cody Joe.

"I don't want her hurt, either," Cody Joe went on. He paused. "Say, do you think you can help me get back together with McCall?"

Good grief. Austin groaned again, huffed and moaned. "Every level of hell would freeze first before I even considered doing something like that."

Now, Cody Joe seemed offended. His shoulders went back. His forehead bunched up, and Austin would have made a significant bet that Cody Joe was about to launch into all the reasons why that'd be a good idea.

Really stupid reasons, no doubt.

But there wasn't time for arguing his really stupid points because at that exact moment McCall drove up.

Despite Cody Joe's presence, Austin was both happy and relieved to see her. He couldn't say the same for McCall, though. She practically skidded to a stop when her attention landed on Cody Joe, and then she stormed out of her car.

"What are you doing here?" she demanded, aiming her narrowed gaze at Cody Joe.

"I was hoping Austin would help me get you back." Either Cody Joe was an idiot or… Yeah, an idiot, all right, because he went to McCall with outstretched arms as if ready to hug her.

"Get back with me?" she said, batting his hands away. "There's no chance of that, and you shouldn't have come here to pester Austin."

Cody Joe sighed. "You're still mad at me," he muttered, taking *stating the obvious* to a whole new level.

"Yes, I am," McCall verified. "And I'm especially not happy about you trying to drag Austin into this."

"Well, your granny said you might be here with him so it's obvious he's your friend." Cody Joe stopped, his gaze suddenly whipping between the two of them. Then he huffed and put his hands on his hips. "Say, there's not something going on between you two, is there?"

Obviously, there were a few brain cells in Cody Joe's head, after all, but Austin didn't respond. He just waited for McCall to take the lead on this.

"My relationship with Austin is none of your business," she snapped.

Even though this wasn't anything to celebrate, Austin had to fight back a smile. A *relationship* sounded like a good start to him and was a hell of a lot better than McCall and him just being friends.

"Of course it's my business," Cody Joe argued. "*You're* my business. I care about you, McCall."

She didn't exactly roll her eyes, but it was close. "I suspect you care more about how your mother's reacting to all of this. I can't imagine that Alisha is happy about how things turned out."

"She's not." Cody Joe lowered his head, shook it. "But my mom's not the only reason I want you back. We were good together, McCall. We belong together."

This time she did fully roll her eyes, and Austin could see that she was having a battle between reason and a temper tantrum. Even though it wouldn't accomplish anything, he was rooting for the temper to win out. This cocky ass needed to be taken down a few notches.

"No, we don't belong together," McCall assured him. Her words were low and had just a *you're treading in shark-infested water* warning to them. "You publicly embarrassed not only me but also the foundation. I might be able to forgive you for the first but not the second. And even if I did forgive you," she quickly added, "I wouldn't be getting back together with you."

"But, McCall—" That was as far as Cody Joe got because she cut him off with a nasty glare.

"You're leaving," she told him. "And I'll begin the paperwork to sever ties with you on the foundation."

For a couple of moments, Cody Joe just looked dazed as if McCall had slugged him with her fist and not just her words. "You can't," he eked out.

"Oh, yes, I can." No eke for McCall. Her voice was steady and firm. "And don't bring up how much this will disappoint your mother. I know it will, but after what you did, I don't think she'll blame me."

Austin could almost hear her adding an "I hope not, anyway" to that.

Cody Joe stared at her for a long time. "You'd really do this? Miss Watermelon meant nothing to me."

McCall sighed. "That's the problem with you, Cody Joe. It meant nothing, and yet it blew up in our faces. Because of that *meant nothing* stunt, the foundation lost thousands of dollars in donations."

Cody Joe opened his mouth, closed it. Then, by degrees, his stare turned to a glare. Obviously, it was sinking in that he'd just screwed up by screwing around.

"Ditching me won't help with those foundation donations," he snapped. "And it won't help with my mother."

"No," McCall admitted. Now, there was an even deeper sigh and resignation in her voice. "But as far as I'm concerned, a clean break is the only way to go. I'll get that paperwork started first thing in the morning."

That definitely didn't help with Cody Joe's glare, and he turned it on Austin. "You need to talk some sense into her."

"McCall sounds pretty sensible to me." Austin went to stand beside her for some moral support.

Cody Joe made a few flustered sounds that were part snarl, part growl. He glanced around as if looking for something, anything, that would help his current lousy situation before his attention slowly came back to them.

"Peekaboo," Cody Joe spat out like profanity. His eyes flared when he looked at McCall. "Does your boyfriend here know about that?"

"I do," Austin volunteered. He was doing some glaring of his own now because he was dead certain he knew where this was going.

Apparently, so did McCall because she shook her head and muttered a barely audible, "No."

"Yeah," Cody Joe said with what Austin could only describe as a thoroughly pissed-off smile. "Ditch me and everybody for miles around will know the secret you've been trying to keep." Sneering now, he leaned in. "Just how many donations will you lose when folks hear you own a strip club, huh?"

CHAPTER THIRTEEN

McCALL WATCHED CODY JOE storm away and back to his truck. He didn't wait around for her to respond to his question, but she knew the answer.

Just how many donations will you lose when folks hear you own a strip club?

Plenty. That's how many donations she'd lose, and she had the sickening feeling in the pit of her stomach that she couldn't do anything to stop it.

"Wait up," Austin called out to Cody Joe, and he hurried after him.

McCall seriously doubted that Austin had a civil conversation in mind. Not with the anger practically coming off him in waves. Nope. This could lead to some shouts, maybe even some punches, and it wouldn't resolve anything. However, it could make things worse not just for her but for all three of them. Trying to deal with Cody Joe right now would be like pouring kerosene on an already blazing fire.

"No," McCall told Austin, and she ended up running after him.

Austin made it to Cody Joe ahead of her, and he caught on to Cody Joe's arm, whirling him back around to face them. Cody Joe must have taken the move as a threat because he tried to connect his right fist with Austin's jaw. Austin dodged it and muscled Cody Joe against his truck.

"Just please let him go," McCall pleaded.

"You want to have this out?" Cody Joe challenged Austin. "You want us to settle it here and now?"

McCall stepped in between them. Not the brightest idea she'd ever had because the men were moving toward each other just as she did that, and she ended up squished between them. Not the kind of personal contact she'd expected when she'd decided to come to Austin's house and confess that she was ready to move past that foreplay stage. There was little chance of that now. The air was zinging not with lust but with temper.

"Stop it," she warned both of them.

Since she was facing Austin, she took hold of his arms and started backing him away. It didn't work. He was still moving forward so she kissed him. Again, it wasn't the brightest idea she'd ever had, but it stopped him in his tracks. It really stopped him when she let her mouth linger more than a moment on his.

"Shit," Cody Joe spat out. "So, that's how it is."

McCall supposed it would have been a good time for her to look back at Cody Joe and do more diffusing of this situation. But she simply didn't care if he was pissed off and stayed that way.

"That's how it is," she assured him. Austin's and her eyes stayed locked, and he ran his thumb over her bottom lip, gathering up the moisture from their kiss. He then brought that thumb to his mouth and flicked his tongue over it. Tasting her.

Which was exactly what McCall wanted to do to him.

That little tongue maneuver weakened her knees and reminded her why she'd come over here in the first place. Of course, hearing Cody Joe's grumbled profanity reminded her that she should do some adulting and deal with him first.

"Goodbye, Cody Joe," she said.

She didn't shout it or say it with all the anger and frustration she should be feeling. Maybe because that kiss had mellowed her out or simply distracted her. Either way, she slid her arm around Austin's waist and got him moving toward his house.

McCall half expected Cody Joe to shout out some kind of "you'll be sorry" threat, but he thankfully just got in his truck and sped off. She allowed herself one kiss, letting Austin's mouth work his magic to give her a nice buzz of pleasure.

Pleasure that didn't last, of course.

The second she pulled back, McCall felt the fresh wave of dread come over her. Mercy. What was she going to do?

Austin pushed her hair from the side of her face and brushed a chaste kiss on her cheek. "Cody Joe might not tattle once he cools off."

She wanted to latch on to that, but McCall doubted that'd be the outcome. Yes, Cody Joe could flip-flop on his threat. Heck, he could do that because he didn't want the bad publicity that would backwash on him. But all it would take was for him to tell one person, and it could get around.

"I'm sorry," Austin added. He gently took hold of her hand and led her toward the porch.

She muttered a thanks, one that she genuinely felt, too. It was good to have Austin on her side.

And bad.

Because he shouldn't get caught up in the bad storm that was almost certainly bearing down on her. Still, what choice had she had? She could have given in to Cody Joe's blackmail—and that's exactly what it was—but that would have only delayed what was happening now. There was no way she could get back together with Cody Joe, and that meant he would continue to use Peekaboo to try to pressure her. Still…

Still.

McCall dragged in a deep breath to try to steady herself, and she hoped she didn't start crying. Austin didn't need that, and it wouldn't help. Even knowing that, however, didn't stop her eyes from watering.

Austin took her inside, sat her on the sofa and went into the kitchen. A few moments later, he came back with a glass of wine. She wasn't much of a drinker, but McCall had a few sips now, hoping it would steady her. Of course, that was asking a lot of fermented grapes.

"What can I do to help?" he asked, sitting down next to her and slipping his arm around her.

McCall had an answer for that, but it wasn't one he was going to like. "You can distance yourself from me because, right now, I'm like Typhoid Mary. You could end up getting hurt in the fallout." Possibly the twins, too, though they were likely too young to understand the kind of gossip that would soon come.

He shook his head, brushed a kiss on her mouth. "Not going to happen. This isn't your fault."

Oh, she wanted to latch on to that, but McCall knew she wasn't blameless. "When I inherited the club, I should have come clean then. I kept it secret because I convinced myself that it would hurt the foundation. And it would have. But having a secret like this come out will hurt it even more."

Austin's long sigh told her that he couldn't completely dismiss that. "It'll be gossip fodder for a while. No way around that. You could maybe go ahead and do a statement. A way of getting ahead of it. That way, you could put your own spin on it."

McCall took another deep breath and let that sink in for

a moment. She could call Alisha and ask her to rein in Cody Joe. Alisha would be stunned, but she might help just so the foundation would be safe. Then again, Alisha might be so riled that she would side with her son.

She finally nodded. "Sunny already knows about Peekaboo, but I want to tell Granny Em. After that, I can do a written statement and put it on social media and on the foundation's webpage."

Then, for the next months—heck, maybe even years— she'd deal with the fallout, which she was sure would be legion.

"Thank you," she told him.

McCall might have got up to leave if he hadn't kissed her yet again. And this time, it wasn't a comforting peck. It was full-scale Austin, some lip finesse that was meant to bring her to her knees. It also acted as a truth serum.

"I probably shouldn't tell you this," she said with his mouth still against hers, "but I came over here to offer you sex."

He smiled, the movement brushing over her own lips. "I hope the offer still stands."

"It shouldn't. I should be doing everything to put some distance between us, but I'm having a hard time doing that."

"Good," he drawled, and moved in for what would have no doubt been a brainwashing kiss that her body was aching for.

But his phone started playing a Garth Brooks tune.

He stopped, grumbled out some profanity, but immediately reached for his cell. "That's Edith's ringtone," he said. "Howie and she have the girls today so it might be important."

McCall automatically moved away from him so that the

conversation would be private. However, it didn't take long for Austin to say, "I'll be right there."

That gave her a jolt of alarm and pushed aside the lust and the pity party she was still feeling for herself. "What's wrong?" she asked the moment Austin ended the call.

"Gracie's got a fever. It's not that high, but she's asking for me so I need to go get her."

"Of course you do. I hope she's all right." McCall started for the door. "I should have that talk with Granny Em, anyway."

He grabbed his hat and keys, and they walked out together. Austin even gave her a quick kiss, but she could tell his mind was already on his daughter. Just as it should be. That was also a reminder for her that the girls might be on the receiving end of some gossip when the news about her owning Peekaboo broke.

McCall drove out behind Austin. He headed to the other side of town where Edith and Howie lived, and she took the turn to Granny Em's. With each passing minute, McCall dreaded this more and more. Granny Em probably wouldn't hold this against her, but it was just one more blotch on their lives that'd already had way too many blotches.

Little Cowgirls had literally showcased her sisters' and her embarrassing moments from the time they were toddlers to their teens. It would have likely continued all the way through high school graduation if Hadley hadn't gotten caught joyriding in a stolen car and been arrested. That'd been the final straw for the producers, who'd feared a backlash from the viewers. Badly Hadley had apparently gotten too bad for the show's image.

While McCall hadn't wanted Hadley to get into trouble, she'd been thrilled that the show was canceled. Of course, that hadn't immediately stopped them from living under a microscope what with the fans still wanting info about them. That had died down, but something like Peekaboo would perhaps put her right back in the tabloids that she'd spent her adult life trying to avoid.

McCall parked at Granny Em's and started looking for her grandmother. She wasn't in the kitchen or her bedroom so she called out for her.

Nothing.

There was no sign of Boo, either. McCall thought they might be in the garden, but then she heard the footsteps overhead. She went up the stairs, called out again, and this time she got an answer.

"We're up here," Boo said.

Not one of the bedrooms but the attic. That meant going through Hayes's old room where Boo was staying and up a rickety set of steps. The closer she got, the more she could smell and see the dust. She also saw Boo and Em. Her grandmother was sitting in old overstuffed green-and-yellow flowered chair that'd been in the attic for as long as McCall could remember. Boo was perched on the chair arm. Granny Em had a photo album in her lap, and there was another stack of them on the floor.

"I was just showing Boo pictures of me before I got to be a granny," Em said.

"Em was a knockout," Boo declared. She was smiling, but her expression changed fast when she looked up at McCall. "What happened?"

Granny Em turned her attention on McCall, and both women slowly got to their feet. Obviously, she didn't have a poker face if they could figure out with a single glance that something was wrong.

McCall gathered her breath and got started. "When I got to Austin's, Cody Joe was there. He wanted me to get back together with him. I refused," she quickly added when Boo started to mutter something about kicking Cody Joe in the nuts. "And he said he would tell everyone a secret I've been keeping."

"That SOB," Boo snapped. "I should cut off his nuts."

McCall gave her a nod for her moral support and then turned back to her grandmother. "I own a strip club called Peekaboo."

"She inherited it," Boo quickly piped in. "And she can't sell it or anything. She's stuck with it. That dirthead weasel, Cody Joe, knows that, too, and now he's trying to use it as leverage."

"Yes, he tried," McCall admitted. "But I'm still not getting back with him, and that means soon my secret will be all over town. I just wanted you to hear about it first from me." She closed her eyes a moment, gave a weary sigh. "I'm so sorry."

"Pshaw," Granny Em immediately said. "Nothing for you to be sorry about. It's not your fault that Cody Joe turned out to be so low that he'll have to look up to see the stream of pee he's whizzing."

That was indeed low, and at the moment McCall agreed with Granny Em's assessment. "I'll make a statement," McCall started to explain, but Em waved her off.

Her grandmother went to her and kissed her cheek. "Don't worry about this, sweetheart. I know just the way to fix it."

AUSTIN WASN'T SURPRISED to see the twins still going at full speed when he got to Edith's and Howie's. According to Edith, Gracie's temp had been barely a degree above normal, and Edith had already given her some Tylenol. Gracie didn't look flushed or sick and was playing dress-up when he arrived.

"Gracie insisted I call you," Edith greeted, the apology in her voice and the worry on her face.

That didn't surprise him, either. The girls might be identical twins in looks, but Gracie was still very much a daddy's girl whereas Avery was more independent.

"Daddy," Gracie said, immediately going to him.

Austin picked her up, kissing her forehead and at the same time checking to see if she felt warm. She did, just a little.

"Do your throat, tummy or ears hurt?" he asked, giving her a second forehead kiss.

She shook her head and settled against him. Clearly, Avery was concerned, too, because she stood next to Edith and Howie as Austin sat in the rocking chair with Gracie.

"It's probably just a virus," Austin assured them. "She'll be okay."

"Shouldn't we take her to the doctor?" Edith answered.

Gracie practically made a swooshing sound when her head lifted so fast off Austin's chest. "No, no, no."

"There's no need to go to the doctor," Austin said, more to assure Gracie than Edith. "If the temp doesn't go away by tomorrow or if it spikes, I'll call her pediatrician."

Austin steeled himself for Edith to argue with him about that. If there'd been a dictionary entry for overly protective, Edith's picture would have been there. He could understand why, though, after what happened to Zoey. Still, seeing the doctor would be upsetting for Gracie, and the diagnosis would be Tylenol and to keep an eye on her. Which he would do. He didn't want to put Gracie through a doctor's exam just to ease Edith's mind.

Avery stayed by her sister, offering Gracie a stuffed bear and stroking her hair. Howie kept watch for a few more minutes, and then he headed back to his den where he'd likely turn on the TV.

Edith lingered, and would have no doubt continued to linger had her landline phone not rung. She took the call in the kitchen, but she'd hardly been gone a minute when Austin's own phone dinged with a text message. He smiled when he saw the message there from McCall.

I hope Gracie's doing okay.

"That's my name," Gracie said, looking at the phone screen. She couldn't actually read, but her own name was something she'd recently started to recognize.

"That's right. It's from the fairy lady," Austin told her, and as if she might actually see McCall on the phone, Avery crawled up in his lap and snuggled in his other arm. "Should I tell her you're feeling better?"

Gracie gave it a few moments of intense thought. "Can she come over and play with us?"

"Yes!" Avery endorsed with enthusiasm.

Austin had to smile at that, too. It would have been fun to watch McCall interact with the girls, and they would have certainly enjoyed it, but Edith likely wouldn't want McCall cutting into her visiting time. And Austin didn't think it was a good idea for McCall to be here if Cody Joe ratted out her ownership of Peekaboo.

"The fairy lady can't come play today," Austin explained, and while he texted a response to let her know that Gracie was okay, he got a quick flash of the kiss he'd given McCall. A quick flash of the feelings that went along with that, as well.

Ironically, today should have been an adult playday for

McCall and him, and he hoped that was something he could reschedule soon.

"Can we go see the fairy lady?" Avery pressed.

Austin was trying to work out an excuse why that couldn't happen when Edith came back in the room. One look at her, and Austin knew something was wrong.

Shit.

Cody Joe had likely gone through on his temper tantrum blackmail.

"Uh, that was Annette McKay," she said. Austin knew Annette, of course. She and her husband owned a nearby ranch. "She called to tell me some disturbing gossip."

That was Austin's cue to get the girls out of there so that Edith and he could talk. Balancing them both in his arms, he stood and went toward Howie's den. "I need you to watch the girls for a few minutes," Austin told him.

That put some alarm on Howie's face, but he immediately nodded and made room for the girls on the sofa. He also switched the channel from a baseball game to a cartoon show. That would save Avery and Gracie from fussing about him not continuing the conversation about McCall coming over.

"I won't be long," Austin assured Howie, and he went back in the living room to face the music with Edith. "What did Annette tell you?" he asked so that Edith would cut to the chase.

Best to get all of this out in the open, deal with the blowup, and then he could get the girls home. After that, he could check in with McCall and see how she was handling it.

"It's about Em," Edith explained, surprising Austin. He'd been certain this would be about McCall. "Did you know when Em was young she had a relationship with a man in the mob?"

If Edith had given him a multiple choice, he wouldn't have come up with that answer, but he did remember McCall mentioning something about that.

"Apparently, Em's concerned because this man contacted her and wants to start up things with her again," Edith went on. "Em doesn't want to see him, and she's asked if anyone in town sees a man named Ralphie Devane that we should call her."

Austin smelled a rat. Or rather a distraction that Em was no doubt trying to create to cover up any potential talk about McCall. It probably wouldn't work, though. Even a mob guy couldn't hold a gossip candle to McCall owning a strip club.

"Em insists this man isn't dangerous," she added, "but she doesn't want him coming to her house. I need to tell Howie," Edith tacked on to that. "Don't worry. I'll whisper so the girls don't hear."

Even if Avery and Gracie did hear, they wouldn't understand. Still, it was best if the twins didn't pepper Edith and him with questions about it—especially if they figured out Em was the fairy lady's grandmother.

Austin took out his phone and sent another text to McCall. Are you okay? And what's up with Em?

McCall's response came fast. I'm fine. As for Granny Em, well, this is her way of trying to solve my problem.

She added a weary face emoji that made Austin smile. The smile didn't last, though, because he got a call and didn't recognize the number on the screen.

"Austin Jameson?" the caller asked the moment he answered.

"Yes," he verified. "How can I help you?"

"I'm Alisha Lozano, Cody Joe's mother."

Austin silently groaned, but he held out hope that maybe

Alisha was calling to tell him she'd managed to put a muzzle on her son.

"How can I help you?" he repeated.

"I've just had a chat with Cody Joe, and he told me what's happened between McCall and him."

His version of what happened, anyway. Austin doubted that Cody Joe had spun McCall in a positive light. Or Austin for that matter.

"Cody Joe told me about McCall owning that…club. And while I'm opposed to places like that, I understand she's not an owner by choice. I can overlook it as long as it's not made public."

He nearly snapped, *That's big of you*, but Austin figured that wouldn't help this. Whatever *this* was. "What do you want?" Austin demanded.

The woman paused just a moment. "Cody Joe and McCall need to be together for the good of the foundation. And you're preventing that from happening."

Austin felt the slow, hot rise of his temper. "McCall doesn't want your son," he pointed out. "Cody Joe embarrassed her by screwing around with another woman. And FYI, *that* hurt the foundation."

"Cody Joe made a mistake." Her voice had a crisp, icy edge to it now. "But he'll make up for it, and his name alone can restore donations to the foundation. My name, too. You, on the other hand, can only make things worse."

Austin grumbled some profanity. "It's McCall's decision as to whether or not she'll get back with Cody Joe, and the last I heard, she's finished with him."

"McCall will come to her senses when she realizes this is for the best," Alisha said like gospel.

"Her senses?" He had to stop, take a breath. "From what I can see, the smartest thing she could have done was wash her hands of Cody Joe. Did you know he's threatened to blackmail her, that he'll spill her secret if she doesn't get back together with him?"

Austin figured Cody Joe hadn't mentioned that to his mother.

But he was wrong.

Alisha confirmed it with a simple, "He told me."

"You're okay with your son blackmailing the woman you want him to be with?" Austin snarled.

This time her pause was a lot longer. "In this case, the means justify the ends. My name is linked to McCall, and if her reputation suffers, so does mine. The best thing to do will be for Cody Joe and her to reconcile. Maybe even announce their engagement. That way, her secret will stay safe, and I'll work behind the scenes to figure out a way for her to quietly get out of ownership of that horrible club."

"It would be best to make sure McCall is happy. Cody Joe doesn't make her happy," Austin spelled out.

"Not at the moment, but he can if given another chance." Again, that had a gospel-y tone to it. "Step away from this, Mr. Jameson. You'll not only save yourself and your family an embarrassment, you'll save McCall, too."

Before Austin could say anything else, Alisha ended the call.

CHAPTER FOURTEEN

WHEN THE RINGING of Granny Em's landline phone shot through the kitchen—again—McCall had had enough. She pulled the connection plug. Of course, that wouldn't stop Em's and her cells from ringing and dinging, but it was a start.

Another start was talking to Sunny and Shaw to give them a heads-up about what was going on. McCall had also left a message for Hayes, too, just in case. She didn't know if her brother still heard local gossip, but she went with the "better safe than sorry" approach especially since Hayes had recently helped her out with what could have been another bombshell.

Granny Em didn't seem at all distressed that seemingly every adult in Lone Star Ridge had or was trying to get in touch with her, no doubt to hear any and all dirt to be dished about this fictional Ralphie Devane.

"The distraction's working," Em pointed out while she calmly sipped her coffee at the kitchen table.

"It's working only because Cody Joe hasn't told anyone that I own Peekaboo," McCall reminded her.

Telling was something he would surely do, but waiting around for that to happen seemed just as hard as dealing with the fallout would be. While she appreciated her grandmother's attempt to help, once Cody Joe spilled everything, it would only mean more people calling to get the scoop about what was going on.

"We could maybe hire someone to make Cody Joe keep his mouth shut," Boo suggested. She, too, was at the kitchen table and was playing a solo version of poker. "One of the former strippers at Peekaboo has a brother who does that sort of thing. Breaks legs, twists arms, busts faces."

McCall scowled at her. "Let's not make this worse than it already is." Though she was pleased that Boo had said *former stripper*. McCall didn't want to employ anyone who had body-maiming connections like that.

Unlike Boo and Granny Em, she couldn't sit, so McCall started to pace across the kitchen. "Making up that story about Ralphie Devane wasn't a good idea," McCall muttered. It was about the thirtieth time she'd said a variation of that, but Granny Em only smiled as she'd done the other twenty-nine times.

"The name's made up," Em explained. "So is the part about him trying to get in touch with me. But I did have a boyfriend in the mob. It's not really lying if a part of the story is true."

Yes, it was lying, and McCall only hoped this didn't come back to bite them in their butts. Especially since it was only a temporary smokescreen.

"Speaking of names," Boo said, "my name change isn't legal yet, but I could still tell everyone that I'm the McCall Dalton who owns the club."

"Thanks, but no one will believe that." Plus, it wouldn't be that hard for anyone to check the club's ownership and see that it was not only McCall's name but her address, as well.

When McCall's cell dinged with a call, she started to automatically hit the decline button, but then she saw Austin's name on the screen. She answered it as fast as she could.

"Is Gracie all right?" McCall immediately asked. She certainly hadn't forgotten about the little girl, but with everything else going on, she'd pushed it to the back burner.

"She's fine," Austin quickly assured her. "I'm here with her at Edith and Howie's. How about you?"

McCall didn't answer until she'd stepped out of the kitchen. "Not fine." And she realized Austin was one of the few people outside of family that she could be honest with. "I feel as if I'm sitting on a time bomb."

She heard the heavy sigh he made before he spoke. "I'm sorry about that." Austin sighed, then paused. "This makes me feel a little like a tattletale, but I got a call from Alisha."

"Alisha? Why would she—" McCall stopped when the answer to her own question came to her. "She's trying to get Cody Joe and me back together."

"Bingo. And she thinks I'm in the way." Another pause. "Am I in the way?"

"No," she blurted out, and then rethought that. "No," McCall repeated. "I wouldn't get back with Cody Joe even if you weren't in the picture."

"I'm in the picture," he said, and she could practically see him smiling.

Not good. This wasn't a smiling matter.

"Austin, you need to distance yourself from me," she reminded him.

"Shouldn't you let me decide that for myself?" he countered.

She wanted to shout, *No!* That it was only a matter of time before her toxic state rubbed off on him, but her phone beeped with a message from Sunny. At that same moment, she heard Granny Em's cell ring from the kitchen.

The rat Cody Joe ratted, Sunny had texted, and McCall read it aloud for Austin to hear.

"Yeah," Austin verified. "I just got a text about it from my mom."

Even though McCall had been steeling herself up for over an hour, it clearly hadn't helped. Every muscle in her body tensed and filled with dread. She got a flash of all the calls and texts that were going on right now, and face-to-face gossip would soon follow.

"Cody Joe and Alisha didn't waste any time," Austin added. "I figure Alisha knew her call to me hadn't worked, and she gave Cody Joe the green light to take a shot at you."

Sadly, McCall could see it playing out just like that. From the kitchen, she heard Granny Em snarl, "Yeah, so what if McCall owns a place like that? Your husband's making eyes at the new waitress at the Lickety Split. Seems to me you oughta be talking more about that than McCall owning a legal business that provides a service to husbands just like yours."

Good grief. McCall didn't want to get in a tit-for-tat match.

"You heard me right," Em added, no doubt responding to some kind of denial or outrage from the person who'd called her. "Your Eddy always had a roving eye. Other roving parts, too, from what I've heard. I know plenty of other gossip about him and you, and if you pester McCall, you'd better grab a shovel to scoop up the crap."

McCall groaned and pressed her fingers to her head to try to ease the throbbing. "I have to go," McCall said to Austin. "I'll call you when I can."

She put her phone away, heading for the kitchen to do some damage control, but the knock at the door stopped her. McCall was certain it'd be someone she didn't want to see, but when the knocking continued, she threw open the door and saw a surprise visitor.

Cait.

Austin's sister was on the porch, not looking at McCall but rather at the two cars that had pulled up in the driveway. McCall recognized both drivers. One was Hattie Monroe, the biggest gossip in town, and Tandy Baker, the second biggest.

Cait made a circling motion with her index finger followed by a hitch of her thumb to indicate she wanted the women to turn around and leave. Both stayed put, and Hattie even opened her car door and stepped out. Without saying a word, Cait tapped her badge, put her hands on her hips and aimed a hard stare at her.

"I'm here to see Em," Hattie protested. "She probably needs someone to lend her a shoulder and an ear."

"Em's already got two shoulders and two ears of her own," Cait fired back. "I suspect that's plenty enough."

"I doubt that." Hattie's attention shifted to the doorway, and she gave McCall a serious dose of stink-eye. "Your poor grandmother must be devastated over what you've done. Of course, I guess it's not really your fault what with the terrible upbringing you had."

McCall suspected there wasn't even a tiny smidge of real concern in Hattie's tone. Or in her heart. The woman just wanted to dice up this savory topic and pass on to other gossips what she could learn from the horse's mouth. And the grandmother of the horse's mouth.

Cait made that *get out of here* waving motion again to Hattie and Tandy. "This house is under quarantine because Em found some black mold. It can cause a respiratory infection and some other nasty stuff. It's got to be inspected before anyone can come in."

Hattie pulled back her shoulder, scowled. "*She's* in there," she said, pointing to McCall.

McCall started coughing as if hacking up a lung. Yes, it was sort of lying to go along with Cait, but she really didn't want to deal with Hattie and Tandy just yet. Nor did she want Em to have to see them. Considering Em's already snarky mood, this could turn into an ugly scene.

Hattie must have at least believed the mold claim/McCall's hacking, because she leaned back as if putting some distance between McCall and her. The woman also got back in her car, and she drove away with Tandy right behind her.

"Thank you," McCall told Cait. She stopped coughing, drew in a normal breath.

Cait shrugged. "Glad to help. Those two have got enough tongue for ten rows of teeth. Do you really own a strip club?" Cait tacked on to that without pausing.

McCall sighed, nodded. "I do."

"She inherited it," Boo added, coming up behind them. "Hi, Cait."

McCall wasn't sure where or how Boo and Cait had met, but clearly they knew each other. Of course, in a town this small, Boo had likely already crossed paths with just about everyone.

Cait greeted Boo back and turned to make sure the gossips were leaving. They were. Maybe Tandy and Hattie would even spread the news of why they'd been turned away.

"Other nosy folks will come," Cait pointed out. "That mold scare won't hold them back for long. Heck, threat of Ebola or typhoid won't keep them away once the gossip mill heats up."

"No," McCall agreed. "If I thought it'd do any good, I'd stand in the middle of Main Street, admit to being the owner of Peekaboo and answer any questions people wanted to ask."

"Won't do any good," Cait immediately verified. "Tongues will just start wagging about you having gone bat-shit over the embarrassment of your secret being out."

Yes, and that added another knot to McCall's stomach. There was nothing she could do to stop this gossip avalanche. Well, nothing that would help her, anyway. She could maybe still keep Austin out of the fray. If she saw him in person, he might finally see how serious she was about this, but she didn't want to bother him what with Gracie being sick.

"I can put up a quarantine sign at the end of the road," Cait said, glancing around. "Maybe set up a spike strip on the driveway that'll flatten the tires of anyone who goes past the sign."

It was tempting, but McCall shook her head. Damaged tires would only add to the gossip and create a whole lot of ill will for Granny Em. Her grandmother lived in this town and would therefore have to live with anything that followed the Peekaboo scandal.

"The way I see it, I have two options," McCall said. "I can hide out here at Granny Em's, which will only cause more and more people to come looking for dirt." She had to pause and gather her breath because the second option was going to *hurt*. "Or Boo and I can leave and go back to Dallas."

Silence. Both Boo and Cait stared at her for a long time, and McCall could practically see them working through that. Leaving meant her giving up on Austin. The thought of that felt like a fist gripping her heart, but staying would do more than a fist-grip. It could crush both of them.

Cait was the first to break the silence. "You plan on talking to Austin about that?"

McCall nodded. "I can explain to him that my leaving will make the gossip die down faster."

Boo made a sound as if she wasn't buying that. McCall didn't buy it, either, but this way the gossips might leave Austin alone. *Might.* Of course, the gossips might zoom in on Austin and Granny Em if she wasn't around to deflect the chatter.

McCall was still mulling that over when there was the sound of another approaching car engine. Not Hattie or Tandy this time, but it was someone she hadn't wanted to see.

Edith.

Since Austin hadn't given her a heads-up call, it likely meant he hadn't known Edith would be making this trip. Maybe because Austin had already taken the girls back to their house. Or Edith could have stormed out. If so, then Austin might be right behind her.

Edith's car practically screeched to a stop in front of the house, and the woman barreled out. "Is it true?" Edith asked, her attention zooming in on McCall.

"Want me to arrest her?" Cait muttered to McCall. "I'm sure I can come up with something. Disturbing the peace, a traffic violation or two."

"No, but thanks," McCall whispered back. She dragged in a couple of long breaths and came out of the house and down the porch steps to face Edith.

"Is it true?" Edith repeated before McCall could say anything.

"It's true," McCall verified.

"She inherited the club," Boo called out.

McCall made a sound of agreement to indicate that was true, but she doubted it would soften this with Edith. And she was right. Edith's iron expression got even harder.

"You own a strip club," Edith ground out like profanity. "You own a strip club, and yet you spent time with Austin and my grandbabies."

McCall wanted to point out that she hadn't stripped in front of them. Nor had she even talked about it so the girls would hear. Even if she had, McCall doubted Avery and Gracie were old enough to understand. Still, they would certainly grasp that something was wrong, and McCall hated putting them through even one moment of uncertainty.

"McCall inherited Peekaboo!" Boo repeated, a little louder this time. "She can't sell it or give it away. I'm just as much the owner as she is."

Along with the second part not even being true, that clearly didn't help because it caused Edith's eyes to narrow even more. The woman's face also started to turn red. "Does Austin know?" Edith demanded.

Oh, this was shaky ground. Since McCall didn't want Cait getting in on this and because Edith looked ready to implode, McCall gently took hold of Edith's arm and led her to the shade tree. She had Edith sit in the swing.

"Does Austin know you're here?" McCall asked.

"No. Austin and Howie are with the girls, and I sneaked out. I told them I had a headache and needed a lie-down." Edith groaned, rubbed her hands over her face. "How could you do this?" she pled, obviously forgetting her previous question about Austin knowing. "And here I was about to give you the card from Zoey."

McCall froze, then shook her head. "Zoey left *me* a card?"

Edith's mouth twisted as if annoyed with herself for mentioning that. "Zoey didn't specifically leave it to you, but she was certain that Austin would end up seeing someone else after he got past his grief. I thought that someone else might be you."

Oh.

Considering that she was a counselor, McCall wished she knew how to respond to that. She didn't. First, she doubted that Austin would ever be finished grieving for Zoey, and second, he wasn't exactly seeing her. Yes, they'd kissed. Had even planned to have sex. But that was a long way from being a part of his and his daughters' lives.

McCall mentally repeated that last part to herself.

Then she added some mental curse words—also meant for herself. It certainly felt as if she *wanted* to be a part of their lives, and that was a stupid thing to feel.

"I didn't read the card that Zoey left," Edith went on. "But I'm guessing she wanted to give her blessing for Austin to get on with his life."

That seemed, well, logical. And very loving if that was true. If McCall had been in Zoey's place, she wouldn't have wanted Austin to grieve for her forever. Still, Austin needed someone who fit better into his life here in this small town.

And that wasn't her. Not as the owner of a strip club.

"I'm worried about Austin," Edith continued a moment later. She looked up, connected gazes with McCall. "He's a good man so he might not tell you if all of this is playing havoc with him and the girls."

Havoc was a good way of saying how all of this could play out. Austin could end up getting peppered with gossip. Heck, it could even end up hurting his business just as it would hurt her foundation. She knew how important his ranch was to him. It wasn't just his livelihood but also his home.

"Will it help if I leave town?" McCall came out and asked.

"Yes," Edith immediately blurted out. She pressed her fingers to her mouth and held them there for a moment.

"But if I ask you to leave, Austin might not forgive me for doing that."

That was possible. He already resented Edith's interference. "This would be my decision," McCall said. "I won't go see him today because Gracie's not feeling well, but I can talk to him tomorrow if she's well enough to go to preschool."

Edith nodded, murmured a thanks and stood. "I think that's for the best," she said as she walked back to her car.

The best. That was another good saying for McCall leaving. She just hoped it was a decision she could go through with. Hoped it didn't crush her heart, either.

But McCall already knew that a heart-crushing was exactly what she was going to get.

CHAPTER FIFTEEN

WHILE HE RODE his appaloosa toward the barn, Austin tipped back his Stetson and used his forearm to swipe the sweat from his forehead. Of course, since his forearm was wet, too, it didn't help much, but it was better than having the sweat trickle down into his eyes where'd it'd sting like hell.

He enjoyed hard, backbreaking work, most of the time, anyway, but he'd pushed himself today, trying to cram a full day's work into a morning. First, by repairing a stretch of fence and then by moving some horses to a different pasture. The second had been a necessity to prevent overgrazing, and it was a chore he hadn't been able to put off any longer.

Thankfully, Gracie had helped Austin just by being well so that he could send them both to preschool. Then Cait had added to that helping out by asking if she could take the girls for the afternoon since it was her day off. That meant after he'd showered, he would drive over to Em's.

Where he'd have it out with McCall.

It'd been nearly twenty-four hours since the news had broken about her owning Peekaboo. Nearly twenty-four hours since she'd issued that *I have to go* and *I'll call you when I can* when they'd been talking on the phone. Austin had figured she'd need some time to try to deal with the fallout. Time for her to figure out how to deal with him, too. But he was more than ready to chat with McCall as to what she was considering.

Austin suspected she'd try to run.

And Edith might have had a hand in encouraging Mc-Call to do just that.

Cait had told him that Edith had shown up at Em's while she was there. His sister hadn't overheard exactly what Edith had said to McCall, but Austin was betting his former mother-in-law had told McCall to get out of town. Or words to that effect. Unfortunately, in McCall's state of mind, she just might think that was the best thing for him.

When he made it to the barn, Austin untacked the appaloosa, hosed her down and gave her a quick brush. He filled her water trough before turning the hose on himself. It wouldn't replace a shower, but it felt damn good. Stripping off his now wet shirt, he went out of the front of the barn to head to his house, and he came to a dead stop when he saw McCall.

Wearing flip-flops and a loose white cotton dress that fluttered in the breeze, she was standing by the side of his porch and had her purse hooked over her shoulder. Obviously waiting for him. Good. This meant he wouldn't have to go to her, after all.

He walked closer, studying her expression and looking for signs that she'd been crying or was upset. But that wasn't what he saw at all. Her mouth was slightly open, her face a little flushed, and her wide, interested eyes were practically sliding right over him.

"Whoa," she muttered. "Would you mind going back in the barn and walking out like that again?" She patted her chest. "This is sort of a fantasy of mine."

It took him a moment to realize that *he* was the fantasy. Or rather him being wet and half-naked was. And he was pretty sure the look on her face was good old-fashioned lust. A surprise, but much better than any other mood he'd been anticipating.

Austin went to her, hooked a still damp arm around her waist, pulled her to him and kissed her. Again, he felt no hesitation. She melted right into him, giving him no resistance when he deepened the kiss with his tongue. She tasted sweet, hot and capable of quenching any thirst he'd ever had.

"Whoa," she repeated when she eased back. Her breath hit against his mouth. "Fantasy fulfilled."

"Then you need another fantasy," he drawled. "Maybe I can fix that for you."

Austin kissed her again and slid his hand down her back. He would have done a lot more sliding, a lot more kissing, too, but then he remembered he still needed that shower.

"I'm sweaty," he reminded her.

"I know." Her voice was a little dreamy, and she caught on to handfuls of his wet hair and kissed him.

All right. So, sweat was also part of the fantasy. He could go with that. Or so he thought, but McCall ended the kiss and stepped back.

"Damn it," she grumbled. "I came over here to tell you the reasons why I should leave town."

Bingo. He'd nailed it. "Then I'm glad I distracted you."

Austin caught on to her waist again, nudged her closer, but he didn't kiss her. Too distracting. And it was obvious they needed to do some talking before they moved on to that re-creating a new fantasy part.

"Come inside," he said. "I'll grab a shower, and then I can tell you all the reasons why you should stay."

He thought he saw some panic go through her eyes. Eyes still glazed some from the lust. Since he didn't want the panic to win out, he took her by the hand, led her inside the house and straight to the bathroom.

"Stand right here," he instructed. "Don't move."

When he was certain she wouldn't bolt, he turned on the

shower and started stripping off the rest of his clothes. She pinched her eyes shut when he made it to his boxers. So, apparently that wasn't the fantasy.

Or maybe it was.

"You have an amazing body," she grumbled. Her voice wasn't dreamy now but strained, and she set her purse on the vanity. "If I look at you, you'll distract me. That can't happen because then you might be able to talk me into staying."

It was as if she'd just handed him the keys to the universe. Or rather the keys to fixing the problem of her wanting to run.

Bare-assed naked, Austin stepped under the warm spray of the shower, took hold of her hand again and yanked her in with him. McCall let out a little yelp that he quickly caught with his own mouth.

The kiss was wet, of course, because the water was slushing down them, and her yelp turned to a laugh. A short one, anyway, before she pulled back and gave him what she probably thought was a very serious look. Hard to look serious, though, with her hair soaked and clinging to the sides of her face.

And while plastered against his naked body.

"I shouldn't be doing this," she said. "I'm sending all the wrong signals."

They seemed very right signals to him, but he didn't want this to take a bad direction. "Let's table the you-leaving discussion for now. I promise once we're done here, we'll talk."

By then, maybe the aching fire in his body would allow him to think so he could come up with a convincing argument for her to stay.

Because she didn't seem to have doubts when he kissed her, Austin dived back in for another one. He was very thankful for a hot-water-on-demand heater that wouldn't leave them shivering in the cold if this led to where he wanted it to lead.

Sex.

Austin was ready for that. Ready to move in for more kisses, but then he caught McCall looking at him. No panic this time. She was doing the same gaze-sliding as she had when she'd seen him come out of the barn. Her gaze went from his mouth. To his chest.

Then lower.

Her breath hitched, and she started to breathe through her mouth. "You have no right to look this good," she mumbled after she cursed him.

"Same goes for you."

He did some looking, too. Yeah, she was dressed, but the fabric was clinging to her in all the right places. He had no trouble seeing the outline of her breasts. Her nipples were now hard and puckered, just begging to be tasted.

Which he would soon do.

He wouldn't mind tasting what was behind the outline of her panties, too.

"You didn't have this body when we were in high school," he said, cupping her breast and flicking his thumb over her nipple. "McCall, you are one hot fantasy."

She shook her head, and since Austin didn't want her arguing with him about her amazing curves, he anchored her back against the clear glass of the shower wall so he could kiss and touch her at the same time.

Too many clothes—that was his first thought, and her dress was heavy and soggy now. Still, he didn't want to move too fast by shucking it off her so he ran his hand down her leg, pushing up her dress to her waist. That gave him some bare belly-to-belly contact. He upped that by shoving her dress up even farther, pushing down the cups of her bra and sampling her nipple. He sucked it into his mouth and nipped it lightly with his teeth.

She had a nice moaning reaction to that so he slid his hand over the front of her panties. This was semifamiliar territory for him because of what'd happened in his truck, but he intended to make this a whole lot better. He caught on to her panties, shoving them down to the floor of the shower.

Lowering himself, he gave her a kiss that he was sure she wouldn't forget anytime soon. Just as he'd done to her breasts, he did some sucking and nipping. McCall did some cursing and bucking, but she wasn't trying to get away from him.

Nope.

She thrust her hips toward his mouth and fisted her hand in his hair. Austin was reasonably sure he could have finished her off then and there, but he wanted to be inside her this time.

"Wait here a sec," he told her, and he went ahead and yanked off her dress before he stepped out of the shower to get a condom from the boxes that he'd put in the cabinet below the sink.

He hurried, not wanting to risk her changing her mind. It turned out, though, that mind changing wasn't a problem, because when he stepped back in the shower, McCall still had that heated look in her eyes, and she was struggling to get off her bra. Austin helped her with that, flinging it aside.

No way could he resist her naked breasts so he dropped a few more kisses there while he put on the condom. By the time he hoisted her up against the shower, he was as hard as stone and ready to plunge into her.

So, that's what he did.

One hard long stroke, and he was inside. Oh, man. She was tight, wet and already moving. Austin moved with her, thrusting his hips to match her moves.

The position put them not only body-to-body but also face-to-face. That meant he could manage some more kisses, but soon the intense pleasure made even that impossible.

Everything inside him built, built, built. The need, the heat, the urgency to take her and finish this. Fast. Then faster. Deep. Then deeper. Until it all pinpointed to this one single moment where he had to finish this. Where he had to finish her.

Thankfully, McCall was right there with him. On a low silky moan, she gave in to the thrusts, and he felt her climax take hold of him. Squeezing and gripping his erection until Austin had no choice but to give in to it.

Holding on to McCall, Austin let himself go.

Wearing a pair of Austin's boxer shorts and his T-shirt, McCall sat at his breakfast table, sipping a Coke, while she waited for Austin to come out of the laundry room that was just off the kitchen. She soon heard the thunk-thunk of her clothes tumbling in the dryer, and each thud was a reminder that this visit sure hadn't gone as planned.

After Cait had called to tell her that she'd have the girls for the afternoon, McCall had come to Austin to explain why she had to leave town and had instead ended up having shower sex with him.

Amazing shower sex.

The kind of sex that zoomed to the top of the list as the best ever.

She supposed if she had to fail at a particular mission, then that was the way to go. At least her body was sated and humming even if her mind was whirling with the possible outcomes of what she'd just done.

Good grief. How could she have possibly screwed things up this much? Now, Austin would think she was some sort of tease or an idiot who couldn't make up her mind.

McCall preferred to think of it as temporary insanity.

When she'd seen him walk shirtless out of the barn, any and all logical thoughts had jetted right out of her head.

She'd been teleported back to those days when she'd had a serious crush on him and had wanted him more than her next breath.

McCall wanted to think it wouldn't happen again, but when he came strolling back in the kitchen, she felt a fresh flood of heat. Of course, that probably had something to do with the fact that he was only partially dressed again. No shirt, bare feet. He had on jeans, and while they were zipped, the metal button was undone, leaving the denim to shift and flap a little with each step. Her heart did some shifting and flapping, too.

"Something on your mind?" he asked.

His voice was sex, smoke and a kilo of triple-strength testosterone. No smugness but rather a teasing confidence that let her know he knew exactly what was on her mind. Unfortunately, she couldn't be mad at him for seeing into her soul. Or maybe he hadn't had to go that deep to do any *seeing*. There was probably plenty of telltale signs of lust still on her face, and her body was no doubt giving off some triple-strength hormones of its own.

"I wanted you to know that you don't have to worry about the black mold scare at Granny Em's," she said, and managed to sound serious, too.

He smiled, and yes, that managed to send all female parts of her into a tailspin, too. "I'm guessing Em came up with that as a way to keep the gossips away?"

"Actually, it was Cait's idea. Your sister thinks fast on her feet."

"That's one way of putting it," he joked, and then tipped his head to her. "My clothes look good on you."

McCall glanced down at the T-shirt that clearly showed her braless breasts. Her nipples had gone hard and were highly visible, which was yet another reaction to all of Austin's studliness. The boxer shorts clung to her like a second skin, and her body wasn't letting her forget that Austin's butt—and other parts of him—had once worn them.

He took a beer from the fridge, opened it and had a long pull from it before he sat down across from her. "How are you holding up with the gossips?"

She nearly gave him the automatic answer of "Fine," something she'd been saying a lot to Granny Em to keep her from worrying, but it didn't seem right to lie to a man when you were wearing his boxers.

"I go back and forth between a pity party and wanting to crush Cody Joe's balls in a garlic press."

Austin exaggerated a wince, then chuckled before his expression grew serious. "I'm guessing Edith's visit didn't help."

It shouldn't have surprised her that he knew about that. Cait would have told him. "She's worried about Gracie and Avery," McCall settled for saying, which, of course, wasn't much of an answer.

"She told you to leave," Austin filled in for her.

McCall shrugged and decided there was nothing she should say about the woman. No, it hadn't been pleasant for Edith to visit her like that, but McCall wasn't sure how she would have reacted had their positions been reversed.

"Alisha shouldn't have called you," McCall added a moment later. "I'm betting that wasn't a pleasant conversation."

"It wasn't." Austin had another sip of his beer. "I should have spelled out to her that she raised a whiny dickhead who thinks he can crap all over everyone and still come out smelling clean."

That was Cody Joe in a nutshell, but McCall couldn't put all the blame on him. No, she was just as much at fault as he was.

"Secrets don't always stay secrets," she said. "In hindsight, I should have 'fessed up to owning the club as soon as I inherited it. Now, it's hurt the foundation, and it could hurt you. Don't say it won't," she quickly added when she saw the argument in his eyes.

"It'll create some talk among my customers," he admitted. "Maybe I'll get a few questions about whether or not you've done a striptease for me." He paused. "Do you know how to do a striptease? Because if so, I might be interested in seeing that."

She scowled at him, but there was no heat in it. Actually, it felt, well, good to play it down like this. Even if it shouldn't. The effects of this could be very real. Very harmful. And that's why, despite what'd happened in the shower, she needed to tell him that she should leave town.

"Don't go," he blurted out as she stood. He slapped his beer on the table, went to her and pulled her to him. "Don't run because you think it'll spare me some gossip. It won't," Austin assured her.

McCall had an argument for this. No, her leaving wouldn't immediately spare him gossip, but "out of sight, out of mind" might soon apply to those doing the talking about her. That would eventually spare Austin from hearing it. From having to explain it to his girls, too, if somehow the talk got back to them.

But McCall didn't get to voice a word of that well-thought-out argument.

That's because Austin kissed her. There was just as much heat in this one as the others, but there seemed to be something else. Some emotion that frightened her. And drew her right in.

"Give it a week," he said, their mouths still touching. "One week. Then decide if you want to stay or go."

CHAPTER SIXTEEN

Main Street was now her own personal fishbowl. McCall had no doubts about that when she came out of the lawyer's office.

One step outside the door, and it was as if all conversations and movement stopped, and McCall figured the dozen or so people milling around had been waiting to get a glimpse of her. Maybe even more than a glimpse. Perhaps they were trying to hear some snippet to clue them in to why she'd had an appointment with the town's attorney, Rick Downing.

If that's what the townsfolks were after, they'd be sorely disappointed if they learned this had nothing to do with Peekaboo. Her visit to the lawyer was about the other scandal. The first one Cody Joe had set into motion with Miss Watermelon. And now, McCall had started the process to sever foundation ties with him.

Whether or not Cody Joe would actually agree to do that was anyone's guess, but McCall was hoping, now that he'd done his best to ruin her life, he'd also washed his hands of her in all areas, including the foundation.

"I'll have the paperwork ready for you to sign later today," Rick told her in a voice low enough to let her know that he, too, was aware people might be trying to listen.

He'd walked her to the door and now looked out on Main Street as if gauging what she might face. Judging that she still had a lot to "face," he gave her a pat on the back. "Hang in there," Rick murmured before he stepped back in his office and shut the door.

At least he hadn't tried to reassure her that all of this would die down soon. It wouldn't. Her sister Hadley had taken a joyride in a stolen car nearly two decades ago, and people still brought it up. Apparently, there were no issues with memory loss when it came to her and her family.

McCall pulled in a long breath. "Does anyone have a question or something they want to say to me?" she called out.

Well, that was one way to put a stop to the stares and the behind-the-hand whispers. Everyone suddenly got very interested in something else. Of course, if Hattie or Tandy had been on Main Street, they would have taken her up on that offer. Someone would likely call them to let them know about it, which meant they could still show up before she walked the two blocks up the street to the parking lot.

McCall almost wished for conversation. Anything to get all of it more out into the open. Then she wouldn't have to think about the request Austin had made the day before.

One week.

That's what he'd asked her to take before making up her mind. One week to make a decision that would change her life forever.

If she left Lone Star Ridge, it would pretty much put an end to any relationship she might have with Austin. If she stayed, it could do the same but in a much messier way. Either way, Austin would likely end up getting hurt. Ditto for her, but there was no *likely* about it. Somehow, the kissing, lusting and the shower sex had caused her to feel more for him than kissing, lusting and shower sex.

She was falling in love with him.

And that wasn't good for either of them.

Her phone rang, and she groaned softly when she saw Mr. Bolton's name on the screen. Since they didn't have an appointment, she considered letting it go to voice mail, but it'd been several days since he'd contacted her, so she didn't want to blow him off. Especially since she thought she could lose clients once they heard about Peekaboo.

"One hour?" Mr. Bolton demanded the moment she answered.

McCall immediately thought she knew what this was about. Mrs. Eidelman. Judging from Mr. Bolton's snappish tone, the woman and he had gotten together and he wasn't pleased about the time delay she'd suggested for foreplay.

"Some women need more time," McCall pointed out.

"One hour," he repeated in a protesting grumble. "That's too long. I fizzle out by then and go a little limp. Do you know what I mean?"

Yes, she'd deciphered his complex code of communication. "Some men need help in that area. If it continues to be a problem, there are medications—"

"I don't need no stinkin' pills. I just need to get on with it before the fizzling happens."

"Well, maybe your partner needs that time to take her from fizzle to sizzle."

McCall groaned. Mercy, had she just said that? Apparently so, and judging from the way Sherman Graham's head whipped up, he'd heard it even though he was a good fifteen feet ahead of her on the sidewalk. He looked back over his shoulder at her, his eyebrows raised, but the shift in his position allowed her to see something else.

Edith.

The woman was ahead of Sherman and was making a beeline toward McCall. Okay. *Be careful what you wish for.* McCall had wanted conversation, and she was apparently about to get it.

"See if your partner will be willing to reduce the time for one hour to forty-five minutes," McCall advised Mr. Bolton. "Call me tomorrow morning at ten, and we can talk more about this."

She had just put away her phone by the time Edith made it to her. "You're still here in town," Edith *greeted.*

"For now." That was all she got a chance to say before Edith continued.

"Austin won't like me talking to you," the woman said. "He called and told me to back off, that he didn't want me pressuring you. Well, I thought pressure was needed so that's why I went to Em's to see you."

"Yes. You made your opinion clear on this." McCall didn't say it in anger, but even she could hear the chill in her voice. She had a right to that chilly tone, but Edith also had a right to her concern. "I know it's uncomfortable for you that I own Peekaboo. Trust me, at times it's uncomfortable for me, as well."

Edith gave an acknowledging nod and glanced around, no doubt to see if anyone was listening. Other conversation and movement had stopped again, so yes, people were listening. Or rather trying to do that. It wouldn't surprise McCall if a few of those folks were attempting lip reading.

"Your assistant, Boo, also called me and gave me an earful," Edith added, her voice practically a whisper now.

Now, McCall was surprised. She had no idea Boo had done that, nor did she think it was a good idea.

"Boo explained to me the changes you've made at the club," Edith went on. "And explained, too, that you'd considered just letting the business go bankrupt but how that would hurt the…*women* and other employees who work there."

Obviously, Boo had gotten very chatty, and it appeared to have given Edith some food for thought.

"I still don't think you're good for Austin and my grand-babies," Edith went on.

So, evidently that *food for thought* hadn't changed her opinion about this. "There'll always be talk about it," McCall admitted. "But I still haven't made up my mind if I'm leaving town or not."

McCall would have added more, but the footsteps behind her caused her to turn around. It was Leyton, and he was eyeing Edith as if he might want to arrest her.

"Are you okay?" Leyton asked, and McCall realized he meant the question for her.

She nodded. "Thanks, I'm fine." But she did appreciate Leyton looking out for her.

"I wasn't badgering her," Edith insisted. "So, there's no need to call Austin and tell him I was talking to McCall."

"No need to call him," Leyton agreed. He tipped his head to the sidewalk across the street. "Because Austin can see it for himself."

When she shifted in that direction, Edith went stiff, but then she smiled. McCall soon saw why. Austin wasn't alone. The girls were with him.

"The fairy lady," Avery squealed.

Maybe because Gracie and she were too eager to get across the street, Austin scooped them both up, and he made his way toward them. He, too, was smiling. Sort of. He smiled at Leyton and McCall, anyway, but there seemed to be a warning in his eyes when he looked at Edith.

"The fairy lady," Gracie greeted when Austin set them down on the sidewalk.

Both Avery and she hurried past Edith and greeted Mc-Call as if she were their best friend who they hadn't seen in

ages. They latched on to McCall's legs for a hug. Since she
didn't think she could pick them up the way that Austin had,
McCall stooped down and cuddled them in her arms for a
moment. She also automatically checked Gracie's forehead
with her wrist but didn't feel any fever.

"Can we play fairy tale rules?" Avery asked. "Can we?
Can we peaze?"

McCall couldn't help but smile at that, but clearly Edith
wasn't feeling the love. Her expression had gotten even ston-
ier, and that's why McCall gave the girls a vague, "We'll
play it soon." Then she steered the girls in their grandmother's direction. Edith stooped to give them hugs as McCall
had done.

When McCall stood, she practically bumped right into
Austin. He reached out, taking hold of her arm to steady her,
and just like that, McCall remembered how they'd ended
up in the shower. Good grief. She needed to make herself
immune to him or at least learn how to put her body in the
chill mode whenever she was around him.

"Hey," Austin drawled, and he leaned in and brushed
his mouth over hers.

McCall was certain she wasn't the only one shocked by
that kiss. Even Leyton made a sound of surprise. The girls
giggled. Edith looked ready to keel over.

"Can you come over later?" Austin asked McCall, clearly
ignoring the other responses.

"Yay!" Avery and Gracie squealed, and that was accompanied by some jumping up and down. Anyone within hearing or seeing distance was definitely getting some gossip
fodder right now.

"The girls and I can cook dinner for you," Austin added
as if to sweeten the pot on his invitation. The twins were all

for that, too, and started with the *pleases* while they tugged on McCall's hand.

Again, that didn't please Edith.

Neither would McCall's answer, but she realized she didn't want to say no just because Edith disapproved. Obviously, Avery, Gracie and Austin wanted her there. And it wasn't as if an evening with them would sway her whether to stay in Lone Star Ridge.

Well, *maybe* it wouldn't.

"I'd love to come over," McCall said, earning her not just a grin from Austin but another of those short kisses, as well. *Short* in this case didn't equal sweet. Even the brief mouth-to-mouth contact was like a flashfire.

"Now that Gracie's feeling better, I was hoping to get some playtime with the girls," Edith piped in.

"Maybe you can do that on Saturday," Austin agreed just as Leyton stepped away to take a call.

Edith would have almost certainly preferred to have the girls today, and that way they wouldn't be around Austin's strip-club-owner friend. And that riled McCall. Yes, Edith had a right to be concerned about her grandchildren, but McCall wasn't going to corrupt them with tales of Peeka-boo. Plus, the girls clearly wanted to spend time with her.

"Gotta go," Austin said. "I'm taking Gracie in for a checkup."

"Oh, I can go with you for that and watch Avery," Edith insisted.

Austin didn't tell her no, but McCall got the feeling that's because he intended to talk to the woman and make sure she wasn't bothering McCall.

McCall got a second round of leg hugs from the girls, and she watched as the four of them headed up the street toward the small medical clinics attached to the hospital. She was about to go to her car when Leyton stopped her.

"Hold up a sec," Leyton said, still talking on the phone.

She waited, expecting some kind of a pep/hang-in-there talk from Leyton, but after seeing his expression, McCall knew something was wrong. "What happened?" she asked the moment he ended the call.

"That was Em. She said Cody Joe Lozano just showed up at her house. He won't leave, and she wants me to come over and run him off before you get home. She didn't want him upsetting you. And she especially wanted him gone before Boo got back from running errands. Em thought Boo might punch him or something."

With each word Leyton spoke, the anger came. Building and building until she felt like a pressure cooker about to spew. She groaned, fisted her hand in her hair and pulled hard. The gesture would no doubt get tongues wagging—again—but she hoped the pain in her scalp would stop her from yelling in anger. The SOB Cody Joe just couldn't stay out of her life.

"I'll handle it," McCall said, but then realized she'd spoken through clenched teeth.

"Uh, I don't think so. Come on," Leyton instructed. "You can ride to Em's in the cruiser with me, and when we're done, I'll bring you back into town to get your car."

Her first thought was to refuse. She wanted to storm over to Granny Em's and carry out the threat to crush Cody Joe's balls, and she wouldn't need a garlic press to do it, either. She could crush them in her fist. But that would only escalate this feud that in no way needed such escalation. Cody Joe had already done the damage, and there wasn't anything that could undo it. Especially anything related to garlic presses, fists and balls.

On a resigned sigh, she followed Leyton to his cruiser, which was parked just outside the police department. "Thank you for this," McCall said as they got in.

He didn't say something like "This is my job," and even though it was, it hadn't been his job to come out and check on her when she'd been talking with Edith. That'd been a duty to his brother.

"If you can stand to hear any more advice or interference," Leyton said, driving toward Em's, "I don't think you should leave town because of anything that's happening. Or leave because of or as a result of an asshole causing trouble."

"Even if that trouble could affect Austin?" she asked.

"Even then. It's been a long time since I've seen my brother truly happy. You make him happy."

"The jury's out on that," she mumbled. "I don't want him hurt," McCall added. "Austin's already been through enough, and he doesn't need me causing trouble between Edith and him."

"Edith's not blind," Leyton commented. "She saw Austin smile, saw the way Avery and Gracie reacted to you. Oh, yeah. And Edith also saw those kisses."

Plenty of other people had seen those kisses, too, and by now the brief lip-locks had likely made news in the tricounty area. Austin shouldn't have done that. Heck, she shouldn't have stood there and enjoyed each and every one of them.

McCall stayed quiet a moment, wondering if this conversation was meant to cool down her anger or if Leyton was just trying to smooth things over for Austin's sake. No matter which it was, she thought Leyton might be straight with her.

"Do you think Edith seeing that smile and the girls' reaction will cause her to back off with her custody threat?" McCall came out and asked. "Or will it make her dig in her heels because she's worried about having to share them?"

He lifted his shoulder and made brief eye contact with her as he took the turn to Em's. "I think it could go either way. Edith's still grieving for Zoey, and she lets that grief play into the decisions she makes. And FYI, not all those decisions are anywhere near the right ones for Austin and his girls. Just remember that when it comes to making your own decisions."

All of that sounded like something a counselor would say. Wise words, yes, but wisdom wasn't always easy to carry out.

"Since you're not telling me to mind my own business," Leyton went on, "I should probably ask if you staying here is even doable. I know you've got businesses to run back in Dallas."

"It's doable," she admitted. "But it's taken some juggling. Boo is fine for now, but she'll definitely want to go back. Maybe, though, I could talk her into taking a bigger part in running the club."

Boo would no doubt jump right on that. So would most of her clients if she switched them to phone consults. Still, that was a lot of rearranging and then possibly rearranging the changes if things didn't work out between Austin and her. Of course, she could just stay for Em. That was plenty enough reason, considering that Em might soon need more help than she was getting from a part-time housekeeper.

However, McCall had to put her decision making aside because Leyton pulled to a stop in front of Em's.

She immediately spotted Cody Joe. It would have been impossible to miss him because he had a massive bouquet of red roses tucked in each of his arms, and he was pacing across the porch. He appeared to be muttering to himself, but his expression brightened when McCall stepped from the cruiser. He hardly spared Leyton a glance.

"I knew you'd get here sooner or later," Cody Joe said right off. "Your grandmother wouldn't let me in."

At that moment, Granny Em opened the door. "Darn right I wouldn't. I told him to leave, but he wouldn't budge."

"Because I had to see McCall." He flashed McCall a smile that he probably thought was charming. Considering what he'd done to her, it just made her want to use a garlic press on his mouth and tongue, too. "I'm so sorry, baby. Real, real sorry. I came here to try to make you understand that. I brought you flowers," he added when McCall glared at him.

Em rolled her eyes, scowled at Cody Joe. "That boy's so thickheaded you could hit him in the face with a tire iron, and he wouldn't yell about it until morning," she grumbled.

Maybe it was indeed stupidity that had caused him to come here like this. Or it could be another case of mama pressure. Perhaps this scandal hadn't played out the way Alisha wanted. The woman might not have realized that some of this dirt could sling onto her, too.

"McCall, baby," Cody Joe said, coming down the steps toward her. "I miss you real bad. We could even do a big announcement about us making up and stuff. That'll help with what folks are saying."

Every word pissed her off even more, and McCall could see it was doing the same thing to Granny Em. Rather than wait for her grandmother to give in to the rage and try to kick Cody Joe's butt, McCall stormed toward him, yanked the flowers from his hands and threw them on the ground. It wasn't exactly adult of her, but she started stomping. She smashed and ground the petals into the ground.

"Hey, baby," Cody Joe protested. "Those were for you. They're a makeup offering."

"You can see what I think of your offering," she snapped while she continued stomping.

Cody Joe reached for her as if to stop her, but Leyton

stepped up. "Give me a reason to arrest your sorry ass. And FYI, I'll consider you touching McCall even with a fingertip to be a good enough reason."

Cody Joe stopped moving, frowned. "I wasn't gonna hurt her. I just need her to listen."

"Listen?" McCall hadn't intended to shout that, but it was so loud that even the horses in the corral whinnied from the sound. "You listen," she went on, lowering her voice but not reining in her tone. "I'm done with you. I'm done with your mother. And I'm done with any association whatsoever that you have with the Saddle Up for Tots Foundation. I want you out of my life and out of my town."

"*Your* town?" Cody Joe asked.

With everything she'd just thrown at him, McCall was surprised he would zoom in on that. "My town," she verified, not having a clue if that meant she'd actually be staying. But hell in a really big handbasket, Lone Star Ridge would always be her home, and she didn't want any reminders of Cody Joe here.

Cody Joe stared at her for several long moments, maybe expecting her to change her mind or at least give him some kind of peace offering. That wasn't going to happen. Leyton's and Granny Em's glares didn't soften, either, and finally on a muttered oath, Cody Joe kicked at the slaughtered bouquets of roses, and he went to his truck. He sped away.

"I hope that's the last I see of him," McCall grumbled.

"If it's not, just give me a call." Leyton gave her arm a gentle squeeze. "I'll follow him to make sure he leaves town, and then I'll come back to get you to take you to your car."

The thank-you was still on her lips when McCall heard the sound of an approaching engine. She groaned, steeled herself up for round two, but it wasn't Cody Joe. However, it would likely be a different kind of round two because it was Edith.

Leyton cursed softly under his breath. "That woman has some very bad timing. You want me to hang around and make sure she behaves herself?" he asked.

McCall shook her head. Her mood was just sour enough that she wouldn't be taking any more flak from anyone, including Edith.

Leyton got in his cruiser, but he kept an eye on Edith as he backed out of the driveway. McCall waited until he was gone before she turned to Edith.

She faced Edith head-on. "If you're here to pressure me to leave or tell me what an unsuitable person I am for inheriting a strip club, then you need to go."

Edith didn't fire back an angry response to that. In fact, she didn't look angry at all. She glanced at the stomped roses, stepped around them, and when she lifted her hand, McCall saw the white envelope she was holding.

"If that's some kind of threat or legal action—" But McCall stopped, remembering what Edith had said earlier when they were on Main Street. "It's from Zoey?" McCall asked.

Edith's nod was a little shaky. So was her hand when she gave the envelope to McCall. "Zoey left me instructions to give this to the next woman in Austin's life…and his heart. After seeing you with him today, I realized that woman is you."

Without saying anything else, Edith left, leaving McCall in stunned silence.

CHAPTER SEVENTEEN

AUSTIN STARED AT the envelope that Shaw had just handed him. He instantly recognized the handwriting and knew it was from Zoey.

Just as he had with the other cards he'd gotten, Austin's chest tightened, and he felt the punch of grief. Grief mixed with relief that he still got to have this small piece of her.

From the twins' bedroom, Austin could hear chattering about them playing dress-up. They obviously didn't know their uncle Shaw was here or they would have run out to greet him. Austin hoped they'd stay in their room a little longer just to give him a minute to pull everything in.

"I didn't expect to get another one from her this soon," Austin managed to say.

Shaw nodded, and there was plenty of sympathy in that simple gesture. "This one came with more instructions than usual. Zoey's note said to give it to you when Edith called and told me it was time. Edith called me about a half hour ago."

That would have been about the time Gracie was finishing her checkup and not long after he'd run into Edith, McCall and Leyton on Main Street. Austin had seen the disapproval—or something—in Edith's eyes when he'd kissed McCall, but he couldn't figure out what that had to do with her giving Shaw a call to let him know to deliver the card.

"These are for the girls," Shaw said, handing Austin two

more envelopes. "The instructions Zoey left with Edith are that these are the last ones. Not just for the girls but for you, too."

It suddenly felt as if someone had reached into his chest, latched on to his heart and was squeezing every drop of life right out of it. Hell. It shouldn't hurt this much. It should be a welcomed gift to have this contact with her. And maybe it would be. Once he'd gotten over the initial punch.

"I can stay for a while if you want," Shaw offered when Austin didn't say anything.

Austin considered it but shook his head. "Thanks, but I'll be okay." He wasn't at all sure of that okay part, but if he fell to pieces, he didn't want even his brother around for that. Of course, falling to pieces would have to wait because he didn't want Avery and Gracie to see that, either.

Shaw hesitated a little longer, but he finally turned and left. Austin took a few moments of his own before he tucked his card into his back pocket and walked toward the girls' bedroom. By the time he reached it, he'd managed—he hoped—to get his mouth working into what was a passable smile.

Gracie, who obviously wasn't feeling any leftover effects from her fever, had donned a superhero cape, complete with a tiara and a pair of his old cowboy boots that were way too big for her. Avery was wearing a fireman's hat, a white doctor's coat and a badge. Apparently, she was covering multiple career bases at once.

The trunk with the other costumes was open, and various clothing items had been tossed on the floor. They were obviously having fun with this, and he could thank Edith for putting the dress-up stuff together. She also kept the inventory fresh by bringing over new items every couple of months.

"Your uncle Shaw just brought these over," he said, holding up the envelopes for the girls to see. "They're from your mom."

Austin didn't mention that these would be the last ones they'd get. No need since the girls never asked if more cards were coming. If they ever did, he could tell them then. And he hoped it wouldn't have this gut-punching effect that it was having on him.

The girls ran to him, each of them reaching up to take a card. They swapped, though, when they saw their names on the envelopes. As usual, they both tore into them, but Gracie took a little more care with hers, clearly trying not to rip the envelope.

They pulled out the cards, both immediately smiling and showing each other theirs before they handed them to Austin. "Read 'em to us, Daddy," Avery insisted.

Since he still wasn't feeling steady, he sat on one of the beds and snuggled them on each side of him. "Which one first?" he asked, remembering that they usually took turns doing this.

"Me," Gracie said.

Avery didn't balk at that and even wiggled in closer so she could see the card better. On the front was a cute white bear seated at a table loaded down with cupcakes and ice cream, but the plate directly in front of him was empty.

Austin read the question written beneath the table. "'Why did the teddy bear say no to dessert?'" He flipped the card open. "'Because he was already stuffed,'" he read.

The girls cackled with laugher, and he wished he hadn't had to fake his own laugh. Still, it was so like Zoey to want to leave the girls with a smile.

"'Gracie, I'll love you bunches and bunches forever and ever,'" Zoey had written at the bottom.

"My turn," Avery immediately said once Austin had handed Gracie back her card.

He took Avery's and read the caption underneath a Dalmatian with an empty food dish in front of him. "'What did the Dalmatian say after he finished his lunch?'" Then, inside was the punch line. "'That hit the spot.'" Beneath that, Zoey had written, "'Avery, lots of love and hugs from me to you.'"

The girls took their cards to study the pictures and the words they would someday soon be able to read for themselves. Austin stood to go into the kitchen to read his, but before he could do that, there was a knock on the door. Figuring it was Shaw returning to check on him, he threw the door open.

And he saw McCall on his porch.

It wasn't anywhere near dinnertime so obviously she was early. It was obvious, too, that she was upset, and Austin found himself silently cursing before he blurted out, "What happened?"

"Edith," McCall said, causing him to curse again. Then she added, "She gave me this."

She thrust out the card for him to see, and Austin nearly choked on the quick breath he sucked in. He made a weird sound, one that didn't qualify as manly or dignified on any scale, but it was the best he could manage because he saw right off that the card was from Zoey.

"Uh, why did Edith give that to you?" he asked.

Shaking her head, McCall stepped in and glanced around. Probably looked for the twins.

"They're in their room," Austin told her. He shut the door and took the envelope from her to have a better look. Yep, it was Zoey's handwriting, all right, and on the front she'd written, "For the next woman in Austin's life."

Hell. He hadn't even steeled himself up yet to read his

own card and now this. Obviously, McCall was looking for some steeling, too.

"Why'd Edith give it to you?" he repeated. But as soon as the question had left his mouth, he waved it off.

Clearly, Zoey had left Edith instructions to do this, and it meant that Edith had figured out that Austin had feelings for McCall. Deep feelings. The kind that could turn into love. What surprised him, though—no, it actually stunned him—was that Edith would accept those feelings enough to give McCall the card.

With her hands trembling just a little, McCall took the card out the envelope, opened it and showed it to him. "Since my mom gave this to you," Zoey had written, "I know you're as good, kind and amazing as Austin believes you are. Hold him and my babies close and don't look back. I'm their past, and I'll always be part of them, but you're their future."

When McCall looked up at him, he saw that she was blinking back tears. Well, crap. Were the tears because she didn't want that whole future part or because Zoey's *blessing* had touched her? It was more than just Zoey's seal of approval, though. This was one from Edith, too.

Even after having two daughters, he still wasn't good at dealing with crying, but he pulled McCall into his arms. "Don't worry. All of this doesn't come with strings. I want strings," he quickly added. "But I don't want you to have them unless you're sure."

McCall pressed her face against his shoulder. "I just wasn't expecting it."

Ditto. He was right there with her, and it felt as if a rug had just been pulled from beneath his feet. Unfortunately, he might have to weather a second rug-pulling.

"Shaw brought over a card for me, too," Austin said, taking it from his back pocket.

Because she was still in his arms, Austin felt all of her muscles go stiff. McCall lifted her head, her gaze colliding with his. "What did yours say?"

"Let's find out."

This was a first. He'd never read one of Zoey's cards in front of anyone, but Austin was pretty sure his was connected to the one that McCall had gotten. He only hoped that he wouldn't need to be held once he'd read it.

Easing back from McCall, Austin opened the card fast. As usual, it was a funny card with a dorky-looking guy in a hat asking a beautiful woman, "How do I look?" The guy's shadow was in the shape of a huge dick.

McCall made a sound as if she'd started to laugh but then had pulled back on it. She clamped her teeth over her bottom lip.

"It's okay. The cards make me laugh, too," he said. But not this one.

Again, Austin went with fast when he opened it. There was no caption inside, only Zoey's handwriting.

"This is the last one," she'd written. "It's time for you to cut the training wheels and start riding again. I want you to live a long happy life with this new woman you've found. Oh, and if that woman is Mindy Sue Brookhouse, well, consider me overlooking your bad taste. But I'm okay with anyone else."

That got a smile out of him. Until the last line. "Goodbye, Honey Buns."

Honey Buns was her name for his butt. Sappy but Zoey loved her some sap. She had also managed to get to the heart of everything with just those three last words. There'd be no more pet names for him. No more goodbyes.

This was it.

McCall didn't say anything, which said everything, and she didn't touch him. She just sat there while he read the card again and again and again.

Austin braced himself for some tears. He often cried when he got a card from Zoey. But this time his eyes didn't burn and his throat didn't close. This time the card and what she'd said felt…right.

It was time for him to move on.

It was time for him to say goodbye to the woman he had and always would love. She just wouldn't be the reason he didn't love someone else.

The moments crawled by, the silence punctuated by the girls' laughter from the other room. Austin wasn't sure how much time had passed before he tucked the card back into the envelope and turned to McCall. There were tears in her eyes, but she was blinking hard to keep them from falling. That caused a different kind of emotion to go through him. Not like a punch or a flood this time. But a warm trickle.

He leaned in and kissed her.

There was some heat in the kiss. There always would be when it came to McCall. But Austin felt more of that warm trickle, too.

"I want to stay," she said, her voice a whisper.

Good. Because he wanted her there, right where she was. "Of course. You can help us cook."

McCall shook her head. "No. I want to stay in Lone Star Ridge. I want to be with Avery, Gracie and you."

This time when he kissed her there was indeed some heat.

"Fairy tale rule," Gracie muttered through a yawn. "One more story. Not from you," she added to Austin.

"Yeah, from her," Avery piped up, and she pointed her finger at McCall. "We want a story from the fairy lady, peaze." She stretched out that last mispronounced word a few syllables and completed it with hands clasped in hope.

"McCall might be tired of reading stories," Austin pointed out. "Especially since she's already read two, and she told you one about magic ponies while we were eating dinner."

"McCall," Gracie repeated as if testing that out. It made Austin wonder if he should have insisted they call her Miss McCall or something other than just her given name. "I like fairy lady," Gracie added.

So did Austin, and if McCall and his girls didn't know that, they soon would. As far as he was concerned, McCall had given him a big bright green light when she'd told him she wanted not only to stay but to be with him and his daughters. It didn't mean this was a forever kind of relationship, but it was a good start.

"I can read one more story," McCall said, plucking one of the books from the huge basket filled with them.

Since it was on top, it was one of the girls' favorites, a story about a lazy duck named Slackers that McCall's sister Sunny had illustrated. And Austin's father, Marty, had actually written—something that Marty had only recently made known. Austin had told the girls that their grandfather was the author, but it hadn't made much of an impact since they really didn't know the man. Marty hadn't done any better being around for his grandkids than he had his own children.

McCall seemed to be familiar with the story because she started doing the voices of the characters right from the first line. However, she'd only made it to the third page before both Avery and Gracie were completely sacked out.

Austin adjusted the covers and kissed them both on their heads while McCall put the book away. They tiptoed out of the room and eased the door shut.

"Thank you for doing that," he whispered. Then he debated if he should tell her she didn't have to feel obligated to do it again.

"It was fun," she said, but she was rubbing her hands along the sides of her dress, making him think that there'd been something uncomfortable to go along with the fun.

Austin didn't want there to be an awkwardness between them because of the cards. Or the moments they'd shared after the cards. A connection, he supposed. Coupled with lust. Most would have considered that a recipe for a mighty fine start.

"I don't know if I'm doing the right thing with Avery and Gracie," McCall went on. "I mean, it's a fine line. I want to be with them, but I don't want them to think I'm trying to replace their mother. Or that I'm worming my way into their lives."

She wasn't exactly babbling, but it was close enough.

"Would it help if I put on the tutu?" he asked.

Judging from the way she blinked, she hadn't been expecting that question.

"The tutu will make you smile," he explained.

The breath she released seemed to be one of relief, and he got that smile from her. It still had a little edge of nerves to it, but she was relaxing some.

"Come outside with me," he said, taking the baby monitor from the kitchen counter. They wouldn't be able to go too far since he wanted to hear the girls if they woke up, but the monitor had a good enough range to cover even if McCall and he decided to walk down to the barn.

He shoved the monitor in his back pocket, took out two

long-neck beers and motioned for her to follow him through the kitchen and onto the back porch. It was still hot—Texas summer nights usually were—but there was a breeze. Just enough to cool things off a little and maybe keep the mosquitoes and gnats away.

Austin handed McCall her beer, set his and the baby monitor on the railing, and he looked out at his place. To him, there wasn't a prettier view on earth what with the milky white moonlight on the pastures and the horses grazing in the distance. So many stars. And the lightning bugs sparkled on and off, putting on a show for them.

While there was the smell of feed, the horses and grass, he also got a whiff of the gardenia bushes that his mom had planted for him shortly after he'd bought the place. The flowers stirred with McCall's own scent, which only added to his "nothing prettier" opinion.

Man, she was beautiful.

The moonlight was on her, too, angled just right as if to say, *Hey, look at this, look at her*. So, Austin did some looking.

"Cicadas," McCall said, having a sip of her beer.

"Yep." That rattling buzz was distinctive along with being a little early. The cicadas didn't usually come out until July, but they were serenading them tonight. "They're looking for a mate," he said almost idly.

Then realized it probably hadn't sounded so idle to McCall. It maybe sounded like a lame come-on, but at least she was smiling when she turned to him.

"Ditto for the frogs," he added when he heard one croak.

"And the lightning bugs?" She was still smiling and moving in closer to him.

"Definitely looking for a mate. The horses probably are,

too. Don't look out in the pasture if you don't want to catch a glimpse of horse sex."

She leaned in as if she might press her smiling mouth to him but no kiss. McCall just slid a long look over him. "I'd rather catch of a glimpse of you shirtless coming out of your barn."

Surprised and pleased, Austin slid a look over her, as well. "That really did it for you, huh?"

"It really did it for me," she verified. She moved in closer, and he was pretty sure there would have been a kiss this time, but he moved away from her and barreled off the porch.

"I'll be right back," he said, running to the barn.

He heard her laugh as he peeled off his shirt along the way. Austin didn't linger even a second in the barn. The moment he was inside, he turned around and started back toward her. He did linger this time, but that was only because he wanted to savor the way she was looking at him.

Yeah, there was some definite hunger in her eyes now.

And some definite hardening in his jeans. He was sporting a full-fledged erection by the time he stepped back on the porch. Austin hooked his arm around her waist, pulled her to him and pressed her against his hard-on.

Then he kissed her.

The taste and feel of her was even better than he'd thought it would be, and his expectations had been mighty high when it came to McCall. After all, she was his fantasy, too.

He deepened the kiss, letting the heat from it slide them right into a slow, lazy sway that caused her middle to brush against his. Nice and more than a little mind-blowing. Austin figured it would be a whole lot mind-blowing in a hurry, but then McCall pulled away from him.

"I can't have sex with you inside the house, not with the girls in there," she said in an almost frantic whisper.

Austin shrugged, pulled her back to him. "Then we'll have sex here on the porch. I have a condom in my wallet."

"Here?" Her voice squeaked, and her gaze fired around.

"No one other than the horses for miles around. Who knows, maybe this will be part of your new fantasy. Like shower sex."

When her gaze came back to his, he saw her process that. Saw the arousal creep back in when she slid his body against his. All in all, that was the perfect move to make. Another big green light. And yeah, they might end up with splinters in their butts, perhaps a mosquito bite or two, but Austin figured that'd be totally worth it because of what was about to happen.

And what was about to happen was sex.

He didn't play around the next time he kissed her. Austin took hold of the back of her neck, moving her so that the kiss had the right angle. And he touched, too. No sense not going for all the bases at once. He ran his hand between them, cupped her breasts and played with her nipples.

If McCall had any doubts about what was happening, they seemed to vanish right then, right there. She took hold of the back of his neck, dragging him down even closer to her. Not that getting much closer was possible, but McCall took care of any gaps in contact. While he had her mouth for supper, she made sure every possible inch of them was touching.

Touching was good. Very good. But, of course, it only caused the heat to soar. Austin cursed himself again when he felt that urgent need to hurry. He really wanted to take his time with her. And maybe that could happen. Once he had sated this first fireball, anyway.

He caught on to her, lifting her so that she hooked her legs around his waist, and without breaking the kiss, he backed them toward the porch swing. It squeaked and lurched when he dropped down onto it, but all in all, it put them in a good position with McCall on his lap.

And the battle began.

Since he wasn't wearing a shirt, she went after the zipper of his jeans. He had a lot more to do to rid them of any barriers, but her loose dress was easy enough to pull off over her head. He sent it flying, opened the front hook of her bra and would have gotten his tongue on her nipples if she hadn't managed to get her hand in his pants first.

His eyes crossed.

He cursed it.

And he loved every bit of what she was doing to him.

He'd never thought much of hand jobs when the real deal was available, but McCall was carrying this to a new level. A level that Austin had to stop, though, if he stood any chance of giving her a climax the old-fashioned way. Well, as old-fashioned as you could get considering they were in a porch swing. Also, considering that he was keeping an ear on the monitor in case either of the girls woke up.

Austin eased aside McCall's stroking, massaging hand that was sliding up and down the hard length of him. He skipped the nipple kisses, too, and went after her panties. It wasn't easy to maneuver, and he nearly pitched them forward and out of the swing, but he finally managed to shimmy the panties off her. Then he did some turnabout, fair-play stuff, by reaching between her legs and sliding his fingers into all that wet, tight heat.

She froze a moment, threw back her head and made a sound he wished he could bottle. It would no doubt be a cure for impotence and low sex drive. It sure as hell speared his own sex drive through the stratosphere.

"Condom," he reminded her. But he managed to keep up the stroking while he fished his wallet from his back pocket.

In fact, all that wiggling around might have only added to McCall's pleasure. By the time he got on the condom, he could feel her muscles tighten around his fingers.

Then tighten around him when he thrust inside her.

McCall was definitely a dirty talker when she got this hot, something that clashed with the good-girl image she'd had way back when. And man, she could pump her hips and ride him hard.

Just exactly the way Austin liked to be ridden.

Of course, since this was McCall, he doubted if there'd be anything she could do that would cool him down. Nope. She just kept it up, slip-sliding over his hard-on until he was ready to beg for mercy. She gave him mercy, all right. When the climax hit her, those slip-sliding muscles started to tighten, squeeze and give him something a whole lot better than a hand job.

And Austin gave it right back to her.

CHAPTER EIGHTEEN

MCCALL PARKED AT the end of the driveway and hoped the sound of her car engine didn't wake up Boo and Granny Em. It was barely five in the morning, much too early for them to be up yet.

Much too early for her to be out so late, McCall mentally added.

She hadn't intended to fall asleep at Austin's, but that's exactly what'd happened after they'd come in from the porch and snuggled up together on his sofa. It'd been wonderful. An amazing night that she wasn't sure she deserved. However, she'd take it and any other nights like that Austin could give her.

Easing her car door shut, McCall walked to the porch. And stopped in her tracks when she spotted the person curled up by the door.

"Cody Joe," she muttered like an oath, and she stormed up the steps to give him an earful that would almost certainly wake up Boo and Granny Em. But when she got closer, she saw that it wasn't the idiot bull rider, after all.

It was her sister Hadley.

Hadley stirred, her heavily made-up eyes opening. She sat up, stretching and yawning at the same time. The bangles and bracelets on her wrists and ankles jangled as she pulled her knees to her chest and stared at McCall.

"Morning," Hadley greeted, her voice sounding like a rusty gate.

"Good morning," McCall cautiously said, and she went closer to have a better look. No signs of injury, nor was there the smell of booze. Then again, she'd never known Hadley to be a heavy drinker.

"What are you doing here?" McCall asked, and that question not only applied to why Hadley was in Lone Star Ridge but also why she'd been sleeping on the porch. The front door likely wouldn't have been locked, and even if had been, Hadley would have known that Granny Em hid a key in the geranium plant to the right of the door.

"Didn't want to wake up Em," Hadley answered. "I flew a red-eye into San Antonio, caught a taxi here and had the driver drop me off at the end of the road. I got in about two hours ago."

Her sister stood, shaking out the wrinkles of her loose black pants that had a silver stripe down the side. No, not a stripe. Interlocking snakes with lethal-looking sparkly fangs. It was possibly one of Hadley's own creations since she was a costume designer. One with "out there" taste in what she came up with for movies, ad campaigns and even clients looking for something unique.

There were more of those silver fangs woven into strands of her long hair that was dyed as black as the pants. Those fangs clanged as much as her other jewelry, which would qualify as legion. Triple earrings in each lobe, necklaces and rings along with chains on her pants pockets and the pocket of her sleeveless black leather shirt.

"Walk of shame, huh?" Hadley said, tipping her head to McCall's disheveled clothes.

"Yes," McCall admitted.

Then McCall went to her sister and pulled her into a hug.

Hugs were automatic with Sunny, something she didn't have to think twice about, but she always "thought" with Hadley. As usual, her sister went a little stiff. That didn't stop McCall, though. She held on.

And she got flooded with a boatload of childhood memories.

So many good ones. Others not so good.

Once, they'd been so close in part because they'd had to stand together under their mother's manipulations and the prying eyes of the camera crew that followed them seemingly everywhere. But that had changed around the time they'd hit puberty. Around the time that Hadley had started really living up to the name the producers of *Little Cowgirls* had given her.

Badly Hadley.

The name had always seemed like a cartoon outlaw to McCall, but it had been one that Hadley had seemingly taken to heart and tried to live up, or down, to. Hadley had acted out by cutting school, breaking curfew, slipping out at night and finally by getting caught riding in a stolen car with her friends. She'd been arrested, and while she hadn't actually spent time in lockup, she did get a juvie record out of it. That in turn had gotten the show canceled.

"Come inside," McCall said when she finally let go of her sister. "I can fix us some coffee, and you can tell me why you're here."

"Tit-gate," Hadley said, causing McCall to turn back and look at her. "I guess you haven't been reading any tabloids?" Hadley added.

"No. I've been avoiding them since I know there'll likely be stories in them about me and the strip club I own."

"Yep, there are stories, all right. Who would have thought

Good Girl McCall would end up owning a place called Peekaboo?"

"Certainly not me," McCall said under her breath. "It's caused me and everyone around me some embarrassment." And she would always regret that even if it didn't seem to bother Austin.

"I might have taken some of the publicity pressure off you," Hadley explained a moment later. "A costume I designed for Myla Livingston had a malfunction during her live performance at a big-deal charity ball."

McCall knew that Myla Livingston was a big-name pop singer. Practically a legend now that she was in her forties. And she was also a diva with a temper and a serious mean streak. Considering that Hadley had called this Tit-gate, it wasn't hard for McCall to figure out what part of the costume had malfunctioned or that it'd caused tabloid-worthy publicity.

"I'm sorry," McCall said, keeping her voice to a whisper when they went inside. "Is it going to cause a lot of trouble for you?"

Hadley made a sound of agreement, confirming it had indeed already caused her trouble but also blowing it off with the same breath. McCall doubted, though, that it was anything to blow off if news of it had hit the tabloids. Something like that could hurt Hadley's business, and Myla could maybe even get her blackballed.

When they made it to the kitchen, Hadley sat at the table, stretched again and pushed her tousled hair from her face. McCall got the coffee started.

"You were with Austin?" Hadley asked. Then she added, "Hayes told me that Austin and you were getting back together."

McCall automatically frowned. "We *might* get together," she clarified, though she wouldn't mention that she'd now had sex with him twice along with some heavy fooling around in his truck. "We need to take things slow because of his twin girls."

Hadley made another of those sounds of agreement, but this one had a slightly different edge to it. "I always thought you'd be a good fit with Austin. The same with Sunny and Shaw. Sunny's been in love with him ever since she sprouted tits."

Maybe even before then. McCall didn't have a single childhood memory of Sunny's love interest that didn't include Shaw. Unlike Austin and her. She'd lost the dice roll to Zoey, and that had been the end of that.

Well, until now.

"Some people thought for certain that you'd get together with Leyton," McCall pointed out. She poured them both a cup of coffee and sat at the table. "There was that hot make-out session you had with him at the back of the barn, the one that got caught on camera."

"Yeah, that." Hadley blew at her coffee while she stared down into the cup. "Leyton got all embarrassed about it."

McCall couldn't disagree about that. Even as a teenager, Leyton had always seemed to walk the straight and narrow. Maybe because he didn't consider himself a real Jameson since he'd been born out of wedlock. In many people's minds, he'd always be just another of Marty Jameson's *love children*. It didn't matter that Lenore had legally adopted him or that Cait, Austin and Shaw thought of him as their brother. Leyton had always seemed to have that need to be perfect and not cause any waves that would disgrace a family name.

Ironic since Marty disgraced it often.

"I doubt Leyton has any fond memories of that night," Hadley remarked.

No. Because the cameraman had caught the sixteen-year-old Leyton playing a raunchy game of "frisk the suspect" with the town's bad girl, Hadley.

Granny Em had tried to stop the footage from being aired. So had McCall, Sunny, Leyton and Hadley. But in the end their mother had won out because she still had the control to decide what would or wouldn't make it into the episode. Anything that was embarrassing to the triplets or Hayes automatically made the cut because their mother saw that as a way of boosting ratings. It hadn't helped either that Leyton and his parents had signed release forms at the beginning of that season of *Little Cowgirls*. Forms that had given the producers the right to use any footage of Leyton.

"I won't be making a Jameson threesome by hooking up with Leyton," Hadley insisted. "You and Sunny will have to settle for twosomes." She paused, quit staring into her coffee and lifted her eyes to meet McCall's.

Crap.

McCall saw it then—the sympathy—and that look almost certainly had something to do with why Hadley was here.

"There's going to be a problem," Hadley said, her words slow and deliberate as if she'd rehearsed them. "Hayes tried to fix it, but it's a no-go. McCall, you need to brace yourself for another shit-storm."

"You're grinning like an idiot again," Leyton pointed out while he hoisted another bale of hay off the flatbed and dropped it on the barn floor so that Austin could stack it.

Austin had no doubts that he was doing just that. Even if his mouth wasn't sporting that particular expression, he was grinning inside. It'd been a long time since he'd felt this good, and he wasn't about to try to stop himself.

Despite Leyton's comment, Austin knew that his brother was happy for him. All of his family had shared his grief over losing Zoey, and all of them would be breathing a little easier that he'd climbed out of that particular dark hole. He could thank McCall for that climb, and Austin hoped like the devil that she continued to be around.

"Just how serious are you about her?" Leyton asked.

"Serious," Austin admitted. "And yeah, I know McCall hasn't been back that long, but she...fits."

It had taken him a few seconds to come up with that word, but it was the right one. McCall fit not only with him but also Avery and Gracie.

"McCall's staying in Lone Star Ridge," Austin added a moment later.

Leyton's eyebrow rose on his sweat-drenched forehead. "What about her counseling practice?"

"She'll make some trips back to Dallas for some clients, move others to appointments over the phone. Maybe she'll even open a new practice here." That was something McCall had mentioned when they'd snuggled up on the sofa after porch-swing sex.

"The town could use a counselor," Leyton said. "Every now and then a person gets a sentence of court-appointed therapy, and they have to drive into San Antonio for that."

Austin hadn't considered that angle, but yeah, McCall could probably do that along with getting other clients going through a divorce or something like that. He frowned, though, when he thought about the phone conversation he'd overheard. He couldn't see anyone local spilling their sex problems with such ease, but maybe they would.

"Does that mean Boo will also be staying?" Leyton asked. He dropped another hay bale off the flatbed.

Austin hoisted up the bale and mimicked Leyton's earlier eyebrow hike. "Are you interested in her?"

"No way. She's as far from my type as it gets." Leyton's answer was fast and firm. "But plenty of guys wouldn't mind hooking up with Boo. I was just wondering, that's all."

Austin believed him about the lack of interest, which made him think of something else. "How are things going with you and the kindergarten teacher from Bulverde?"

Leyton shrugged. "It didn't work out, and don't tell Cait," he quickly added. "I don't want her fixing me up with anybody."

Austin made a sound of agreement. Their sister was definitely a busybody when it came to her brothers' love lives. Ironic since Cait didn't seem to spend nearly as much time on her own relationships. Or rather she didn't spend any time at all. Unless she had some secret lover stashed away, Austin figured it'd been nearly a year since she'd been out on a date.

"I need to make sure the girls are getting ready," Austin said, checking the time. His half sister, Kinsley, was in there with them. *Supervising.* But Avery and Gracie were pros at convincing Kinsley to play games with them. "I'll need to drive them to preschool in another half hour."

Leyton checked his watch, too, and jumped down from the flatbed. "I need to get showered and dressed for work, but I can come back late this afternoon and finish helping you with the hay."

"I'd appreciate that." They started toward the house with Leyton falling in step beside him. "How's Kinsley doing, anyway?"

Leyton took his time answering. "Better." Then he paused. "A little better," he amended.

Instant guilt. Austin knew Kinsley had had it rough what with only recently finding out that Marty was her dad. Then a double rough when her useless turd of a mother had basically abandoned her. He should have tried to help her adjust—just as his siblings and his mother were no doubt doing.

"The custody papers are final," Leyton explained.

Austin did know about that and was thankful that Shaw had stepped up to take legal custody of the girl so that she wouldn't have to go into foster care.

"Shaw and Sunny are having an addition built onto his house so that Kinsley will have her own space. In the meantime, Kinsley's splitting time staying with Cait, your mom and me. Mostly me," Leyton added in a mumble.

Austin pulled back his shoulders. "With you?" Out of the three places to stay—Cait's, his mom's and Leyton's—Austin would have figured Kinsley would have preferred hanging out with Cait.

Leyton shrugged again. "I guess Kinsley sees me as the kindred spirit brother. I mean, because I'm a bastard like her."

Austin cursed. "The only bastard in this scenario is Marty."

And their father probably still hadn't learned to keep his zipper up. Every other year or so, another of Marty's kids would turn up at the ranch, each of them wanting some kind of fatherly acknowledgment or love that Marty just wasn't capable of giving. Some like Leyton and Kinsley stayed. Others drifted in and out like smoke.

Like Marty.

Austin's childhood wasn't an especially bad one, but he'd learned never to count on Marty for anything. Still, Marty had "given" them Leyton, and while that hadn't been intentional on Marty's part, it had turned out to be a damn good thing. Leyton was Austin's brother in every way that mattered, and he figured one day he'd feel the same way about Kinsley being his sister.

When Austin reached the back porch, he heard the sound of the approaching car engine, and he went around the front to see McCall. He automatically smiled. Then frowned.

Because one look at her face, and he knew that something was wrong.

"Shit," Leyton said under his breath. Obviously, he'd picked up on McCall's troubled expression, too.

Austin's stomach dropped. He hoped that McCall hadn't changed her mind about staying. Or about him.

"I have to talk to you," she said once she made it to Austin.

Since Austin figured McCall wouldn't want an audience for this, he glanced back at Leyton. "I'll make sure the girls are dressed," Leyton said. "And if McCall and you need a little more time, I can drive them to school."

The thanks he gave his brother was heartfelt. And almost certainly necessary. Because Austin didn't think this was going to be a short and sweet conversation with McCall. Apparently, McCall didn't want an audience for it, either. She motioned for him to follow her as she started for the barn.

"When I got back to Granny Em's this morning, Hadley was there," she said, and he could hear the worry and strain in her voice.

Hadley. That actually caused the muscles in his chest and stomach to relax some. Maybe whatever had happened didn't have anything to do with McCall and him.

"Is your sister okay?" he asked when McCall didn't continue.

She made a so-so motion with her hand. "She's in some trouble over a costume, but that wasn't the only reason why she came to Em's." She stopped again, muttered some profanity and groaned. "Remember that picture of me in the skimpy waitress outfit when I worked at Peekaboo?" McCall didn't wait for him to answer. "Well, it's surfaced again."

Austin repeated the "Shit!" that Leyton had belted out earlier. "Hayes has a recording of that idiot who blackmailed him to keep quiet about the picture."

McCall nodded. "He wasn't the one who leaked it. Apparently, it was his girlfriend. She saw the picture on his phone, got jealous and posted it on social media. Someone realized that it was me and alerted the tabloids."

Austin added a couple of "hells" to his other profanity. He'd known, of course, that there was always a chance the picture could resurface, but the timing sucked. This could start up another round of gossip.

And another round of guilt for McCall.

It could send her running for fear of bringing this down on him and his girls.

"I don't know how long it'll be before everyone knows," she went on. McCall turned her head, but he saw her swipe a tear that spilled down her cheek.

He reached for her, and even though she tried to push him again, Austin held on. He pulled her into his arms.

Just as his phone dinged with a text message.

Just as McCall's buzzed with one, too.

Even though Austin doubted that he would want to see what was on his screen, he took out his phone, anyway. "It's from Edith," he grumbled.

And yep, he'd been right about not wanting to see what was there because Edith's message read, We have to talk now. It's about McCall.

CHAPTER NINETEEN

MᴄCᴀʟʟ ᴡᴀs ᴄʟᴏsᴇ enough to read the message from Edith, and she knew it would be about that photo. It didn't matter that it'd been taken a dozen years ago. It was still a picture of her in a strip club.

She looked at her own phone screen. It was an I'm sorry from Hayes, and a string of texts quickly followed her brother's. One was from Alisha, another from Cody Joe. More came from foundation donors. She didn't answer any of those but zoomed in on the one from Em.

I can create a distraction for you, Em had messaged.

No, McCall immediately texted back. Whether or not that would actually stop her grandmother, she didn't know, but the last thing they needed was more publicity to cover up what was already out there.

You're sure? Em answered. Hadley said she could go into town if you think that'll help.

McCall sighed. She wasn't sure exactly how Hadley thought she could help, but she didn't want her sister involved in this. Hadley already had enough troubles. Plus, McCall was certain there was something that Hadley wasn't telling her. If this picture scandal hadn't blown up, McCall would have pressed for whatever it was bugging her, but for now that would have to go on the back burner.

"I need to go," McCall told Austin. "I have to try to do some damage control—again."

Austin stepped in front of her when she started to walk away. "I don't want you to leave because of this."

She knew what he meant. Leave as in run for the hills and get out of town. It was tempting. Mercy, was it tempting, but other than trying to distance Austin from this, it wouldn't solve anything. The scandal would just follow her wherever she went. It was time to give another statement to the press. And more. It was maybe time for her to step away from the foundation.

It squeezed at her heart to consider doing that, but it was for the best.

"I don't want you to leave," Austin repeated.

McCall sighed again, looked him in the eyes. She realized it would do a lot more than squeeze her heart if she had to quit seeing him. It would crush her. And that made her silently curse.

Crap.

She'd fallen in love with him.

Great day in the morning. She so didn't need this now. Nor did she need the kiss he gave her when he leaned in and pulled her close. But she certainly wanted it. Wanted him, too.

She let the kiss linger a moment longer than it should have. Let it deepen, too. It was wrong to take comfort from it, to take comfort from him, but McCall didn't stop it. She kissed him right back and held on to Austin until she felt herself steady a little.

"I'm sorry," she managed to say when she eased away from him. "Not for the kiss," she quickly added.

The corner of his mouth lifted into that damnable smile that had her hormonal number. Of course, pretty much everything about Austin had her number.

"I'll call you," she promised. McCall brushed another quick kiss on his still smiling mouth and hurried to her car.

She wouldn't cry, and McCall kept repeating that to herself as she drove away. Crying would be a pity party, but she would yell and curse. No pity in doing that. So with no one around to hear, she cursed like a sailor with zero volume control. She peppered in Alisha's name. Cody Joe's. And Mindy Sue Brookhouse, who'd flung a snotty Kleenex into McCall's hair when they'd been in second grade. She moved on to her worthless mother and generically added anyone who'd been mean to animals.

Like the kiss, it actually seemed to help release some of the anger.

By the time McCall had made it into town, she'd actually started to come down a little. But the coming down came to a screeching halt when she saw Edith coming out of Rick Downing's office on Main Street. Rick was a lawyer, and McCall instantly got a very bad feeling.

McCall pulled over to talk to Edith, and immediately got everyone's attention with the squeal of her brakes and when her tire hit the curb. Of course, even if she'd successfully managed a silent approach, word would still get around that Edith and she had "talked."

Edith stopped and stared at her as McCall made her way to her. However, the woman did glance around, no doubt trying to gauge who was in listening range. There were a few people milling around, which was probably why Edith didn't say a word until McCall was close enough for her to whisper.

"Enough is enough, don't you think?" Edith managed to make that a snarl enough, though she was whispering, and she didn't wait for McCall to answer. "I'm not going to stand by while my granddaughters are exposed to this sort of thing. Exposed to *you*," she added.

McCall nodded. "I'm sorry about that picture, but I wasn't doing anything illegal. And it was taken a long time ago."

"Do you think that matters? You're practically spilling

out of that little outfit you're wearing." In case McCall had been confused by that statement, Edith pointed in the general direction of McCall's breasts.

"The uniform didn't cover much," McCall agreed, also keeping her voice low, "but it stayed on me the whole time I was waitressing. I didn't strip. I only served drinks."

"Well, it certainly doesn't look that way, not to me and probably not to anyone else who sees it."

McCall suddenly wished she could have another cursing/yelling session to tamp down the temper she felt rising as fast and hot as August heat. It wouldn't help matters for her to get in a shouting contest with Austin's mother-in-law. Especially a mother-in-law who might be thinking about cutting him off at the knees.

McCall glanced up at the sign: Rick Downing, Attorney at Law. "Why were you in there?" she came out and asked. Yes, it was rude, but McCall thought she knew exactly where this was going, and she didn't like the destination.

Edith hiked up her chin. "Even before you came back to town, I wasn't sure Austin should be raising two little girls. Girls need a mother figure."

If McCall's temper had been on a thermometer, it would have shot right through the little bulb end. "The girls need their father. He loves them, and they love him." She had to say that through clenched teeth, but McCall managed to get out the words. She couldn't do anything about the glare she aimed at Edith.

Edith glared back. Apparently, her temper was on the rise, too. "I could have handled Austin having the girls if he'd continued to be a good role model for them. But you ruined all of that. You've done nothing but bring one embarrassment after another to my family. So has your grandmother and now your sister Hadley. Everyone who isn't talking about your picture is talking about the costume Hadley rigged to expose that singer's breast."

Tit-gate. McCall wanted to insist that Hadley hadn't "rigged" it, but she had no idea if that was true. "Leave my sister out of this," McCall settled for saying.

"That's hard to do when she's all over the magazines and the gossip TV shows," Edith countered. "She's been practically booted out of Hollywood, and that's why she came running back here."

"Actually, she came to warn me about the picture," McCall said, though she was afraid of the consequences Hadley might face over the costume scandal.

Edith groaned, dismissed that with a flick of her hand and shook her head. "My, God. What will the girls think if they see that picture of you?"

There weren't many things that Edith could have said that would have immediately dissolved McCall's temper.

But that did it.

The shame flooded through her. Shame not because she'd done anything wrong but because she really didn't want Avery and Gracie to see her like that. McCall didn't want Austin or her having to explain to toddlers what a strip club was and why the fairy lady had been working there.

Edith's chin came back up, and she likely saw that what she'd said was getting through to McCall. "The way I see it, you've got two choices," Edith went on. "You can stay, and I'll have Rick file the custody papers I just started. Papers that will lead to a court battle for me to get my granddaughters."

McCall didn't respond. She just stood there and waited for the rest of what she knew Edith would say.

"Or you can leave town. *Leave Austin*," Edith clarified.

"Leave my granddaughters and never come back. Your choice," the woman added.

With that, Edith turned and walked away.

IN HINDSIGHT, AUSTIN realized he probably should have dropped off Avery and Gracie with a sitter before coming over to Em's. But this visit had been sort of spur of the moment—especially since he hadn't heard a peep from McCall after she'd left his house earlier that morning. He just wanted to see her for a couple of minutes, just to make sure she was okay.

And to make sure she wasn't thinking about leaving.

That's why he'd come straight to Em's after picking up the girls from preschool. Having Avery and Gracie along for this could put some limits on what McCall and he said, but Austin hadn't wanted to wait. Even if McCall hadn't had enough time to do all that damage control she wanted, he still needed to see her.

"Granny Em's," Avery announced when Austin pulled to a stop in front of the house.

He was surprised that Avery remembered because it'd been a while since he'd brought Gracie and her here. The last time had to be about four months ago when the vet hadn't been able to come out and Em had asked Austin to check one of her horses. The horse, a paint gelding, had been fine so Austin had visited with Em while she stuffed the girls with homemade cookies and hot chocolate.

"McCall lives here," Austin told them, which created a whole lot of excitement.

"We can play fairy tale rules," Gracie said, "and she can read us a story."

"Three stories," Avery corrected.

"There might not be time for stories today," Austin told them. "McCall might be busy."

Heck, she might be crying, as well, and that was another reason he'd wanted to see her.

He glanced but didn't see McCall's car, and he hoped she'd parked it in the garage. If not, well, he'd deal with that after he talked to Em.

The moment Austin had the girls out of their car seats, they took off running to the porch ahead of him. The front door opened, and he got a nice jolt of anticipation when he thought it was McCall. It wasn't.

It was Hadley.

Of course, since Hadley and her sisters were identical triplets, there were very similar facial features, but Austin could have never mistaken Hadley for McCall—especially now that Hadley had black hair.

The girls practically skidded to a stop and looked up at Hadley. Gracie cast an uncertain glance back at Austin.

"You the fairy lady's sister?" Avery asked. No timidness in her tone. Just disappointment that it hadn't been McCall who'd come to the door. Austin completely understood that.

"Yeah," Hadley said as if that was a question she got all the time. She kept her attention on the girls. "Are you the fairy tale twins, Griselda and Humperdink?"

They giggled. "Gracie and Avery," Avery clarified. "And that's our fairy tale daddy."

Now, Hadley's gaze went to him. "Hey, Austin. How's it hang—going?"

He nodded to let her know he appreciated her pulling back on saying *hanging*. Austin didn't want to have to explain that in toddler-speak. "I'm okay. You?" he risked asking.

Her mouth twisted into a snarky smile. "One misplaced costume hinge, and I'll never hear the end of it." Hadley motioned for them to come in. "McCall went into town about fifteen minutes ago to do an errand, but she should be back soon."

"An errand?" he questioned as they made their way to the kitchen where they found Em. Maybe the woman had ESP about this visit because there was a cooling rack of what appeared to be freshly baked snickerdoodles on the counter.

"Just in time," Em said, beaming at the girls. "Would you two like some cookies and milk?"

Before the last words had even left Em's mouth, Avery and Gracie said two very enthusiastic "Yes, peaze."

"What kind of errand did McCall need to run?" Austin pressed. He probably sounded obsessed or something, but he wouldn't be able to push aside this worry until he saw her.

"She didn't say," Em answered, helping the girls into the chairs at the kitchen table. "But I can tell you that she was u-p-s-e-t," she spelled out.

That sure as hell didn't help the worry. "Is Boo here?" Because he'd likely be able to get some answers from her.

Hadley shook her head. "She's in Dallas, dealing with some business."

Probably business connected to Peekaboo. McCall had said something about sending Boo back up there to handle that, but Austin hadn't thought it'd be this soon.

Em served the girls each a cookie, poured them a glass of milk and then went closer to Austin. "I figure E-d-i-t-h is in a horn-tossing mood over that p-i-c-t-u-r-e of McCall."

Em probably hadn't had to worry about the girls overhearing that because they were focused on the cookies. Nor would they have gotten the horn-tossing/pissed-off reference, either.

"You're sure Edith knows?" Austin asked. Like Em, he also kept his voice low. "She hasn't called me about it, and I think she would—"

"She knows," Em interrupted. "McCall wouldn't say

what was said, but plenty of folks let me know that Edith and McCall were talking right there on Main Street outside of Rick Downing's office."

Well, shit. This was one time that Austin wished he hadn't been kept out of the gossip loop. He was about to tell the girls to finish their cookies so he could drive into town to try to spot McCall's car, but then Austin's bad feeling skyrocketed.

"Did McCall say anything about leaving?" he asked.

"Loads," Hadley answered, and Em verified that with a nod.

"McCall came back here ready to leave, but I told her just to wait it out and things would get better," Em added.

Austin looked at Hadley to get her take on that. *"Loads,"* Hadley repeated. "She was crying when she went up to her room, and then about thirty minutes later, she came down and said she had to do something. She didn't use the word *errand*," Hadley spelled out. "She said she was going out."

He mentally repeated his *well, shit.* "Did she take a suitcase with her?"

Both Em and Hadley gave variations of a shrug. "I didn't actually see her leave," Em admitted. "She called out to Hadley and me when we were in the kitchen."

"I want to check her room," Austin said. "Avery and Gracie, wait here with Granny Em."

The girls didn't protest, especially when Em said they could have another cookie. With Hadley right behind him, Austin headed for the stairs. Fast. He wasn't even sure if McCall had brought a suitcase with her to town or if she'd had her things shipped, but he intended to look for any signs that Edith had sent her running.

And he quickly found it.

There was a note lying in the center of McCall's bed, and

since it wasn't folded or in an envelope, he had no trouble reading it.

"I'm so sorry," she'd written. "I just need to get away for a while."

Now, Hadley joined him in some cursing, and he took out his phone. When McCall didn't answer, he sent her a text. Call me now.

Whether she would answer or not was anyone guess, but he quickly fired off another message that just said, Please. Then he tried Edith. Unlike McCall, she answered on the first ring.

"What did you say to McCall?" Austin demanded to moment Edith was on the line.

Edith, however, wasn't so fast to answer. "What did McCall tell you I said?"

He probably should have held back on the cussing, but Austin couldn't stop himself. He didn't like shitty word games like this. "What did you say to her?" He not only raised his voice, he also made sure that Edith knew he was pissed.

Still, Edith didn't jump to say anything. Several moments creeped by before she finally said, "I told her I didn't think it was a good idea for her to stay in town." Another pause. "And I let her know that I'd just had Rick start drawing up those custody papers."

Austin didn't trust any profanity then because he would have called her some bad names. Names with *coldhearted* and *bitch* in them. And while the grandmother of his children might indeed be just that, he wouldn't cross that petty line with her.

"Let me guess," he said once he got his temper under control so he could speak. "You told McCall you'd file those papers if she stayed in town."

Austin didn't actually need that confirmed. He knew that's what Edith had done. But he wanted to hear it. And he did.

"Yes," Edith admitted, but this time she didn't pause. She jumped right into an explanation that Austin knew from the get-go would be bullshit. "It's the right thing. You can't have the girls exposed to this sort of thing."

"But I can have them exposed to a manipulating woman like you who tried to bully McCall into doing what you think is *right*?" Okay, he wasn't even sort of successful in keeping the anger out of his voice. Except this was many, many steps passed the mere anger stage.

"I didn't bully her. I simply told her what I would do, and I'm telling you, too. Austin, if you don't put an end to your affair with McCall, I'll file for custody."

Austin considered how to answer that and decided the best way to go was just to hang up. So, that's what he did.

"If you squeeze your phone any harder, it'll break," Hadley pointed out. She walked around him to stand in front of him. "Look, I'm not what anyone would call a champion of justice, but I don't like people dicking with McCall. That whole good-girl image isn't crap. It's the real deal."

Yeah, it was, and it didn't matter that none of this had been McCall's fault. She'd just gotten caught up in it.

"Is that what Edith is doing—dicking with McCall?" Hadley asked.

Austin sighed, scrubbed his hand over his face after he loosened the grip on his phone. "Unintentionally dicking with her," he admitted. "But I think Edith truly believes she's doing the right thing. She's not." Austin snapped out that last part.

Hadley held up her hands in a *don't kill the messenger* gesture. "If I thought it would help, I'd volunteer to make Edith an outfit that would give her an embarrassing moment or two when it malfunctioned. And I know this dude who does voodoo dolls."

Austin managed a smile and patted her on the arm. "Thanks. I'll keep that in mind as plans B and C."

"What's plan A?" she asked.

"To hell if I know," he grumbled, and he headed out of the room and back down the stairs.

Maybe McCall just needed some time to think, but he thought if he could just talk to her, he could make her see that leaving shouldn't be in part of plans A, B or C.

The girls weren't in the kitchen where he'd left them, but Austin soon found Em and them in the living room. No cookies, but Em was showing them something that was hanging in the coat closet. Something big, white and sparkly, and it looked familiar.

"Look, Daddy. It's the fairy lady's dress," Avery announced.

"A costume?" Hadley moved in for a closer look. "And what's with Miss Watermelon?" she added, running her fingers over the tacky runner-up banner.

"It's the dress McCall had on when she came back to Lone Star Ridge," Austin supplied. "She wore it for a charity beauty contest. Obviously, a rigged one since she didn't win."

That garnered a smile and nod of agreement from Em. Hadley just continued to study the ball of white puffy fabric.

"You know what's missing from that dress?" Hadley asked.

All of them looked at her.

"McCall," Hadley supplied. She turned to the girls then. "What do you say that we find her and bring her back?"

The girls clearly thought that was a good idea because it started some loud squealing and jumping up and down. Austin didn't jump or squeal. But he did smile.

Because, yeah, he finally had a plan A.

CHAPTER TWENTY

"CLARA EIDELMAN'S A TEASE," Mr. Bolton snarled.

McCall was betting that most women in their eighties didn't get called that, but then it perhaps wasn't common for such a woman to get pressured for sex by a man that McCall had secretly labeled a horndog. That wasn't a very kind term for a therapist to use, but Mr. Bolton was trying her patience today with this phone call.

Of course, considering her own sour mood, any one of her clients likely would have done some patience-trying. Heck, anyone period would have tested her.

McCall hadn't wanted to take his call while she was driving back to Dallas, but after she'd seen his name pop up on the Bluetooth screen in her car, she'd remembered they had an appointment. Since she'd already rescheduled with the man twice, she'd taken it. And was now regretting that decision. Her mood wasn't anywhere good or focused enough to dole out any sage advice or counselor's empathy.

Physician heal thyself indeed.

She wasn't going to be able to talk herself out of the heart-crushing that she'd just gotten. Nor would she be able to shove aside what she felt for Austin. Still, she couldn't ruin his life or the girls', and that's what could happen if she'd stayed around Lone Star Ridge. It would have given Edith the fodder to try to tear Austin's family apart.

"Well?" Mr. Bolton prompted with some obvious aggra-

vation. "What do you have to say about that? Clara Eidelman's a tease," he repeated.

"I think you focus on sex because you don't want to deal
with your grief over losing your wife five years ago," Mc-
Call firmly stated.

It was the first time she'd said something that blunt to
him, and she was met with silence. Which was okay. Maybe
it meant Mr. Bolton was actually considering that.

While he did his considering, McCall did some of her
own. Sex hadn't been Austin's way of dealing with grief.
She knew that all the way to the marrow. He'd been with
her because that's what he'd wanted, and he hadn't used her
as a fix. That made all of this even more painful.

Damn it.

Now, she was battling the blasted tears again. Not only
was boo-hooing not safe because she was driving but crying also wouldn't do any good. She just needed to focus on
the future. Whatever that would be. But once she had that
focus, it would help.

She hoped.

"I miss my wife," Mr. Bolton finally said. That was another first. McCall heard some grief in his voice.

"I know you do. The two of you were married for a long
time, and there's no timetable for grief, Mr. Bolton. Maybe
you should take a breather from sex and just deal with the
feelings you're still having."

More silence for a while. "How long of a break?" he finally asked.

That had her smiling despite the tears. "At least a week.
And then we'll talk." That way, she would know if the break
had actually helped and if she needed to advise him to make
it even longer. Mrs. Eidelman would almost certainly appreciate that, too.

McCall arranged a follow-up session with Mr. Bolton, but she'd only been off the phone with him for less than a minute when another call came in. No surprise there. She had been getting a steady stream of calls and texts from Granny Em, Sunny, Hadley and Austin since she'd left town. McCall hadn't wanted to take those, but she did answer this call from Boo.

"It's true?" Boo immediately asked. "You're leaving Austin?"

"Who told you?" McCall countered.

"Em. She called me about ten minutes ago and hoped that I knew where you were. Where are you?"

McCall looked at the sign for the next exit. "I'm on I-35, just a few miles from San Marcos." Not that far, really, from Lone Star Ridge, but she'd had to stop for gas. That and she was driving slow since she knew she likely wasn't being as attentive to the road as she should be.

"Hold on a sec," Boo said. "I need to answer this text." McCall did wait, huffing a little, but it wasn't long before Boo came back on the line. "I'm supposed to tell you that your leaving Lone Star Ridge is dumber than a bag of hair."

No doubt directly from Em. "I'll call Granny Em later and talk to her." Not that talking would help her grandmother accept McCall's decision to leave, but it'd been the right thing to do. "For now, I just want to get to Dallas. How's everything at Peekaboo?"

"Same ol', same ol'," Boo said, "but I want to do something about that. I thought about it all the way up here, and I think I've come up with a fix. We can change the name."

McCall groaned. "It's too late for that. Everyone knows I own the strip club so changing your name to mine won't help."

"No." Boo laughed as if that'd been the stupid idea that

McCall had insisted it would be. "I meant change the name of Peekaboo. And change Peekaboo right along with it."

Maybe it was because her head was clogged from all the crying, but McCall had to say, "I don't get it. Change it to what?"

"Change it to not a strip club." Boo sounded excited now, and her words ran together she was talking so fast. "I have this idea, and it wouldn't mess up the conditions of Lizzie's will because you'd still own it, and you wouldn't be selling it. Nor would you be running it in the ground just for the sake of it going bankrupt."

"I'm listening," McCall assured her, though she didn't have much hope that this would be a helpful solution to her problems.

"We could make it a place for women's fantasies from books and movies. We could set it up like a tea parlor, one of those fancy Victorian ones that serves the little sandwiches. I love those."

"Sandwiches?" McCall questioned.

"Yeah, and other food that fits with the themes. In some rooms, the servers could be Vikings serving mead and whatever it is that Vikings eat. Hunks of meat, maybe. Then, in another room, the waiters could be dressed like Mr. Darcy and could serve tea and scones. We could put cowboys like the tasty Austin in others to serve some kind of beef finger food."

McCall waited Boo out until she'd finished. "Peekaboo isn't a restaurant," she pointed out.

"But it has a kitchen, and we could have the food catered if you don't want to get that up and going. There'd be no groping or anything hinky, just some yummy treats to eat and equally yummy eyeball candy for women looking for a fantasy experience."

McCall didn't automatically jump to playing devil's advocate. She gave it some real thought and decided that it actually wasn't a horrible idea. A shocker since most of Boo's ideas were often well off the mark.

"We could call it Fanta-tea," Boo went on, chuckling now. "You know, as a play on *fantasy*."

Okay, that wasn't especially good, but as excited as Boo was about this, she'd probably come up with plenty of other options. But McCall immediately thought of a hitch.

"What about the strippers?" McCall asked. "How would they feel about basically being replaced by a bunch of male waiters?"

"I'll bet some won't be excited," Boo admitted. "But I think they'd all get on board with it as long as they have jobs. We could even work them into the playacting with some of the hot guys. Again, nothing gropy or sexual. They could just play the fantasy role of whatever room they're serving."

McCall figured there'd be no way to stop the sexual thoughts, but as long as they stayed thoughts and not actions, that'd be okay. And they already owned some costumes from when McCall had wanted the strippers to try out more conservative dance routines.

"Maybe we could even have some of the current strippers transfer to management," McCall said, thinking out loud.

"Does that mean you'll be too busy with Austin to do any management duties yourself?" Boo immediately said.

"No." McCall answered fast, too. "I'm not sure what'll happen with Austin. I just want to give him some time to sort out his feelings."

And time to get Edith off his back with this custody suit.

"Write up this idea," McCall told Boo, "and we'll talk about it when I get to Dallas."

She ended the call with a still enthusiastic Boo only to have her phone ring again with another call. It was Austin's name that popped up on the screen again, and while McCall wanted to put off talking to him, she didn't want him to worry about her.

Well, not worry more than he already was.

She could give him a quick assurance that she was okay and say that she'd call him back tonight. By then, McCall would have figured out what to say. She could hope so, anyway.

Taking a long breath, McCall hit the answer button on her steering wheel and expected to hear Austin's voice pouring through her car. She didn't.

"We're playing cops and bobbers for real," the little voice said. McCall was almost positive it was Avery. "And you're the bobber."

McCall knew that *bobber* was Avery's word for *robber*, but she had no idea how that applied to her.

Then McCall heard the siren.

Her gaze flew to her rearview mirror, and she saw the flashing lights of the cruiser. And if she wasn't mistaken, it was a Lone Star Ridge cruiser with Leyton behind the wheel.

Good grief.

"Sorry," the voice said. Not Avery this time but Austin. "Please take the next exit so we can talk."

McCall gritted her teeth, furious that he'd come after her like this, but she couldn't verbally blast him because obviously he had Avery and Gracie in the cruiser.

Leyton kept on the flashers until McCall turned at the next exit, and he finally turned off both them and the siren. McCall pulled into the parking area of a gas station, stormed out of her car, whirling in the direction of where Leyton had stopped. She was ready to give Austin a piece of her mind, but the anger did a flash burn and was gone as fast as it'd come when she saw his face.

Yes, he'd been worried.

Austin came toward her, and she saw more of that worry in his eyes. He frowned. "You've been crying."

Apparently, she wasn't the only one without a poker face.

He went to her, pulled her into his incredibly strong arms and brushed a gentle kiss on her cheek. "I'm sorry for what Edith said to you."

She so wished she could just dismiss that as not having played into her decision to return to Dallas, but she couldn't. It hadn't just *played into it*. It'd been the sole reason.

"My leaving is the only thing that makes sense," she said.

He shook his head. "Nope, it's the only thing that doesn't make sense."

McCall might have been able to argue that if he hadn't kissed her. Not a peck on the cheek, either. This was a full-blown one on the mouth. Completely French, completely Austin. It seeped right into all the cold places that had gotten colder with each mile of distance she'd put between them.

"Hi, fairy lady," Avery called out.

That pulled McCall out of the kiss trance, and she looked over Austin's shoulder. Leyton had gotten the girls out of their car seats, but he had hold of their hands to keep them from rushing forward. He probably figured that Austin and she had to talk. They did. But they wouldn't be able to solve anything here.

"Boo texted me and told me where you were on the interstate," Austin explained. "We were already headed this direction so it wasn't hard to catch up with you. Thank God that you drive well below the speed limit."

She wanted to be pissed off at Boo, but the anger wouldn't

do any good right now. McCall kept her voice as level as she could considering she was still recovering from the scorching kiss. "We both could use some time to think," she said.

"Bullshit." And Austin kissed her again.

That threw her off-kilter once more, and when he finally let go of her, McCall tried again. Well, she tried after she regained her breath. "I don't want you to lose your girls because of me."

"I won't, and I don't want to lose you because of Edith." He took her by the shoulders, looked her straight in the eyes. "McCall, I'm in love with you."

CHAPTER TWENTY-ONE

AUSTIN HADN'T BEEN sure what McCall's reaction would be when he told her he loved her, but he hadn't expected her to get choked on her own breath. It wasn't a little cough, either. She sucked in a huge chunk of air and then followed it with a hacking, strangling sound.

"Is you okay?" Gracie asked, pulling Leyton's hand until he took the girls toward McCall.

McCall nodded, but she didn't manage to actually say anything. She just kept coughing until Austin went back to the cruiser and got her a bottle of water that he'd brought along for the girls.

"It's all right if you don't wanta be a bobber," Avery added, clearly concerned about McCall.

McCall shook her head, gave Avery a weird little wave that she'd likely meant to reassure the girl. It didn't. Both Gracie and Avery looked on, and Gracie got bold enough to venture forward and pat McCall on the arm.

"I'm okay," McCall eked out, and she guzzled down a huge amount of water when Austin uncapped the bottle and handed it to her.

Her expression definitely didn't agree with her *I'm okay* assurance so she'd obviously said that to stop the girls from worrying. Once she had the coughing under control, McCall even stooped down and gave them a smile. "I don't mind being a bobber at all," she said.

"Good," Avery declared, shifting her attention back to Leyton. "Book 'er, Nuckle Leyton."

McCall laughed, though it was a little strained, and Leyton clearly picked up on that. Even though he hadn't heard Austin tell McCall that he was in love with her, his brother knew something was up.

"Why don't I take the girls in the gas station for a treat?" Leyton suggested. Of course, that got him a big yes, some jumps and squeals from the girls. "I'll try to find something that isn't total junk," he added to Austin before he led them away.

Obviously, this wasn't the best place to have a heart-to-heart talk with McCall what with the cars pulling in and away from the pumps, the smell of gasoline fumes and the sticky heat, but it would have to do. He didn't want McCall to leave until she understood how he felt about her. Then he still wouldn't want her to leave.

"You didn't mean what you said," she insisted when Leyton and the girls were out of earshot.

"Yeah, I did." And he turned her again to face him so that she could see this wasn't BS. "I suppose you're going to say that we haven't been together that long. It's true, but it's plenty long enough for me to know my own feelings. I'm in love with you, McCall."

That still wasn't a "jump into his arms and let's celebrate" kind of expression she was giving him. McCall was looking at him as if his confession had screwed up everything.

And in some ways, it did.

Because if McCall insisted on leaving, it was going to put his heart through the wringer. However, Austin was taking a gamble here that it would do the same to her heart. She might not be in love with him—not yet, anyway—but he was pretty sure her feelings for him ran deep. Hopefully, *deep enough*.

She kept staring at him as if he might take it back or say it was some kind of joke. That's when Austin kissed her again so that she'd know he was serious. Also, he wasn't an idiot and knew that his kisses did things to her body. Did things to his own body, too. And while the attraction between them didn't equal love, it sure didn't hurt especially when the attraction was this strong and hot.

McCall was a little breathless and starry-eyed when he pulled back from her. He saw the heat simmering. Saw it cool, too. "Edith," was all she said.

His mother-in-law definitely played into this whether Austin wanted her to or not. "I heard she was at Rick's to have him draw up the custody papers."

And while he'd said that with as little emotion as he could manage, there was plenty emotion inside him. He despised Edith for what she was doing.

For what she felt she had the right to do.

"I find it hard to believe that a judge would take my kids because I'm in love with a woman who worked as a cocktail waitress twelve years ago," Austin continued.

"I own a strip club," she reminded him.

He nodded. "That doesn't mean you're a bad person, and it damn sure doesn't mean I'm a bad father. You care about my daughters, I can see that—"

"I do," she interrupted, but then had to repeat it when a passing car practically drowned out her voice. "That's why I don't want to see them hurt. I don't want you hurt."

This, he thought, was one of the reasons he'd fallen in love with McCall. She would put him and the girls ahead of her own feelings.

"Then trust me," he said. "Trust that I won't let Edith get custody."

Austin was certain he could do that. Well, almost certain. And it was that *almost* that ate away at him and only added to his whole despising feelings for Edith.

McCall stayed quiet, which he thought meant she was actually considering what he'd said. Again, though, there was no indication that she was about to jump on his bandwagon.

But then she nodded.

As far as Austin was concerned, that nod was as good as gold. He smiled, and this time when he kissed her, it wasn't to cloud her mind or heat up her body. It was because seeing that nod had made him feel damn good.

"Daddy," he heard Gracie call out. Both McCall and he turned in Gracie's direction. "We got treats."

They did indeed. Surprising, Avery and she were eating bananas, so Leyton had managed to find something healthy for them, after all. However, they also had boxes of chocolate milk, and Austin suspected that Leyton's bulging shirt pocket held some kind of candy. That was okay. He allowed some spoilage rights when it came to aunts and uncles.

"We getta go back with Nuckle Leyton in the police car," Avery announced, speaking through a mouthful of banana. "We getta play cops and bobbers the whole way."

Austin lifted his eyebrow, looked at Leyton. His brother shrugged. "I thought maybe McCall and you would need some time to talk. I can take the girls back with me while you go with McCall in her car."

It sounded like the perfect plan to Austin. They were only about thirty minutes from Lone Star Ridge, but that would indeed give McCall and him some time alone. However, when McCall didn't voice any kind of agreement with that plan, all attention turned to her.

Austin didn't like putting her on the spot like this, but he would have liked even less having her drive off before they had a chance to work this out.

"All right," she finally said, and Austin did a fist pump before he could stop himself.

The gesture caused Gracie to giggle. "Will you getta play a game with the fairy lady?" she asked.

"I sure hope so," Austin muttered, flashing McCall a grin.

That grin was a risk because he could tell she was still on the fence about what she should do. And she certainly didn't grin back. However, she did hug the girls goodbye. Hugged and thanked Leyton, too. Before she started for her car.

"Come on," McCall said, her voice as neutral as her expression. "Let's go to your place and straighten things out."

CHAPTER TWENTY-TWO

McCALL WAS PRETTY sure going back with Austin was a mistake, but her crushed heart just didn't have the strength to turn him down. And no, it didn't have anything to do with him kissing her.

Well, not much, anyway.

It had to do more with her making sure that he understood that she wouldn't be able to bear it if she caused him to lose custody of his girls.

"If I cave in to Edith on this," Austin went on once they were in her car, "what's to say that she won't keep using that threat? What if she objects to the way I discipline the girls? Or don't discipline them?"

He had a point, a good one, but apparently Austin felt the need to drill that point home while she got back on the interstate, heading south toward Lone Star Ridge.

"What if Edith just gets pissed off at me about anything, or nothing, and then decides that makes me an unfit father?" He shook his head. "I can't live my life by her rules. That would make me an unfit father."

Again, another good argument, and McCall could admit that something—something that didn't have anything to do with her—could crop up. Maybe something to do with another woman in life. It was entirely possible that Edith might never approve of anyone who she saw as replacing her daughter.

Still…

"Edith gave me that card from Zoey so she must know that you're moving on with your life," McCall reminded him.

"Yeah, moving on with *you*. And yes, she's riled right now over that picture, but she wouldn't have given you that card if she hadn't seen something in you that would make her believe you'd be right for me and the girls. I have to believe that Edith will eventually remember that and back off."

Again, that was a solid argument, and McCall wanted to latch on to every word of it. Actually, she wanted to latch on to Austin. Leaving him was one of the hardest things she'd ever had to do, and she wasn't sure she could make herself do it again.

So, where did she go from here?

To his bed, came the little voice in the back of her head, but McCall doubted that sex would be the fix for this. However, before she could figure out possible fixes, her phone rang again, and she saw Boo's name on the screen on her dash.

"I need to take this," she told Austin. "I'll have to let Boo know that I won't be back in Dallas today." She hit the button on her steering wheel to answer the call, but Boo started speaking before McCall could say anything.

"The Fine Booty or Studly Desires," Boo blurted out.

McCall was certain she got a blank look on her face. Austin grinned.

"Those were two of the suggestions for names when I ran the idea past some of the girls," Boo added a moment later.

Oh, this was about Peekaboo, and it took McCall a few seconds to shift conversational gears. "Just put all the name possibilities in a report, flesh out your other ideas about how to set up the serving rooms, and I'll go over it. I think it's good idea that just might work," she admitted. "Thank you for coming up with it."

"You bet your fine butt it'll work," Boo insisted. "And speaking of fine butts, any word from Austin?"

Before McCall even slid him a glance, she knew he'd be grinning. He was. And it was that grin that made her a little weak in the knees. Of course, just about everything Austin did or said made her feel that way.

"Austin's with me now," McCall answered, then added, "You're on the car speaker."

"Hey, Boo," Austin greeted. "Thanks for letting me know where McCall was on the interstate."

"No problem. Do right by her, okay?"

"That's the plan," Austin answered.

McCall cleared her throat. She should probably scold Boo for ratting her out to Austin, but McCall just didn't have it in her. "We're heading back to Lone Star Ridge," she told Boo. "I'll call you later and let you know when I'll be back in Dallas."

"I hope that's never," Boo quickly said. "I mean, never as in you coming back to Dallas."

McCall hadn't been expecting that. Nor was she positive she wanted it. Heck, she wasn't positive of anything right now.

"I can handle things here," Boo went on, "and even the old meddling biddy won't be able to object when we turn Peekaboo into a tea room."

Oh, Edith could and probably would still object since it seemed as if this new idea would still have a sexual edge to it. An edge aimed toward women, yes, but McCall doubted Edith would be eating finger sandwiches in the Viking room served by burly bare-chested guys.

CHASING TROUBLE IN TEXAS   261

"One more thing," Boo said a moment later. "Cody Joe called me a few minutes ago."

McCall groaned, and Austin even dropped his grin. "What the hell did he want?" Austin snarled.

"He said McCall had blocked his number—"

"I did," McCall verified. "Anything he has to say to me, or to you, should go through my lawyer. I don't want to talk to him."

"Yeah, I pointed that out to him in the bitchiest way I could manage and called him King Dickhead. Don't think he liked that much, but it got him to turn off that sappy fake charm fast so I didn't have to listen to any of his bullshit excuses about why he screwed up. Anyway, he wanted you to know that he'll sign the papers severing his ties to the foundation."

McCall had geared up to call him a much worse name than King Dickhead, but that stopped her. "Why didn't he just tell the lawyer?"

"My guess is that he thought this was a way of making amends. He said he was sorry and all. I told him he was indeed sorry, and I didn't mean the kind of sorry that went with an apology."

Something was fishy about that, but then maybe Alisha had pressed for him to make that call. Alisha didn't want continued bad publicity any more than McCall did.

"Cody Joe didn't have any conditions for signing, did he?" McCall pressed, and she took the exit off the interstate for Lone Star Ridge.

"Nope, but he did say that his mom would probably want to talk to you soon."

Great. McCall couldn't imagine that being a fun conversation. And it might not even be a necessary one. Once she was at Austin's place, and after they'd talked things out, she'd call her lawyer and ask him to field any communications that came from Alisha.

"So, Studly Desires?" Austin asked when she'd ended the call with Boo.

"It won't be called that," she assured him. "The idea is to class up the place, not make it sound tawdrier than it already is. But Boo came up with the idea of converting Peekaboo to a tea shop where hot costumed male waiters serve the food and drinks. Obviously, it'll be geared toward female customers."

"Does that mean you'd need to be in Dallas for the changes?" he asked after a long silence.

Good question. "Maybe, just until everything is set up. But if it works out as I want, Boo will be the manager and she'll hire some of the current strippers to work with her. That doesn't mean I think it's a good idea for me to stay in Lone Star Ridge," she quickly added.

Austin paused again. "What would make you think it was a good idea to stay?"

Now, that was a bad question, one that could lead her to say things she shouldn't say. Like she wanted to stay. Desperately wanted it. That she wanted him with that same desperation. And that if she stayed there was no chance that she'd be able to hide her feelings from Austin.

"I just don't want you and the girls to get hurt," she settled for saying. It was becoming her broken record response, one that she'd no doubt be repeating even more.

Of course, that caused him to huff, but then he followed it with what seemed to be a sigh of resignation. If he was resigned to her leaving, then maybe this talk wouldn't be as tough as she'd thought it would be. That was the mind-set she had, anyway, when she turned into his driveway and pulled to a stop in front of his house.

"Tell me you don't have feelings for me," Austin challenged.

There were some lies that would just stick in the throat. That was one of them. So McCall didn't even attempt it. "My feelings shouldn't play into this."

"Uh, then whose should? And please don't say Edith's. I've already told you that I don't want her to have a say in my personal life."

"But that's just it. She has a say because she's your daughters' grandmother," McCall argued.

"She doesn't have a say in my personal life," he repeated. "I'm not putting the girls in danger. I'm not mistreating them. I'm being the best father I can be, and that means Edith has to butt out."

All of that sounded, well, logical, but she wasn't so sure that Edith would stick with logic. The woman could and would skew all of this to convince herself that Avery and Gracie could indeed be harmed.

McCall took a moment to figure out how to convince Austin of that before she turned to him. That wasn't a good idea, though, because looking at his face put a serious dent in her willpower.

And he knew it.

That cocky half grin he flashed her was lethal.

McCall muttered some profanity and nearly told him that she shouldn't go inside. Even if that's what she wanted. Especially because it was what she wanted. But she hesitated just a little too long, and she didn't do diddly to turn away from him when he leaned in and kissed her.

There it was. The pleasure and sensations that she'd missed in few short hours she'd been away from him. She'd missed his arms, too, and he helped her out with that by popping her seat belt and pulling her to him. Across the console and into his lap.

Suddenly, they were face-to-face, body-to-body, and he was kissing her as if starved for her. McCall totally got that because she was starved for him. And Austin was doing a really good job of feeding that need.

"I feel like an idiot," she managed to say. "Because I should be stopping this."

Austin pulled back just enough for their eyes to meet. "Do you want me to stop?"

McCall knew that he would do exactly that. All she had to do was say the word. A word that just wasn't going to come especially since she was the one to start the next round of kissing.

"We should take this inside," Austin said. At least, that's what she thought he said. Hard to tell with their mouths going after each other in the most carnal kind of way.

Part of her wanted to stay put and just enjoy this especially since his erection was pressing right in the center of her thighs. It was creating some amazing pressure that only made the kissing more incredible. But he was right. Austin's place wasn't on the beaten path, but someone could come driving up at any moment and see them. That definitely wouldn't help either of their reputations. Still, if they moved, she might come to her senses.

At the moment, her senses was the last thing McCall wanted.

And her body agreed.

Austin opened the car door, and they nearly fell out. That brought her back some. Not enough, though, because Austin just righted their balance and kept kissing her. Somehow, he also managed to get out of the car without dropping her.

McCall hooked her legs around his waist, keeping that

amazing contact in the center of their bodies. Austin made that pressure even better by sliding his hand to her bottom and pushing her even tighter against him. He kicked the car door shut and headed toward the house.

Not easily, though.

Basically, he was walking blind, and coupled with the distraction of her touching his chest and trying to get his shirt unbuttoned, he stumbled a few times. There was more stumbling when he got her on the porch and inside the house. He didn't even head to the bedroom, though. They only made it as far as the sofa where he dropped her down and followed on top of her.

Exactly where she wanted him to be.

One day they might have sex in an actual bed, but apparently it wasn't going to be today. Not with this urgent battle going on between them. She was fighting with his shirt, and he was at war with her dress. Every part of her body was demanding that she have him now, now, now.

Austin was thankfully in on that *now*, and he finally got her dress off over her head. In the same motion, he flicked open the front hook of her bra and did some breast kisses that only made her want to up that *now* to *immediately*. She gave up on his shirt and went after his belt and zipper instead.

McCall freed his erection from his boxers. No easy task since he was huge and hard. She wouldn't have minded dropping some kisses all the way down him and doing some tasting of her own, but those breast kisses only sped things up for both of them.

Cursing, he pushed her panties down below her knees, fumbled for his wallet and pulled out a condom. Something McCall was certain she wouldn't have remembered. Thank goodness one of them still had a shred of sensibility, but she was certain that even Austin lost that shred when he got on the condom and thrust into her.

The world turned to warm honey. All sweet and delicious. That lasted for the first few strokes, but warm honey couldn't hold up against a need for fierce and primal that it was all-consuming. McCall needed one thing right now.

Release.

And Austin was working hard to give her just that.

The orgasm rippled through her, consuming her and sending her flying. Austin joined right in there with her. Every nerve and muscle got in on the pulsing, causing the pinpoint of pleasure that was certainly the best she'd ever had. And because it was the best, it fogged her mind, and McCall found herself blurting out something she had no intention of blurting out.

"I love you, Austin."

WELL, HECK. MCCALL decided she needed her head examined. Admitting she was in love with Austin solved nothing, and in fact could make things worse. Still, she'd said it, and the only thing she could do now was own up to it.

And leave.

The leaving was especially necessary because it was the only way she was going to think straight and figure out how to do some damage control. Which, of course, Austin didn't help with when he grinned down at her. It was surprising that he could manage that within seconds after an orgasm, but he did.

"Want to repeat that now that I can actually hear?" he asked.

McCall didn't have to think about this answer. "No. I need to go."

His grin didn't waver, and he moved off her as if he'd

expected her to say exactly that. He didn't stop her when she scrambled off the sofa, pulled up her panties and put her dress back on.

"I love you, too," he said, not in a snarky, judgmental way but with the honest to goodness tone that she knew was genuine. Austin did love her. And she apparently loved him. Now, they'd have to deal with the fallout.

"I'll call you later," McCall said, hurrying out the door.

The moment she was outside, she immediately dragged in some fresh air, hoping it would help, but nope. Her thoughts were flying a mile a minute, and none of those thoughts spelled out a good solution as to what she was going to do. She seriously doubted that it would cause Edith to back off simply because McCall had made the mistake of not guarding her heart carefully enough.

Of course, maybe there wasn't enough guarding in the universe to have stopped it.

From the moment she'd seen Austin that night of the Cody Joe debacle, McCall had felt that her heart was on a collision course with Austin's. Even if she'd tried harder to stop it, she doubted she would have succeeded. No. This seemed to be something akin to destiny. Too bad that destiny could seriously screw them both over.

She drove back to Em's, hoping that she could sneak in and shower, but no such luck. Cait's SUV was in the driveway, and her grandmother was right there waiting in the doorway. Granny Em probably knew some of what was going on and deserved to know more. However, McCall was hoping she'd hold off on the questions.

Granny Em took one look at her and pulled her into her arms. McCall hadn't even realized she needed a hug until Em did that.

"You figured out you're in love with Austin," Em said with complete conviction.

No need to deny it when apparently she was wearing her stupid collision-course heart on her sleeve. "Yes."

Em patted her back, released her from the hug and looked her in the eyes. "Nothing makes you feel more miserable than being in love."

McCall frowned. That wasn't the brightest assessment of love, but in this case, it fit to a T.

The giggling caught McCall's attention, and those were giggles she instantly recognized. "Cait is here with the twins?" she asked, hoping she was wrong. She wasn't sure she was up to facing Avery and Gracie just yet.

Em nodded. "They got here a couple of minutes ago. Leyton had something he had to take care of at work, and Cait wanted to see Hadley. If you want to go on upstairs, I'll make excuses for you."

It was tempting, and McCall had just about convinced herself that an escape was what she wanted, but then she heard the girls giggle again. She realized it might help her mood if she saw them. Still, she had to freshen up first.

"Give me a few minutes," McCall said. "Are they in the kitchen?"

"No, in the old sewing room with Hadley and Cait."

McCall nearly asked what they were doing in there, but she'd soon see for herself. She hurried upstairs, grabbed a quick shower and changed her clothes. She didn't bother with makeup, and with her hair still wet, she went back down and made her way to the sewing room.

It'd been years since McCall had been in that particular room, which had apparently once been her grandfather's home office where he ran the daily goings-on of the ranch. After Hadley had taken an interest in making clothes,

Granny Em had converted it to a sewing room. One that Hadley had considered off-limits for anyone else.

Well, it certainly wasn't off-limits now.

There was still some giggling going on when McCall stepped inside and spotted Cait helping Avery into an old Spice Girls Halloween costume with a British flag. Mc-Call remembered Sunny wearing it way back when, and even though it was miles too big for Avery, Hadley had obviously made some adjustments so that it wasn't dragging on the floor.

Hadley was also fitting a costume on Gracie, one that McCall recognized since she'd been the one to wear it when she was ten or eleven years old. It was a rather elaborate fake satin aqua-colored Marie Antoinette dress, complete with a powdered white wig made out of knitting yarn.

Cait looked up at McCall and tipped her head to Gracie. "I'm guessing the *Little Cowgirls* producer or your mother chose that outfit for you?"

"You'd think, but no, it was my choice. Granny Em and Hadley pieced it together from some prom dresses they got from the thrift shop." And clearly, Hadley had had talent even back then.

"McCall," Gracie greeted just as Avery said, "The fairy lady!" Despite the bulky outfits, they hurried to her for a hug.

Yes, she'd been right about the girls lifting her mood. This was what she needed.

"This one's mine for our fashion show," Cait said, holding up a ghost costume. Or rather a sheet with eyeholes cut out from it. That'd been Hayes's costume, and Cait pulled it on over her head. "Yours is over there." Cait pointed to the fairy tale dress that McCall had worn for the ill-fated charity beauty contest.

Since Granny Em was getting into the spirit, too, by donning a vampire cape, McCall pulled on the fairy dress over the one she was already wearing. She couldn't zip it, of course, what with the added bulk of her regular clothes, but she got enough of herself in it. Hadley put on some music from her phone.

Inappropriate music because it was the old classic "The Stripper."

It was an instrumental so thankfully there were no words to go along with the sultry beat. Hadley's grin let McCall know that it was her way of paying homage to Peekaboo.

"Maybe you should play something else," McCall *suggested.*

"We could use one of my favorites," Em quickly said.

Cait, Hadley and McCall were all quick with their "nos." All of them knew Em's taste in rap music with explicit lyrics, and since McCall wasn't sure of Hadley's alternatives to "The Stripper," she took out her own phone and hit the play button for Pharrell's "Happy."

The girls obviously knew the tune because they clapped and jumped.

And the fashion show started.

Cait strutted around the room giving exaggerated model poses and a few breakdance moves that were genuinely bad and weird because she was wearing a sheet. When she stopped and propped her hands on her hips, she motioned for Avery and Gracie. The girls went together, moving much as their aunt had done except there was a lot more giggling involved.

They were such happy kids, and it was hard to stay down around them. However, McCall did wonder how they'd react if they found out she'd fallen in love with their father. Maybe that would also make them happy.

Or it might be too much too soon.

For just a moment McCall let herself imagine how things could be if Austin and she did end up together. She'd be with not only him but also with the girls for plenty of moments just like this. For bad moments, as well, since that was part of life. She knew from her counseling experience that blending a family took work. And that it didn't always work out.

"Your turn," Avery insisted, pointing at McCall. The timing was spot-on because it saved McCall from slipping into a blue mood.

McCall did the walk, or rather the dancing strut, to the other side of the room where Avery, Gracie and Cait were standing, and when she was done, she curtsied and winked at the twins. Then Em followed, kicking up her legs like a can-can dancer. Not exactly graceful moves and it didn't go with the beat of the music, but it got laughs from Avery and Gracie. No laugh from Em, though, because her attention froze on the doorway. McCall quickly shifted in that direction and saw someone she definitely hadn't expected to see.

Rick Downing, the lawyer.

McCall's stomach dropped because she seriously doubted that Rick had just dropped by for a visit. The timing fit that this had something to do with the visit Edith had made to his office.

"Uh, the door was open," Rick said. He looked as if he was trying to figure out what the heck was going on. "I knocked, but you must not have heard me."

McCall hit the stop button on the music, but the girls immediately protested. She handed her phone to Em so the fashion show could continue with music, and she stepped out into the hall. She shut the door behind her—again to Avery and Gracie's protests.

That's when she saw that Rick wasn't alone. Edith was standing at the end of the hall.

"I'm sorry," Rick said. "Edith insisted I come."

The sewing room door opened, and Em glared out at Edith. "You'd better not have come here to cause trouble."

Judging from Edith's stern expression, that's exactly why she'd come, but her expression changed when Cait, Em, Hadley and the twins all came out. It was a tight fit, especially with the costumes, and they were practically squished against each other.

"Avery, Gracie," Edith said in such a surprised way that it was obvious the woman hadn't known they were there.

"We're having a fass show," Avery announced.

"Yes, I see." Edith looked at McCall. "Uh, maybe we can talk outside?"

McCall wanted to refuse just on principle because she hadn't wanted Edith to bring any of this custody mess into Granny Em's house, but digging in her heels wouldn't help the situation. Besides, McCall didn't want to talk to Edith in front of Avery and Gracie.

"I'll go with you to talk to her," Cait insisted, yanking off the ghost sheet. She no longer sounded like the fun aunt but rather a cop. One with a mean attitude.

"I'll go with you, too," Hadley piped in. She also sounded mean, and considering that today she was wearing snake fang earrings, she looked it, too.

"I'll go wift you," Gracie volunteered, taking hold of McCall's hand. No mean look for her, but there was some concern on her sweet face.

There's nothing that could have softened McCall more than that. In fact, it immediately brought tears to McCall's eyes. Gracie likely had no idea what was going on, but she obviously wanted to add her support to Cait's and Hadley's.

And apparently so did Avery. "Me, too," the girl insisted. "Where we goin'?"

McCall stooped down so that she'd be at an even level with Avery and Gracie. "It's okay. I just need to speak to your grandmother for a few minutes. Why don't you go back in the sewing room and find another costume for the next round of the fashion show?"

Neither Avery nor Gracie showed a lot of enthusiasm with that suggestion, and that told McCall loads. The girls had obviously picked up on the vibes that something wasn't right. But that vibe all changed in the blink of an eye.

"Daddy!" the twins called out in unison, and they began to babble about their costumes.

McCall stood and turned to see Austin working his way past Rick and Edith and toward his daughters. He scooped them both up, kissed them. Then he gave McCall a kiss, too, before he turned back to Edith.

"Is there a problem?" Austin asked the woman.

Edith made a flustered sound and tipped her head to the girls. That was probably her way of saying she didn't want to discuss any of this in front of them. When she didn't give Austin a verbal answer, he turned to Rick.

"Are you here as Edith's lawyer or is this a social visit?" Austin pressed.

"Edith's lawyer," Rick verified. He lifted the envelope he had gripped in his hand. "I have papers that Edith wanted McCall to read."

"To give her one last chance to make things right," Edith piped in.

It didn't take a genius to figure this out. Edith wanted McCall to see the papers, to show her that she was serious about pursuing custody. But Edith intended this to be a sort of blackmail.

"Make things right," Austin repeated, and he sounded as mean as Cait and Hadley had earlier.

McCall heard the shuffle of footsteps behind her. Clothes swished and squished. There was a lot of body-to-body contact, but Granny Em, Hadley and Cait all moved forward, surrounding her. No doubt to show their support, and it was sort of working. McCall felt the united front against Edith. Even Rick was giving the woman some "this was a bad idea" glances.

"And how exactly do you expect McCall to make things right?" That came from Cait, but honestly with the tempers now zinging in the tight space, any one of the women or Austin could have said it.

With a twin in each arm, Austin turned to McCall. Yes, he was angry, all right, but it softened some, and after a few seconds he managed a smile. That was partly because of Avery, though.

"Sorry, I tooted," the girl said.

She had indeed, and the stinky smell seemed to get trapped in the jammed hall. Gracie made a "ewww" sound, pinched her nose and shifted her weight, reaching out for McCall to take her. McCall caught her as she practically leaped into her arms.

"Maybe we should all go out for some fresh air," McCall suggested. She gave Avery a quick kiss on the forehead to hopefully reassure her and turned to head out.

But Austin stopped McCall by stepping in front of her.

"McCall," he said amid the squished bodies, stinky air and glaring mother-in-law. "Will you marry me?"

CHAPTER TWENTY-THREE

WELL, AT LEAST McCall didn't have a coughing fit with this latest surprise that Austin had sprung on her. But she was surprised, no doubts about that. She stood, silent and stiff, while she stared at him.

Even though her mouth had dropped open only a little, Austin touched the bottom of her chin to move her lips back together. Then he kissed her. Because of this audience, he kept it short and sweet.

"Marry you?" Edith repeated, the first to break the silence. "You want McCall to marry you?" And yeah, there was plenty of surprise in not only her voice but her expression.

"Get married?" Gracie asked, looking over at Austin.

He nodded and figured this was something he should have run past his girls, but it'd been a spur of the moment thing. Maybe in part because of his reaction to Edith, he admitted, but also because he was in love with McCall.

Austin made sure he had both Avery's and Gracie's attention when he talked to them. "I'd like to marry McCall. How would you two feel about that?" He didn't have to wait long for their response.

"Yay!" Avery squealed just as Gracie said, "I'd like that." Gracie's smile let him know that this particular "I do" would get her seal of approval. But clearly not everyone else in the hall felt that way.

"Uh, we need to talk," McCall muttered to him.

Austin had known that was coming, and he'd even counted on the skeptical glances that he was getting from Hadley, Em and Cait. Of course, their approval would be, well, nice, but the only ones that really counted right now were Avery's, Gracie's and McCall's.

He stood Avery on the floor next to Cait, and McCall did the same to Gracie. However, McCall and he didn't make it even a step before Edith's surprise turned to anger.

"I know what you're doing," Edith blurted out, her voice a shrill accusation. One that wasn't just aimed at him but also at McCall. "You figure you can get married to try to weaken my custody case. But it won't work. I won't let you get away with this."

"Grandma's mad?" Gracie asked, and her bottom lip quivered as if she might start to cry.

Austin made sure Gracie and Avery didn't see the hell-freezing look he shot Edith, and he scooped up Gracie, holding her close to him. "No, she's not mad," he assured his little girl, but he wasn't quite able to rein in his temper enough to make it sound believable.

"What's a cuss-ody case?" Avery asked, tugging on McCall's fairy dress. "Is it like bad words?"

Edith apparently realized what she'd just said and how she'd said it in front of the grandchildren that she seemed hell-bent on snatching away from him. "No, it's not bad words." Edith's bottom lip wasn't doing any trembling, but her words were calmer now. "It's just something that I need to talk to McCall and your dad about."

"Is cuss-ody case like gettin' married?" Avery pressed.

A crappy father might have tossed Edith to the wolves and demanded that she explain it to Avery and Gracie. But he loved his kids too much to use them to put Edith in her place. He was about to offer Edith an out and tell the girls that he needed a private word with their grandmother, but Edith spoke before he could do that.

"A custody case is doing what's best for you and your sister," Edith said. She came closer and looked down at Avery.

Avery gave that a moment of thought. "Like gettin' married?"

Edith gave a frustrated sigh. "No. It's more like giving you girls the best home you can possibly have."

Gracie smiled. "With the fairy lady."

Now, Edith frowned. "No, not with McCall but with me and your grandfather."

That certainly didn't bring on any cheering. Not from the girls. And especially not from Austin. Edith probably didn't know that just hearing that felt like deep cuts with a very sharp knife.

Cait moved next to him, closing ranks. Em and Hadley did the same to McCall. Austin was sure all but McCall were glaring at Edith. Like him, McCall was trying to hold this situation for the sake of the girls.

"I gotta toot again," Avery announced—after she'd broken wind. Silent but deadly.

Obviously, his daughter had some kind of stomach issues because it stank up the air enough that Rick and Edith started out of the hall. Austin would have preferred to stay put and give them some distance, but he also needed some air.

With Gracie still in his arms, he took hold of Avery's hand to lead them out toward the foyer. "Can you marry the fairy lady now?" Avery asked him.

"No," Edith answered before Austin got the chance to say anything. "Your father and I have some things to work out."

"Like cussody," Avery supplied.

"Yes." This time Edith's sigh seemed to be one of relief. "I'm going to talk to someone, a judge, because I want Gracie and you to live with your grandpa and me." She plastered on a smile. "Wouldn't you like that?"

Everyone stopped again, and Avery and Gracie looked at Edith as if she'd sprouted an extra nose. Avery latched on to Austin's leg, anchoring herself there.

"No," Avery said, shaking her head. "I want to stay with Daddy."

"Me, too," Gracie piped in, and her lip started quivering again.

Enough was enough. "You're staying with me," he assured the girls, and he hauled up Avery into his arms.

Edith managed to keep that plastic smile. "But living with me will be fun."

Austin gave the woman a look that he was certain would freeze every ember in hell. "You should go now," he managed to say.

"Now," Em repeated. She moved pretty fast, considering she was wearing vampire garb, and she marched down the hall toward Rick and Edith.

Rick was smart enough to turn and go, but Edith stayed put. For a few seconds, anyway. "You might think you're as tough as a stewed skunk," Em said, her voice a low growl, "but you're about to find out different."

As threats went, it was a strange one, but Austin was thankful it was one the girls likely wouldn't understand. Heck, he wasn't sure he understood it. However, it was enough to get Edith finally moving. That didn't stop her, though, from issuing one last set of fighting words from over her shoulder.

"This isn't over," Edith snapped.

Austin had no trouble understanding that threat. And he didn't think it was a bluff. No. This wasn't over.

MCCALL PUSHED ASIDE everything that'd just happened, and she whirled around to make sure Avery and Gracie were okay. The girls were quiet and looking more than a little confused, and McCall suspected they were picking up on the thick tension in the air. She silently cursed Edith for having this showdown in front of them.

Shifting her attention, McCall then looked at Austin, who was also quiet. She didn't think that was because of any confusion but because he was too pissed off to say anything. Avery and Gracie had already heard enough angry words for one day.

"It's okay," McCall said, brushing her hand on first Gracie's cheek and then Avery's.

"Is cussody okay?" Gracie asked at the same moment her sister said, "Can we get married now?"

Despite everything that'd just happened, McCall smiled. Then she didn't. Because she remembered Austin's marriage proposal was on the table. First and foremost, though, he'd need to talk this out with the girls—not just the marriage thing but also Edith's custody demands.

"Why don't the four of us take a walk?" Austin suggested, and his gaze on her let McCall know that she was included in that foursome. "We can take the girls to the swing."

Until he added that last part, neither Gracie nor Avery seemed the least bit interested in getting out of the house, but that perked them up. Good. McCall was all in for anything that didn't make them feel confused or sad.

"I can take them to the swing if you and McCall want some time alone," Cait suggested.

It was tempting, but McCall doubted that Austin wanted to be away from his daughters right now. And she was right. Austin kissed Cait's forehead, thanked her and then motioned for McCall to follow him.

"Can we get married now?" Avery repeated.

Obviously, the girl wasn't going to let that drop. "McCall and I have to talk about that," Austin said.

Thank goodness he hadn't put McCall on the spot by having her answer Avery's question, but she doubted that the girl was just going to drop the subject.

Despite the costumes, they went out of the house. McCall immediately glanced around but didn't see Edith or Rick, thank goodness, as they made their way to the tree swing. The shade helped with the brutal temperature but not much. Still, the girls didn't seem to notice when Austin sat them side by side on the wooden seat of the swing.

"Hold on," Austin told them. It took some maneuvering to have Avery reach behind Gracie and vice versa so that both of their hands could grip each side of the ropes. Then he gave them a little push. Even though they only moved a couple of inches, the girls giggled with delight.

Austin looked at McCall, and he lifted his eyebrow, obviously waiting for her to respond to his proposal. However, since the girls were right there, she needed to be mindful of her words and not let her anger over Edith play into this.

"The timing isn't good for any big changes in your life," McCall reminded him, moving in front of the girls so she could not only keep tabs on their reactions but also to be there in case one of them started to fall out.

"I love you," Austin simply said.

"I love you," Avery and Gracie echoed.

The girls' attention was on the swinging, but Austin's gaze was still fixed on her. "I love you," McCall muttered. It was true, but it didn't fix anything. "That's why I have to say no. I don't want to do anything to create another scene like the one that just happened."

There was no need for her to fill in the blanks. If she backed away, then Edith might, too, and right now that was for the best.

Clearly, Austin didn't agree with her.

He certainly wasn't smiling now, and he huffed. But she saw more than disappointment and anger in his eyes. McCall saw the hurt. Damn it. This was exactly what she'd been trying to avoid. Austin had been through enough.

But apparently *enough* wasn't over.

Because Howie drove up.

"Grandpa," Avery and Gracie greeted. Obviously, they were delighted with their visitor and tried to pump their legs to swing higher to show him what they were doing.

Howie smiled at them. A smile that definitely didn't make it to his eyes. "That looks like fun," he told the girls.

"It is," Avery said, beaming. "We gonna get married."

"We don't want cussody," Gracie added, frowning.

Despite Gracie's mispronunciation of the word, Howie evidently figured out what'd happened because he groaned and shook his head. "I'm sorry," he muttered, moving behind the girls probably so they wouldn't see that his expression was no longer a happy one.

"Edith crossed a big line today by coming here," Austin answered. He kept his voice low, practically a whisper. "She tried to strong-arm McCall into leaving."

Avery didn't seem to pick up on that, but Gracie's expression grew more serious. To distract her, McCall started singing the only song that she thought the girls might know. "The Wheels on the Bus." Yep, they knew it, all right, and joined right in on the repetitive lyrics.

"I'm sorry," Howie repeated, barely audible over the cheery chorus of "round and round." "I tried to talk her out of doing this. I honestly did. But I think her grief's gotten all mixed up with the gossip and embarrassment."

It was hard for McCall to keep up the cheeriness over the reminder that she was the reason for such embarrassment, but she forced herself to keep tuned into the girls when they moved on to the next stanza. "The people on the bus go up and down."

"I'm a good father," Austin insisted.

Since there was plenty of raw emotion in his voice, McCall went a little louder with her "up and down" portion of the lyrics. Still, she heard Howie when he said, "You are."

"The driver on the bus says move on back," the girls belted out. McCall hadn't remembered these specific lyrics, but it was easy to follow along.

"If Edith keeps this up," Austin went on, "she'll do something that can't be fixed."

Howie's weary sigh was drowned out by the whaa-ing/ baby's crying sounds of the next stanza. "I know," Howie admitted. He opened his mouth as if to three-pete another "I'm sorry," but then he stopped and shook his head. "I'll talk to her again," he said, but he didn't sound very hopeful that he'd be able to change Edith's course of action.

"Grandpa's gotta go," Howie told the girls, and even managed goodbye kisses before he went back to his car.

Howie had no sooner pulled out of the driveway when Granny Em walked out onto the porch. She was still wearing her vampire cape and had likely been watching from the window. That cape swirled in the breeze as she came toward them. Not scowling or angry. Granny Em was all smiles.

That worried McCall even more than a scowl would have.

"I know how to fix this," Em announced. "I can throw a party. A big one for everyone in town."

Oh, God. McCall groaned, but the groan didn't put Granny Em off one bit. She kept on smiling.

"Just give me a day or two," Em added, sounding very pleased with herself. "And I'll have everything worked out. You two will be saying those 'I do's' before you know it."

CHAPTER TWENTY-FOUR

"BA-OONS," AVERY ANNOUNCED the moment Austin pulled to a stop in Em's driveway.

Yep, there were indeed balloons. Dozens of them tied to anything that could be used to tie them down. The Mylars floated, sagged, bobbed and bopped with each gust of wind.

Em or whoever had done the decorating obviously hadn't been picky about the choice of balloons. Some had cartoon figures, superheroes, dinosaurs and even a disturbing grinning witch with a hairy wart on her chin. At least a dozen of them said Happy Birthday. Others had Get Well Soon, Happy Anniversary, Congrats, I'm Sorry, Thank You, It's a Boy and Enjoy Your Retirement. One announced a tire sale at Big Bob's.

Apparently, Em was covering all celebratory bases for this shindig.

Austin had a bad feeling about this. Of course, he rarely had good feelings about any of Em's plans, and this one was no different. That's why for the last two days he'd actually tried to tap into the gossip mill to try to learn what she was up to with this party, but that tapping had turned out to be a lousy idea. The speculation he'd heard was worse than what Em's plan would actually be.

He hoped.

According to the gossips, Em was plotting some kind of revenge against Edith. Maybe like the pig's blood scene from *Carrie*. Or that Em was using those mob connections she'd recently spilled to have Edith threatened in *The God-father* kind of way. Austin had heard way too many "I'm gonna make him an offer he can't refuse" variations.

Since the gossips hadn't been at Em's to actually hear what the woman had said to McCall and him, the gossips hadn't pushed into the area of any "I do" possibilities. But that had been a biggie in what Em had promised. Or threatened.

Just give me a day or two, and I'll have everything worked out. Austin and you will be saying those "I do's" before you know it.

Austin wanted those "I do's." Maybe not right away. But he wanted that somewhere down the line for McCall and him. What he didn't want was Em doing anything to try to hurry that along. A scheme like that could send McCall running, and that was the last thing Austin wanted.

Ditto for some kind of public humiliation for Edith.

After all, with Em inviting the whole town, it meant kids would be there. Including his own kids. And Austin didn't want them to witness their grandmother being taken down a notch. Even if that's something Austin wouldn't have minded happening.

Austin parked on the side of the house with the family vehicles, making sure he left enough room if he had to make a fast exit with the girls. According to the instructions Em had given him, he was to arrive an hour before the start of the party, and he considered that a good thing. This way, he could suss out Em's intentions, check on McCall and if necessary get Avery and Gracie out of there.

Of course, McCall wouldn't stand for the girls being exposed to something that would hurt them. Especially something like their grandmother's public humiliation.

Austin got out with the girls, and while keeping a good

grip on their hands, they made their way to the backyard where he saw rows of picnic tables set up. There were also of couple of tents, a bouncy castle and several large barrel grills that looked ready to go. So, the party would be a picnic, but thankfully there was no banner announcing engagement plans for McCall and him.

Avery and Gracie squealed when they saw the bouncy castle or maybe their reaction was also for McCall, who was coming out of it. Her haired was mussed, her face a little flushed and she was smiling. Considering that she was also barefooted, Austin guessed that she'd been doing some bouncing.

Her smile did a lot to ease some of that bad feeling. Maybe there was nothing to worry about, after all.

"I couldn't resist trying it out," McCall said, stepping down from the inflated castle.

The girls bolted toward her, and she did a scooping spin, whirling them around once she had them in her arms. "Do you want to jump?" she asked them, and got the fastest answers in the history of fast answers.

"Yes!" the girls squealed. The moment McCall stood them on the ground, they started taking off their shoes.

"Want to jump?" she offered to Austin.

Because she looked so happy, Austin would have agreed to pretty much anything. He sat down on the bench outside the castle and started shucking off his boots. The twins finished ahead of him and darted inside.

"So, Em's party really is only a party?" Austin asked.

McCall shrugged, and he hated that her smile faded. "She says it's just a way of bringing together the town."

"And you believe her?" he pressed.

"No, but she won't spill. I do know she invited some of the big donors for Saddle Up for Tots. I have no idea if they'll come." McCall paused. "She also invited Howie and Edith."

Austin got that flash of *Carrie* and *The Godfather*. He really did need to have a chat with Em before the party started.

"Granny Em's in the kitchen," McCall said as if reading his mind. "The party's a pot luck, and the volunteer firemen will be manning the grills, but Boo and she are fixing some things."

"Not Hadley?" he asked.

McCall shook her head. "She went back to California this morning."

"I'm sorry." Austin stood, pulling her to him. In part to comfort her. In part because he just wanted her in his arms. Things always seemed a lot better when he was holding McCall.

She didn't resist and seemed to melt against him, definitely taking some comfort. "If this party takes a wrong turn," she whispered, "I've set up some playthings and books for the girls in my bedroom. You can take them there if you need to leave in a hurry."

Austin eased back, looked at her. "And that's one of the reasons I'm in love with you. You always think of my girls."

The flush on her face returned, but she kissed him, and the kiss might have lasted longer had Avery and Gracie not started squealing. Not from pain. Austin would have picked up on that. No, this squealing was no doubt from having their little bodies flung and hopped around in the castle.

Taking hold of McCall's hand, he stepped inside. Not easily. You'd think since he was a cowboy that he had a good balance, but he learned differently when he went down—and bounced on his butt.

Since he still had hold of McCall, she went right down with him, their bodies bumping together in a nice way. Chest to breasts. It would have been even nicer if they'd been alone and could have done more. That made him wonder just how many times people had had sex in a contraption like this. Maybe McCall and he could sneak back in here after the party finished.

"Jump high!" Avery insisted, and she showed them how it was done. She fell and bounced, too, into Gracie, causing the girls to giggle.

The giggling went up a notch when Austin took hold of McCall's waist and jumped together with her. Of course, the girls wanted to get in on that, probably because it lifted them higher, and soon they were all in a sweaty, out of breath mess. A sweaty, out of breath mess having fun.

Man, he was lucky. Even with all the crap Edith was trying to pull, yeah, he was lucky.

"Woohoo?" Em said, stepping into the castle with them. Like them, the woman wasn't wearing shoes, and she made a wobbly walk toward them. Then she started bouncing. "I knew this would be fun. The whole party will be fun."

Austin and McCall shared a glance, and McCall bounced her way closer to Em. "I don't want this to be an engagement party," McCall insisted. She kept her voice low, but if the girls stopped giggling for even a second, they'd be able to hear her.

Granny Em either nodded or her head bobbled when she jumped. Austin couldn't be sure which. "Because you haven't told Austin you'll marry him," Em supplied. "Have you?" she added a moment later.

McCall certainly wasn't giggling. "No."

Austin wanted more. Actually, he wanted a yes, but he understood that McCall wanted more time. He just hoped she didn't take too long.

"If this isn't an engagement party, then what is it?" Mc-Call asked.

Again, Austin had trouble interpreting the jiggling of Em's shoulder, but it was possibly a shrug. "I thought we could celebrate, uh, the future."

He saw the instant suspicion in McCall's eyes and was sure it was in his, as well.

"The future," Em repeated. "Because soon Sunny will be pregnant if she isn't already. Soon, the papers for Kinsley's custody will go through. And soon you'll have money pouring into the foundation." She paused and grinned when she looked at the girls. "We can celebrate the pony, too. Did you two decide on a name for him?"

"Rose Poopy-head," the girls immediately answered.

"Excellent choice," Em declared even though it wasn't. Still, both girls seemed satisfied with the name, and it wasn't always easy to come up with a compromise.

"What do you mean about money pouring into the foundation?" McCall asked.

Again, it was possible Granny Em shrugged. "I set up a big donation jar on the front porch. I told folks that it was going to be an interesting party what with all the stuff going on, and that the price of admission was donations to Saddle Up."

McCall groaned, but she didn't spell out that it sounded a little like blackmail. Or selling tickets to a spectacle. Especially since most of those folks wouldn't be able to resist seeing how things played out between Edith and him.

"I also called in a few favors," Em went on. "I reminded the business owners of how much money they made when *Little Cowgirls* was being filmed here. Heck, Breakfast at Tiffany's made out like a bandit. I just said how nice it'd be if folks gave some money to a good cause. A cause that doesn't have any secrets. Unlike *Little Cowgirls*."

That sounded a little like a guilt trip or maybe even extortion if Granny Em had suggested she might verify a *secret* or two. Like the owner of the Breakfast at Tiffany's café had fooled around with one of the *Little Cowgirls'* cameramen.

"Cody Joe's mom won't be coming," Em went on a moment later, obviously not speaking to the girls now. Considering her age, Em was a darn good jumper. "But she called, and I suggested she could still make a donation. I explained that I thought it'd make her look as if she's climbed above the fray. Then I reminded her that everybody was talking about how the fray was of her own son's making."

McCall didn't groan again, but Austin suspected that was because she knew it wouldn't do any good.

"Anyway, Alisha said she'd consider a donation," Em added.

The woman might just pony up some money, and if so, that would not only be good for the foundation but also for McCall. She might finally be able to start putting that whole Cody Joe fiasco behind her.

"So, you'll swear to me that you won't bring up Austin's marriage proposal?" McCall pressed Granny Em.

"Nary a word about it," Em assured. "Can't guarantee that others won't, but you'll not hear it from my lips." Em smiled with those *nary a word* lips and bounced her way out of the castle.

McCall glanced over at the girls, who were in the process of running headfirst into the castle walls and giggling like mental patients when they fell back on their butts.

"Any news on the custody papers?" McCall asked him while the girls were occupied.

Austin hated to put a damper on things, but he didn't

want to keep this from her. "Edith is proceeding. I've had to hire a lawyer from San Antonio since Rick's representing her."

Austin felt exactly what he expected to feel. The anger. It came in waves any time he thought about it, which was often. This was going to cost him time and money to fight, but the worst was the emotional toll.

"I'm so sorry," McCall said. Her footing was wobbly, but she still managed to get her arms around him. "I wish there was something I could do to stop this."

He brushed a kiss on her mouth and knew that was true. McCall would do anything—including not saying yes to his proposal—if she thought it would help.

"The custody hearing will have to go before a judge," Austin added. "And my lawyer thinks the judge will either throw out the petition or else ask us to go to mediation."

In other words, talk. Something that wouldn't help because Edith had dug in her heels. So had he.

"We don't want cussody," he heard Avery said.

Austin silently cursed. Obviously, the girls hadn't been as occupied as he'd thought. He turned toward them and saw that Gracie and Avery had both stopped bouncing. Stopped giggling, too. And his daughters were looking at him with very concerned eyes.

"We don't want cussody," Gracie repeated.

There was no way Austin could stay on his feet and pick them up so he sat down and motioned for them to come to him. They did, falling into his lap, and the motion sent McCall tumbling down beside them.

"Peeze don't make us go with Grandma Edith," Avery said, issuing her plea first to Austin and then to McCall.

"I'm going to try to make sure that doesn't happen,"

Austin assured her. That started a group hug, which they all needed, and he made sure McCall was in on it.

"We love you," Gracie said as if she had to convince them. "We love McCall. We don't wanta go with Grandma."

Obviously, the hug hadn't given her any reassurance, and Austin wasn't sure he could do that with words, either. Still, he had to try. It crushed his heart to see his girls upset.

"I love you, too," Austin said.

"So do I," McCall added.

"And we don't want you to worry about custody," Austin added. "We want you to have fun. This is a party, remember. We've got to celebrate naming the pony."

Clearly, that still wasn't working. The girls weren't bouncing and they sure as heck weren't smiling.

"Say, I saw a couple of cakes in the kitchen," McCall said. She was attempting a smile and pulling it off. "How about we sneak some before the party starts?"

With the girls' collective nods and "Yays," there went their dark mood. He wished his own mood could be fixed with sugar and fat.

They stood, again not easily. McCall helped up Avery. He helped up Gracie. But they hadn't even made it a step when Austin saw Edith standing in the castle entry. Her grave expression and church clothes didn't mesh with the cheery blown-up surroundings.

"We don't want cussody," Avery said. Not a shout. But a whisper. And she moved behind McCall, holding on to her as if she were an anchor.

"Peaze, no cussody," Gracie contributed, moving behind Austin.

Edith probably thought he'd put them up to saying that, but he hoped like the devil that the woman could see what she was doing to the girls.

"Please," McCall repeated. "No custody."

Well, heck. Austin joined in on that chorus, too, but he simply said, "Please."

Edith stood there, staring at them and saying nothing. Not anything verbal, anyway. But Austin could see that she was blinking back tears and that her mouth was no longer set in such a firm line. Her lips were quivering a little.

"No custody," Edith finally said.

Because Austin truly hadn't expected her to say that, he didn't respond. Neither did McCall or the girls. Not at first, anyway. Then, as if they'd just been given eight pieces of cake, Avery and Gracie started cheering and bouncing again.

Edith didn't go to them, but she managed a smile with her trembling mouth. "I'm sorry," she said. "I just didn't want the girls to forget their mother. I don't want you to forget her."

Austin had to force down the lump in his throat. "I won't. Zoey gave me two beautiful kids, and I see her every time I look at them."

"You can live with that?" Edith asked, and then shifted her attention to McCall. "You can live with the man you love seeing another woman in his children's faces?"

"Absolutely," McCall said without hesitation. "Because I see the same thing when I look at them. They're my friend's daughters. And the daughters of the man I love. How could I not love them, too?"

Austin got another lump in his throat. And a very warm feeling in the center of his chest. McCall had already told him that she loved him, but it felt good to have it all rolled together like this. The timing was perfect.

Well, perfect-ish.

He'd already talked to the girls about this and had gotten their enthusiastic approval to proceed.

He reached in his pocket and took out the box. He flipped it open to reveal the diamond engagement ring just as he went down on one knee. That last part failed. Hard to do a knee proposal on a bouncy surface, and he landed on his butt again.

"Yay!" the girls yelled. They landed next to Austin and pulled McCall down with them. "Will you marry us?" Avery asked.

This was it. The showdown of sorts. If McCall said what he wanted her to say—yes!—then it would take the *ish* out of perfect-ish. And it would hopefully have Edith see just how happy this would make him and the girls.

"Will you marry us?" Gracie repeated.

McCall looked at the ring. At the girls. At Edith, who was still in the doorway. And then at him. Austin figured this wasn't the most romantic proposal that'd ever been, but he could tell from McCall's smile—and the happy tears in her eyes—that it was a surefire winner.

"Yes," McCall said. She kissed Austin and gathered them into her arms. That tipped them all over on their backs like long-legged turtles. "I'll marry all three of you."

* * * * *

THAT NIGHT IN TEXAS

CHAPTER ONE

WHEN HE SPOTTED the pregnancy test, Harley Garrett's hands froze under the stream of running water in the bathroom sink. Heck, his entire body froze. Possibly the entire state of Texas did, too.

Blinking to make sure he was focusing, he stared down at the white Magic Marker–sized stick in the trash can on the tiled bathroom floor. He wasn't an expert about such things, but it was definitely a pregnancy test.

Harley gulped in his breath. Not a very manly reaction considering he was a tough cowboy and champion bull rider, but there were just some things that could shake him to the core.

Turning off the water and wiping his hands to dry them, he stooped down for a better look. Harley could see the little screen on the stick, which was blank, but he had no idea what it meant. Unfortunately, he had an idea of who'd put it there.

Crap.

This was the bathroom off the reception area for his family's guest ranch, Rustler's Ridge, and while guests did occasionally use it, at the moment they didn't have anyone staying in the main house, only in the cabins. The ranch hands didn't normally head in here, either, since there were bathrooms in the bunkhouse. The only reason Harley had ventured into it was because a meeting with a buyer had run late, and he'd needed to make a pit stop before heading back to the barn.

The doorknob jiggled, causing Harley to jolt, and the

jolting just continued when he heard the voice on the other side of the door. "Harley? You in there?"

It was his kid sister, Liv. The very sister who was involved with a scumbag cowboy on a neighboring ranch in their hometown of Lone Star Ridge, Texas. The very sister who was barely twenty-four and frequently used this bathroom because she often worked out of their mother's office when she was setting up schedules for the riding lessons she gave.

Harley mumbled some very bad curse words, threw open the door and faced Liv. He didn't bother to tamp down the glare that was surely on his face. "Are you knocked up?" he demanded.

He'd been so sure that she would look guilty, maybe even sputter out a not-so-convincing denial, but his sister only stared at him as if he'd sprouted multiple sets of eyeballs.

"Uh, no," Liv said, exaggerating that two-word response. "But thanks for asking me a question that's basically none of your beeswax."

"It is my beeswax." Though he hated using that term. "You're my sister, and there's one of those pee sticks in the trash can."

Her expression went from surprised sisterly annoyance to curiosity, and Liv stepped around him to have a look for herself. She gasped.

"It's not mine," Liv insisted, shaking her head, and as he'd done, she leaned in to no doubt check if it was a positive or negative result. "It's blank."

"Yeah," he confirmed, "but someone obviously felt the need to take the test." And it was possible the test had indeed given the result before fading.

However, at the moment the results weren't the big question here. Someone had put that pee stick in the garbage can, and he'd just ruled out one of the possible females who could have left it there.

That left him with two other prospects.

"Darla," he said, referring to Darla Givens, the receptionist who'd worked at the ranch for the past two years.

"No way," Liv concluded. "She doesn't have a boyfriend. Believe me, if she did, she would have told me."

Maybe. But if he excluded Darla, then there was only one other likely candidate.

"Hell," Harley grumbled just as Liv gushed out, "Holy crap. You think Mom's pregnant?"

That was indeed the only remaining female who made regular use of this particular bathroom. His forty-eight-year-old mother, Tracy, who'd had Harley when she'd been only seventeen in what had sure as hell been an unplanned pregnancy. One that'd had her parents tossing her out of their house. To make matters worse, Harley's father, whom he'd never met, had skipped town and never shown his face again. If it hadn't been for Tracy's great-aunt leaving her Rustler's Ridge, Tracy and he wouldn't have even had a roof over their heads.

When Harley was four, Tracy had married a local mechanic, Jerry Darlington, and they'd had Liv three years later. Jerry and Tracy had divorced shortly thereafter, and there'd been a string of relationships after that.

Messy, broken relationships.

Harley loved his mother, most days anyway, but she'd made an art form out of hooking up with dirtbags and other turds who could give her the most trouble. She'd become a cautionary tale to Liv and him about not getting involved too deep in their own relationships.

Maybe that was what'd happened again—another messy relationship for Tracy—but this time it'd led to something more permanent. Like another kid.

Harley repeated his "Hell."

Liv repeated her "Holy crap." But then she shook her head. "Isn't Mom too old to get knocked up?"

Harley gave his sister a flat look to remind her that not only didn't he know that sort of thing but it also wasn't something he *wanted* to know. Still, he had to consider it.

"Maybe it was someone who just dropped by for a visit," Liv speculated.

He hoped she was referring to the person who'd left the pee stick and not someone who'd possibly gotten their mom pregnant. But the moment the thought went through his head, Harley got a bad feeling. Apparently so did Liv because at the same time they blurted out, "Marty Jameson."

It wasn't a stretch for them to come up with that name when connected to a pregnancy test. Marty Jameson was an aging country-rock music star who'd fathered more than a few kids, including the ones with his ex-wife. He was staying in cabin number three on the ranch, something he did from time to time. Supposedly, he was there to work on some new tunes, but maybe he'd taken a break from music writing to knock up yet one more woman.

"I'll talk to Mom about this," Liv volunteered.

Harley had no trouble hearing the subtext in that. Liv thought she could ask the question with more finesse. And she probably could. But he didn't want to wait around to hear a rehashing of that conversation. He wanted to get to the bottom of this right now.

With Liv by his side, he hurried out of the bathroom and headed straight for Tracy's office. She wasn't there and neither was Darla, who was on her lunch break. However, Harley did spot someone through the large bay windows that fronted the house.

Amelia Wade.

Seeing her didn't nearly cause a heart attack as the pregnant stick had, but Harley got a jolt of a different kind. A good one. One that arrowed right to his groin and other parts of him.

He'd had a thing for Amelia since he was old enough to have things, and the years hadn't cooled it down one bit. Thankfully, it was the same for her. Amelia worked for a cattle broker in Wrangler's Creek, which was about thirty miles away, but she often made trips to the ranch since Harley and his mom bought livestock from her boss.

Harley usually found a reason to go to her place, too, but if weeks went by without them contacting each other, neither of them got bent out of shape about it. That was because Amelia was no more interested in anything serious than he was. Between the two of them, they had enough emotional baggage to derail any hint of serious.

"I'll find Mom," Liv said when she followed Harley's gaze to the parking lot, where Amelia had just exited her truck.

That pulled him out of his gawking, something he was prone to do whenever Amelia was around. The woman was definitely a looker without even trying. Amelia managed to make worn jeans, boots and a plain shirt look amazing. Ditto for her long brown hair that she had scooped away from her face and into a ponytail. Her brown eyes were in the same amazing category, too, but today she had them covered with sunglasses.

"Don't talk to Mom about the test until I'm with you," Harley warned his sister.

Liv certainly didn't agree to that, and she headed to the back of the house to look for their mother, just as Amelia came through the front door.

Harley experienced more of that groin tightening, and despite the possible situation involving his mom, he found himself smiling at Amelia.

"I didn't know you were coming to Rustler's Ridge today," he greeted, walking toward her.

Harley wanted to kiss her, but then that wasn't a new reaction. Nor was it one Amelia would appreciate. She didn't exactly keep their friends with benefits relationship a secret, but she didn't announce it to the world, either. Even though her folks knew she was seeing Harley, she wouldn't want them kissing in public and becoming fodder for gossip. Gossip that her parents wouldn't like one little bit.

The Wades might overlook their high-society-born daughter working for a cattle broker, but they wouldn't want their friends to know that she occasionally bedded a cowboy who'd been born on the wrong side of the sheets. That was why Amelia and he had adopted the saying of "what happens on Rustler's Ridge stays on Rustler's Ridge." That had worked out well for going on three years now, and Harley didn't want to stir up anything that would put an end to Amelia's visits or give her any grief with her snooty folks.

Amelia smiled, too. It wasn't quite as dazzling as usual, and she immediately hitched her thumb in the direction of the road that led to the ranch. "There's a reporter with a wide-angle-lens camera parked at the end of the road. Looks like he might be up to something."

Harley sighed, cursed under his breath. "Marty Jameson's staying here."

Amelia didn't seem surprised about that. Marty didn't often draw interest from the paparazzi, but there were occasional rabid fans who wanted to meet the former heartthrob. If the reporter didn't leave, Harley would need to have a chat with him. With Marty, too. But that would wait until after he'd figured out why Amelia had come.

She took off her sunglasses, hooking them over the neck

of her shirt, and she glanced around. "Is your mom here?" she asked.

So, this was business. Odd, though, that his mom hadn't mentioned it. Then again, if his mother had been preoccupied with pregnancy tests and her latest scumbag, then it might have slipped her mind.

"She's around somewhere," Harley said, going closer to Amelia.

Because he just wanted to touch her, he reached out and ran his fingers over her bunched-up forehead. He would have asked her what had given her those worry lines, but her phone rang. She pulled it from her pocket and muttered something he didn't catch. Not a happy muttering, either, but Harley thought that was possibly because her father's name, Patrick Wade, had popped up on the screen.

Harley saw the debate she had with herself about answering the call, but she finally hit the answer button. "No, I haven't found her," Amelia said without so much as a hello. "I'll get back to you if she's here."

Frowning at that, Harley waited for Amelia to end the call, and she looked at him. "My parents had a big argument, and my mother left," Amelia explained. "She might have come here."

That only deepened Harley's frown. Rustler's Ridge seemed like the last place in Texas where the old-money heiress Nadine Wade would go, but he went to the now empty reception desk to look through the reservations. They used computers for keeping info like that, but his mom also liked to keep an old-fashioned guest book that people signed. Other than Marty and a family in cabin number six, there were no other guests.

"If she's here, she didn't sign in," he relayed.

"She wouldn't have signed in," Amelia immediately verified. "It's possible she's with Marty Jameson."

Well, hell in a big-assed handbasket. Harley certainly hadn't expected to hear that. "They know each other?" He had to ask.

"Apparently," Amelia said on a heavy sigh.

For such a short answer, it carried a crap load of emotion. The wrong kind of emotion, too. Marty had plenty of fans, many of them about the same age as Nadine, but she sure didn't seem Marty's type. Then again, maybe Nadine had done some fan-girl slumming. Or perhaps she'd simply lost her mind, which seemed far more plausible to Harley than it did for Nadine to be voluntarily hooking up with Marty.

"You really believe your mom could be with Marty?" Harley pressed.

She shook her head, shrugged. "His name came up in the argument, and my dad seems to believe she left to come and see him. How long has Marty been here?" Amelia asked.

"About two weeks for this visit."

And before Amelia had shown up, Harley had been thinking that'd been enough time for Marty to knock up his mother, but it seemed a stretch for even Marty to impregnate one woman while keeping company with another. However, if anyone could manage that, it'd be Marty.

"I haven't seen any other cars headed toward his cabin, but I can call him so you can ask him about your mother. Or I can take you there," Harley offered.

"Take me there," she said after a couple of moments of hesitation.

Harley motioned for her to follow him, hoping this didn't lead to some big blowup between Nadine and Amelia, but before they even reached the door, Darla Givens, the receptionist, walked in.

As usual, Darla was dressed, well, like no one else in Lone Star Ridge with her pink poofy overalls, pink hair and, yeah, pink sandals. The woman gave a beaming grin to Amelia while she tugged off her—what else?—pink sparkly sunglasses.

"You're back," Darla said. "And I see you found Harley."

Harley didn't think it was his imagination that Amelia also hesitated before giving Darla a nod.

"Amelia came by earlier to see you, but you were still in your meeting," Darla added.

This time Amelia didn't just hesitate. She seemed to freeze, and she didn't look at him when she said, "We need to talk."

Harley had been about to say the same thing to Darla. Despite Liv's assurances about Darla not having a boyfriend, he wanted to ask her about the pregnancy test. Obviously, though, it would have to wait because Amelia clearly wanted to get out of there.

Darla wasn't exactly a gossip, but Harley understood why Amelia would want to keep it quiet that her mother might be in Marty's cabin. That was why Harley went ahead and led Amelia outside. The cabin wasn't far, only about a quarter of a mile from the main house, and it sat just off a tree-lined curvy dirt road. So with Amelia right by his side, Harley headed in that direction.

"I'm sorry you didn't get a chance to see me earlier," he said, giving her hand a gentle squeeze. "Obviously, this situation with your mother has shaken you up."

Amelia stopped, pulling her hand from his, and with her mouth already open as if ready to say something, she whirled around to face him.

But she didn't say anything.

After a few seconds, she groaned and squeezed her eyes shut. For the second time in the same day, he nearly had a heart attack when Amelia finally did speak and said what was on her mind.

"Harley, I think I'm pregnant with your baby."

CHAPTER TWO

AMELIA BRACED HERSELF for Harley's reaction. Which she was certain would be *bad*.

He had a right to be stunned and furious. After all, they'd practiced safe sex, and making a baby hadn't been on either of their radars. Yet, here they were, facing the real possibility that their noncomplicated relationship had just crossed over into a huge complicated zone.

"Say something," Amelia finally insisted, just to break the silence.

He nodded but still didn't speak. That was because he seemed to be gathering his breath and trying to shake off the stunned and furious reaction she'd been expecting. At the moment, though, there didn't appear to be any fury on his face, but he had the shocked look down pat.

And it made her realize that she'd never seen him like this.

Harley was usually rock steady. *Hot* rock steady with his rugged cowboy looks and laid-back ways. Which was why she'd been attracted to him in the first place. Troubles just seemed to slide off him. Unlike her. Amelia always felt wound too tight, always felt one step off from who she was supposed to be, but when she was with Harley, he had a way of keeping her level. She was hoping he could do that now.

First, though, he apparently had to level himself.

He tugged off his Stetson, wiping his forehead with his

arm and pushing the dark blond strands of hair away from his face. She always thought he looked more like some Viking god than a cowboy, but he was indeed the latter. A real honest-to-goodness cowboy. And he was wearing the championship rodeo buckle to prove it.

"The pregnancy test in the bathroom was yours," he finally managed to get out, after he swallowed hard.

Of all the things she'd expected he might say, that wasn't one of them. Amelia pulled back her shoulders and shook her head.

"Uh, no," she answered. She studied him a moment, trying to figure out if his comment was because he was in shock, but she didn't think it was that. "There was a pregnancy test in your bathroom?"

Good grief. She hoped there wasn't someone else out there who might be carrying his child. But she immediately rethought that. Harley wasn't the sort to sleep around. Neither was she. In fact, the only people they slept around with was each other, and that was one of the reasons their relationship was uncomplicated. That and because they didn't put demands on each other.

"Not in *my* bathroom," he corrected. "But in the one off reception." He paused, stared at her with his now intense brown eyes while he took in more of those long, steadying breaths. He looked as if she'd punched him in the gut, and in a way she had. What she'd just told him must have packed a wallop, and now the wallop was on top of the one he'd gotten from what he'd seen in the bathroom.

"So, whose test was it?" she pressed.

"Don't have a clue. Well, I actually have a clue," Harley amended. "Liv says it's not hers, so that leaves Mom and Darla as the most likely candidates. But Liv says Darla doesn't have a boyfriend."

Amelia didn't know about Darla's personal life, but she did know a little about his mother. Tracy had been a teenager when she'd had Harley, so it was possible she was still young enough to get pregnant. And it was sad that any gossipmonger who got wind of the pregnancy test in the bathroom would almost certainly jump right to that conclusion. Yes, Tracy seemed to gravitate toward men with less than stellar reputations. But that didn't mean Tracy was pregnant. Heck, even if she was, Amelia certainly wasn't in a position to judge her for it.

"Maybe one of the people staying at the ranch came in when Darla was at lunch and you were in your meeting," she suggested. If so, then this was the day for pregnancy scares and tests on Rustler's Ridge.

"You're really pregnant?" he asked. He still looked shocked, but he was coming out of it.

"I think I might be."

She groaned, and because she could no longer stand still, Amelia started walking. Not ideal weather for it, though, since the temps were already in the nineties and without so much as a stirring of a breeze.

"I've taken one of the home tests. It was negative, but I'm over a week late. I've never been late before," she added.

Both of them did more deep breathing, and she figured it was somewhat of a miracle that they both managed to keep taking steps toward Marty's cabin.

Harley was likely doing some mental math right about now. She certainly had when she'd first realized she was late. The last time they'd been together was exactly one month ago today. He'd come over to her house in Wrangler's Creek and had spent the night. As usual, the sex had been great. It always was with Harley. Also as usual, they'd used protection. Still, no form of birth control was 100 percent.

"I'll repeat the home test," she went on a moment later. "I also made an appointment with the doctor here in Lone Star Ridge for tomorrow since they didn't have any openings today. I couldn't go to my regular doctor because she's friends with my parents."

Of course, considering her parents' rift, they might not even tune in to any gossip about her. Which was something at least. They always seemed to be breathing down her back and judging her for the career she'd chosen. They would have preferred her having a job that required her to wear designer clothes. Or better yet, no job at all since they wanted her to be married to the "right" man.

Harley was in no way *right* in their eyes, but then her folks weren't right in his, either. He wasn't the sort to put up with their snooty insults and lofty expectations, and that was yet another reason why he suited Amelia.

"I'm sorry," Amelia continued a moment later. "I swear, I didn't mean for this to happen." She paused, nibbled on her bottom lip. "I considered not telling you until I was sure one way or the other. But I couldn't keep this to myself, and there wasn't anyone else I could talk to about it."

She hadn't realized that she was holding her breath until her lungs started to ache, but she was indeed waiting for Harley to tell her that everything would be okay, that they'd somehow get through this. In other words, she needed a miracle.

Harley glanced at her, groaned and then seemed to steel himself up. She was certain he would have attempted to give her that miracle or maybe some kind of reassurance, but someone called out to them.

Darla.

"Did you see your mom?" Darla asked, hurrying toward them.

Harley shook his head. "Where is she?"

Darla shook her head as well. "Not your mom. *Yours*," she said to Amelia.

"Uh, she's really here?" Amelia glanced around as if she expected her mother to materialize out of thin air.

"I think so. I mean, I've never actually met her, but I've seen her pictures a lot on the society pages and on social media. I'm pretty sure she drove by the main house a little while ago, just as I was taking my lunch break."

"She's with Marty," Amelia muttered under her breath.

She hadn't actually believed her mother would come here, but maybe she'd been wrong about that. It seemed too much of a coincidence that Darla would see someone resembling her mother on the very day that Amelia had reason to believe she'd come to the ranch. Of course, Amelia still didn't know why her mom would want to see Marty, but the singer's name had come up during the part of her parents' argument that she'd overheard.

"Thank you," Amelia managed to say to Darla, and she started walking toward the cabin area as the receptionist headed back to the main house.

"I think we both need at least a couple of minutes to wrap our heads around all of this," Harley said, taking hold of her hand.

By *this*, he probably hadn't meant her parents' argument. No. This was about the possible pregnancy. Amelia hated that she had done this to him. Hated that she'd done it to herself, too. Amazing sex evidently came with a price. A huge one that Harley and she might have to pay. But there was something that she hated even more. Part of her was actually a little thrilled at the possibility of having a child.

A part of her that she needed to tamp down.

Because this wasn't just about her and her thrilled parts. It was about Harley, and he'd told her too many times to count that he wasn't a family man. Which led her to something she needed to say to him.

"If I am pregnant, you don't have to do anything. I can raise the baby by myself." She said it just as she'd rehearsed it, but during her rehearsal, she hadn't anticipated seeing anything but relief on his face.

This wasn't relief.

His eyes narrowed a little. His mouth tightened. "We need to talk."

That didn't sound like the start of what would be a pleasant conversation, and Amelia nearly repeated that comment about her being able to raise the baby herself. But his steely expression stopped her. Apparently, they did indeed need to talk. Very soon. However, first she needed to find her mother.

"Marty's cabin," she reminded him, tipping her head in that direction.

The steel in Harley's expression remained. "If your mother's with Marty, you should put off seeing her. For now anyway." That didn't sound like a suggestion, either. "We need to talk," he repeated. "And we can go to my place to do that."

Harley tried to get her moving toward the road that led to his house, but Amelia held her ground. "I just need you to hear me when I say that I don't expect anything from you."

He stared at her. Nope, that was a glare. And then Harley leaned in and kissed her.

Amelia didn't know who was more surprised. With all his usual finesse, which was plentiful, his mouth moved over hers as if he were claiming every inch of her. That wasn't unusual. Harley always gave it his all when he kissed her. But normally those kisses were the beginning of foreplay that would lead them straight to bed. Nothing about this could be foreplay. Or hot.

But it was.

Mercy, it was.

She wasn't sure why Harley had always been able to make her body zing and turn her mind to mush, but he was proving that he still had that ability despite their situation.

He didn't stop with just a kiss, either. He hooked his arm around her waist, pulled her to him and added some delicious body to body contact. It should have reminded her that such contact wasn't a good thing when they had something so important to hash out. But it felt so good to be in his arms. To have him hold her like this. To have his mouth on hers.

She could feel her nerves settle. Could feel herself melting into him.

Again, not good.

A month ago, this would have been yet another amazing start to some great sex, but at this moment it was a deflection and a distraction that they didn't need. Even though it took great effort on her part, Amelia mustered up every ounce of willpower and tore her mouth from his.

"Why did you do that?" she managed to ask. Of course, since she didn't have much breath left in her body, it came out not as a demand but rather a silky whisper. Very much like the way she whispered things when they were in bed.

Harley didn't hesitate. "To remind you of how we got into this position in the first place."

She was about to tell him that she needed no such reminder and that the kiss in no way helped this discussion they needed to have. However, Amelia didn't have time to say anything because someone cleared their throat, and it caused them to whirl in the direction of the sound.

"Uh, this might not be any of my beeswax, but this isn't exactly a private place for you two to make out," Liv commented.

Liv was already close, very close, and Amelia had no idea how she'd gotten just a couple of feet away without either of them hearing Harley's sister's approach. Of course, it was hard to hear much of anything with her pulse throbbing in her ears and the rest of her body buzzing from the heat the kiss had caused.

Since Amelia didn't have a comeback for Liv, she waited for Harley to respond. "You're right. It's not any of your beeswax."

Liv slid suspicious glances between the two of them, and Amelia hoped that in addition to witnessing the scalding kiss that Liv hadn't also heard any of the conversation about the possible pregnancy.

"Something you want to tell me?" Liv asked, her right eyebrow winging up.

Amelia sighed. Obviously, Liv knew about the test that Harley had found in the garbage can, and even if she hadn't heard that part of the conversation, Liv wasn't stupid. She could put one and one together. However, in this case, the one and one didn't lead to Amelia.

"No, there's absolutely nothing I want to tell you," Harley insisted.

That didn't appease Liv because she simply shifted her attention and her still raised eyebrow to Amelia. Amelia would have given her a nicer version of what Harley had said, but she didn't get the chance. That was because Amelia spotted Marty coming up the road toward them.

It'd been over a year since Amelia had seen him and that'd been on one of his trips back to Lone Star Ridge. He'd been in the diner when Harley and she had gone in for breakfast. Even though Marty was in his sixties, she could still see the "been there, done that" hot rocker looks that had no doubt attracted many women over the years.

Maybe had even attracted her own mother.

It was hard to imagine the prim and proper Nadine hooking up with Marty, but the man's name had definitely come up during her parents' argument.

"Ah," Marty said with a sheepish smile. "You're here."

It took Amelia a moment to realize the comment was aimed at her. "Have you seen my mother?" she asked.

Marty smiled again in a way that she figured most would consider "good ol' boy charming," but it didn't charm her one little bit. Amelia got a knot in her stomach. Correction—the knot that was already there tightened as if multiple fists and wrenches had been applied to it. Along with her parents' argument and the pregnancy bombshell she'd had to deliver to Harley, this day definitely wasn't going well.

"Nadine's in my cabin," Marty admitted. "I ran out of coffee, so I thought I'd bum some off that cute receptionist."

So, it was true. Nadine had come to Marty. "Do you want to tell me why my mother came to see you?"

Marty didn't hesitate. "That should come from her." He started walking toward the main house.

"And what about my mother?" Harley asked, causing Marty to stop.

Marty eyed him, and Amelia thought the man might be trying to suss out exactly what Harley meant by that question. Unless Marty knew about the pregnancy test in the bathroom, though, he probably wouldn't make the connection between Tracy and the hard stare that Harley was now giving him.

"She's with Nadine," Marty answered after several crawling moments.

"Mom's in your cabin with Amelia's mother?" Liv sounded as stunned by that as Amelia was.

With good reason.

Nadine and Tracy weren't friends. In fact, the only encounter that Amelia remembered the women having was when Nadine came to Rustler's Ridge to see if she could convince Tracy to run some interference in Amelia's relationship with Harley. Tracy hadn't taken the bait on that, and even though Amelia wasn't sure exactly what had been said in that particular conversation, she doubted it'd been pleasant for either woman.

Marty nodded in response to Liv's question. "I think it'd be a good idea to give them some time. They're talking."

Harley, Liv and Amelia all just gaped at him, and Amelia figured the three of them were on the same thought page. She couldn't imagine what Tracy and her mother had to discuss.

Unless...

Oh, God. Was it possible her mother had learned about the pregnancy scare? Amelia didn't live at home, hadn't for years now, but her mom had a key to her house in Wrangler's Creek. If Nadine had gone snooping, she might have found the pregnancy test or the note that Amelia had scribbled about her appointment time with the doctor in Lone Star Ridge. It wouldn't have taken much digging to figure out that the doctor was an ob-gyn.

The anger rolled through Amelia, a low simmering boil because once again her mother might have stuck her nose where it didn't belong. Not only was she going to have it out with her mom, she was also going to change the locks on her doors so there wouldn't be other surprise visits.

Amelia started toward the cabin, not caring if she interrupted the chat time that Marty seemed to think the women needed. Liv and Marty stayed put, but Harley hurried to keep up with her while calling out to Marty.

"There's a paparazzo at the end of the road," Harley told

Marty. "You need to take care of it." Then he turned his attention back to Amelia. "I can see the fire in your eyes. Maybe it's not a good time to see your mother."

"She might know about the pregnancy," Amelia spat out.

He nodded right away, so obviously he'd come to the same conclusion. Of course, Harley had personally witnessed one of her mother's impromptu visits when Nadine had dropped by unannounced while Harley had still been in her bed.

"Just hold up a second," Harley said, taking hold of her arm. Despite her huff, he turned her to face him. "Maybe we should settle some things between us first before you tackle dealing with your mother." When she gave him a blank stare, he added, "We have to do the right thing, Amelia."

"The right thing?" she repeated. "And what exactly would that be?"

"Simple." Harley shrugged. "We need to get married."

CHAPTER THREE

"Wh-what?" Amelia stuttered out.

Harley watched as the color drained from her face, letting him know that she hadn't been expecting his offer of marriage. Of course, maybe it had something to do with the way he'd worded it. In hindsight, it had sounded more like a demand than a proposal.

"Will you marry me?" he amended.

That didn't help her regain her color, but she did start shaking her head before she even spoke. "You can't marry me just because I might be pregnant."

That wasn't the only reason, no. Harley wasn't one to explore his feelings, but he knew he cared for Amelia. *Deeply* cared for her. And he hadn't been with another woman in years, not since Amelia and he had become lovers. Maybe that wasn't enough for her to say yes and deal with the criticism she'd almost certainly get from her parents. Still, they were adults, and he could see himself making a life with her.

The question, though, was could she make a life with him?

Apparently, Amelia had no intentions of answering his proposal right now. "We can discuss this later," she insisted.

Crap. Yeah, he'd messed up all right. He should have laid some groundwork first before popping the question. He should have emphasized the pros of them getting married. But for him to be able to do that, he had to come up with a pro that didn't involve a baby or those deep feelings for her. Amelia would want more.

A hell of a lot more.

And she deserved it, too.

She'd want, well, love and other stuff. He groaned and wanted to punch himself in the face. The fact that he could tack on *and other stuff* with a big-assed word like *love* meant that he needed to have a serious sit-down with himself to figure out how to get his head screwed back on straight.

"Later," Amelia emphasized, and she started walking again toward the cabin that Marty was renting.

The moment the cabin came into sight, the front door opened, and his mother and Nadine stepped out onto the porch. Even though they were still a good twenty feet away, Harley could feel the thick tension in the air. Tension that he didn't believe had anything to do with Amelia's possible pregnancy or his botched marriage proposal.

What the devil was going on?

Whatever it was, he was positive he didn't want to deal with it right now. Especially since he hadn't gotten his stomach un-clenched over hearing Amelia's baby news. But apparently babies, marriage proposals and personal conversations were going to have to wait because Amelia made a beeline for the porch.

Harley didn't have to guess if Nadine was happy to see her daughter. She wasn't. The woman gave a weary sigh and folded her arms over her chest in a defensive position.

"Why are you here?" Amelia demanded, looking just as defensive as her mom. "What happened between Dad and you?"

Those questions didn't help with Nadine's attitude, and she expressed some of that disapproval by aiming a glare at Harley before she shifted her attention back to her daughter.

"I came here to think," Nadine snapped, which really didn't explain much of anything. There were plenty of places more suitable for someone in her economic bracket.

"You're in Marty's cabin," Amelia pointed out. She matched her mom's snappish tone. "Why?"

Nadine opened her mouth, made a sound of frustration and shook her head. "I plan to stay here for a day or two to work some things out. Not *here here* with Marty," she amended. "But at the ranch. Tracy has a cabin for me to rent."

Harley looked at his own mother to see what her take on this was, but she only lifted her shoulder in a gesture that could have meant anything.

"Marty said you two had to talk," Harley relayed, sliding his gaze between Nadine and his mother. "Care to share the topic of conversation with Amelia and me?"

Apparently, the answer was "no" because the women exchanged a glance and promptly followed it up with double head shakes. That sure as heck didn't please Amelia, who huffed and stormed closer as she looked her mother straight in the eyes.

"What the heck is going on?" Amelia demanded.

Nadine didn't keep the direct eye contact with her daughter. Nope. Instead, the woman dropped her gaze to Amelia's stomach, and it was as effective as a mountain-sized red flag. Hell's bells. Nadine knew about the possible pregnancy.

No way would Harley confirm or deny anything. Doling out that info to Nadine was Amelia's call. However, he did motion for his mother to join him in the yard so he could ask her about the pee stick he'd found. It took a second motion of his hand before Tracy finally started walking toward him—slowly and with much hesitation.

"Excuse us a second," Harley said to Nadine and Amelia.

He didn't want Amelia to have to face Nadine's possible wrath alone, so he'd keep this short.

"There was a pregnancy test in the bathroom by your office," he whispered to Tracy once she was in front of him.

Considering the fact that Tracy had been here chatting with Nadine, Harley had to consider that his mom knew about Amelia possibly being pregnant. He wasn't sure what Tracy's reaction would be to that or to the test itself.

But what he saw on her face was shock.

Tracy's eyes widened, and she made a shivery sound as she sucked in her breath. Of course, that shock could be because he'd just discovered her secret.

"Liv," she managed to eke out.

"No," Harley quickly assured her. "It's not hers." He paused, studying her expression to see if there was even a whiff of BS going on here. There wasn't. "You really don't know who put it there?"

Tracy didn't look back at Amelia, which made him believe that she wasn't privy to Nadine's stomach-glancing suspicions. "No."

Harley pushed a little harder, wanting to make sure he'd gotten to the bottom of this as far as his mother was concerned. "The test I found in the bathroom wasn't yours? You're not pregnant?"

The burst of air that left her mouth was a sort of laugh, the kind a person made when they'd just heard something stupid to beat all stupid. It was a welcome sound for Harley, and while it didn't clear up who'd left the pee stick, it meant he didn't have to worry about his mother becoming a mom for the third time.

"You found a pregnancy test in the bathroom?" Nadine asked, getting Harley's complete attention. His mother's, too, because they both turned in Nadine's direction.

Crap.

Nadine knew something about it. Harley could hear it in every word of her question. Amelia saw it as well because she stepped back while glaring at her mother.

"What do you know about that test?" Amelia demanded.

Nadine didn't get defensive, but her mouth did tighten a little before she said, "I found it in your house, and I brought it here to confront you." She paused, probably because of the look on Amelia's face. "After I got here, I realized it wasn't a good time for a confrontation, so I tossed it in the trash in the bathroom. I didn't know anyone would actually see it."

"You're pregnant?" Tracy asked.

"To be determined," Amelia answered without looking at her. She kept her narrow-eyed gaze nailed to Nadine. "It wasn't a good time for you to snoop in my house," Amelia spelled out, her words clipped and raw. "In fact, there's never a good time for that."

Nadine nodded as if that'd been exactly the reaction she'd expected. "This is another reason I didn't want to confront you. I knew it'd turn into a big blowup, and I don't have the mental energy for it right now."

No mental energy? Well, that was a first. Nadine hadn't had any trouble in the past mustering up enough snootiness to blast Harley for being in Amelia's life. And in her bed. Now that he'd maybe gotten Amelia pregnant, he would have thought Nadine would come at him with every snooty weapon in her arsenal. But nope. Which meant there was something hellish bad going on here. And it obviously had something to do with Marty, or else Nadine wouldn't be at the ranch.

"You're maybe pregnant?" Tracy pressed again while she nibbled on her bottom lip and studied Amelia.

Amelia groaned. She was obviously still battling the temper demon that her mother had sprung loose. "I won't know until I see the doctor tomorrow."

His mother seemed to go through a couple of stages of re-action. A little shaky at first, but by the time she started nod-ding, he thought there was some acceptance in there, too. Of course, the acceptance might end when she found out that he'd proposed to Amelia. His mother liked Amelia well enough, but she wasn't blind to the trouble that Nadine would likely cause for him on a daily basis if he became the woman's son-in-law.

"Okay, now that we've got that cleared up," Harley said, "I'd appreciate it if one of you told Amelia and me what's going on."

Tracy and Nadine exchanged another volley of those glances, and Harley didn't think it was his imagination that they were trying to mentally suss out what to spill or maybe how to spill it.

"The truth," he added. "The whole truth. We're past the point of doling out any half-assed answers."

Dragging in a long breath, Nadine nodded and turned not toward him but Amelia. "A few months ago, I came here to talk to Tracy about how displeased I was about you seeing Harley. I thought Tracy could help convince Harley to end things."

Oh, the anger came. Really bad pissed-off anger. But Harley knew this shouldn't surprise him. Nadine would always see him as low and as useless as hoof grit. Even if she didn't have a clue what hoof grit was.

"I told Nadine I wouldn't interfere," Tracy jumped in to say, probably because she saw the venom in Harley's eyes and didn't want it aimed at her.

"All right," he said because he believed her, but he made a circling motion with his index finger for Nadine to continue with her explanation.

She did, after the longest pause in the history of long pauses. "When I came here to talk to Tracy, I met Marty." Her forehead bunched up, and her mouth twisted as if she'd tasted something sour. "I'd had I guess you could call an infatuation with him, the way you do sometimes with celebrities, so I was…dazzled to meet him in person."

"Dazzled?" Amelia prompted when her mother didn't add anything else.

Nadine nodded. "Marty can be quite charming."

Harley groaned, and he wondered how many women had fallen for that charm. The man certainly had a knack for separating women from their panties.

"You had an affair with Marty Jameson?" Amelia asked. It wasn't anger in her voice. Nope, this was pure shock.

"No. Not an affair," Nadine insisted. "A single dazzle-induced indiscretion. I got caught up in his whole celebrity status."

That was snooty code for a one-night stand, something that Marty had no doubt had plenty of, but Harley figured it was the first and only time for Nadine.

"Did Dad find out?" Amelia asked. The shock was fading, and in its place came plenty of concern.

After another of those excruciatingly long pauses, Nadine nodded. As if she'd turned on a tap, her eyes filled with tears. "Yes. Someone told him, A 'fan' of Marty's." She put *fan* in air quotes, and her expression turned bitter. "Apparently, that fan also happened to be staying here at the ranch, and she snapped some pictures of Marty and me as we were coming out of his cabin."

"The fan sent the pictures to Amelia's father," Tracy filled in after making a sound of frustration. "Nadine doesn't know why the fan waited several months before doing that, but Patrick got them in an email."

So, that explained her parents' argument. However, it didn't explain why Nadine had come to Marty today. Or how she'd been able to get in touch with him. Marty didn't always broadcast his whereabouts to just anyone, including members of his own family.

"I was afraid this fan would try to blackmail Marty," Nadine went on, "so I called him. He'd given me his personal number after, well, after. I came here to talk to him in person."

Since Amelia didn't look too steady on her feet, Harley slipped his arm around her waist.

"Oh, God," Nadine said, touching her fingers to her trembling mouth. And she repeated that a couple of times before she blurted out, "Your dad is talking about divorcing me."

AMELIA PACED ACROSS the guest cabin that she'd rented for the night. Since it wasn't a big space, it didn't take her long to get from one side to the other. Too bad, because it might have helped her burn off some of this restless, angry energy if she could pace to the point of exhaustion.

When she'd left her place that morning in Wrangler's Creek, she'd thought the worst of what she would have to face would be Harley's reaction to her possibly being pregnant. If she had just stayed home to wait for her doctor's appointment, she wouldn't have run into her mother. Wouldn't have had the triple whammy of a possible baby, her mother's affair and her parents' divorce.

But maybe the divorce fell into the *possible* category, too.

There was no way to know since her father wasn't answering his phone. Knowing him, though, he was probably doing some cleanup, making sure that the pictures of Marty and Nadine didn't make it to social media. Or fixing things so that the photos didn't lead to some kind of blackmail to keep them secret.

Amelia froze when there was a knock at her cabin door. She definitely didn't want to go another round with her mother, and she didn't want to see Tracy, either. But it was Harley who called out to her.

"It's me," he said.

She wasn't sure she wanted to see him, either, but she couldn't shut him out. Some women went through pregnancy alone. Not her, though, unless it was absolutely necessary. If she was indeed carrying Harley's child, he would be as much of a part of that as he wanted.

Judging from his marriage proposal, he wanted to be a large part.

More likely, though, he had popped the question out of duty and without thinking it through. Harley was a decent man, but she didn't want him pressured into doing something that could ultimately sour their friendship and make him resent her. Or worse, resent the baby.

Amelia opened the door, surprised that it was already dark outside. She'd closed the blinds and curtains, and she hadn't once noticed the time. Not with so many thoughts and worries stewing in her head. One look at Harley's face, though, and she realized he'd had his own worry stew going on.

The moment he was inside, Harley immediately pulled her into his arms for a hug. Thirty seconds ago, she wouldn't have thought she needed such a thing, that a hug couldn't have helped. But it did. It soothed some of her jangled nerves, and judging from the way his muscles relaxed, she thought that maybe it did the same for him.

"Sorry that I didn't come by sooner," he said, shutting the door behind him. "But I had some things to take care of. Besides, I thought you could use the alone time."

Oh, yes. She'd needed these hours to herself. Too bad she didn't feel any better about things, but at least no one else had had to put up with her gloom and doom mood.

"I talked to Marty," he went on, and he led her to the

kitchen, where he had her sit down at the table. He snagged two bottles of water from the fridge and took the seat next to her. "He's had a chat with the fan who took the pictures of him and your mom. She promised to give him the photos and not send them to anyone else."

That was indeed progress. "How'd Marty manage to get her to agree to that?"

Harley shrugged, and the corner of his mouth lifted into a quick smile, causing a dimple to flash in his cheek. "The man's got charm."

"Apparently so, if he could talk my mother into bed." A reminder that added only another gallon of gloom and doom to her mood.

Good grief. Her mom had slept with Marty Jameson, the man who supposedly went through lovers as frequently as many people changed their sheets. When her mom had fallen from her snooty tower, she'd fallen long, hard and fast. Along with forgetting that she was a married woman.

"Yeah," Harley agreed, as if he'd known exactly what Amelia was thinking. "The fan said she sent the pictures to your father because she thought it would cause trouble for your mother. She was jealous and didn't want Marty seeing Nadine again. But when Marty pressed the fan, she admitted that she hoped your father would be willing to pay for the pictures."

"He might have done that," Amelia agreed, but then she paused. "But he could also use them if there's a divorce."

A divorce. Something she'd been trying to wrap her mind around for hours. Obviously, her mother hadn't wanted to end her marriage or have a possible life with Marty or she would have told her husband what she'd done. Her mom had tried to keep it a secret. But now that the secret was out of the proverbial bag, that meant the divorce decision rested with her father.

"My parents aren't overly affectionate with each other," Amelia admitted, "but I didn't expect their marriage to end. I didn't think either of them would want to go through the scandal of a divorce. And they might not. My father might overlook a *single dazzle-induced indiscretion* just to avoid gossip."

Of course, that was provided the gossip wasn't already out there. Amelia wasn't sure just how effective Marty's pact with this fan would be.

Harley reached out, sliding his hand over hers. "FYI, your mother is still against us being together. Yeah," he verified when Amelia groaned. "Apparently, Nadine still thinks she has the right to judge us. She said something along the lines of she didn't want you using what she'd done to make a bad decision." He flashed another quick smile. "Guess I'm the bad decision."

Like the hug, the smile actually helped, and Amelia found herself smiling, too. Not in a happy rah-rah kind of way, but one more of resignation. Harley didn't deserve her mother's condemnation.

"I'm sorry," Amelia said, her voice filled with the emotion that she'd been battling all day.

No smile this time. Harley just gave a heavy sigh and stood, pulling her back to her feet and straight into his arms. She thought he might give her a lecture to try to convince her that there was no reason for her to be sorry.

But instead he kissed her.

His mouth came to hers, and she immediately felt the warm jolt of pleasure. Heat mixed with need. It was there even after all the years they'd been together. No kiss from Harley ever felt ordinary or like the same old move. And as it always did, it sent her body into overdrive.

This was so much better than a lecture on many levels, and the heat from his mouth leveled her, revved her up and sent her flying. Then he deepened the kiss and made her legs go weak.

She wanted to know how he managed to give her so much pleasure by using only his mouth. Of course, she couldn't figure it out because he didn't just keep the contact lip to lip. Tightening his grip around her waist, he angled them so they were hip to hip as well. All in all, it was an amazing fit of his body against hers.

"You're trying to convince me to say yes to your marriage proposal," she managed to say, mumbling the words against his mouth.

He pulled back a little and flexed his eyebrows. "Obviously, I wasn't doing it right if that's what you got from the kiss."

Amelia couldn't help herself. She smiled. "Oh, you did it right," she assured him. "You always do it right."

Now those flexed eyebrows turned a little cocky. "Always?" he drawled. Then, as if to claim that particular title, he kissed her again.

Since her body was already heated up to the point of scalding, she was the one to pull him back to her. Chest to chest this time. And she did some kiss deepening of her own. Part of her knew she should be trying to keep some distance between them so she could think with a clear head, but this was a heck of a lot more fun than thinking.

And that fun had led her to possibly being pregnant.

The reminder did stop her because this felt as if she was leading him on. Of course, he was likely trying to coax her to bed so he could finish this kissing the right way along with getting her to say yes to his proposal. But Amelia wasn't ready for either of those things. Not with the pregnancy test looming over their heads.

When she eased back from him, she saw that Harley understood that bed coaxing wasn't going to happen tonight. He wasn't upset. Not even frustrated. Okay, maybe he was a little frustrated. She certainly was, and her body was trying to nudge her into stepping right back into his arms. However, he gave her a chaste kiss.

"I'll get us something to eat from the café," Harley offered, "and we can talk if you want."

She did want to talk. Amelia could feel every nerve in her body, and the one person who could help ease all that hot tension inside her was Harley.

A knock on the door had them both groaning at the interruption, but Amelia soon heard something else that alerted her that there'd likely be a lot more groans to come.

Her mother.

"Amelia," her mother said, and it was obvious she was crying. No, not just crying, but rather sobbing. Loud, hiccupping wet sobs punctuated with more knocks on the door. "Let me in, please."

Even without the rare *please*, Amelia wouldn't have just ignored her. But that was what she wanted to do. Mercy, did she. Her mother wasn't on her good side right now, considering that she'd gone snooping in her house.

Harley stayed back when she went to the door and opened it. Her mother practically threw herself into Amelia's arms. Nadine blurted out something through the sobs, something that Amelia couldn't decipher, but apparently Harley figured it out.

"Your father," Harley muttered, coming closer.

Swiping away tears, Nadine nodded, and with sob-filled breaths, she said, "Your father went through with it. He filed for a divorce."

CHAPTER FOUR

HARLEY TRIED TO throw himself into work, and it wasn't as if he didn't have plenty to do. He'd already moved some of the horses to the back pasture and drawn up the monthly work schedule for the hands, but he wasn't sure if he'd done either of those things well. Because his mind kept straying back to one thing.

Well, two actually.

Amelia and a possible baby.

Their baby. And no matter how many times he mentally repeated that, it caused his worries to soar. He hadn't exactly had a good role model in the father department. Or the mother department for that matter.

The notion of fatherhood seemed overwhelming in a good/bad kind of way. Good because it'd be Amelia's and his son or daughter. Bad because he wasn't sure how Amelia would react to a positive test result. Or even a negative one. Either way the test turned out, she could decide to end things with him and make a fresh start.

Amelia hadn't wanted him to go with her to her doctor's appointment, and Harley had respected her wishes. Waiting, however, was a bitch, and that was why he'd decided to work while he waited. That way, he wouldn't be under the prying eyes of his mother, Liv, Darla or any guest who happened to show up if he'd gone into his office at the main house.

Harley had just about convinced his body to go off high

alert and give his worries a rest when he heard a truck pull up in front of his place. He saw Amelia through the front window, and the high alert returned with a few of its friends to add to the level of intensity.

As she walked toward the porch, he examined her face, looking for any clues, but he saw only the fatigue and worry. He opened the front door, and she kept on walking until she was right in his arms. All in all, that was the best place possible.

"I don't have the test results yet," she immediately said and sort of sagged against him. "The doctor put a rush on it at the lab, and he's going to call me."

So, another wait, but Harley figured this one would be easier on him because Amelia was there. Now he needed to make sure it was easier on her as well.

"Are you okay?" he asked.

Amelia didn't answer, but she eased back, looked up at him. "Are *you* okay?" she repeated.

He could give her this. The reassurance that he wanted her to have. So he smiled, nodded and kissed her. He wasn't sure which of those three things had helped to relieve the troubled look on her face. Maybe it was the combination of all of them, but at least her forehead wasn't bunched up as much when he pulled back and studied her.

"I'm okay," he verified. "And we'll both be all right no matter how this turns out."

He had to believe that. Wanted her to believe it, too.

Harley didn't push on his marriage proposal and instead went with a reliable way of giving a "get out of here" shove to the rest of her worried expression. He kissed her again. It obviously wasn't a chore for him. Kissing Amelia never was. But it sure felt as if they both needed this more than usual.

This time when he started to move back, Amelia caught

on to him, grabbing a handful of the front of his shirt and pulling him back to her. Judging by the look in her eyes, he kissed her again, and this time with some of his own tension gone, he felt that slide of heat that only Amelia could give him.

And what a nice slide it was.

It went straight from her mouth to the parts of him that wanted to make this a whole lot more interesting. Of course, one particular part of him believed that *interesting* was just another word for sex. Thankfully, the rest of him knew that foreplay would make that slide of heat even better.

Amelia made a sound of pleasure when he deepened the kiss. It was music to his ears not just because it meant she was aroused but also because she wasn't going to let a possible pregnancy stop her from enjoying this.

But it gave Harley a mental stop.

Was it okay for a pregnant woman to have sex? It had to be. Either that or there'd be a lot of horny pregnant women and their partners in the world. He dwelled on that for another couple of moments, until Amelia pressed her hand to his stomach and moved her kissing to his neck.

Harley forgot all about horny pregnant women and test results. He possibly forgot how to speak. He didn't test that theory because he decided to use his mouth to make Amelia as crazy as he already was.

He went after her neck, too, and he didn't make nice with his hands. They went after her breasts, which he knew from experience were two of her prime hot zones. Forgoing her kisses on his own neck, he dropped lower so he could put his mouth on her nipples. They were hard and pressed against her shirt.

This time her moan of desire was a lot louder, and as he'd

known she would do, she surrendered to it. Her head rolled back while she soaked up the pleasure he was giving her.

Soon, though, shirt kisses just weren't enough. The fire kicked up a flame or two, which urged him to go for skin to skin. Harley shoved up her shirt, pushed down her bra and put his tongue to good use on her puckered nipples.

Her next groan had an edge of urgency to it, and she fisted her hand in his hair, anchoring him against her breasts while her other hand dropped to his butt. No anchoring there. She gave him a push, aligning them in the best possible way. With his erection right in the vee of her thighs.

"I want you now," she demanded, "and don't you dare say no."

If he'd been able to speak—which was still to be determined—there was zero chance that a no would come out of his mouth. Especially not with her right nipple still rolling around on his tongue.

Amelia clearly meant that *now* part because she started walking him backward toward his bedroom. This was familiar ground for both of them. They'd had sex plenty of times at his place, in his bed, but this seemed…different. As if they had been on a severe sex diet and were now breaking the fast. Harley felt starved for her.

They made it to his bedroom with only minimal bruising. A hazard that came with walking, groping and kissing at the same time.

Oh, and with Amelia unzipping him and sliding her hand down into his jeans and onto his erection.

He nearly got a concussion from that when he banged his head on the doorjamb. The injury was totally worth it, though, because the pleasure that spiked through him could have gotten him through any pain. Heck, it could have gotten him through major surgery.

Since Amelia was still driving the motion train, she pushed him onto the bed and quickly followed on top of him.

"Don't say no," she repeated, rising above him and stripping off her top and bra.

Harley figured this was a sort of sexual sign language, his way of saying yes, and he unzipped her jeans and did a turnabout fair play. He dipped his hand down into her panties. Into her. And got the reward of her loud moan of pleasure along with some creative profanity.

He smiled. It was one of the things he liked about this cowgirl with the silver-spoon roots. She had a dirty mouth when he stroked sensitive parts of her. Well, one specific sensitive part anyway.

She *tolerated* his strokes for a few moments before horny Amelia emerged and went after him. He'd seen this transformation many, many times, and it never got old. Using that dirty mouth to whisper equally dirty suggestions, she tugged at his clothes. Fast and urgent. Wild. Begging him to hurry. If he hadn't already been hard as stone, seeing that kind of need in her would have done the trick.

Harley hurried, helping her shimmy out of her jeans. Her, helping him peel off his shirt. Fast and furious didn't mean, though, that he couldn't take in the sights. And what a sight it was. Amelia had an amazing body. All those curves. All that soft skin.

He got in a few more fondles before she leaned over to get a condom from his nightstand drawer. Thankfully, just doing that didn't give her a safe-sex flash that would cause her to think of those looming test results. Her putting on the condom was rote. Their routine.

But there was nothing routine when she took hold of his erection and guided it into her.

They could do this a million times, more, and it would

still give him that crazy mix of scalding pleasure and send him soaring to new heights. He was never sure how she managed that, but he was thankful for it.

Amelia liked being on top, which suited him just fine because it gave him the chance to watch her while she rode him. Her hair was loose now, the long dark locks shifting and spilling onto her breasts as her body moved with the thrusts. She wouldn't take long, he knew. Couldn't. Something this intense just didn't have a long shelf life and would burn out fast. The good side to that was they could usually have a slower, second round after they caught their breaths.

For now, though, Harley didn't want his breath. He only wanted Amelia and those long, deep thrusts that slid over his erection. Squeezing him. Torturing him. Until he finally felt her release. The torture kicked up another fiery notch as her climax caused her muscles to contract, squeeze and coax him to the only place he wanted to go. He got off right along with Amelia.

With her breath gusting and her face flushed, she took a moment before she leaned down and kissed him. "Please don't tell me you regret us doing that," she murmured against his mouth.

Finally, Harley rediscovered his vocal abilities and said the one word she'd been telling him not to say. "No."

AMELIA HAD TOLD Harley not to regret them having sex. And she'd meant it. She didn't want him having any regrets.

But she certainly did.

Sex had a way of clouding judgment at a time when Harley and she needed every shred of judgment they could get. If she was pregnant, then she needed to be thinking about the future. And figuring out a way to turn down his marriage proposal without crushing him. She cared for Harley, maybe even loved him, but she didn't want him to be locked into a marriage for the sake of a child.

Of course, that judgment-clouding reminder hadn't stopped Amelia from having shower sex with Harley.

She could curse herself now for lapsing into that, but at the time it'd seemed necessary. It was strange how often things felt necessary with Harley.

She'd just finished putting her clothes back on when her phone rang, and Amelia practically sprained her wrist yanking it from her pocket. It got Harley's complete attention, too, and he stopped in mid-zip to look at the phone with her. They both groaned when they saw that it wasn't her doctor's name on the screen.

It was her mother.

Unable to deal with the woman right now, she pressed the decline button. Just as someone knocked on the door.

She wouldn't put it past her mother to have already been on the porch when she made the call, and while Amelia couldn't hit a decline button for a knock, she could ignore it. Or rather she could have if the knock hadn't turned to a pounding that seemed to shake the door.

"Amelia, it's me," someone called out.

This time Harley and she didn't groan. They cursed instead. Because it was her father, Patrick.

Even though she wasn't especially pleased with his visit, Amelia did want to get his side of the story of this breakup with her mom. She glanced in the mirror long enough to run a hand through her mussed hair, and even though she looked as if she'd just had shower sex, she still went to the door to answer it.

Her father didn't look as if he'd been having a good day, either. There were bags under his eyes, probably from lack of sleep, and his suit was wrinkled. He also hadn't shaved in a day or two. Or combed his hair. In a contest of which one of them looked more disheveled, her dad would win.

"Harley," her father said, looking over her shoulder.

"Mr. Wade," Harley greeted back.

There wasn't any friendliness in either of their tones. Just as there hadn't been the one and only other time they'd met. That'd been at Amelia's house when her father had dropped by one morning for a surprise visit. But he'd been the one to get the surprise when Harley had come out of her bedroom wearing just his boxers. Other than a cool nod and an indifferent hello, her father hadn't said anything else to Harley before he'd excused himself and told her that he'd call before he came over the next time.

Unlike her mother, her dad most likely hadn't made any snooping trips to her place where he could have uncovered pregnancy tests.

"Your mother told you what's going on?" her dad asked, and then he walked into the house invited.

Amelia nodded but didn't shut the door. If her father started yelling, which was a strong possibility, she was going to get him out of Harley's place. She might have still had some afterglow from two rounds of great sex, but her fun meter for other stuff—like her parents' baggage—was at an all-time low.

"She slept with that singer," her father added, making Marty's career title sound like an unidentified fungus.

Amelia had been about to nod again, but then her father flung his hand in the direction of Harley's small front yard. That was when she saw Marty standing there. It was amazing, but he managed to look charming even though there was nothing for him to be charming about.

"I tried to explain to Patrick that I was only with Nadine one time," Marty volunteered.

"That's like saying you're a little bit pregnant," her father grumbled, and when his narrowed gaze came back to hers, she realized someone, probably her mother, had ratted her out.

Amelia didn't need to ask how he felt about possibly becoming a grandfather. He didn't approve of Harley and her. But before she could borrow Liv's word and tell her father that Harley was none of his beeswax, she heard another voice.

Her mother.

"Oh, God," Nadine frantically called out. "You two aren't going to fight, are you?"

Since her father and Marty weren't anywhere close to each other, Amelia thought that possibility was jumping the gun, but there was some venom in her father's eyes. She wasn't sure if that was because Harley might have gotten her pregnant or because of Marty. Maybe it was both. Patrick Wade wasn't used to having his perfect world getting a kick in the butt.

"I should punch him," Patrick snarled, turning to face Marty.

Marty held up his hands in what might have been a charming surrender, but then he shrugged. "It seems to me, though, that you should punch yourself for not paying more attention to an attractive woman like Nadine. She wouldn't have strayed had she been happy at home."

"Ah, hell," Harley cursed, summing up completely how Amelia felt. For such a charmer, Marty was clearly an idiot, and he'd just thrown word gasoline on a blaze created by a *single dazzle-induced indiscretion*.

"Excuse me?" her father said, which was man-code for you're about to get your ass whipped.

Marty, who was perhaps accustomed to men trying to

kick his ass, adjusted his hands. No more gesture of surrender. He waggled his fingers in a challenge.

"Hell," Harley repeated when her father turned to storm out.

Amelia did some storming, too, to stop him, but Harley was faster. With a couple of long strides, he bounded down the steps and got between the two men.

"They're going to fight," her mother yelled to no one in particular. Apparently, her socialite training had prepared her to watch, fret and wring her hands, but it was training that Amelia had obviously failed because she ditched the hand wringing and fretting and went to stand by Harley.

"There'll be no fights," Amelia warned her father and Marty, and she made sure there was some meanness in her voice.

"Marty, don't hit him," Tracy yelled. She came running from the direction of the main house, and Liv and Darla were right behind her.

"I didn't start this," Marty insisted. "But I'll damn well finish it."

Spoken like an idiot because he had in a way started it when he'd slept with a married woman.

"You heard Amelia," Harley snarled. "There'll be no fights."

"I called the sheriff," Darla shouted. "He'll be here any minute."

Great. Just what they didn't need. Amelia knew Sheriff Leyton Jameson, and he had a reputation for being a good cop, but he was also one of Marty's "love children." The law wouldn't help this situation. They all needed to calm down. Unfortunately, what she was about to say probably wouldn't accomplish that, but it might get her parents to leave.

"You filed for a divorce," Amelia reminded her dad.

"If you truly believed that was the right thing to do, you wouldn't be here. Did you come to try to reconcile with Mom?"

"No," he spat out with far more volume than necessary. People three states away had probably heard him. "I just want an explanation from him and your mother as to why they'd do something like this."

Amelia sighed. This was like shower sex with Harley all over again. There was no reasonable explanation other than sexual attraction for what had gone on between Marty and her mother.

Except...

There was more between Harley and her. What she had with him wasn't only a *single dazzle-induced indiscretion.* It was multiple emotion-induced beddings. Along with dinners, long conversations and shower sex. And it hit her like a massive bag of bricks. She couldn't lose that.

Correction—she didn't want to lose that.

She didn't want to lose him.

Where the devil had her head been all this time for her not to have already realized that? Maybe the great sex had just caused her to focus on that and not see the big picture here.

Amelia turned to Harley, and he must have seen some of what she was feeling on her face because it put some alarm and worry in his eyes. He shot warning glances at both Marty and her father before pulling her into his arms. He brushed an incredibly tender kiss on her temple.

"You're the big picture," Amelia murmured.

Of course, Harley didn't understand that. He wasn't a mind reader. Apparently, neither was her mother.

"You're upsetting Amelia," Nadine declared. "And that's not a good idea in her possible condition."

Amelia could hear her mother hurrying to her, and some part of her appreciated the concern, but this moment was about Harley and her. It was that big-picture deal, so she tuned out Nadine. Tuned out everything except him.

"Will you ask me to marry you again?" Amelia blurted out, and she wasn't sure who she surprised the most. Maybe herself.

Harley smiled. However, he didn't get a chance to say anything because her phone rang, the sound shooting through the sudden silence. Amelia hated to break the moment, but this call could be important. One look at her screen, and she knew that it was.

"It's the doctor," she whispered to Harley. And answering it, she went back onto the porch.

"Amelia," the caller said. "This is Dr. Mendoza, and I have the results of your pregnancy test."

CHAPTER FIVE

HARLEY COULDN'T BE SURE, but he thought all the people in his yard were holding their collective breaths. He certainly was, and he kept his attention pinned to Amelia. Either way this went, he wanted to be there for her.

She might not let him, though.

It was promising that she'd asked him to propose to her again. That meant she was at least thinking about saying yes. However, this call from the doctor might send her into an emotional tailspin no matter what the test results.

In the distance, Harley heard the sound of sirens, and he cursed. Sheriff Leyton Jameson was obviously on the way. The threat of a fight seemed to be gone. For now anyway. But they wouldn't just be able to send Leyton on his merry way without giving him some kind of explanation as to what was going on. That meant slogging through all the messy details of Nadine and Marty's affair when Harley didn't care a rat about it. Not with what Amelia and he could be facing.

"Thank you," Amelia murmured into the phone, barely loud enough for Harley to hear.

She ended the call, turned slowly back around, and her gaze zoomed right to him. That was all Harley needed to hurry to her. He definitely didn't want an audience for this, and to the chorus of groans from everyone else in the yard, Harley led her back into his house. He couldn't tell from her expression if the test had been positive or negative, but whatever the result, it could wait a few more seconds.

"Before you say anything," he told her, "I want you to know that I'm in love with you."

She'd already opened her mouth to say something, but Amelia paused, shook her head. "I'm not pregnant. The test confirmed it."

Harley figured news like that would have caused some men to feel a whole lot of relief. He didn't. And he thought Amelia was experiencing the same thing. He was almost positive there was disappointment in her eyes.

"I'm sorry," he said. That was as far as he got because the sirens stopped blaring in front of his house, but the yelling started up again.

Hell. Judging from the cursing, threats and thuds, Marty and Patrick were now actually fighting.

"Let me take care of this, and then we'll talk," she whispered.

On a heavy sigh, Amelia went back outside, and Harley was right behind her. No way would he let her deal with this alone. Of course, there was no *alone* in this scenario since there were now even more people in his yard, including some guy with a camera. Probably the reporter that Amelia had spotted the day before.

Two of those people, Patrick and Marty, were indeed fighting. Or rather they were attempting to fight. There were punches being thrown, nearly all of which missed their targets unless Patrick was aiming at Marty's elbow. Marty was mainly ducking, and considering there wasn't a mark on him, he appeared to be doing a good job of it. Maybe he'd had lots of practice because Harley doubted this was the singer's first experience with an irate husband.

"Stop them!" Nadine yelled.

Leyton was trying to do just that, and he got a punch on the shoulder for his efforts. A punch from Patrick that earned him a very badass glare from Leyton. Obviously, the sheriff had had enough, and he latched on to the back collars of both of the fighters' shirts.

"If either of you tries to hit anybody again, I'll bash your heads together," Leyton warned them. "Then I'll arrest you for being stupid."

That stopped the attempted punches, but it didn't cool tempers one bit. Marty and Patrick stood there, glaring and with their breaths snorting out like angry bulls.

"Now, using your inside voices and keeping the cursing to a minimum, tell me what's going on here," Leyton said, and despite his calm tone, no one in the yard mistook it for anything but an order from a cop.

Patrick went first. "She cheated on me." He flung a finger at Nadine. "With him." The finger got flung at Marty that time.

Nadine also got in on finger flings. She aimed hers at her husband. "He's divorcing me."

"Who are you people?" the reporter asked, earning him glowers, narrowed eyes and some cursing from everyone but Marty.

"They're just some fans of mine," Marty said. The man was smooth as spit, and he smiled at the reporter. "And you are?"

"Dan Deavers." The reporter couldn't have been more than twenty, and he grinned in a proud way that proved he was also an idiot. There was nothing about this situation that warranted a grin. "I do freelance work for a couple of magazines."

In other words, a paparazzo out for a story. Sadly, he'd gotten one.

Proving that he was an idiot, too, Marty matched the reporter's grin, and he went to him, sliding his arm around Dan's shoulders. "You and I need to talk. Give us a minute," he added to Leyton. "I'm about to offer Dan Deavers here the interview of his life. Not just with me but plenty of my music friends. In exchange, he'll hand over any pictures he just took and develop amnesia about anything he heard."

So, maybe Marty wasn't an idiot after all. Apparently, neither was Dan because he went right with Marty as they strolled out of Harley's yard. They didn't go far, just out onto the road, and Leyton cast them a warning glance before turning back to Tracy, Liv and Darla.

"Do the three of you need to be here?" Leyton asked them.

All three women not only hesitated, but in unison they turned their gazes to Amelia. Harley didn't have to guess what they were waiting for. They wanted to know Amelia's test results.

"I'm not pregnant," Amelia announced.

The yard went silent again, but Harley saw some reactions that surprised him. His mother and sister looked disappointed, and there wasn't a lot of relief on Patrick's and Nadine's faces, either.

Maybe because they could see Amelia's sadness.

It was strange that just the day before the pregnancy had been a heart-stopping scare, but today there was no "scare" to it. Harley felt the loss of there not being a baby, and he was pretty sure that Amelia was feeling that right along with him.

Nadine went to Amelia and pulled her into a hug. "I'm sorry if you didn't get the test result you wanted."

That was a huge concession coming from Nadine, but maybe it proved how much she loved her daughter. Of course, that didn't stop her from being a snooty busybody who couldn't mind her own business, but her loving Amelia could make her at least tolerable in Harley's eyes.

"This was for the best," Patrick said, making him intolerable in Harley's eyes. What an asshole thing to say to his daughter, who was clearly hurting.

Just when Harley was ready to give Patrick a piece of his mind, the man also went to Amelia. He hugged her, too, and since Nadine still had her arms around Amelia, it turned into an awkward embrace. Then again, *awkward embrace* was another term for family as far as Harley was concerned.

"I love you," Patrick told Amelia.

Okay, so Harley didn't have to launch into that whole "piece of mind" lecture or put the man on an intolerable list.

"I love you, too," Nadine told her daughter, and it didn't seem as if she'd done that only because her husband had. It appeared to come from the heart, and there were fresh tears in Nadine's eyes. These didn't seem to be tears for her own marital situation, either.

"I love you," Amelia said, glancing first at her mother, then her dad.

Then at Harley.

Amelia kept her gaze on Harley. "I really love you," she repeated.

Those few words helped to wash away the disappointment over the test results. But it did a heck of a lot more than that. His heart swelled, and for some stupid reason, the rest of his body took that as a signal that he should haul Amelia off to bed so they could celebrate.

Later, he'd do just that.

For now, though, he extracted her from her parents' hug so he could kiss her. All in all, it wasn't a bad way to start that celebration. When Harley finally eased his mouth away from hers, they were both smiling.

"You love me," Harley said, his smile stretching to a big-assed grin.

"I love you," Amelia confirmed, matching his grin.

Harley didn't believe he'd ever get tired of hearing her say that, but he remembered they had an audience. Too many people were still on his lawn, including Marty, who'd obviously negotiated terms with the reporter since the guy was gone.

"Now that you've heard that Amelia's not pregnant and that Harley and she are in love," Leyton said, pointing to Tracy, Darla and Liv, "you can go back to wherever you should be. FYI, where you should be right now isn't here," Leyton clarified.

Liv and Tracy were grinning, too, and his mother blew him a kiss before she hooked her arms through Darla's and Liv's and escorted them away.

Leyton turned to Marty next. "Please tell me you're not going to be stupid enough to try to press assault charges against this man." He tipped his head to Patrick and then stared at Amelia's father. "Same goes for you. Pressing charges creates paperwork, which in turn causes gossip. I see no need for Amelia and Harley to have to deal with such talk. Do you?"

That "do you?" came out as a very threatening challenge. The kind a person might ask while aiming a baseball bat at your head. Leyton wouldn't do anything like that, but for a nice guy, he sure could go all mean cop.

"I won't file charges," Marty said, and that was followed by a grumble from Patrick where he stated the same.

Leyton nodded, pointed to Marty. "You've got some other place to be. Go there right now."

Marty shrugged as if that'd been his plan all along, and he strolled off in the direction of his cabin.

"You two also have some other place to be right now," Leyton continued, talking to Harley and Amelia. "I'm guessing that'll involve some kind of personal celebration that's none of our business. You can get started on that if you want."

Amelia shook her head. "But what about my parents?"

"Your mom, dad and I are going to have a little chat," Leyton assured her. "Maybe at the café behind the reception desk. I'm going to suggest counseling, which I hope they'll consider since they obviously love you. They probably love each other, too, and I'm going to say that they shouldn't throw the good out with the bad...and other crap like that. They'll listen because of that whole part about loving you and each other."

In the next few seconds, a lot of glancing went on. Amelia to her parents. Her parents to her and each other. Harley even got a few of those glances, including a glare from Patrick. Harley wasn't going to hold that against him. It was practically a duty for a father to want to murder anyone who'd had sex with his daughter. After all, Amelia was still his little girl.

"I'd be willing to go to counseling," Nadine admitted.

Patrick opened his mouth, and his expression made Harley think he might lash out at Nadine. That he might remind his wife that she was the one who'd cheated. But the man looked at Amelia again and nodded.

"Counseling," Patrick agreed.

This time, it was Amelia who initiated the group hug, pulling both of her parents into a family celebration of sorts. She caught on to Harley's shirt, hauling him into the mix. Yeah, it was awkward. Maybe it always would be with her folks, but Harley would make it work for the simple reason that Leyton had said. Because Harley loved Amelia, too.

"Let's go to the café and give Harley and Amelia some alone time," Leyton suggested as soon as the group hug ended.

Both Amelia and her mother had tears in their eyes, but Harley thought those were happy ones. Patrick still shot him another glare, which was decidedly not happy, but then offered his hand for Harley to shake.

Harley accepted it.

If Patrick squeezed a little too tight and if he still had that murderous look in his eyes, Harley accepted that, too.

There was another round of short hugs, murmured good-byes and only a smidge of awkwardness left by the time Leyton led Amelia's parents in the direction of the main house. If anyone could get Patrick and Nadine to bury the hatchet and work on their marriage, it was Leyton.

Once Amelia and he finally had the porch and yard to themselves, Harley slid his arm around her waist. "Are you okay with not being pregnant?" he asked.

She looked at him, nodded. "I'm all right. And I'm all right with you, too." She added a smile that let him know she was a lot more than just okay.

He tightened his grip on her and coaxed her inside. That way, he could kiss her, touch her, tell her how much he loved her.

And get her naked.

Thankfully, Amelia was on the same page he was because she started the kissing and getting naked part the moment they were inside his house. While nakedness and sex were indeed the end goals here, Harley stopped her from unzipping him.

"I'm waiting for an answer to my question," he reminded her, and had to speak through his gritted teeth when her nimble fingers located his erection pressed against the front of his jeans. "Will you marry me?"

She stopped fondling him and looked into his eyes. "But I'm not pregnant."

He checked his watch. "Plenty of time left in the day for that."

She laughed, and mercy, it was a good sound to hear. A good expression to see, too, on her face. In fact, it was so good that Harley just had to sample some of it. He kissed her long and deep. The kind of kiss that led to shower sex.

And a future together.

"Yes, Harley," Amelia said, whispering the word against his mouth. "I'll marry you."

* * * * *

Read on for a sneak peek at
USA TODAY *bestselling author Delores Fossen's*
Wild Nights in Texas,
a story about reunited love and the bonds of family.

CHAPTER ONE

THE ROOSTER STARTED IT.

Sheriff Leyton Jameson saw it all go down from the window of his office at the Lone Star Ridge Police Department. Squawking and flapping its wings, the Rhode Island Red came out of the alley at lightning speed. A blur of feathers and spindly yellow legs, it arrowed off the sidewalk by the hardware store and into the street.

And right in front of the Jeep.

The driver swerved to avoid hitting the rooster. Barely. The brakes squealed before the Jeep slammed into the four-foot-high concrete cowboy boots sporting the name Hank's Hardware. Leyton heard the sound of crunching metal, followed by a spewing radiator.

Leyton set his coffee aside and hurried out of his office, through the now-empty bull pen for the deputies, past reception and out onto Main Street. Even though he hadn't dawdled, he wasn't the first to make it to the now-wrecked Jeep. That honor belonged to Carter Bodell, the town's mortician, who was sporting a T-shirt that said I Will Bury You. Since that probably wasn't something an accident victim would want to see right off, Leyton muscled Carter aside and stepped in front of him.

Leyton immediately spotted the airbag. It had deployed like a tire-sized marshmallow and was now squished against the driver's face. A fog of the talcum powder that had come out with the airbag fluttered around the cab of the Jeep, falling onto the woman's black hair.

"Crap," the driver grumbled, batting away the bag and sending some of that powder right at Leyton. The motion caused the dozen or so thin silver bracelets she was wearing to jangle. Her earrings did some jangling, too. There was a trio of what appeared to be Goth-clad fairies in her right earlobe.

He helped her with the batting, unhooking her seat belt, but Leyton stopped her when she tried to get out. "You need to stay put," he told her. "I'll call for an EMT to come and check you."

Leyton fired off a text to the dispatcher to get that started. Since the hospital was just a couple of blocks up the street, it wouldn't take them long to get there.

"Crap," she repeated, turning her head in his direction.

Their eyes met. Familiar dark blue eyes. And despite the fact the woman's face was covered in talc, the rest of her was familiar, too.

Hadley Dalton.

Leyton got the jolt he always did when he saw Hadley. Which wasn't very often. But it was sort of a gut-punch mixture of red-hot lust and cold, dark dread. The lust because, well, this crap-muttering woman would apparently always ring his manly bell. The dread was because there wasn't another woman on earth who could give him as much trouble as Hadley.

It'd been a while, years, since Leyton had seen Hadley, but he had heard that she'd come back for a visit about six weeks earlier. A short visit where their paths hadn't crossed. Considering how small Lone Star Ridge was, that likely meant she'd purposely avoided him. Judging from the scowl she gave him, she would have preferred for that avoidance to continue.

"It's Badly Hadley," Carter said as if making an announcement to the entire town.

Hadley immediately shifted her scowl from Leyton to Carter. With good reason. *Badly Hadley* was the nickname Leyton knew she hated. She'd gotten dubbed with it when she and her triplet sisters had been the "stars" of the reality show *Little Cowgirls*. The episodes had documented plenty of embarrassing moments of the triplets' lives and been filmed right here at her grandmother's ranch in Lone Star Ridge. The show had stayed on the air for a dozen years. A dozen years of TV viewers tuning in to see just how bad Badly Hadley could be.

Leyton knew for a fact that she could be very, very bad.

"Are you drunk?" Carter asked her because he, too, knew about the very, very bad. In a generic sort of way, that is. Unlike Leyton, whose knowledge of Hadley was a bit more… personal.

"No, I'm not drunk," she snarled. She blinked as if trying to focus and looked at Leyton. Her gaze slid from his face to the badge he had clipped to his belt. "I wrecked because I dodged a chicken."

"A rooster," Leyton corrected.

Though the rooster was now nowhere in sight. He made a mental note to find it so it didn't cause any other accidents. There were plenty of ranches and farms nearby that had poultry, but this was a first for one making its way into town.

Still scowling and groaning, Hadley turned in the seat and would have gotten out had Leyton not stopped her again. "Just wait until the EMTs get here."

"I'm fine," she insisted. "But I need to move this unicorn horn. It's poking my thigh."

Of all the things Leyton had thought she might say, that wasn't one of them. "Unicorn horn?" he questioned.

Hell. She probably had a concussion or was maybe in shock if she was hallucinating about something like that.

Hadley nodded as if she'd just explained everything to him, and she practically oozed off the seat. Leyton caught her in his arms. Good thing, too, because Hadley wobbled when she stood, and she looked down. Leyton followed her gaze, and that's when Leyton saw that there was indeed a, well, unicorn horn.

It appeared to be a hat with a hard plastic horn jutting out from the rainbow-colored head. The horn was jammed and tangled in the laced-up side of Hadley's black jeans. She yanked it out, winced, and Leyton saw some blood. Not much, but it appeared to have broken the skin.

"It's something my grandmother wanted me to make," she said, her voice a little steadier now. "It was on the seat next to me when I wrecked."

Hadley was a costume designer in California so that made sense. Well, sort of made sense. Her grandmother Em wasn't the most conventional person, but a unicorn hat seemed on the extreme side even for her.

"You're bleeding," Carter blurted out the way a weatherman would warn of a tornado bearing down on him. There was volume, urgency and panic in his voice, and he hooked his arm around Hadley's waist.

Hadley gave Carter a look that could have frozen lava. "Carter Bodell, if you're going to shock me or have some kind of device on you to make farting noises, I'll knee you in the nuts," she snarled.

Unlike the unicorn horn, this particular comment hadn't come out of left field. Carter was a prankster. One with the sense of humor of a third grader. He often had shocking/farting devices on him that went off when he shook hands with someone or slapped that person on the back.

"And if you try to feel me up again like you did in high school," Hadley added to the snarl, "I'll also knee you in the nuts."

Leyton wasn't sure if Carter had intended to do any feeling up, but that got the undertaker backing away from Hadley. However, she hadn't given the same warning to Leyton, which was ironic since he had indeed felt up Hadley many times. Not now though.

Definitely not now.

Hopefully, not ever again. He needed an entanglement with Hadley about as much as he needed a unicorn horn in his thigh or a wreck-causing rooster on Main Street.

"Is she okay?" someone called out.

Ty Copperfield, the young, fresh-faced EMT, was running up the sidewalk toward them. Leyton knew him, of course. He knew everyone in town and vice versa since Leyton had lived here most of his life.

"I'm fine," Hadley grumbled, and she wiped some of the talc from her face.

With enough of the airbag powder gone, Leyton got a better look at her. No cuts or nicks as there sometimes was with an airbag deployment.

"Her leg's bleeding," Carter said, pointing in the direction of the wound.

"It's just a scratch," Hadley insisted, but that didn't stop Ty from stooping down and checking it for himself.

"You're right," Ty said a moment later. "Just a scratch, but you'll need to have it cleaned."

Ty stood, waved a little penlight in front of her eyes, made a sound of approval and then as Leyton had done, he continued to check Hadley for other injuries. So did the crowd that was gathering on Main Street. But the crowd did it from a respectable distance.

Everyone who'd been in the shops and businesses was now outside, and the possibility of heatstroke from the sweltering July temps wouldn't stop them from milling around to find out what was happening. Leyton saw a lot of texting and calling going on, and soon it would be all over Lone Star Ridge that Hadley was back and had been involved in a wreck. There'd be embellishments to the gossip, no doubt. Gossip that might include him since he still had an arm around Hadley.

Ty halted his once-over exam of Hadley and snagged her gaze. He grinned. "Say, you're Badly Hadley. Man, I can't believe it's you. I used to see you on that TV show when I was a kid."

"Little Cowgirls," Carter supplied as if being helpful. "Hadley used to be a star."

Talk about some ego slamming. *Used to be a star* was the same as saying a has-been, and Ty's *when I was a kid* remark sure hadn't helped. Hadley was just thirty-three, only a year younger than Leyton, but to the twenty-two-year-old Ty, she probably did seem old-ish. Added to that, *Little Cowgirls* had been off the air for eighteen years now, so Ty had indeed been a kid when he'd watched the show.

"I need to go," Hadley muttered, and she stepped out of Leyton's grip so she could turn and look at the Jeep.

Hadley groaned, then cursed when her gaze skimmed over the airbag debris in the front seats, the bashed-in front end and the still-spewing radiator. The engine was no longer running, which meant there'd been enough damage that the Jeep would have to be towed.

She certainly made an odd picture standing there in loose laced-up jeans, black tank top and bloodred flip-flops. Her long straight hair was black—which he knew was dyed from her natural dark brown—and was pulled back in a ponytail.

Not fussy but that only seemed to draw more attention to it. Just like the woman herself. Hadley might have been born and raised here, but she looked city. And very much out of place on a small-town main street where a rooster could cause a wreck.

"I need to go," she repeated, this time aiming her comment at Leyton. Ty resumed his exam and began checking Hadley's head. "I have to see Em."

It wasn't a surprise that she'd want to see her grandmother. Em had practically raised Hadley, her sisters and their brother since their own parents had been pretty much scum. But there was a high level of concern in Hadley's voice that made him think this was more than just a visit.

"Is Em okay?" Leyton asked. When Hadley didn't jump to answer that, Leyton felt the knot form in his gut.

"I'm not sure," Hadley finally said.

And just like that, the knot tightened. Em had always been good to him. Unlike plenty of others in town, Em had never judged him, either, for being a "love child" instead of being born with the Jameson name.

Hadley batted away Ty, who was now examining her neck, and she grabbed her purse from the passenger seat of the Jeep. "Em called me late last night and insisted I come home," Hadley told Leyton.

She opened her mouth, no doubt to add to that explanation, but she must have realized she had Ty's and Carter's complete attention. The attention of the dozen or so townsfolk, too.

"I'll call the rental company and report the accident," she continued, still gripping the unicorn hat in her left hand. "First though, I need to see Em."

Leyton hesitated, nodded. He should probably insist on taking her to the ER and then getting her statement about the accident, but the gut knot won out. Those things could wait. "I'll drive you."

And just like that, their *uncomfortable* past washed over her expression. "I can walk."

Yeah, she could since it was less than a half mile, but Leyton had no intention of letting her do that. "I'll drive you," he insisted, and he grabbed the large suitcase from the back seat of the Jeep.

Since he wasn't sure if she was steady on her feet, Leyton took hold of her arm and maneuvered Hadley and her suitcase around the crowd and across the street to the police station parking lot, where his cruiser was parked.

It occurred to him that had this been her sisters, Sunny or McCall, more folks would have greeted her. There would have been more smiles, too, and *welcome home* would have been doled out for the friendlier sisters. But Hadley always seemed to have an invisible back-off sign.

"I'll need to have the Jeep towed," Hadley muttered, glancing back over her shoulder at it before she got into the cruiser.

"I can help with that." He could also arrange for anything else in the Jeep to be brought out to her grandmother's ranch. For now though, he wanted answers. So, he put her suitcase in the cruiser, got in and started the engine. "What do you think is wrong with Em?"

She shook her head, causing more of the talcum to fall and her ponytail to swish. "Like I said, she insisted I come. I asked her why and she said she just had something important to tell me." Hadley cursed under her breath. "She also asked me to bring her the unicorn hat."

Leyton met Hadley's gaze before he pulled out of the parking lot. "Why the hat?"

Hadley made a frustrated sigh. "She said it was for a costume party at the preschool where she does story time. She sketched out a picture of what she wanted and asked me to make it for her. Apparently, she already has the actual costume but wanted the hat to finish off the look." *Look* went in air quotes.

Well, Em did do story time, but he couldn't imagine that the hat would be safe to have around kids. However, it did ease the gut knot some. Things couldn't be that bad for Em if she still planned on going to the preschool. Then again, maybe the hat was some kind of ploy. Exactly what kind of ploy, he didn't know, but it could have something to do with the rumors he'd heard that Hadley had recently been fired from her job. Maybe this was Em's way of giving Hadley busywork?

"I got stuck in a traffic jam in San Antonio," Hadley went on, "so I took out the unicorn cap from my luggage and did some work on it. Em wanted rhinestones added to the horn."

He heard the tension and worry in her voice and pushed for more info. "Do McCall and Sunny know if anything's wrong with Em?"

"No. I called them right away, and they said that Em seemed fine. McCall's in Dallas, closing down her office there, so I told her to stay put, that there was no need to worry."

He knew about McCall being in Dallas. Knew, too, that she was shutting down her counseling practice there so she could move it to Lone Star Ridge. McCall was living at the ranch with Em, but that would change as well once her fiancé, Austin Jameson, and she got married. Since Austin was also his half brother, Leyton had stayed apprised of their plans.

"Sunny's on a book tour for the next couple of days," Hadley added. "I told her to stay put, too."

Again, Leyton knew about that. Sunny was an illustrator for a popular graphic novel series, *Slacker Quackers*, and she'd gone on a tour to promote the latest issue. In fact, he knew plenty about Sunny as well since she was engaged to another of his half brothers, Shaw.

"I hadn't texted Em my flight info because I didn't want her coming to the airport to pick me up," Hadley went on. "I didn't want her making that drive. So, I called her when I landed to tell her I was getting a rental car and would be here soon, but she didn't answer."

She took out her phone from her purse, and with the call on speaker, she tried again. The call went straight to voicemail. "Em hasn't answered any of my six calls or texts," Hadley added.

Hell. He hoped the woman hadn't fallen or something. Em was in her seventies, and while she seemed in good health, that didn't mean she hadn't had an accident.

Leyton pushed the accelerator, going well past the 30 mph speed limit, and he pushed it even more when he took the turn on the road that led to the ranch.

Whenever he came here to Em's, he always got the same feeling. That time had somehow stopped. The house and the grounds hadn't changed since *Little Cowgirls* had been filmed here.

Maybe Hadley was also seeing that because she dragged in a long breath, and he didn't think it was his imagination that she seemed even more unsteady than she had right after the wreck. Home usually held plenty of memories, and in Hadley's case, there were just as many bad as good ones here.

Hadley barreled out of his cruiser the moment Leyton came to a stop, and he had to hurry to catch up with her. By the time he was on the porch, she already had the front door open—it was unlocked—and she rushed inside.

"Em?" she called out.

No answer.

"Em?" Hadley tried again.

Still nothing, but Leyton tried to tamp down any real

concern. The ranch was a big place, and it was possible that Em was in the barn or outside in her garden.

Obviously, Hadley wasn't tamping down anything. Moving fast and leaving a trail of the talcum in her wake, she raced through the maze of rooms and to the kitchen. Em wasn't there, either, so Hadley headed toward the woman's bedroom suite. And she stopped cold.

Because Leyton was behind her, it took a moment for him to see why she'd frozen. Another moment to figure out what was lying on the floor. Or rather what was *possibly* on the floor. It appeared to be a stretchy rainbow unicorn costume, and it was in the middle of the hall as if someone had dropped it there.

Hadley picked up the costume, taking it with her into Em's room. Again, no sign of the woman, but her dresser drawers were wide open, and there were more clothes and shoes strewed around.

"Is this usual?" Leyton wanted to know since this was the first time he'd been in this part of the house.

Hadley shook her head. "No. She's usually a neat freak." And still clutching the costume, she walked to the bed, her attention zooming in on something there.

A note.

"Is that Em's handwriting?" Leyton asked.

She nodded and picked it up. "'Hadley, I'm fine, but I had to go on a short trip to visit an old friend,'" she read aloud. "'Remember that secret box we buried when you were twelve?'"

"Box?" Leyton repeated, but he didn't wait for an answer. Looking over Hadley's shoulder, he read the last part of the note, his voice blending with Hadley's.

"'Well, it's time for you to dig it up,'" they read, "'because there are some things about me that you need to know.'"

CHAPTER TWO

HADLEY REREAD HER grandmother's note several times, and she tried to steady herself with Em's *I'm fine*, but nothing about this felt anywhere near fine. Something was wrong.

"Do you know anything about these old friends she's visiting?" Leyton asked, and he sounded very much like the cop that he was.

She shook her head. "I've never heard her mention any *old friends*." Hadley looked at Leyton. "You'd know as many of her friends as I would. Maybe more."

After all, Leyton had lived in Lone Star Ridge since he was a kid when he'd moved in with his biological father, Marty Jameson, and his then wife. Unlike Hadley, who'd left town when she turned eighteen, Leyton had stayed.

And he'd become the sheriff.

It didn't surprise her that he had gone the good-guy route, but it always felt a little like salt in an old wound to her.

"What about this secret box?" Leyton pressed, tapping what Em had written.

Hadley drew in a long breath and took a quick mental trip down memory lane. "When I was a kid, I was feeling down about…something, and Em said we should make a time capsule of sorts. She wanted us to put things in the box that'd made me happy. Then, any time I needed to be cheered up, I could think about the box."

Hearing it all aloud, Hadley knew how silly it sounded.

How caring, too. Em had loved her and had done this silly, caring thing to try to pull her out of a dark mood. It had worked. For a little while anyway.

"I haven't thought of that box in years," Hadley admitted. But she certainly thought about it now. Thought about what she'd put in it, too, and she silently groaned.

"What's in the box that Em now wants you to know?" Leyton pressed.

Hadley tried to visualize everything that Em had added to the stash. "I don't have a clue. I remember she put in an old 8-track music disk and a peach pit that she thought looked like Elvis."

She had to hand it to Leyton. He didn't give her a flat look or good belly laugh. That's because he knew that Em wasn't exactly conventional. However, neither an 8-track or a peach pit explained the last line of that note.

Because there are some things about me that you need to know.

Well, unless there was something hidden in those items. That was possible, she supposed, but Hadley certainly hadn't picked up on any vibes that Em had been trying to hide anything.

"It's been twenty-one years since that box went in the ground, and until now Em's never said a word about it." Hadley paused. "I have to dig up the box," she added, already heading out of Em's bedroom and toward the back door off the kitchen.

Of course, Leyton was right behind her, but he took out his phone and made a call. "Cait," he said to the person he'd called.

Cait Jameson, his half sister. Also his deputy sheriff.

"Ask around and see if anyone knows where Em is," Leyton told his sister. "She's not at her place, and the scene looks, well, disturbed."

Hadley couldn't hear Cait's response, but she figured the deputy would jump right on that. *Disturbed* was the right word. Something had gone on in Em's bedroom. There'd been clear signs of that frantic rush to either pack or find something. Maybe Em had done that.

Maybe someone else had.

But Hadley quickly pushed that last thought aside. It wouldn't help her to jump to a worst-case scenario even if the dread and worry were starting to pulse through her.

By the time they reached the barn, Leyton had finished his call, and he took the shovel from her when she plucked it from its hanger on the wall.

"Where's this box?" he asked, obviously planning on doing the digging himself.

Hadley didn't argue with him. The truth was she was still feeling a little light-headed. Maybe because of a combination of the wreck, all the stupid talcum powder she'd breathed in, the blistering heat and the fear that something had happened to her grandmother.

She led him to the large oak that still sported a swing, and then with her back to the tree, Hadley started walking, pacing off the fifty steps that Em and she had taken twenty-one years ago.

It'd been much cooler that day. A drizzly March morning when her mother, Sunshine, had taken "Good Girl" McCall and "Funny" Sunny to the ice cream shop to film a scene for *Little Cowgirls*. Hadley had been grounded—again—so she hadn't been invited. Em and she had had the ranch to themselves that day.

A rarity.

Hadley had much preferred being at the ranch alone with Em than she had going with the cameraman and producer, who would record an ordinary outing and try to make it into something that would entertain viewers. That meant doing whatever it took to create an embarrassing or memorable situation.

On that specific outing, the writers had scripted that McCall drop her ice cream in her lap. Even if McCall hadn't gone along with it, Sunshine would have made sure it happened. Made sure there was drama and embellishment, too. Even though Hadley didn't know all the details of how things had played out, McCall had come home in tears that day.

There'd been lots of tears on lots of days, and her mother had been at the root of so many of them. So many. No happy mother-daughter relationships for Sunshine and the Little Cowgirls. Heck, not between Sunshine and Hadley's brother, Hayes, either. Hayes was just as messed up as the rest of the Dalton sibling gene pool.

"You okay?" she heard Leyton ask.

Maybe he'd picked up on the fact that she was doing more than counting paces and was reliving a thing or two that shouldn't be relived. The past could be a mean, bitter bitch. So could her mother. That was the reason Hadley hadn't seen her in over a decade. It'd been longer than that for her father, who'd left after *Little Cowgirls* had gotten canceled when Hadley had been fifteen. Not only had he not returned, he also hadn't bothered to contact any of his kids.

Hadley now thought of herself as a self-orphaned orphan. Still, the estrangement had its benefits. Along with not having to see or speak to her folks, she didn't have to worry about picking out Mother's and Father's Day cards. Good thing, too, because it would have been pretty hard to find one that conveyed the sentiment of "you don't have a single parental bone in your entire bodies."

"I was just thinking about greeting cards," she muttered.

Not exactly a lie, but Hadley didn't want to open a vein

when she already had so much weighing on her mind. She needed to keep the emotional bloodletting to a minimum.

Hadley stopped at the fifty paces and glanced around, hoping this was the right spot. There'd been no trees or shrubs back then, but there had been a large landscape boulder, and it was still there.

Next to it was a birdbath, and the base was a concrete statue of, well, *something*. A squat little creature with a winking eye and an extremely large butt. A *bare* butt that revealed dimpled cheeks. And its nose was missing. It'd been lopped off, maybe by design or Mother Nature.

"What is that thing?" Leyton asked, tipping his head to the noseless figure.

Hadley shook her head. "Your guess is as good as mine." Which applied to so many of Em's decorating choices.

"I think we buried it here," she said, pointing to the right of the birdbath. "It's a green metal fishing tackle box."

Unlike twenty-one years ago, the ground wasn't soft today, but Leyton jammed the shovel into the grass and dirt in one strong, fluid move. A reminder that he wasn't just a sheriff but that he also worked on his family's ranch. It was no doubt the reason he had all those muscles to flex and remind her that he was a well-built cowboy.

She watched as he hefted a shovel full of dirt, tossing it to the side before he went back in for another.

"We didn't bury it deep," she added. "Maybe a foot down, so if you don't hit it soon—"

Hadley broke off when she heard the crack of metal against metal. She dropped to her knees for a better look. It was the fishing tackle box all right, but it was no longer green. It was now a rectangle of flaking rust. Leyton loosened it from the ground, and together they pulled it out.

She immediately went for the latch. It wasn't a lock, but

the rust had fused it together, so Hadley couldn't open it. Leyton helped with that, too. He motioned for her to move back and struck the latch with the point of the shovel. It popped right open.

And they both groaned.

Because the white packing paper that Em had put on top of the contents was now a mess that resembled dirty clots of lard.

"The water leaked in," Leyton grumbled, causing Hadley's stomach to drop to her ankles. She hadn't been sure what they'd find in this box, but it'd been their best bet for figuring out what had happened to her grandmother. Well, if Em's note had been accurate.

Leyton put the shovel aside, took out his pocketknife and began to flick out the packing paper blobs. When he'd cleared the path, she saw the peach pit. It didn't look any more like Elvis now than it had way back then, but it was still intact. There was also a plastic sandwich bag that contained an index card with a handwritten recipe for Sweetie Pie, a chocolate pecan concoction.

Despite this situation, Hadley did indeed smile about the recipe. "It was my favorite. I wanted her to add it to the box."

Hadley took out the bag, flipping it over so she could see if Em had written anything on the back, but it was blank. No cryptic messages to decode anything that might be going on now.

Leyton took out the next sandwich bag. The water hadn't into gotten to it, either, but the flower inside had definitely seen better days. It was dried and flat. He looked at her, his eyebrow lifted to let her know he was waiting for an explanation. But Hadley didn't give him one.

"I don't remember what this is," she lied. She took the

bag from him, putting it behind her, and reached for the next one.

But Leyton beat her to that, too, and like the recipe, it was in pristine condition in the baggie. Not a drop of moisture had gotten on the picture.

Of Leyton.

It was a photo Hadley had taken of him by the corral when he'd come over to do some work for Em. He wasn't looking directly into the camera, but Hadley had still managed to catch him grinning in that cocky way that only a thirteen-year-old boy could grin.

Once again, Leyton's eyebrow came up, and once again, Hadley didn't want to explain it. She just snatched it from him, dropping it with the dried flower, and she pulled out the 8-track. The water had definitely done some damage here, but the label was still easy enough to make out. It caused Leyton to groan.

"My father," Leyton grumbled in a "toenail fungus" tone.

It was indeed music from his father, Marty Jameson, who'd once been a country music star. Well, sort of a star anyway. He'd had some hits and successful tours. He'd also abandoned his family and slept around enough to produce many offspring. Three from his marriage, and many, many others born on the wrong side of the sheets. Leyton was one of those.

"Em loves his music," Hadley commented while she looked on the back of the 8-track and then down into what she could see of the actual tape. Nothing there, either. "Maybe one of the songs means something. Or the album title, *Running Ragged*. Any idea if your dad wrote a song for Em?"

"Not that I know of," Leyton said almost idly.

That's because like hers, his attention was no longer on the 8-track, but the envelope that had been beneath it. It, too, was in a bag, but it wasn't completely dry. The moisture has smeared the writing on the front, but she still had no trouble reading it.

For Hadley.

"I don't remember her putting this in there," Hadley said, taking it out. "But I left the box with Em when I went to the barn to get a shovel. Em could have slipped it in there then."

Hadley's hands were a little unsteady when she opened it and pulled out the single page of paper that'd been inside. Like the writing on the envelope, the ink had smeared here, too. In fact, there were huge ink blotches over most of the paper. It was anyone's guess as to what the first paragraphs said, but Hadley could make out the line below it.

"'I had a life before here,'" Hadley read. "'I used to be somebody else.'"

Hadley's mind did a little mental stutter, and she read it again. And again.

"Somebody else?" Leyton asked. Obviously, he was also having a hard time figuring out what it meant.

Hadley continued to study the letter. Or rather the nonsmudged parts she could make out, but she could only get a word here and there. *Love. Safe. Sorry.* She finally looked at Leyton to see if he had gotten more of it than she had, but he just shook his head.

"Maybe Em had a different name before she moved here," Leyton suggested.

She thought about that a moment. "It's possible, I guess." And it frustrated her to realize that she knew so little about a woman she loved. "Em moved here from East Texas after she met and married my grandfather. This was his family's ranch."

"And what about her family?" Leyton pressed.

Hadley tried to shuffle through the memories she had of Em, but she didn't come up with much. "She didn't talk a lot about her past, but I remember her saying her folks died when she was very young. I never met any of her relatives."

The sound of a car engine got their attention, and Hadley lifted her head to see an SUV pull to a stop in front of the house. Leyton's sister, Cait, got out. Like Leyton, she had a badge clipped to her belt, and she made a beeline toward them.

"Please tell me that's not where Em buried the dead skunk she found on the road when we were kids," Cait remarked.

"No," Hadley assured her. But she remembered the incident. Despite the horrible stench, Em had indeed buried the critter in a Dick's Sporting Goods shoebox.

"Thank God." Cait went to her and pulled her into a hug. "Heard you had a run-in with Rosco the Rooster. You okay?"

Hadley nodded and tried not to go stiff from the hug, but she didn't quite manage it. It wasn't that she didn't like Cait, she did, but it always felt weird to be welcomed in a place where Badly Hadley had done so many unwelcoming things.

"Rosco?" Leyton asked, standing.

Cait let go of Hadley and turned back to her brother. "Yep. It belongs to Delbert Watley. He'd brought it into town with him to do errands, and it jumped out of his truck window when he was parked behind the hardware store. I gave him a warning and told him if he didn't want to leave Rosco alone, then he should look into getting a rooster sitter."

Propping her hands on her hips, Cait tipped her head to the metal box. "I'm guessing that has something to do with Em...and with you?" she added for Leyton when she saw his picture in the plastic bag. Cait frowned. "And our worthless excuse for a father."

Hadley quickly scooped up the plastic bags and the 8-track. No way did she want to explain Leyton's picture to his sister. Or to Leyton.

WILD NIGHTS IN TEXAS

"This was a memory box that Em and Hadley buried," Leyton explained. "Any news about Em?"

"Maybe," Cait answered. "Late yesterday afternoon, Howie Hargrove and Hildie Stoddermeyer saw a black car with Louisiana plates. They think Em was in the passenger seat."

Howie was the mayor and Hildie owned the diner so they were reliable when it came to this sort of thing. Still, Hadley had to shake her head. "I don't know of any family or friends that Em has in Louisiana."

And that caused Hadley's worry to soar.

Maybe Em had been kidnapped.

"Did Em look scared?" Hadley blurted out.

Cait shook her head. "Nope, but Howie and Hildie only got quick looks. The car was heading toward the interstate. Any idea where she'd be going?"

Hadley looked down at the items from the tackle box. Em had said there'd be answers in these things, and maybe there was. Maybe in the smeared portions of the letter. Or in some portion of the 8-track. Since it'd been one of Em's favorites, it didn't feel right to toss the 8-track on the ground and stomp on it so the plastic would crack and she could see inside. However, it might come to that.

"No idea," Hadley told Cait. "But I need to take a better look at these things. A better look at her room, too."

Cait and Leyton started walking with her when she headed toward the house. "Keep asking around town," Leyton instructed his sister. "Press to see if anyone remembers any of the numbers on the license plate of that black car."

"Will do," Cait said. "You want me to do something about the wrecked Jeep? I can go ahead and call for a tow truck."

Hadley hadn't forgotten about the Jeep, but it wasn't a high priority right now. "Yes, please. But ask around about Em first."

Cait repeated her "will do," and she gave Hadley's hand a quick squeeze before she peeled off to go to her SUV.

With Leyton right behind her, Hadley carried the items from the tackle box inside and spread them out on the kitchen counter. She zoomed right in on the smeared letter, trying to make out the words. Beside her, Leyton appeared to be doing the same thing.

I had a life before here. I used to be somebody else.

Those were still the only clear sentences so she moved on to the 8-track, taking out a butter knife so she could pry open the plastic case.

"Why'd you put my picture in that box?" Leyton asked.

Hadley's hand slipped, and she almost stabbed herself with the knife. Huffing, Leyton took both it and the 8-track from her. "Why?" he repeated.

"Because I was twelve." When she'd still believed that she could have something good.

Or rather *someone* good.

Someone with a hot face to go along with the goodness. And the hot face had been pretty important to her back then. All that dark brown hair and those smoky gray eyes. Even that cocky grin had been on her list of reasons to lust after him. The DNA gods had sure been generous when it came to the Jameson brothers, and Leyton had gotten more than his fair share of hotness.

Once, they'd come very close to being lovers. A lifetime ago when she'd been fifteen and he sixteen. Then, teenage life as she'd known it had come to an end when one of their make-out sessions had been secretly filmed by the camera crew. They'd been clothed, but there had been full-body fondling with lots of tongue kissing. And sounds. Moans and grunts of pleasure. Whispered wants.

Hickeys.

Things that teenagers definitely hadn't wanted a camera to record.

Well, not most teenagers anyway. Leyton and she hadn't been into the whole "let's get stupid and film ourselves so we can watch" thing.

All in all, the recording wasn't as revealing as it could have been. Other times when they'd made out, Leyton's hand had made it into her pants. And vice versa. They could thank pollen and perhaps hay for being alerted before that had happened on this particular night. The cameraman's allergies must have gotten the best of him, and the loud sneeze blast caused Leyton and her to fly apart and notice the camera that had been aimed at them.

Hadley had begged her mother and the producer not to air it. But they had anyway. And when he'd found out that it was all going to be on TV, Leyton had broken up with her. She couldn't blame him, not then, not now. Leyton had always had to walk a line because he's Marty Jameson's illegitimate son, and that had made him a "like father, like son" joke around town.

She put all of that aside to focus on the present. Specifically, focus on the questioning look that Leyton was giving her. He was obviously waiting for her to explain that *Because I was twelve*, but that wasn't going to happen.

Thankfully, she got a change of subject when Leyton popped open the 8-track. She saw the spool of tape with the recorded music and a little plastic wheel to feed the tape through the playing surface. What she didn't see was a note or message from Em.

"Anything about this that'll help us?" Leyton asked, tapping the pressed flower in the plastic bag. "Why is it in there?"

Because I was twelve would be the truthful answer, but like the picture, it would require too much explaining. Had-

DELORES FOSSEN

ley just settled for shaking her head, and she started back to Em's bedroom.

She got another gut punch when she took a second look at the disorder there. Before today, Hadley couldn't remember ever seeing anything out of place in here, and it only confirmed that something was indeed wrong.

"This might sound a little like a Hardy Boys mystery, but maybe there's some kind of secret code in the recipe," Leyton said from the doorway. He had the baggie with the recipe card and was studying it.

Since that was as good a theory as any, Hadley went to him to take it and examine it again. While she did that, Leyton began to look around the room.

The ingredients for the recipe all looked legit. So did the baking instructions, but Hadley found herself trying to analyze each word, even the little smiley face that Em had put at the bottom of the index card. But Hadley doubted that meant anything other than Em was happy when she doodled it. Any real clues had to be in the letter.

"Can a crime lab analyze the letter?" she asked.

"Since there's no evidence of a crime, no. But I know of some private labs that can do it."

She glanced up at him to say they should get right on that, but Hadley saw what he was holding. Or rather what he was reading. It was a trashy tabloid, *Tattle Tale*, and it had her picture on the cover with the headline "Badly Hadley Strikes Again."

"Where'd you find that?" she blurted out.

"On the nightstand next to Em's bed. It was open to the story about Tit-gate," he said, skimming the page.

Considering that Leyton didn't hesitate over the stupid Tit-gate headline, that meant he likely knew all about the wardrobe malfunction of a costume that Hadley had designed for an aging pop star legend, Myla Livingston. Myla hadn't reacted well to the incident, which was a serious understatement, and then she'd done her best to smear Hadley's business. It turned out that Myla's "best" was plenty good enough because Hadley had been fired from her contracts.

All of them.

And other than a very low budget movie that would never see any real distribution, she didn't have any future prospects of work. As much as that stung, and it stung bad, Hadley had to push that bad down deep inside her and focus on figuring out what was going on with her grandmother.

Leyton flipped through the tabloid and came to a page where the top corner had been folded down. Hadley went to him, hoping that maybe Em had written something on the page. But no. It was just an ad of a hot guy in snug boxer briefs that framed his superior junk.

"I don't think that's a clue to her whereabouts," Leyton commented.

Hadley made a sound of agreement and kept looking, not at the hot guy's junk, but around the rest of the room. There was a notepad on the nightstand, and Em had written *Waterstone Productions* with a phone number.

Her stomach sank a little.

"'Waterstone Productions'?" Leyton read aloud when he looked over her shoulder. "That's the company that wants to do a reunion special for *Little Cowgirls.*"

"You knew about that?" Hadley asked.

"Em and Sunny mentioned it. Apparently, some guy's been calling them and trying to convince them to do it. Sunny and McCall aren't interested."

Neither was Hadley. In fact, she had no intentions of going down that road again. Especially when she had to find out what had happened to Em.

Considering the best way to approach this, she took out her phone and composed a text.

I've been in a car accident.

Hadley showed the text to Leyton before she sent it to Em. And Hadley waited, already second-guessing herself. She didn't want Em to worry about her, but she didn't want her own worry to continue, either.

Even though she'd been hoping for the sound of a text response, the sound of her phone ringing was even better. She nearly pulled a muscle hitting the answer button when she saw Em's name on the screen. Relief washed over her. But so did the questions.

"Are you all right?" Em blurted out at the same moment Hadley asked her the same.

"I'm fine," Hadley assured her. "It was little more than a fender bender." Okay, that was a lie, but she hadn't been hurt. "Where are you?"

"I'm fine, too," Em said, even though that didn't answer Hadley's question. "Did you dig up the box?"

"I did. Where are you—"

"Did you read the letter and look at the 8-track?" Em interrupted.

Hadley gave a frustrated huff. She didn't want to talk about this. She wanted to know where her grandmother was and why she'd left. She decided to put the call on speaker so Leyton could hear the conversation. "The letter has a lot of water damage so I couldn't make out what it said. What did you mean that you had another life?"

"I mean, I used to be someone else. But that's not important right now," Em continued, rolling right over Hadley's repeated *where are you?* "I just need a little time to myself.

Time to work out a few things. But I promise I'm fine and that I'll be back home soon. You're sure you looked at the 8-track?" Em added.

Leyton added his own frustrated huff to the conversation. "Em, where are you?" he pressed.

"Leyton. Oh, good. You're there with Hadley. I'd hoped you would be. Make sure she doesn't worry too much."

"I am worried too much!" Hadley snapped. "Why'd you leave? What's going on? Where are you?"

"I'll be able to tell you that soon. But for now, please keep an eye on the house until I get back. Oh, and you might want to keep your distance from Sunny's pet duck, Slackers. She left him there when she went on her trip, and he's been in a sour mood. His food's in the barn."

Hadley sighed loud enough to drain every ounce of breath from her body. She didn't want to talk about a sour-mood duck.

"Where are you? When are you coming back?" Leyton's demands were more like the interrogation of a suspect.

But he was talking to the air because Em had already hung up.

* * * * *

Don't miss Wild Nights in Texas
by Delores Fossen,
available October 2020
wherever HQN Books and ebooks are sold.
www.HQNBooks.com

Chapter One

In the dark of his apartment, Brady Wyatt considered getting drunk.

It wasn't something he typically considered doing. He stayed away from extremes. If he drank alcohol, it was usually two beers tops. He'd never smoked a cigarette or taken a drug that wasn't expressly legal.

He was a good man. He believed in right and wrong. He believed wholeheartedly that he was smarter, better and stronger than his father, who was currently being transferred to a maximum-security federal prison, thanks to a number of charges, including attempted murder.

When Brady thought of his twin brother nearly dying at Ace's hands, it made him want to get all the more drunk.

Brady wished he could believe Ace Wyatt would no longer be a threat. His father wasn't superhuman or supernatural, but sometimes…no matter what Brady told himself was possible, it felt like Ace Wyatt would always have a choke hold around his neck.

Once he could go back to work, things would be fine. Dark thoughts and this sense of impending doom would go away once he could get out there and do his job again.

The fact he'd been shot was a setback, but he'd taken his role as sheriff's deputy for Valiant County, South Dakota, seriously enough to know being hurt, or even killed, in the line of duty was more than possible.

He'd been shot helping save his soon-to-be sister-in-law. There was no shame or regret in that.

But the fact the wound had gotten infected, didn't seem to want to heal in any of the normal ways no matter what doctors he saw, left him frustrated and often spiraling into dark corners of his mind he had no business going.

When someone knocked on his apartment door, relief swept through him. A relief that made him realize how much the darkness had isolated him.

Maybe he should go stay out at his grandmother's ranch. Let Grandma Pauline shove food at him and let his brother Dev grouse at him. Being alone wasn't doing him any favors, and he was not a man who indulged in weakness.

He looked through the peephole and was more than a little shocked to see Cecilia Mills standing there.

Any relief he'd felt at having company evaporated. Cecilia was not a welcome presence in his life right now, and hadn't been since New Year's Eve when she'd decided to kiss him, full on the mouth.

Cecilia had grown up with the Knights, on the neighboring ranch to his grandmother's. Duke and Eva Knight's niece had been part of the fabric of Brady's life since he'd come to live with Grandma Pauline at the age of eleven—after his oldest brother had helped them escape their father's gang, the Sons of the Badlands.

While Brady had been friends with all the Knight girls, Cecilia was the one who'd always done her level best to irritate him. Not always on purpose, either. They were just…diametrically opposed. Despite her job as a tribal police officer on the nearby reservation, Cecilia bent rules all the time. She saw gray when he saw black, and even darker gray when he saw white. She was complicated and they didn't agree on much of anything.

Except that their fundamental function in life was to help people. Which, he supposed, was what had made them good friends despite all their arguments.

Until she'd kissed him and ruined it all.

Don't miss
Isolated Threat *by Nicole Helm,*
available June 2020 wherever
Harlequin Intrigue books and ebooks are sold.

Harlequin.com

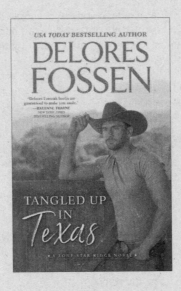